"What does it matter what I might want? Who would care?" he whispered, deliberately crowding her, leaning in when she began to draw back. "Do you, Lady Emmalyn?"

"What do you mean?" she asked on a shaky breath of air. She backed away from him, a subtle half step that edged her closer to the wall of trees at her back. Her dusky lips parted as she stared up at him, all guileless beauty and feminine promise. "W-what is it you want?"

He was fairly certain she knew. After all, he has done little to conceal his desire for her since his arrival at Fallonmour. More than anything now, he wanted to taste that pert, rose-colored mouth. He wanted to lose himself in the moment, lose himself in Emmalyn's kiss. Lose himself in the bliss of her body.

She could make him forget his past—forget himself—if only for a few exquisite moments. God help him, he wanted nothing more than to claim every sweet ounce of her passion and fill her with his own. He wanted to take her. He knew he could have her . . . but he could never keep her.

He decided he damned well didn't care.

Without another word, Cabal bent his head down and pressed his lips to hers.

By Tina St. John
Published by The Ballantine Publishing Group:

LORD OF VENGEANCE
LADY OF VALOR

Lady of Valor

Tina St. John

IVY BOOKS • NEW YORK

An Ivy Book
Published by The Ballantine Publishing Group
Copyright © 2000 by Tina Haack

www.randomhouse.com/BB/

Library of Congress Card Number: 99-68879

ISBN 0-449-00424-4

Manufactured in the United States of America

First Edition: April 2000

10 9 8 7 6 5 4 3 2 1

This one is for my little sister, Nicole.
Thank you for being such a wonderful friend.

Thanks to my other "sisters," too:
Faboo, Babette, Coco, and Fifi,
for keeping me sane and grounded,
and, most of all, for reminding me to laugh.

Love always to John,
for a million reasons
and then some . . .

Prologue

The Holy Land. September 1, 1192

The dead man lay there, motionless and sprawled on the dirt floor of the tent where he had crumpled moments before. A bleeding wound at his side spread out like spilled wine, staining his Crusader's surcoat and the ground beneath him a deep crimson-black. Left arm outstretched, his now unmoving fingers were curled into the hard-packed earth mere inches from the boot of an English foot soldier.

Cabal—Blackheart, as he was better known these more than two years on campaign—stood in the dim illumination of a sputtering candle that had been upset during the struggle and considered that clawing, desperate hand with sober reflection, like a man awakened from the depths of a black and heavy dream.

Outside the tent, darkness had settled over the desert, cooling the vast sea of scorching sand but doing little to calm the bloodlust of the Crusaders camped there. The bonfire that King Richard's army had lit hours before would burn long into the night, as would the men's drunken voices, raised in celebration of the day's small victory.

Camped for more than a sennight and wanting for action, the soldiers had raided a village that afternoon, taking with it scores of Muslim lives. Never mind that the numbers included women and children; they were all soulless heathens according to the church. As such, they had been afforded less regard in their slaughter than would the lowliest vermin. But

1

the dead were the fortunate ones. They were spared the horrors suffered on those left living as prisoners of the Cross.

Staring down at the dead officer, Cabal ran a hand over his grimy dark-bearded face and blew out a weary sigh. Damnation. What manner of beasts had they become in God's name? Worse, he wondered, could it actually be starting to matter to him?

Before a long-forsaken conscience could rouse to needle him further, Cabal's ear was drawn toward the approaching sound of footsteps scuffing in the sand outside the tent. The flap was thrown open and a laughing soldier ducked inside, bleary-eyed, stinking of sweat and overmuch wine. "Sir Garrett, ye selfish bastard! Do ye mean to keep the chit all to yerself?" The mercenary drew in a choking gasp, stumbling back on his heels. "God's wounds, what happened—"

When he made to advance, Cabal held him off with a dismissive flick of his hand. Crouching beside the fallen nobleman, he reached out for a jeweled dagger that lay next to him, slick with its owner's blood. "I came upon the struggle too late," he offered blandly. "There was no saving him."

"She killed him! The damned Saracen whore killed him!"

"She was no whore, Rannulf. Only a child." Cabal could scarcely contain the edge of disgust in his voice. "No more than ten summers if she was a day."

"Child or nay, the filthy bitch will suffer—"

The soldier's sputtered exclamation broke off as Cabal rose to his full height and faced him, forced to incline his head under the cramped slope of the tent's ceiling. "The girl is gone."

The mercenary frowned, looking past Cabal to a severed length of rope that lay on the earthen floor. Sir Garrett of Fallonmour had leashed the thick braided cord about the young Saracen's neck when he plucked her from a crowd of screaming villagers that day, intent on keeping her for his own base amusement. Though Rannulf seemed hesitant to voice his doubts about the prisoner's escape, his expression was suspicious, questioning.

Cabal answered frankly. "I set her free."

"Set her free? So she can stab another man in the back? The murdering little wench should be run down and gutted!"

"Any man who goes after the girl or any other peasant in retaliation for this will answer to me."

Rannulf gaped at him in disbelief. "God's blood, Blackheart! Ye fought beside Sir Garrett for nigh on two years. Why, to hear ye now, that peasant slut's life meant more to you than his!"

Cabal met and held the incredulous stare without responding. Garrett of Fallonmour was certainly no friend of his, but then Cabal did not place much value on anyone's life, not even his own. He took a small amount of satisfaction in seeing that bleak understanding register fully in the other man's eyes.

"Jesu," the mercenary whispered suddenly, as if just now realizing the breadth of his folly. Few dared challenge the man whose reputation deemed him among the worst of King Richard's savage henchmen. Face fading to an unhealthy pallor, Rannulf swallowed hard. "Sir Cabal, please. I assure ye, I meant no offense—"

Casually, Cabal wiped Garrett's bloodstained blade on the edge of his surcoat, biding his time in contemplative silence while Rannulf spewed a fretful string of apologies. Better that the mercenary's immediate worry for his own neck blind him to the disturbing truth behind Cabal's actions regarding Garrett's innocent young hostage. A truth that Cabal himself was only recently coming to realize . . .

Though his heart was every bit as black as a desert night, it had, of late, begun to beat.

Damnation, how he needed to feel the crush of battle! Too much idle time was making him soft. Weakening him. His feet itched to be on the march again; his muscles craved combat. If Richard and the Saracen leader did not resolve their standoff soon and get on with the business of war, Cabal reckoned he would likely go mad with the waiting.

"Clean up this bloody mess," he growled to Rannulf. The

harsh command sent the soldier to his knees on the tent floor, scurrying to pick up the smoldering candle and right the upended table. "See to disposing of the body as well. Doubtless the king has no desire to see one of his noble vassals left behind for sport among the infidels. Not even this one."

Cabal tossed Garrett's dagger to the floor, then turned and quit the tent. Outside, the smoke-filled night air was thick with the sounds of conversation and drunken laughter. Flames from the camp bonfire climbed high into the moonless sky, illuminating hundreds of faces that watched surreptitiously as the king's most feared warrior strode through their midst on his way to the royal pavilion at the end of the avenue.

Four men-at-arms stood outside the massive striped silk tent that sheltered King Richard, England's finest son. Though the king had been ensconced within most of the day for solitary contemplation and meetings with his officers, his guards granted Cabal immediate entry, as they would any high-ranking vassal. One of them swept aside the square of silk that served as the tent door, allowing Cabal to pass beneath. That he had earned this brand of respect out of fear more than status irked him somewhere in the far corners of his mind, but Cabal pushed the feeling away as he came into the tent and bowed before the presence of Coeur de Lion.

"Ah, Cabal. I thought perhaps you might have been Fallonmour, come at last to join us. His tardiness for this conference is beginning to try my patience." The king had assembled five of his officers inside, the noblemen all seated before him around a large ornately carved table that was strewn with countless maps and papers. His legendary royal temper beginning to flare, Richard barked, "Will someone go fetch the impudent bastard, or must I do it myself?"

Only Cabal dared speak in the moment of panic that followed. "That will not be possible, my lord." He met Richard's puzzled stare, his blunt statement also gaining the attention of the two servants who had scrambled toward the tent's exit. "There was an incident with one of the prisoners in the camp a short while ago," Cabal explained. "Fallonmour was killed."

The king remained silent amid the aghast exclamations of his officers, his tawny brows arched only slightly in reaction to the news. "Well," he said to Cabal, "that Fallonmour survived more than a week past his arrival in Palestine is a credit to your skill more than his value to me as a soldier. I wager he'd have been dead long before this had you not been there to guard his back."

Cabal stared but took no esteem in a compliment that was merely stated fact. Though he had despised Garrett for his carelessness in battle and faulty leadership of his regiment, as was his duty, Cabal had delivered him from the killing end of a Saracen blade on more than one occasion. But not tonight, and the thought plagued him anew.

"Come in, then," the king offered, indicating a vacant X-chair beside the gathered noblemen. "It should please you to know that I have reached a decision regarding the infidels' proposed treaty."

Cabal seated himself at the table with the others, unaffected by the cool glances of the officers as he, a baseborn mercenary, took his place amongst their titled ranks. He accepted a cup of wine passed to him by one of the king's servants, then watched over the rim as Coeur de Lion rose from his chair and began to pace slowly behind the desk.

"I have decided to accept the terms of Saladin's agreement," he stated without preamble, his distaste for the resolution made clear in his constricted tone of voice. "I leave to meet with him in the morn."

The king's vassals did nothing to conceal their relief, each of them rushing forth with congratulations, offering words of support for the decision to end the strife. Interested only in being on to the next battle alongside his king, Cabal remained stoic, drinking his wine in emotionless silence as Richard explained the details of the settlement, then gave orders for the officers to inform their regiments.

"Prepare the ships to sail for England in the coming weeks," he instructed. "I, however, will needs take an alternate route from the rest of you. It seems my advisors fear I might be set upon if I travel in the open. I tell you, 'tis damned inconvenient when one's enemies lie in wait within and without the realm. Not to mention among one's own blood kin." Alluding to the known treachery and scheming of his younger brother, Prince John, the king's wry humor lacked its usual bravado.

"What of Fallonmour's holdings now, Your Grace?" inquired one of the assembled men, his concerned tone scarcely masking the glint of avarice in his eyes. " 'Tis far too valuable an estate to leave in the hands of Sir Garrett's new widow—or his brother, Hugh de Wardeaux."

"Indeed." The king's broad, leonine brow furrowed in consideration. "I know not of the widow Fallonmour's politics, but Hugh has made no secret of his loyalties to John. 'Tis one more alliance I can ill afford to ignore." Richard met Cabal's confirming nod, then retrieved a quill and a blank square of parchment from his desktop and began writing. "Until I am back in London and have the leisure of deciding upon a worthy vassal to install as lord, I think it best to place Fallonmour under the wardship of someone I can trust."

Cabal lounged negligently in his chair, watching with mild interest as five sets of eager eyes rooted on the king, five noblemen waiting like vultures for a chance to increase their wealth upon the sudden death of one of their own. Idly, he wondered which would get the boon, at the same time thankful that his pledge in service to the Crown had removed him from such meaningless concerns.

As of its own accord, his hand stole to the center of his chest, where the solid weight of that obligation rested so insidiously against his skin. A cold reminder of who he was, and what he would never be.

The king ceased writing midway down the page and glanced up at his officers, seeming to assess the lot of them each in turn. His cool, careful gaze traveled over their expectant faces as if visually measuring their honor, questioning it. "There is only one man here whom I would trust to selflessly guard my interests at Fallonmour," he said. "One man I would install without worry that he might harbor his own designs for the place." Coeur de Lion's commanding stare came to rest pointedly on Cabal. "I will send him."

Chapter One

England. June 1193

That particular day dawned much the same as the hundreds that had come before it, still, Lady Emmalyn of Fallonmour felt an odd quickening in her veins—a queer sense of hopeful anticipation that roused her before the sun's first rays lit her chamber. Something was in the air; she could feel it.

Would today be the day?

Excited to find out, she washed and dressed quickly, then quit her chamber and descended the stairwell that spiraled through the heart of the castle. She moved hastily and on light feet, knowing she would have only this short while to claim for her own. Before long, the entire keep would wake and her daily duties as castellan would begin anew.

Among the first to seek Emmalyn out this morn would surely be the seneschal, entrusted to oversee Fallonmour upon Garrett's departure three years past. The dour old servant had informed her last eve of his intent to go down to the village at first light for the weighing of the newly sheared wool and an assessment of the fields' bounty. While Emmalyn fully intended to cooperate with the accounting, she disliked the man's tactics, and particularly his harsh treatment of her folk.

She would accompany him to the fields, she had told him firmly, but they would go when she was ready. At present, she had other, more pressing priorities to attend outside the keep.

Fallonmour awaited a new arrival.

Emmalyn crossed the bailey, anxious with anticipation by the time she reached the stables. The head groom, a large, graying bear of a man, was already at work, tools in hand. He greeted Emmalyn with a wide smile when she entered the outbuilding.

"How does she fare this morn, Thomas?"

"Well, milady. Only a matter of a day or two now, I reckon."

"A day or two?" Emmalyn couldn't help but sigh her disappointment. "'Tis the very answer you gave me last week, Thomas. Will she never have this foal?"

The old stable master chuckled. "The first is often late in coming, milady. No cause to fret just now. Minerva will let us know when 'tis time."

Emmalyn looked into her mare's soft brown eyes and smiled. "Did you hear that, Minnie? You're going to be a mother soon." The bay blinked her frondlike black lashes and nuzzled Emmalyn's outstretched palm. Then she nipped her. Gently, but enough to make Emmalyn yelp in surprise.

"'Tis all right," she assured Thomas when he dropped his tools and hastened to her side.

He bent to retrieve something from a bucket on the floor, then cleared his throat. In his hand were an apple and a small knife. Sheepishly, he held them out to her. "Apologies, milady, but I fear I've spoiled the beast of late. She looks fer a treat every morn now—gets downright surly if denied it overlong. I beg pardon, if ye be displeased."

"You have a kind, giving heart, Thomas. You needn't ever apologize for that. Besides," she relented on a soft laugh, "it seems I am as much to blame as you for Minnie's poor behavior. While you have been spoiling her with apples in the mornings, I have been doing the same after supper each afternoon. 'Tis a wonder she hasn't tired of them by now."

Emmalyn had scarcely sliced off the first crisp wedge when the mare nudged forward and stole it from her fingers.

While Minerva munched contentedly, Emmalyn stroked the rough silk of the horse's large head and neck. "I reckon she is due some special treatment, is she not? After all, 'tis not every day Fallonmour hosts a royal birth."

She could hardly contain her pride over the prospect. Minerva's foal was sired by Queen Eleanor's finest stallion, the breeding a gift from Her Majesty on the dowager queen's last visit to Fallonmour, and something Emmalyn prized dearly. At her side, Thomas beamed his assent, then picked up his tools and returned to his tasks with the other horses.

"Milady!"

From the bailey came a preadolescent bark of alarm. The mare started, tossing her head and whinnying, eyes wide. The shout startled Emmalyn as well. She whirled toward the heavy pound of running feet as they neared the stables. One of her fostering pages skidded to a halt in the doorway, breathless.

"Milady, come quickly!"

"What is it, Jason?" she scolded. "You frightened poor Minerva nigh to death—"

"Arlo sent me, milady! You must come at once—he's in the south field! Hurry!"

At the mention of the seneschal's name, Emmalyn bristled. It did not surprise her that Arlo would waste no time in defying her instructions, but what troubled her more was the urgency in Jason's voice. Doubtless Arlo had threatened the boy with some form of bodily harm if he did not carry out the order to fetch her at once. Or perhaps the seneschal had taken it upon himself to terrorize the villeins in the name of commerce. "I've had about enough of Arlo and his bullying ways. Where is he now, Jason? The south field, you say?"

The page shook his head fiercely. "Nay, milady, 'tis not Arlo in the south field, but a rider! He approaches Fallonmour as we speak!"

"A rider?"

"A knight, milady, wearing the white cross of a Crusader!"

Instantly, Emmalyn felt her confidence falter. She drew

in a deep, strengthening breath and made sure her voice remained steady, even if it was little more than a whisper. "A Crusader? Are you certain?"

"Aye! Riding a great black steed and heading for the castle! Milady, think you 'tis Lord Garrett, returned at last?"

Garrett.

Could it be? After three years without a word from him, had he now come home? Although King Richard had been captured by one of his enemies upon leaving the Holy Land, news of his army's return had been circulating for many months now. Inasmuch, Emmalyn had been expecting to see Garrett ride through Fallonmour's gates, preparing herself for the eventuality of her husband's homecoming and how it would affect life as she had come to know it in his absence. But she wasn't prepared. She knew that now, feeling her stomach tighten and twist with every passing moment. She struggled to appear calm. "Tell Arlo to assemble the folk in the hall, Jason. I'll be along in a moment."

Emmalyn turned back to Minerva's soulful gaze and idly stroked the mare's neck. Already her hands were shaking. Mercy, but she had to collect her thoughts. Collect her nerve. Perhaps the war had changed her husband. Gentled him. Perhaps things between them would be different now.

She was different. No longer the child he had married, but a woman of twenty summers. She had managed Fallonmour and its holdings during the more than three years he had been away, acting as castellan and negotiating with tradesmen, even fending off a raid on the village last autumn. So why should the thought of facing one man—her husband—still terrify her so?

Beside her, Thomas's voice was a low, soothing drawl. "Courage, milady."

Emmalyn nodded, but her smile was weak. If the stable master only knew how much she needed his gentle words of support. If he only knew what strength it would take for her to face Garrett again, to return to her role as his wife. But no one knew; Garrett had been careful enough to make sure that the scars she bore were inside, where no one could see them. Not that they were any less ugly, surely no less painful.

Straightening her shoulders despite the weight of her dread, Emmalyn marched out of the stable and across the bailey toward the keep. Castle folk tending their work glanced at her as she passed them, everyone clearly made aware of the approaching Crusader and watching for her reaction to the news. But Emmalyn kept her chin high, her gait purposeful.

To mask some of her own internal disquiet, as she neared the keep she called out orders to a knot of people standing idle in the bailey. "Nell, shoo those chickens back into the roost. Alfred, see to it that straw and fresh water are brought to the stables. And Jane, find Cook. Tell him to warm the venison and lamprey from last eve and use the fresh beans I brought in from the garden yesterday. Bring bread, too, but not the dark—fetch the lightest loaf you can find. Make sure there is wine on the dais, but it mustn't have any grit, so strain it twice before you decant it."

Emmalyn did not slow her pace until she had ducked under the cool shade of the pentice, an arched gateway that led from the bailey to the keep. She stood there a moment, thankful to be away from watchful eyes while she summoned a steady breath.

Dieu, but how quickly Garrett's expectations came back to her, even after all this time. All of the demands he placed on her, from the way he wanted his meals prepared to the way he required her to dress in his presence. She'd had three years to make her life her own, to come out of the shadow Garrett had cast over her. Three years of freedom, yet she felt her hard-won confidence slipping away even before he darkened Fallonmour's threshold.

Could it be so easy to fall back into that life now? Could he control her that effortlessly? Nay! She could not allow anyone to do that to her again. Not now. Not ever.

Knowing Garrett would expect her to greet him dressed in her finest gown, her disobedient hair braided and modestly covered, Emmalyn mounted the keep stairwell, taking a small amount of rebellious pleasure in her current state of drab attire.

She'd had no use for richly toned silks or embroidered slippers in recent days, favoring instead the russet wool tunic she wore now and her practical leather boots. There was no bejeweled girdle circling her hips, only a utilitarian belt adorned with nothing more than a sheathed dagger and ring of jangling keys. Her blond hair she usually plaited, simply to keep it out of her way while she worked, but in her haste to dress this morning she had left it unbound. Its weighty mass tumbled over her shoulders and down her back in a tangle of unruly curls that was sure to set Garrett's teeth on edge.

But she willed herself not to let the thought of his displeasure sway her as she passed her chamber door and climbed the rest of the way up to the tower roof. Two of Fallonmour's knights stood at the farthest parapet, shielding their eyes from the rising sun as they looked to the far hill.

"It has been too long since I last saw Lord Garrett," said one man to the other. "I vow he looks bigger now, does he not?"

"Aye, and hale, too. See how bold he sits in the saddle!"

Emmalyn came up beside them nearly without their notice. She peered over the ledge at the approaching knight, and dread coiled in her belly. The men were right; he did look larger than even she had recalled.

Gone was the rounded slope of Garrett's shoulders; now they looked nearly the width of his steed's broad back. The long red surcoat he wore was faded and torn, a tattered rag that did little to conceal the muscular bulk of the man it clothed. Indeed, from where she stood, Emmalyn could see the power in his thighs, the proud set of his spine as he guided his horse at an easy gait over the plain. There was an

air of calm about him now, a self-assuredness and almost
regal bearing that even this fair distance could not disguise.

Though she fought it, curiosity began to stir in Emmalyn's mind, a subtle interest that made her study him more
closely.

The black destrier she had given Garrett as a wedding
gift—a beast he could never tame and had always despised
for its willfulness—now cantered cooperatively beneath
him, completely mastered. Horse and rider made an admittedly impressive picture, a striking image of the homecoming hero, but something was not quite right. With a
mingling of wonder and suspicion, Emmalyn watched the
firm but respectful way he handled the stallion. The way he
made no move to dominate it, yet managed absolute control.

And then she knew.

" 'Tis not him," she said with quiet utter certainty.

"Milady?"

Emmalyn had turned away from the wall walk to head
back for the keep, but stopped when she heard the guard's
puzzled question. "He rides my lord's mount," she confirmed, "but that man is not my husband."

It took but a glimpse at Fallonmour's grandeur to make
Cabal understand the king's concern for its safekeeping and,
indeed, the avarice that a holding of this magnitude would
inspire in even the wealthiest vassal. Not even recall of the
many nights the regiment had endured Garrett's tedious
boasting of his riches back home in England could have prepared Cabal for the abundance of noble prosperity he saw
unfurled before him. For all the hardship and desolation
he had witnessed along his trek north from the port of
Dover, Fallonmour appeared to have well survived the long
absence of its lord. More than survived, he reckoned: The
place looked to have thrived.

The early-morning sun bathed the stone of the tall, white-
washed keep in brilliant light, gilding its crenellations and
towers and setting the entire castle awash in a spangled,

ethereal splendor. Lush crops of wheat and oats and vetch spread out as far as the eye could see, flourishing and fragrant with the promise of a rich harvest come Lammas. A large flock of newly sheared sheep dotted the fallow lands, grazing on the sprouted weeds and verdant grass.

At the base of Fallonmour's great sloping motte, a village bustled, alive with activity as folk came in from the fields and out of their cottages to see who rode through their midst. Cabal paid no mind to their quizzical faces, cantering forward briskly through the center of the little village and up the hill, headed for the castle and the commencement of his unwanted mission as this demesne's guardian.

As he approached, he saw more clearly the solid indomitability of Fallonmour. The massive wall that enveloped the stone keep and various outbuildings seemed to grow out of the craggy earth itself, from its jutting, flared base to the thirty-foot height to which the ramparts soared. Gathered in the gatehouse, perched between two crenellated towers, stood a half-dozen guards. They stared down at him in defensive silence, as did the like number of crossbowmen lining the battlements.

"I bring word to Lady Fallonmour of her lord husband," Cabal announced in the Norman tongue of England's nobility.

From within the bailey, a female voice ordered simply, "Open."

At her command, the portcullis began its slow grind upward. Cabal urged his mount forward and rode beneath the heavy, spiked gridwork into Fallonmour's wide outer bailey. A gathering of servants, maids, and castle folk had assembled in the courtyard and now stood staring at him expectantly as he rode into the center of the grassy enclosure. The group parted when he dismounted, the men watching him cautiously, a clutch of young maids whispering behind their hands as he passed. But their many faces blurred to nothingness the instant Cabal's eyes lit on Lady Emmalyn.

"Greetings, my lord. I bid you welcome to Fallonmour."

Standing at the base of the steps that led into the keep, she met him with a pale, unsettling gaze so clear and frank, it seemed to look right through him. A wealth of unbound, flaxen curls softened the striking angles of her face but only emphasized the intelligence gleaming in her mist-green eyes.

She did not trust his presence there; he could see it in her rigid stance, in the way she offered him kind greeting but withheld her smile. Like an angel warrior guarding the portal to heaven, she stood before him, garbed in a simple gown and boots, armed with nothing but dagger and keys ... and the power of her intrepid stare. Not at all like the meek young woman Richard had warned he should expect to find in Garrett's new widow.

Lady Emmalyn looked as if she had become more lioness than lost little kitten in her husband's absence—a thought that intrigued Cabal as much as it raised concern. Did her loyalties yet remain with the king? If they did, would they still, once she learned of Garrett's death?

"You say you bring word of my husband," she prompted, her pert chin climbing up a notch under Cabal's lingering scrutiny.

"I do, madam." He stepped forward and offered a perfunctory bow of his head. "I have come by order of the king, a duty impressed on me before his departure from Palestine."

At the mention of Coeur de Lion, the lady grew pensive. "The king sent you?" she asked warily. "Then your news must be of the most grave nature, my lord."

Cabal gave her a grim nod. "It is."

She looked at him for a long moment, unblinking, then glanced to the fine black mount that had belonged to her husband until his death. Garrett's sword belt and a small satchel of his belongings were strapped to the saddle of the destrier, token remembrances to be delivered to the widow at the king's request.

"Garrett is dead?"

"He is, my lady."

"I see," she said quietly.

Her gaze returned to Cabal, lucid with comprehension. He waited for the tears that were sure to come, allowing her a moment to absorb this news before he conveyed the rest of the king's message. But her eyes remained dry. She did not quake or dissolve with inconsolable grief. Instead, she reached out with a steady arm and hailed a young squire to her side. "Alfred will take your mount to the stables, my lord. You will find refreshments and a pallet in the hall, should you wish to rest before continuing on in your travels."

She pivoted and started to walk away.

Cabal cleared his throat. "My lady, I do not think you understand. . . ."

Her step halted. She turned an unblinking gaze on him. "My husband is dead, sir. What more would you have me understand?"

With that, she resumed her cool retreat, heading for the keep without excuse or waiting for his reply. From the schooled briskness of her gait and the rigid line of her back, it seemed to Cabal that he had just been efficiently, albeit mistakenly, dismissed.

Chapter Two

Dead. Although Emmalyn had managed to maintain her composure in front of the dark stranger who had been sent to deliver the news, she walked back toward the keep stunned. She did not want to think that Garrett's death could affect her so, but she was truly saddened. More than saddened, she was guilt-ridden, for how many times had she wished he might never return? How often had she hoped to live the rest of her life without him? Free of his censure, free of his rage. In all her hoping and praying for a peaceable life, could she have brought this woeful fate upon him?

She tried not to think about that as she entered the busy castle. Wanting only a bit of solitude in which to consider the new course of her future, she headed to the stairwell. She had alighted only the first step when she heard a crash of pottery in the great hall, followed by Arlo's shrill voice harshly reprimanding one of the kitchen maids for her clumsiness.

Emmalyn's heart sank. Abiding Arlo's attempts for control at Fallonmour these past years had been trial enough for them all, but in light of this morning's news, she knew that her troubles were about to worsen. Arlo was a nuisance, but not half as dangerous as Garrett's brother, Hugh de Wardeaux. Emmalyn's confirmed widowhood was the very thing her brother-by-marriage had been waiting for. The only excuse that Hugh would need to tighten his grip on Fallonmour. And on her.

Arlo's continued tirade in the great hall brought Emmalyn's attention back sharply. Pivoting from the stairwell in sheer disgust with the man, she walked into the cavernous dining hall. Two pages were on the dais, setting a place at the high table before Garrett's long-unused cushioned chair. Trestles that had been tipped against the walls during the night were now being positioned in neat rows across the large room in preparation for the morning meal. Everyone worked quietly and with haste, as if loath to attract any bit of Arlo's tyranny to themselves. Neither did they come to the defense of poor young Bea, who was on her hands and knees on the floor, picking up shards of pottery from a broken serving vessel.

Arlo stood over her, bellowing, the front of his rich blue robes splashed from hem to knee with wine. He looked up when Emmalyn entered, and the spectacle that surely would have continued until Bea had been reduced to tears, ceased.

"That bumbling, awkward girl has ruined my garments," he groused as he came forward to meet Emmalyn. She did not acknowledge his complaint, merely glared her displeasure and brushed past him. Arlo cleared his throat and wiped idly at the stains. "Am I to understand it, milady, that the Crusader who arrived was not Lord Garrett after all?"

"No."

When Emmalyn invited no further conversation and stepped forth to retrieve a far-flung bit of debris, the seneschal shuffled along beside her with eager steps. Though his greed for information was nearly palpable, his voice was soft, hesitant with calculated concern. "Did this man tell you anything at all, milady? Is there any word of your husband?"

"Yes, Arlo, I have received word." Emmalyn was deliberately evasive, bringing the errant shard of earthenware to Bea and taking a moment to assure the maid that she had done no wrong.

The seneschal huffed his impatience, all thoughts of posturing and gentle persuasion evidently forgotten. "Milady, please, enough of your games! What have you learned of Lord Garrett this morn? Nothing grave, I pray. . . ."

At that blatant insincerity, Emmalyn pivoted and faced him. "Garrett is dead, Arlo."

She ignored his gasp of shock, knowing full well it was done only for politic effect. "Oh, good heavens!" he breathed dramatically, one hand splayed at his chest. "What dreadful news."

"Yes," Emmalyn agreed, nearly able to hear the wheels of opportunity begin to grind inside the seneschal's balding head.

"There is much we should do," Arlo said. "Of course, a messenger should be dispatched to Lord Hugh at once. He must be informed of his beloved elder brother's demise."

"Of course."

The seneschal seemed too caught up in his plotting to notice Emmalyn's sarcasm. Tapping a bony finger against his lips, he rushed on with his thoughts, murmuring the various details that would now have to be addressed. It was not until she started to walk away that he seemed to recall himself. "Emmalyn," he said confidentially, shocking her with both the use of her familiar name and his hand at her elbow. "Rest assured that your needs will be met. I'm certain Lord Hugh will see that you are well cared for upon your removal from Fallonmour."

"No!" Emmalyn wrenched her arm out of the manservant's grasp. Her vehement outburst drew the attention of everyone gathered in the hall. Servants paused in their duties to cast furtive glances toward their lady's distress. Emmalyn steeled herself, struggling to appear confident while inside she was quaking at the thought of losing everything that mattered to her. "Fallonmour is my home now," she informed Arlo tightly. "These folk are my family. No one will remove me so long as I have breath in my body. I will not leave."

"That fact, my lady, remains to be seen."

Emmalyn whirled toward the source of the deep rumbling voice and found the dark Crusader standing behind her, his big frame nearly filling the arched entryway of the hall. He pinned her motionless with a stern gaze, his tousled mane of black hair and thick-grown beard giving him the semblance of a wild beast—a feral hellhound materialized out of the shadows.

He had not looked to Emmalyn like any sort of royal messenger when he stood in her bailey, but even less so now, she acknowledged with a dawning sense of dread. Speechless with startlement, she didn't dare breathe as the knight advanced into the tomblike silence of the great hall. She had not realized the sheer immensity of him until he came within a pebble's toss of her.

Shoulders that seemed the thickness of feast-day hams glided before her face, the bulkiest part of his mailed upper arm at a level with the tip of her nose. His chest looked to be solid as granite beneath his stained surcoat; no sign of indulgences in the trim waist either, its firm diameter cinched with a studded leather belt nigh the width of her hand. Those hard-hewn thighs, which had mastered Garrett's mount with such innate aplomb, were now spread shoulder-width apart, his warrior's frame towering over her like a wall of unyielding stone.

"Whether or not you shall stay at Fallonmour will be determined by Richard, our lord and king. Not you, madam. Until he is able to decide the matter, your keep—and indeed, your person—have been ordered into my charge."

He took a folded square of parchment that was secured beneath his belt and handed it to her. A square of parchment bearing the royal seal of Coeur de Lion. Fingers trembling, Emmalyn opened the letter and read the orders penned some months past in King Richard's elegant script. . . .

The king regretted to inform her that Garrett had been slain in a struggle with a Saracen prisoner. His death meant that Fallonmour's tenancy belonged once more to the Crown; a new lord would be installed at the king's earliest convenience. As for her fate, she was to be wed again, to a man of Richard's choosing. Meanwhile, she was to consider the king's assigned guardian, Sir Cabal, her overlord and protector. She was to welcome him into Fallonmour and

obey him in all matters, affording him the same respect she
would the king himself.

Until the king could decide how to dispense with her
home and her hand, Sir Cabal's will was to be her law.

Emmalyn looked up from the last line of the damning
decree and found the knight's penetrating steely gaze fixed
on her. "Now, my lady, I believe you fully understand."

Beside her, Arlo cleared his throat. "Permit me to introduce myself, sir. I am Arlo de Brois, seneschal here since
Lord Garrett's departure."

"So, you have been responsible for the management of
this place?" asked the knight.

Arlo executed a humble bow. "Yes, my lord."

Emmalyn scoffed at the seneschal's attempt to ingratiate
the king's man, but she was too enraged with the arrogant
knight herself to muster voice enough to dispute Arlo's
false claims of responsibility for Fallonmour.

As if he cared no longer to be bothered with her, Sir
Cabal turned his attention to issues of commerce and management. "I will need a full accounting of the fields and
stores," he told Arlo. "As well as the most recent count of
the folk here in the castle and in the village. How many men
have we in the garrison?"

"Er, a score and ten?" Arlo hedged. "Give or take a
couple, my lord."

"There are eighteen knights and half a dozen squires,"
Emmalyn corrected tightly. If Sir Cabal wanted to know
anything about Fallonmour, he would be the wiser to consult
with her. But he spared her little more than a questioning
glance before heading for the dais and his waiting meal.

"Gather your records and bring them to me here in the
hall," he instructed Arlo. "We will review them as I break
my fast."

Slanting a self-satisfied grin in Emmalyn's direction, Arlo
scuttled out to retrieve Fallonmour's books. She sensed quiet
movement commence once more in the hall as the servants
turned their faces away, taking up their tasks in stunned

silence, loath to look upon her in this moment of forfeit and shame.

Standing there alone in the center of the large room, Emmalyn burned with chagrin. In the blink of an eye, her life had been turned upside down. It was likely only a matter of time—a few weeks, months, mayhap a year—before the king would be released from his captivity and returned to England. And then, she would lose everything: her home, her friends and folk . . . her freedom. This last precious treasure, which she had only begun to taste in Garrett's absence, was already lost to her. She knew it from the sinking feeling in her heart as she watched King Richard's henchman stride across the wide, rush-strewn floor as if he owned the place.

Her keep and her person, now under his charge.

Filled with futile hatred for her circumstances, Emmalyn focused her anger on his broad, retreating back. Her voice arched with the heat of her ire. "Do you expect me to stand by idly as you and Arlo discuss my business?"

Sir Cabal paused to regard her over his shoulder. "Not at all, my lady." A smile lifted the corner of his mouth, but the expression lacked even the slightest trace of kindness. "I would much prefer that you ready a tub of hot water for me in the solar while I confer with the seneschal. My bones are sorely tired from my travels, and my back would welcome a good scrubbing."

Chapter Three

The king's letter still clutched in her hand, Emmalyn paced the solar, verily more steamed than the buckets of boiling water being carried in by her maids and poured into the padded wooden bathing tub. What gall the man possessed, dismissing her as he had before her folk! If the king felt it necessary to send a guard to look after his interests at Fallonmour, Emmalyn did not suppose he could have chosen a more odious example of bullying male arrogance. And to think she must abide his presence for an indeterminate length of time, with the king imprisoned abroad.

She could hear the vague rumble of Sir Cabal's voice in the adjoining great hall, but she could not discern any of the conversation between him and Arlo. Let the arrogant knight feed on Arlo's incompetence and careless accountings, she decided. Temporary or otherwise, she had no intention of making his assimilation as Fallonmour's overlord any easier than was required of her. Emmalyn's hand tightened around the royal decree.

"Shall I scent the water, milady?" One of the maids had uncorked a vial of expensive clove oil, a luxury most often reserved for the lord of the manor and visiting nobility. The spicy-sweet fragrance wafted on the air and Emmalyn frowned, ready to deny Sir Cabal such considerations. At her hesitancy, the maid gave a little shrug and replaced the stopper.

"Wait, Nell," Emmalyn said when the maid turned to leave. "On second thought, I reckon our guest could well do with some sweetening—if not in his disposition, then certainly in his odor."

Stifling a laugh, the maid poured a dollop of the imported extract into the steaming bathwater, then picked up an empty bucket and made to depart the solar. On her way out of the room, she was nearly trampled by Emmalyn's nurse. The big woman rushed forth to enfold Emmalyn in a motherly embrace.

"Oh, milady! I just heard the news about Garrett."

Nurse, whose given name was Bertilda, had accompanied Emmalyn to Fallonmour upon her wedding to Garrett. Having served as her maidservant from the time Emmalyn was a babe, Bertie had been sent along to one day continue her role as attendant to Emmalyn's own children. But there had been no offspring born of her union with Garrett, a loss that Emmalyn felt keenly, even to this day. Bertie was the only other person who understood the depth of that pain. The only person who knew what Emmalyn had endured as Garrett's wife.

"He is no longer your worry, milady," Bertie soothed when the last of the maids had left the solar. "After today, we will waste no more thought on Garrett. Do you agree?"

Emmalyn nodded weakly, still feeling a twinge of guilt for her want to be freed of the bonds of her marriage. How futile that wanting had been, in light of the king's decree. It would not be long before she was matched to another husband—perhaps as wicked as Garrett. Perhaps worse.

Emmalyn drew out of Nurse's embrace and closed the chamber door. "I fear there is more, Bertie. King Richard has determined that I shall wed again, to a man of his choosing. Meanwhile, Fallonmour will be awarded to one of his vassals. The guard who delivered the news has been sent to hold the keep and ensure that I comply."

Emmalyn quickly read the king's order to the nurse.

"Oh, milady. This cannot be!"

"It is, Bertie. 'Tis as real as the mannerless beast breaking his fast in my hall. While the king's man discusses Fallonmour's future with Arlo, I have been relegated to overseeing Sir Cabal's bath."

Nurse clucked her disgust. "And for this news to come mere days after you are asked to contribute a ransom gift for the king's release—'tis an injustice!"

In her shock over the morning's unexpected events, Emmalyn had not given a thought to the special tax being collected from Fallonmour's coffers for delivery to London. All of England's noble houses had been levied handsomely to help meet the ransom price placed on King Richard's head, though there was little hope of reaching the exorbitant sum. It was said that Richard's captor, the German emperor, had demanded a ransom nearly twice as great as all the wealth in England. Emmalyn had been eager to do her part when the request for funds first arrived, but now she felt a pinch of regret in aiding the king's eventual release. His return would only hasten her misfortune.

Evidently Nurse's thoughts were on a similar track. "With the king imprisoned these past months on the Continent, milady, mayhap none of these orders will come to pass. Richard's ransom might never be met, and even if it is, who's to say if he will be released by his captors? He may well never return to England."

"Pray he does, Bertie," Emmalyn countered. "For if not Richard, then England will have to contend with his evil brother, and Prince John will surely have far worse plans for me and this place should he be made king."

"You could appeal to the church," Bertie suggested. "Seek sanctuary there as a nun—many widows have done likewise. The church would protect you, milady."

"And what is to become of Fallonmour if I go?" As tempting as it was to think she might be able to avoid the misery of another marriage, Emmalyn shook her head. "I cannot leave, Bertie. This is my home now. I will not abandon it in fear."

"Then what about going to your sister for help? I'm cer-

tain that Lady Josette and her husband would do whatever
they could for you."

"They would try, I know," Emmalyn said. "But not even
Josette and Stephan have friends high enough to thwart the
king's rule. To seek their help in this would be to invite
greater troubles, for them and for Fallonmour. This is my
problem, Bertie. I must deal with it on my own."

Nurse gave her a sobering look. "I reckon Hugh de
Wardeaux will be none too pleased with the king's plan.
How many times in these past three years did he appeal to
the courts, seeking to lay claim to Fallonmour through his
alliance with John?"

"Too many to count," Emmalyn admitted. "And I do not
expect that he will be content to wait around for King
Richard to return before he attempts more of the same. Perhaps even by force."

"Oh, 'tis so unfair!" Bertie lamented. "You have worked
your fingers raw to ensure that Fallonmour thrived, caring
for the land and the folk far more than your husband ever
did. Fallonmour should be yours, milady. You deserve to
remain here."

Emmalyn's heart warmed at her maid's devotion. "Pride-
fully, I feel likewise, Bertie. But do you think the king will
care a whit what we think? Do you imagine his guard will
care what I have done around here? To them, Fallonmour is
just a prize. Something to be won or traded for another
man's gain."

Much the same as they saw her, Emmalyn reflected bitterly.

"If only there were someone you could go to for help,"
Bertie said. "Someone with influence, who would hear you
out and appreciate all that you have done for Fallonmour."

Emmalyn smiled and laid a gentle hand on the nurse's
arm. "Can you think of anyone who would support me, a
mere woman, over one of the king's chosen vassals? 'Tis
wishful thinking, at best."

Although Emmalyn had heard of widows holding fiefs on
their own in recent years, the instances were few and far

between. None, certainly, of Fallonmour's wealth and size. No man would believe her capable of managing such a considerable holding; she saw that easily enough in Sir Cabal when he so readily assumed that Arlo had been responsible for Fallonmour's progress.

Only another woman would appreciate the work and care that she had poured into Fallonmour. Only another woman would understand her plight. And it would take the interest of a woman with great power to give Emmalyn even a glimmer of hope that there might be a way out of this most recent predicament.

Ideally, someone with proven influence over the king himself . . .

"Bertie," Emmalyn said, an idea dawning. "Perhaps there is something we can do after all. Has the coffer with the royal ransom gift left Fallonmour yet?"

"No, milady. The steward was still collecting taxes for the gift this morn. Do you mean to rescind Fallonmour's ransom portion?"

Emmalyn shook her head. "Not at all. In fact, I will need the driver to make haste for London immediately. But first I must draft a letter to Queen Eleanor."

"Of course," whispered the old nurse, her face lighting with ebullient conspiracy. "The queen has ever been fond of you, milady."

"Let the king's mother determine if I am deserving to hold Fallonmour on my own," Emmalyn said, her hopes buoying with the idea. "And perhaps if we are fortunate, we can be rid of Sir Cabal within a fortnight."

Cabal quit the great hall with a headache beginning to pound in his temples. His meeting with the seneschal had proven an exercise in frustration. Forgetting the fact that he simply did not like the man, Cabal had to wonder how Arlo had been able to so aptly manage Fallonmour when he could scarcely keep his own records organized. Every question Cabal posed had prompted a hasty shuffle through volumes of ledgers and papers, searching for—and most often not finding—acceptable answers. Cabal had finished his meal, eager to be away from the seneschal's self-aggrandizing prattle, and now more than ever he longed to ease his bones in a hot, soothing bath.

Pausing outside the closed door of the adjoining solar, he heard the muffled sounds of women's voices within, their hushed, secretive tones smacking of collusion. He heard his name fairly hissed on the other side of the door and knew it had come from the lady herself. Managing her would prove a challenge to be sure, but it was a challenge, curiously, he found he was more than willing to meet.

Cabal grabbed the iron latch and entered the solar without bothering to knock. From the center of the room, two females whirled to meet him with shocked, guilty-looking expressions. Lady Emmalyn was the first to voice her effrontery.

"Have you no regard for privacy, sir, that you would barge into this chamber unannounced?"

"When last I recalled, madam, this chamber was being readied for my bath. I would take it now."

She impaled him with an icy glare, raking over his travel-worn appearance in blatant disapproval. "Then by all means, do not let us keep you from it. I shall send one of the maids along to attend you."

She and her rotund companion made to brush past him, united in their obvious contempt for him. Cabal understood their anger, but he would leave them no time to conspire against him while he was sitting naked in a tub of water. "Actually, my lady, I would prefer that you stayed instead. There are a few things I would discuss with you."

The older woman gasped in outrage, but Lady Emmalyn remained calm, slanting him a mutinous look. "Surely these matters can wait until you have finished with your bath, my lord. I have duties awaiting me elsewhere; I shall make myself available to you within the hour—"

"I would prefer to speak with you now, madam."

"Sir Cabal," the maid interjected, stepping between the two of them like a protective mother hen. "I hasten to remind you that milady has had a very trying day. To make her tend your bath is asking far too much of her hospitality, not to mention her sensibilities. For pity's sake, milord, she is a newly made widow!"

"A widow who has yet to shed the first tear," Cabal replied, noting the superior tilt to the lady's chin and her blazingly clear, perfectly dry eyes. Inviting no further argument, he turned away from the women and began to unbuckle his sword belt. He placed his baldric and weapons alongside the tub, everything within easy grasp, a habit learned well from his years of battle training and war. A faldstool near the tub provided him a seat while he removed his boots, he well aware of the rebellion brewing near the door.

"If you please, my lady," he prompted when she made no immediate move to comply. "I would bathe while the water remains warm."

A whispered assurance sent the scowling maid trundling off down the corridor; then Lady Emmalyn faced him. "I'm sure you'll understand if I prefer to keep the door open."

Cabal shrugged. "As you wish. I've no particular inclination toward modesty. Come, help me out of my armor."

She could not quite harness the indignant sneer that tugged at her mouth, Cabal noticed with some measure of interest. Lady Emmalyn appeared to be a woman who wore her emotions in her every expression and in her luminous green eyes. A fact that would serve him well in his future dealings with her.

She said nothing as she approached him and knelt before the place where he sat on the stool. He supposed the offended little sniff she made when she drew close had as much to do with his malodor from days of riding as it did with her obvious objection to his presence in her home. Without looking into his face, Lady Emmalyn set about untying the underarm laces of his worn Crusader's tunic, then stood and pulled the garment over his head. Her gaze lingered on the bloodstained faded surcoat as if to count the number of lives that had left their mark on the pale red silk. Too many even for Cabal to hazard a guess now—the last having been this beauty's highborn husband.

"I reckon 'tis good only for the fire," he said, feeling somewhat relieved when she finally set the thing aside.

Her blond head bowed, Lady Emmalyn turned her attention to the leather thongs that secured his chain mail hauberk together at the sides. With deft, fine-boned fingers, she loosened the laces and helped him shrug out of the cumbersome link armor. His padded gambeson vest came off next, then his undertunic, leaving him bared to the waist.

The weight removed, Cabal clamped a hand to his neck and closed his eyes, trying to roll the kinks from his neck and glad for the freedom to stretch his tired muscles. When he lifted his lids a moment later, Lady Emmalyn stood before him, watching. She stared at a spot at the center of his chest, her eyes rooted in curiosity to the small object he wore suspended on a cord around his neck. The cold feel of the amulet against his skin burrowed deeper with every heartbeat that her gaze lingered.

"I can manage the rest," he told her, a terse edge to his voice that actually made her draw back a pace.

She gave him her back and walked to the hearth to stoke the waning fire. Cabal removed his mail leggings, then stripped off his chausses, all the while watching Lady Emmalyn's unpracticed grace as she busied herself with gathering a wedge of soap and a folded linen drying sheet that he would need for his bath. Cabal slowed his progress on the other side of the room, if only to observe her a bit longer, marveling at the tenacity that seemed coiled so tightly within her petite frame.

An enticingly sensual frame, which his long-neglected libido was only too eager to notice.

"Your water grows cold, my lord."

Had she sensed his more than appreciative appraisal? Cabal grinned wryly at the back of her uptilted head, then shed his braies and stepped into the steaming, spice-scented bathwater. The fragrant heat stole his breath as he sunk down into the padded tub, reclining as best he could. The vessel had not been constructed for a man of his size, but even with his knees bent and sticking out of the water and his upper arms pressing against the sides, Cabal felt a bit of his tension begin to melt away. That is, until he felt Lady Emmalyn's hands come to rest tentatively on his shoulders.

"Shall I start with your back or your chest?"

She asked the question with about as much passion as a butcher might inquire after a preferred cut of meat, but the combined effect of her touch and her silky voice so close to his ear rendered Cabal nearly bereft of coherent thought. "Stay there," he growled on a throat suddenly gone dry. "Where you are is fine, my lady."

He shifted in the cramped tub, trying not to let his pleasure show in the tight groan that escaped his lips as Lady Emmalyn dipped her hands into the water and set to work soaping his back. Her touch was light, uncertain—exceedingly more erotic to Cabal than the practiced hands of the washerwomen sent along to Palestine to service the Crusaders. He felt her lathered fingers skim over the various battle scars that riddled his skin, heard her quiet, indrawn breath as she leaned forward to better reach his arms and shoulders.

The rough fabric of her homespun gown grazed his wet skin, her breasts barely touching his back. Unintentional, he was certain, but the whispered contact sent a bolt of lust through him that turned his knuckles white where his hands now gripped the rim of the washtub. God's wounds. He had not been so long without female company that this woman should arouse him so effortlessly.

Cabal exhaled deeply, searching for something to concentrate on aside from his sudden, urgent want to feel her hands all over his body. He found a bit of promise in a tapestry that hung above the hearth on the other side of the room. "Be that one of Fallonmour's high lords on the hunt?" he inquired idly.

A long moment of guarded silence answered before the lady spoke. " 'Tis a depiction of the great king, Arthur. A gift from my father upon my wedding."

"Arthur Pendragon," Cabal mused, needful of the distraction when in that next instant Lady Emmalyn's slick fingers skated down the length of his spine. "My father was a fond admirer as well . . . or so my mother used to tell me."

Behind him, the lady paused, letting a handful of soapy water trickle over his shoulder. "My lord, I trust you do not mean to keep me from my duties simply to engage me in discussion over England's famed, long-dead rulers."

Her impertinence surprised him. It intrigued him. "We will discuss whatever I deem noteworthy," he told her coolly. "And I will keep you no longer than is necessary. Now, continue with what you were doing."

The water at his back lapped around him, the only audible sound as she resumed her ministrations. Obediently, she soaped his neck and shoulders, but her resentment for being forced into the task was made clear in her every brisk, efficient stroke. Her fingernails grazed his nape, and Cabal half expected to feel her tiny hands reach up and tighten around his neck.

"You know, my lady, it was not my choice to be sent here to serve as Fallonmour's guardian. Would that your husband had lived and I had remained with my king. Your life would be unchanged, and King Richard might not be now imprisoned by his enemies."

It was a thought that had plagued Cabal from the day he learned of Richard's capture. He should have been there. He might have seen the danger in time enough to avoid it. He certainly would not have let the king be taken without a bloody fight. Instead he was here, sent to watch over a peaceful country demesne and a willful young widow with an angel's face and a body to tempt a blessed saint.

And Cabal was far from saintly.

He cleared his throat, marshaling his thoughts away from any further ruminations on her unholy appeal. "Truth to tell, my lady, I want to be here no more than you would have me stay. Less, I'd wager."

She scoffed. "I doubt that's possible, my lord."

Cabal eyed her as she came around the side of the tub and washed the length of his arm, suddenly wishing she had been the meek young woman that Richard had described. Far better than this hissing lioness who seemed intent on scrubbing away half of his skin in her spite.

"I assure you, madam, your little plot of land and those who would squabble over it interest me not in the least," he told her irritably. "I am a fighting man, not a farmer. I am here to guard Fallonmour simply because I am the king's best. It is my duty to look after the garrison and the castle's defenses until the new lord is installed. In the meantime, I will expect the full cooperation of you and the rest of your folk. Arlo has already assured me of his continued support as seneschal. Now I must ask for your cooperation as well, my lady."

She dropped his arm into the water with a negligent splash. "You ask for my cooperation, and the king asks for my home and my freedom. Yet I am to expect nothing in exchange for all of this."

"You can expect the security of knowing that with or without you, Fallonmour will not fall into the hands of Hugh de Wardeaux or any other of Prince John's supporters. I trust that means something to you."

He could see that it did, but stubbornly, she would give him no answer. Perhaps she worried more over her own fate once Richard was free to choose a husband for her. Cabal could well understand it if she did; a lady of her youth and beauty would have no trouble attracting suitors for her hand, even in widowhood. She would be wed swiftly, and to the highest bidder more than likely—a dismal future for a lady who had evidently grown attached to her short-lived independence.

But the eventual fate of one headstrong noblewoman was none of his concern whatsoever. He had a mission to carry out, regardless of what might later befall this lady.

"What say you, madam?" he prompted impatiently. "Will I have your cooperation in this?"

She scowled down at her folded hands for a long moment, refusal blazing in the tight line of her mouth. "It seems that I am left with little choice."

Hardly a convincing declaration of good intent. "I would have your solemn vow, my lady."

"Very well." Lady Emmalyn's voice was quietly serene, but there was defiance in the pale green gaze she leveled on him, contempt in her every measured syllable. "On my vow, my lord, I give you my full cooperation . . . for so long as you shall remain at Fallonmour."

He did not trust the stubborn set of her jaw, no more than he trusted her carefully phrased pledge of support. She was plotting something. Perhaps she had already set the wheels of conspiracy in motion. The lady had demonstrated that she was defensive of her home, but would she defy him to retain it? Would she defy her king?

"If you have no more demands of me at the moment, my lord, I will thank you to finish your bath without my further assistance."

She pushed against the tub and started to rise. Before she could take the first step in retreat, Cabal pivoted and caught her wrist cleanly in his hand. She gasped. Startlement and outrage warred in her eyes as she tested his grasp and found it firm and unrelenting. This close, he could not keep his gaze from straying over the length of her, from her strikingly beautiful face to the dampened fabric that clung to her breasts; from the rise and fall of her bosom, to the subtle flare of her hips and the slender outlines of her thighs.

A potent hunger stirred to life inside him as she stared into his eyes, her tiny fist clenched, her lips parted in silent protest. All it would take was a slight tug and she would be in the tub with him, sprawled across his lap. God's wounds, but the image was so vivid, he could almost feel her there now. His grip on her arm tightened of its own accord, his every muscle coiled with tension as his thoughts sped forward on an increasingly illicit path.

He might have let her leave without issue had she not seemed so sure that he would. But she was testing him, pushing the boundaries to see how far he would let her go before reining her in. Touching her had been a mistake, however, even if he meant just to quell a bit of her rebellion. Touching her made it all too easy for him to want more. More of something that already belonged to another.

Something he had forsworn himself long ago.

Cabal released her as if to thrust away the temptation. She stumbled back a pace, staring at him in wild astonishment and rubbing her wrist where he had held her. "Go," he growled when she hesitated to take her leave.

He sunk lower into the tub and closed his eyes, eternally grateful when he heard the sound of her footsteps hastening to the door. He did not move a muscle, not even to draw breath, until the echo of her retreat had vanished down the winding hallway.

Then he shuddered with the sheer power of his want for her.

"Damnation," he swore on a grating whisper. What had he done to offend Richard so that he would sentence him to this brand of torment?

Chapter Four

Emmalyn fled the solar, awash with confusion and panic. She could still feel Sir Cabal's strong hand where it had engulfed her wrist, could still see the hungry look blazing in his ruthless gray eyes. Heaven help her, but the image of his warrior's hard body was still resonant in her mind, every ridge and plane and scar a vivid testament to the violence through which he made his living. She looked at him and saw everything she despised in man: savagery, domination, mercilessness.

Why, then, was her heart still pounding so fiercely in her breast?

She tried to tell herself it was fear that set her pulse racing, worry for her people and her future that made her head spin. Certainly it was anger that fired her cheeks now, outrage over this brash soldier and his arrogant demands that made her blood course hot and furious in her veins. Nothing more.

Dear Lord, she could not allow it to be anything more!

She had to be rid of Sir Cabal, she resolved with new determination. She had to be rid of him as soon as possible. If only the queen would oblige to hear her case. Composing her appeal in her mind, Emmalyn dashed to the stairwell that led to her chambers abovestairs. Arlo met her halfway up.

He took one look at her disheveled, water-stained appearance and gasped. "Saints' blood! What did the cur do, force you to bathe with him?" His probing gaze lingered a heartbeat too long on Emmalyn's flushed face, and his eyes narrowed.

"Or does the high color of your cheeks suggest free will instead, my lady?"

Emmalyn glared at Arlo, refusing to answer to him for anything now. Her problems were far greater than the petty manipulations of Garrett's despised seneschal. She took a step to the side, but Arlo countered, blocking her path up the stairs. "You cannot actually mean to suffer this guard's continued presence here at Fallonmour," he challenged. "Particularly when you must know that all it would take is a message to Lord Hugh and you could have Richard's man ejected from the place on the prince's order."

"I thought you had given Sir Cabal your oath of support," Emmalyn replied caustically. "Although I cannot say that your suggested duplicity comes as much of a surprise, Arlo."

The seneschal chuckled. "And where has your sense of honor gotten you, my lady? Dispossessed and under guard. How the thought must grate on your haughty ideals," he added slyly. "I should think you would be only too eager to seek Lord Hugh's protection now, in light of these new circumstances."

"What Hugh and the prince would offer me is not protection," Emmalyn said. "Do not think for a moment I am naive enough to believe that Garrett's brother would give a thought to my welfare when he's cared little for my rights these past three years. If I must lose Fallonmour, I would rather see it go to any one of the king's chosen vassals before I let Hugh within a league of claiming it for his own. Fallonmour has already endured one tyrant lord; I'll not let it fall into the hands of another."

"A martyr's lot for you, then, is it, my lady?" Arlo jeered. "I wonder to what lengths you would go in this fool's quest to deny Lord Hugh his rightful claim to Fallonmour. Would you sacrifice yourself to Richard's beast if you thought he might somehow help you?" He snickered with malicious humor. "Mayhap you already have."

Incensed, Emmalyn reached up and slapped Arlo across the face. Without a word, she lifted her skirts and brushed past him up the stairs.

"You're making a grave mistake this day," Arlo growled after her. "I might have been persuaded to beg Hugh's lenience on your behalf, but no more. You've chosen your path, my lady; you tread it alone."

Emmalyn refused to acknowledge the seneschal's warning, despite the fact that she knew his ominous words to be true. She was alone in her fight to maintain Fallonmour, now more than ever. She felt that weight tenfold as she climbed the rest of the steps and shut herself in her chamber to pen her letter to the queen.

An hour later, Emmalyn stood in the bailey, watching as the cart carrying a coffer filled with the bulk of Fallonmour's spring profits drove out of the massive castle gates accompanied by two armed guards. She had given the driver an extra tithe on his promise to see her sealed letter was delivered directly to the royal palace. Now all she could do was wait . . . and hope.

Satisfied for the moment that she still had a hand in the shaping of her own destiny, Emmalyn entered the keep. Under her arm she held a large basket of wool brought up from the village. This year's shearing was more bountiful than she had dared anticipate, the quality of the wool among the finest she had ever seen. They should fetch a handsome price for it at the Lincolnshire market next week. Pride swelled in her breast at the thought. The venture that Garrett had refused to consider and what Arlo had called an irresponsible risk, was in fact, paying off.

Emmalyn dropped off the basket in the women's solar, looking forward to spinning some of the wool that evening. Her step lightened, she mounted the stairwell. At the top of the winding ascent, she felt something keenly amiss, something that made the hairs at the nape of her neck rise in warning. Turning in the opposite direction from her chambers, she saw a nimbus of sunlight pouring into the dark hallway through the open door of Garrett's personal chamber, the place where, when she was fortunate, her husband had spent his nights away from her before he left on Crusade.

Since he had been gone, the room had been opened only for cleaning and an occasional airing out. Emmalyn saw no reason to set foot in it elsewise, and she really had no desire to do so now, save to find out who might have invaded the private chambers.

Stepping cautiously, she approached the open doorway and took in the room with one quick glance: the small collection of bound texts lining the far wall, the hooded deep-set fireplace with its orderly stack of logs, the upholstered chair and richly carved desk that her husband had so prized, the papers and ledgers arranged neatly on its surface . . . everything precisely how Garrett had left it. Even her husband's scent seemed to remain, faded certainly, but perceptible enough to chase a cold shiver up Emmalyn's spine.

At the window, with his back to the door, stood a fine-clothed dark-haired man. The sun blazed from without, casting his large frame in silhouette as he leaned one shoulder against the stone embrasure of the window. In a moment of wild panic, Emmalyn could have sworn this man was Garrett, somehow returned and now bigger than life. She must have gasped, for he turned and she found herself face-to-face with Sir Cabal. At least she assumed this handsome man and the dark-visaged knight were one and the same. His expression hardened when Emmalyn could only stare at him, frowning.

"What are you doing in here?" she demanded.

"I will have need of private quarters while I am at Fallon-mour," he answered, stepping out of the shadows and fully into her view. "I saw no reason to take the lord's chamber for myself. You may remain there if it pleases you."

"How very noble of you to think of me, my lord," Emmalyn shot back, but her retort lacked the venom she intended. She could only stare at him, astonished at the transformation that had occurred in the beastly knight she had left sitting in his bath.

Sir Cabal was clean and freshly shaven now, his jet hair still damp from a recent washing. The thick waves were swept back off his chiseled face, falling past his shoulders, their sheen as glossy as a raven's wing. The beard he had worn before had hidden somewhat the strong angles of his jaw, she noted, and as well the fine supple cut of his mouth. And if she thought his gray eyes striking on first glance, now they were absolutely spellbinding, made all the more vivid by the harsh masculine beauty of his face unveiled.

Though this was no longer the savage-looking warrior who had ridden into her bailey a short while ago, Emmalyn still felt an arcane prickle of wariness in his company. Perhaps more so now that he looked every inch a proper gentleman.

His stained and bloodied Crusader's surcoat had been replaced with a silk tunic the color of dried rosemary, which clung to his broad shoulders and thick-hewn arms, the fabric stretching tight across his chest, even unlaced at the collar, as he wore it. Matching hose encased his thighs and disappeared into dark leather boots.

Emmalyn had to shake herself mentally to keep from staring any longer. "You're wearing my husband's clothes," was all she could manage to say.

One black brow rose on his broad forehead as he offered her a rueful half smile. "All I had on return from Palestine were the clothes on my back, my lady. Would you have preferred I don my gambeson and armor for the whole of my stay here?"

"I'm sure I could not care less what you wear," she told him curtly, wishing it were true. Seeing him washed and dressed as fine as any noble lord, Emmalyn decided that she far preferred him in chain mail, for then she would be ever reminded of what he truly was: a cold warrior. The king's best guard, as he was quick to tell her. A trained killer, and now her keeper.

"Arlo advised me there is a ransom gift being assembled here on behalf of the king's release," he said at last, watching her closely as if he could read the jumbled mess her thoughts became in his presence. "I trust all goes well thus far with the collection."

Emmalyn struggled to hold his steady, probing gaze, feeling a twinge of guilt for the note now en route to London. "The driver left with the coffer just a few moments ago, my lord. In fact, I saw him off myself."

"Really?" It was a mild query, edged with his apparent surprise. "Well, I must commend your honor, my lady. Another in your place might have sought to delay the delivery of a ransom that would ultimately speed the passing of an unfavorable edict."

"England needs her king," Emmalyn replied carefully, "and you may believe me when I tell you that I am no less eager than anyone to see that the queen receives what I have sent her."

"Indeed?"

Emmalyn gave a slight nod, sensing the challenge in his deliberate question, certain he knew she concealed some portion of the truth from him. But he did not press her for details. With a gaze that caressed almost as surely as it scathed, he turned back to the open window. "I have been impressed with what I've seen of Fallonmour's accountings, my lady. 'Tis a well-managed estate; doubtless the king will be pleased."

"I reckon no more so than the man he would choose to grant it to in given time."

The knight chuckled vaguely at her sarcasm. "Your seneschal advised me that your time alone had made you headstrong, Lady Emmalyn. On that score, I find I am inclined to agree with him."

He said it with humor in his voice, but Emmalyn found no amusement in his giving credence to anything Arlo would say. "If you were wise, my lord, you would seek Arlo's counsel on nothing of any import. Trust him even less."

Sir Cabal pinned her with a questioning look. "He said much the same of you, my lady. He said you would try to convince me that he was unfit and uninformed as seneschal, that you would insist that you were the one responsible for managing Fallonmour all this time."

"Do you find that so hard to believe, my lord?"

"I find it interesting that Arlo professes sole responsibility for Fallonmour's prosperity, yet your hands are the ones that show the work."

Emmalyn glanced away suddenly, unwilling to accept the complimentary undercurrent to the knight's keen observation. It astonished her that he had divined Arlo's falseness already, but even more shocking was the fact that he would credit her efforts.

"Arlo intends to betray you to Hugh."

She confessed the advice so softly, she was hardly sure she had said it all. But Sir Cabal heard it well enough. "A warning, my lady? And here you've had me thinking you regarded me as your enemy, not an ally."

"I do it not for you or the king, so much as for Fallonmour," she said, refusing to consider that Richard's man could ever be anything but her adversary. "Arlo's only allegiance is to himself and those from whom he feels he has the most to gain. He will pledge his support to you easily enough, but his oath means nothing. He said as much to me this morning after . . ."

After she had fled in shamed alarm from her encounter with Sir Cabal in the solar.

Emmalyn could not finish the thought. She swallowed hard, chagrined to have gotten even this close to mentioning the unsettling experience of bathing Sir Cabal. As it was, the knight studied her too closely, his sharp gaze too penetrating, his vague smile too arrogant, too knowing.

"I thank you for the advice, my lady," he said at last. "Whatever your reasons for offering it. I myself suspected as much of Arlo, which is why I discharged him from his duties."

"Discharged him?"

The knight gave a grim nod. "He left the keep about an hour ago."

The news stunned her—pleased her—but the ramifications

prevented her from rejoicing at Arlo's dismissal. "He will go directly to Hugh." When Sir Cabal did not openly share her alarm, she added, "Once Hugh learns of my widowhood, he will come to claim Fallonmour by force, regardless of what the king has decreed."

"Then he will have to contend with me."

If any other man had made so bold a statement, Emmalyn would have laughed or at the very least thought him mad. But staring into the bleak, ruthless depths of Sir Cabal's eyes, she knew his avowal was not some warrior's idle boast. He was Richard's best; she did not doubt it for an instant.

She wondered how many men he had killed for his king that Richard would be confident enough to send him alone to guard Fallonmour. Though her keep was leagues from London, she had heard the many tales of the king's warrior henchmen, terrible reports of the fear they evoked, chilling accounts of the deaths and decimation. Was this man as merciless as some of Richard's other knights? She was almost afraid to wonder.

Emmalyn was wholeheartedly relieved when Sir Cabal freed her from his gaze, turning his attention back to the open window and the view from beyond the high tower. "Such a vast holding," he remarked thoughtfully, almost to himself.

And it was vast. An awesome sight, as Emmalyn verily knew. She could well imagine what greeted Sir Cabal's vision now: the boundless beauty of the lands that spread in all directions, lush fields and green meadows rolling out as far as the eye could see, every square patch of it contributing to the greater splendor that was Fallonmour.

With the help of the peasants and her folk, Emmalyn had lifted the holding to new heights of prosperity. It was her most proud accomplishment, making Fallonmour strong, and her heart gladdened with the knowledge. Before she could stop herself, she was drifting quietly into the chamber. She came to stand a few paces behind Sir Cabal, just to look upon the land she loved so dearly.

" 'Tis nearly a league, all told," she volunteered hesitantly. "Our wheat and vegetable fields spread to the east; the meadows sweep northerly and to the west. That large hill over there marks the property line to the south."

"There?" Sir Cabal asked mildly, gesturing into the distance.

"Nay," she answered. "Farther south. 'Tis difficult to see from here, I think."

He turned his head slowly toward her, and Emmalyn struggled to tamp down the tremor of awareness that skittered through her at the intensity of his gaze. "Show me."

It seemed a reasonable enough request, she supposed, even if it meant she had to draw closer to him. She stepped to the window and leaned slightly forward, bracing herself at the casement with one palm pressed to the cool flat stone. "There," she said, pointing toward the grassy embankment that marked the southernmost end of her lands.

Sir Cabal seated himself behind her on the wide ledge then, his close proximity generating a nearly palpable heat at her back. In the gentle breeze lofting in through the open window, Emmalyn scented the appealingly spicy undertones of his clove-water bath and a subtle muskiness that, inexplicably, she knew was his alone. She startled when his long arm stretched out beside hers, following her gesture to the area she indicated.

"Ah, yes," he said beside her ear. "I see it now."

His breath was warm, nearly as warm as his dark, rumbling voice. Emmalyn felt something strange rouse within her, something that frightened her as surely as it sought to seduce her. It was awareness, she realized in terror. Awareness for a fighting man—someone who made his living through violence and killing. She squeezed her eyes shut in an attempt to bar him from her senses, which ultimately failed the moment he spoke again.

"I reckon I have never before seen such beauty, my lady."

Emmalyn turned, certain she had not heard correctly. Was he speaking of Fallonmour—the plot of land, which just that morning he had claimed to have no interest in—or did he refer to something else? She stared at him in stunned silence, unable to tear her gaze away from his, not daring to imagine what he meant by his remark, let alone ask.

The air thickened around her, making it hard to breathe, impossible to think straight. Dear Lord, how had she been fool enough to put herself so close to him? He was near enough to touch her. Near enough to kiss her. As if her unwilling thoughts were laid bare for him to read, Sir Cabal's gaze drifted slowly, deliberately to her lips. Emmalyn froze, unable to draw breath, knowing she should flee yet unable to command her legs to action. What madness was it for her to crave this man's kiss? For crave it she did, with every taut fiber of her being.

Her heart thudded a deafening tattoo, accelerating wildly as he reached out to catch a wayward strand of her hair between his fingers. With a movement that seemed too gentle for a man of his strength and size, he swept the errant lock behind her ear. Emmalyn swallowed hard, torn between wanting his kiss and wanting him gone.

As if he sensed her indecision, the harsh line of his mouth softened into a lazy, knowing smile. "Perhaps 'tis time you introduce me to Fallonmour's garrison, my lady."

Chapter Five

Cabal followed Lady Emmalyn out of the chamber, his steps falling hard at her heels. His limbs were still heavy with the weight of his lust for her, his pulse still thundering in his ears. Seating himself beside her at the window had been pure reckless folly. He had recognized that fact in ample time to avoid it, but like a thirsting man drawn to the illusion of desert water, nothing could have stopped him from closing the distance between them. Once there, it had been a damned hard struggle to keep from touching her. It had been next to impossible for him to keep from sweeping her mass of silky blond hair aside and tasting the graceful curve of her neck, a spot he knew was certain to be as sweet and warm as her enticingly feminine scent.

The knowledge that she might have let him do just that haunted Cabal as he exited the keep with her and stepped into the bustle of the castle's inner bailey.

Lady Emmalyn's appearance drew the attention of a clutch of guards positioned at the far side of the grassy courtyard, the majority of them lounging against the shading walls of the enclosure while they drank from flagons of ale and conversed. The elder of the group came forward at once, his proud carriage and seasoned demeanor marking him as the garrison's captain.

"Sir Miles," Lady Emmalyn greeted warmly as the gray-bearded knight approached and gave her a deferential bow.

"My lady, the keep has been abuzz all morning with the misfortunate news brought back from Palestine. I am sorry to hear about Lord Garrett." The grizzled captain turned a reproachful look on Cabal. "My sympathies for the rest of the matter as well, my lady."

"So everyone has heard already of the king's plans for Fallonmour?" she asked.

"Aye, my lady. And as well his plans for you," Sir Miles added, his old-man's voice darkened with obvious defensiveness for his lady's welfare.

"Then you must also know that King Richard has sent one of his guards, Sir Cabal, to watch over the keep until a new tenant is appointed." The captain nodded, slanting Cabal a narrowed, cutting glance that bespoke his disapproval. "Sir Miles has served as Fallonmour's captain for many years," she told Cabal. "He has a great deal of experience with protecting the keep, and the men trust and respect him. I'm certain he will prove a benefit to you in sharing their command, my lord."

"There will be only one captain of this garrison, my lady," Cabal interjected, intent to put a damper on any notion of shared command—to say nothing of past alliances between the guards and their beloved lady. "By the king's order, that man is me."

He was not sure which of the two looked more opposed to surrendering their authority; both the lady and her old guard gaped at him in futile outrage. Sir Miles withered quickly under Cabal's flat stare, developing a sudden interest in his boots, but Lady Emmalyn did not so much as flinch.

"Sir Miles," Cabal instructed, "assemble all of the men. I will join you in a moment to address them." The deposed captain flicked a questioning glance at his lady, hesitating as if to await her confirmation of this new arrangement. "Do it now, Sir Miles."

When the knight had ambled out of earshot to dispense the order, Lady Emmalyn turned to Cabal. "Was it entirely necessary to be so disrespectful of him?" Holding his gaze with a tenacity Cabal was coming to appreciate, as much as it exasperated him, she folded her arms one over the other and glared her reproach. "Sir Miles is a proud man, my lord. If he is defensive of my wishes, it is only because he has Fallonmour's best interests at heart—"

"And I have the king's."

Her slim jaw hardened mutinously at his blunt reminder, an angered flush filling her cheeks. Cabal expected a fiery challenge from the lady but was instead surprised to see her gaze soften almost sadly. When she spoke, her voice was quiet, imploring. "My lord, I realize that you are duty-bound to the king, and I fully understand that you care little for what happens to me or this place. When your mission is over, you will go back to whatever life you left behind and we will all be easily forgotten. But while you are here, I would ask you to have a care with these folk. They are good people, hardworking, devoted. Perhaps that means nothing to you, but it matters to me. They matter to me."

She waited for his reply, staring at him for a long moment as if searching for some trace of compassion in his eyes. Foolish woman; he possessed none. He supposed she would learn that soon enough. "Your concerns have been noted, my lady," he replied, deliberately avoiding an answer. "Now, if you will, I have a garrison to command."

He could feel her hot stare behind him as he pivoted on his heel and walked away from her, striding toward the company of knights gathered near the wall. He heard her infuriated huff as she spun and marched back to the keep, a clear indication of her ill regard for him. She was coming to despise him, Cabal knew, more and more with every hour that he was there. The idea should not have troubled him in the slightest; he had not come there to win the widow's admiration. But strangely, he found that he respected her anger. Her devotion to Fallonmour and its folk intrigued him, perhaps more than he cared to admit.

All the better reason that he should endeavor to keep himself occupied outside the castle and away from her. He needed to be in his element, sword in hand and back on the field, even if it was just in practice. Fortunately on that score, it looked as if he would have no shortage of work with Fallonmour's meager garrison.

Most of the knights were of a middling age, and if Cabal's initial assessment was true, none seemed in any manner of fitness, let alone ready for battle. "Tell me this is not the whole of Fallonmour's army, Sir Miles," Cabal drawled as he approached them.

The captain cleared his throat. "This be it, sir, the whole lot. Two dozen-odd men, I reckon, if you count the fostering squires."

God's bones. Less than thirty guards at most and from the looks of them, long unused to combat. That the keep had managed to escape a serious attack in these three years was in itself a miracle, but to hope that the motley collection of knights assembled before him might one day make an army was utter lunacy. Or impending suicide.

"You have heard, I'm certain, that this keep belongs once more to the king," he told them. "Until he decides on a suitable heir, he has charged me with protecting Fallonmour against all contenders . . . including the prince and the brother of your former lord. If any among you has sworn fealty to John or to Hugh de Wardeaux, speak now and gain your discharge from this garrison."

When no one answered, Sir Miles spoke for the group. "We are pledged in service to this keep, Sir Cabal. We would each of us lay down his life for Fallonmour, and for Lady Emmalyn as well."

"You may be called upon to do just that," Cabal replied. "I expect that once de Wardeaux hears of his brother's demise, he will waste no time in bringing his forces to Fallonmour to secure the holding for himself in the name of Prince John. Our king does not want to see that happen. Neither, for that matter, does Lady Emmalyn."

"Let de Wardeaux come!" shouted one man enthusiastically. "We will be ready!"

Sir Miles's response was slower in forming and decidedly

less bold. "How many men do you reckon he will bring, Sir Cabal?"

"Your guess is as sound as mine. But they will surely be more and better skilled than what Hugh expects to find here at Fallonmour."

The old captain swore an oath and lowered his voice to confer more privately. "Wardeaux Castle is but three days' ride from here and word spreads quickly. It will not take long for Hugh to hear that Fallonmour has no lord. In fact, I would expect that Arlo has already sent a message to him, rot his traitorous soul."

Cabal nodded, appreciative of the old man's insight. "I discharged the seneschal this morning. He left Fallonmour some time ago; no doubt he rides for Wardeaux as we speak."

"Jesu," Sir Miles hissed. "If Hugh should set out immediately upon Arlo's arrival, it will mean we have less than a sennight to prepare to meet him, my lord."

"We have to assume that will be the case."

"But twice that time would not be long enough to take on an army of even equal size." The knight shook his head morosely. "If we do not have time, then we will need more men."

"Precisely my thinking," Cabal replied, knowing their best advantage would be in numbers if not in skill.

Sir Miles frowned. "By the time we send out a herald to gather up lances for hire, de Wardeaux will like as not already be at our doorstep."

Cabal conceded the point with a casual shrug. "We've no need to hire anyone," he said. "I warrant Fallonmour has able-bodied men enough to form a respectably sized army."

That statement drew confused glances from a few of the other knights. Sir Miles regarded Cabal as if he spoke in riddles. "But 'tis just as I told you, my lord. There are no more men than those you see assembled here."

Cabal nodded and spoke to the group. "In Palestine our armies met with resistance from every person capable of wielding a weapon. No one was too innocent nor too lowborn to raise arms in defense of their country and their faith." At the collective look of confusion, Cabal further explained. "The Saracens united—warrior and common man alike—and to their credit, the Holy Sepulchre yet resides in Jerusalem."

A long silence stretched out before one man ventured, "Are you suggesting we arm Fallonmour's peasants?"

"More than that. I am suggesting we train them in combat."

" 'Tis against God's law for a serf to raise arms against a nobleman," one man warned.

"Then we will knight the ones who prove skillful." Cabal watched the offended glances being exchanged between the fallow onetime warriors, well aware of the animosity he was generating. He paused to let it simmer, then tossed a bit more fat into the fire. "Bring me any healthy man from his fields and I warrant I will make of him a soldier. Better, I would wager, than any one of you."

The brash challenge garnered brooding scorn from the lot of knights, as Cabal fully expected. He wanted them angry. He needed every one of them bound and determined to prove him wrong, for their ire would prove a better motivator than anything else he could have said to them at that moment. Only Sir Miles seemed to understand what Cabal was doing. The old captain slanted him a knowing look, then followed him to the periphery of the practice yard while the group of knights picked up their arms and commenced with a robust round of sparring exercises.

"Do you truly think your plan will work?" Sir Miles asked hopefully when he and Cabal were left to their own in the shade of the castle tower.

"I have no misconceptions that I can turn a field full of peasants into battle-ready knights in a few days," Cabal admitted. "But I will train them as if I mean to do just that, and when Hugh comes, he will see an army guarding these walls."

The graying knight let out a heavy sigh, but there was a glimmer of intrigue in his eyes. " 'Tis a serious risk, and not one I would have ever dared, but I believe what you say is possible. I will support your plan in whatever way I can."

Cabal looked down at the captain's outstretched hand, taken slightly aback by the gesture. He was unused to teamwork, much preferring to shoulder responsibility on his own. But something in the old man's conspiratorial gaze tugged at Cabal, and before he knew it, he had reached out to clasp Sir Miles's hand, acknowledging—and accepting—his offered collaboration. "Let's get started," he said with a grin.

Chapter Six

Emmalyn's ears were yet ringing with the sounds of battle practice by the time supper was served that evening. All day long, the bailey below her chamber window had reverberated with the clash of weapons and the coarse shouts of men in training for war. She scowled just to think on it. Less than one day's time and already Sir Cabal had managed to shatter nearly every bit of peace that had once been such an integral part of life at Fallonmour.

In her present frame of mind, she could scarcely concentrate enough to hold a conversation with Father Bryce, Fallonmour's wheezy old clergyman. Seated to her left at the high table, the tonsured chaplain had been carrying on for some time now about his plans to hold a special mass on the morrow to honor Garrett and see that his soul was properly shriven. Despite her private misgivings, Emmalyn would not deny Garrett the service, but she could hardly be concerned with arranging the various memorial details when Fallonmour's future hung precariously in the balance.

When the father suggested that the keep's chapel remain open all day in order that the villagers and castle folk could come and pay their respects, Emmalyn nodded her agreement, though in truth her attention had strayed to the throng of people now pouring into the banquet hall to gather for the meal. At their center was Sir Cabal.

He followed the garrison inside, his face burnished from the sun and exertion, his dark hair roguishly wild about his shoulders. With a glance in Emmalyn's direction, he broke from the crowd of knights and strode toward the dais, his tall form towering head and shoulders over the other men who had once seemed so strong and capable to her. With confident long-legged strides, he approached the high table. "Good eve, my lady."

Emmalyn nodded coolly, hoping her brittle reception would dissuade him from lingering at the dais. The effect was wholly lost in the next instant when Father Bryce rose from his chair, clasping his hands together in warm greeting.

"Sir Cabal!" he exclaimed, as if welcoming a returning hero.

When the father had first arrived at table, he had been singing praises for the Crusader's honor, trying without success to convince Emmalyn that while God had taken her husband, He had sent Fallonmour a bold protector in his place. Emmalyn was more of the mind that they had been traded one devil for another, particularly now, facing the profane appeal of the dark warrior once again.

"I am most eager to hear about your experiences in the Holy Land," Father Bryce said. Then, to Emmalyn's horror, he added, "Come you, my son, join us for the meal. You may have my chair."

Before she could muster an excuse or voice a feasible protest, Sir Cabal accepted the chaplain's offer. He came up on the dais and seated himself beside Emmalyn, his big frame crowding her at the table, his arm nearly pressed against her shoulder. She scooted closer to Nurse at her right, but to her dismay, there was no escape to be had. She could still feel the heat radiating from his body, could smell the muskiness of clean male sweat and horses and leather. Though she fought it, her every fiber seemed attuned to his presence, entirely unable to ignore him.

Nor could Emmalyn ignore how easily the handsome Crusader had won the interest of every young woman in the hall. Once the pages had dispensed with the cleansing bowls and towels, the scullery maids began carrying out the food and drink, the comeliest ones wasting no time in rushing forth to serve the guest on the dais.

"Ale, milord?"

"Trout in cream sauce, my lord?"

The two maids nearly fell over each other in their haste to attend the arrogant knight, who lounged complacently in his chair while the women filled his cup and trencher. The rest of the high table was attended efficiently by other servants, and still Sir Cabal's admirers remained. Emmalyn eyed the giggling flirtatious duo with disdain.

"Jane, Nell, see to the rest of your duties now. There are others in the hall yet waiting to be served."

Nell was quick to bow and take her leave, but Jane lingered a moment longer, tossing her mane of red hair and casting a saucy look over her shoulder at Sir Cabal before languorously departing the dais. Beside her, Emmalyn could feel the weight of the knight's steady gaze, although she refused to look at him for fear he would see that her impatience with the maids actually had little to do with kitchen duties left unattended.

Father Bryce spared her from further consideration of that distressing fact. The priest gave a blessing for the meal, then immediately set about engaging Sir Cabal in conversation of his time on campaign, pressing for details about the harsh beauty of the Holy Land. The knight answered his many questions about religious sites and famed relics but seemed more interested in his meal than in discussing his experiences abroad.

"I am told that the treasures of Acre's many temples boggle the mind," Father Bryce said enthusiastically. "Is it true that the walls of the Saracen mosques are covered in pure gold?"

Sir Cabal took a drink of his ale and gave a bland shrug. "I would not know, Father. The city had been at the center of battle by the Saracen and Christian forces for nigh on two years when the English ships landed in Palestine. Most of the buildings had been looted bare by the Germans and the French. There wasn't much left of Acre when we arrived, even less by the time we departed."

The priest sighed. "A shame, to be sure. But take some comfort in knowing that you fought for what was right and just, my son. If the city was demolished in the efforts to free the Holy Sepulchre for Christendom, then I reckon 'twas good as not demolished by God's own will."

"How can you be so certain, Father?"

What little there was of the conversation halted abruptly at Emmalyn's quiet interjection. She felt Bertie's hand come to rest on her arm, a gentle warning to mind her tongue, but Emmalyn disregarded the caution. "How can we know what God wants?" she pressed. "How can the church determine what is right in God's eyes? Are the Saracens and their beliefs any less honorable than the Christians?"

Father Bryce blinked at her from around the front of Sir Cabal, dumbfounded and at an obvious loss for an answer.

"You do not approve of the Crusade, my lady?" Sir Cabal asked.

"I do not approve of war, my lord, holy or otherwise. To my way of thinking, there is little to admire in any cause that would laud the destruction of whole cities or sanctify the brutal slaying of innocent people."

"For pity's sake, my lady! Have a care with your commentary," gasped the chaplain, chuckling nervously. "Sir Cabal, I beg you endeavor to understand Lady Emmalyn's present state. With the war having claimed her husband, I fear she speaks from overmuch emotion on this subject. She means no offense, I'm certain. Pray, do not take insult."

The hulking knight shrugged. "None taken at all," he remarked, his eyes still on Emmalyn as if to acknowledge that she offered him no such apology. "I am interested to hear more of the lady's opinions on the matter, however." He leaned forward, cornering her in her seat as if to keep the conversation between the both of them. "You do not believe there is honor in defending the rights of the Christians who would journey to Palestine on religious pilgrimage, my lady?"

"Defending their rights?" Emmalyn repeated breathlessly, unable to bite back her rancor despite knowing that she was inviting certain debate. "Is that how the Crusaders justified their actions?"

He paused a moment, considering. "We were there to justify nothing, my lady. We had a mission; we followed orders."

"You make killing sound very simple, my lord."

"Not simple perhaps, but absolute."

Emmalyn weathered the prickle of wariness that washed over her at his light admission. The lethal calm of his gaze bespoke a startling efficiency. By contrast, her husband had ever been brash in his fervor for adventure and combat. Garrett's cruel boasts and bullying ways used to frighten Emmalyn terribly, but somehow Sir Cabal's continued aloofness for how he made his living was even more chilling to her. Something in his easy demeanor, his matter-of-fact tone, convinced her that he was far more dangerous than Garrett ever could have been.

And now the king's order had made this man her adversary.

When she said nothing in reply, could only stare mutely at him, he smiled, the wry curve of his lips seeming less friendly than it did sensual. "We all have certain . . . skills, my lady. If I make my job sound easy, do not think that to mean I particularly enjoy it. War is merely what I do best."

"Then I suppose you believe there is no real harm done, so long as you do not take pleasure in the killing and destruction," she said, his apathy affording her a small measure of courage.

One jet brow quirked on his broad forehead; his sly grin turned dazzling. "Do you think, madam, that Fallonmour can be held without armed conflict? Do you expect to bar Hugh de Wardeaux from your gates without a bit of damage or bloodshed?"

"Defending one's home is far different than conquering a whole people for the sake of greed or political gain," she argued. "Wars are fought because men crave power. You say the Crusaders were upholding the rights of religious pilgrims, but how many Muslims were slaughtered in the name of Christianity, my lord? How many ancient relics were stolen or destroyed by the invading armies?" Emmalyn shook her head, laughing softly at the irony of it all. "How can any feeling person support a cause that would make heroes out of cold-blooded monsters such as that soulless villain, Blackheart?"

She could almost feel Sir Cabal tense beside her at the very mention of the infamous beast's name. The air around her seemed to crackle with the intensity of his silence as he stared at her, expressionless, save that his flinty eyes had narrowed and grown frigidly cold. "Blackheart, my lady?"

"Don't tell me that in all your time serving King Richard you have never heard of his most nefarious henchman, my lord. Why, Blackheart's reputation for evil deeds reached all the way back to England before our men had been gone their first year."

"Lady Emmalyn is quite right," Father Bryce chimed in around a mouthful of food. "Villagers from here to London have since been frightening their children into good behavior with threats that Blackheart will come and get them if they disobey."

"'Tis rumored that he killed a nobleman when he was just a lad," Bertie supplied, stabbing a piece of fish on the end of her poniard. "Sneaked into a heavily guarded castle in the dead of night and slayed the lord in his bed, just as cold as you please."

Emmalyn noticed that Sir Cabal had grown reflective with the sudden turn in the conversation. She watched him lean back in his chair, idly tracing the rim of his cup, wondering if he had heard the same tales she had—or worse, borne witness to them himself. She shuddered to recall the gruesome accounts of Blackheart's lethal skill, stories brought back from Palestine and circulated like wildfire about the realm.

Men had written to their wives of seeing the awesome demon Crusader slay ten infidel warriors at a time, reporting of the brutal raids he led on Saracen villages . . . laying to waste everything in his path. They said he would not die, that he rode into each battle as if to mock death but always emerged from out of the blood and ash and rubble unscathed. Blacker. Stronger.

Not even the gates and temples that towered over Palestine for thousands of years had been able to withstand the wrath of Blackheart's sword.

"Had you ever occasioned to encounter the man while on campaign, my son?"

The knight gave a casual shrug at the priest's query. "I know of him," he answered, then brought his tankard of ale to his lips and drained it.

"Is he as evil as they say?" Bertie asked.

Sir Cabal stared into his empty goblet, his humorless chuckle chasing a queer shiver of dread up the length of Emmalyn's spine. "I couldn't begin to guess on that matter," he replied. "Why? What brand of evil do people say this Blackheart is capable of?"

When Nurse began to recount one of the many purported tales of destruction, Emmalyn pushed her chair back from the table. "If you will all please excuse me, I believe I'll retire early this evening." She rose to take her leave from the dais, sorry to have opened the door on such an unpleasant subject as the demon knight of Palestine. She had no intention of dignifying Blackheart's reputation or his misdeeds by listening to further discussion of them.

"Is everything all right, my dear?" asked the chaplain when she stepped away from the table.

Emmalyn nodded, deliberately avoiding the steady watchful gaze of Sir Cabal. "I seem to have developed a bit of a headache, is all."

Nurse reached out to catch her hand. "Shall I see you to your chamber, my lady?"

"No, stay if you like, Bertie. I'll be fine."

She bade them all good eve and left the hall, thankful to be away from the press of Sir Cabal's body and the heavier presence of his brooding potent regard.

Though she had certainly needed rest, once she had closed her chamber door and slipped into bed, Emmalyn found that sleep held no appeal. She was restless and confused, in need of something to occupy her mind. After several minutes of trying to relax without success, Emmalyn gave up the idea.

Pivoting on her mattress, she slid her bare feet into the warmth of her wool-felt slippers, then dressed in her chainse, a bed gown of soft white linen. Quietly, she quit her chamber and crept along the corridor and down the spiral stairs. Nearly to the base, she spied one of her maids, just returned from the garderobe and hurrying back toward the hall. The girl stopped when she noticed Emmalyn on the stairs.

"Milady, are you unwell?"

"Nay, Bea, I'm fine. Actually, I was on my way to the women's solar. I brought some wool up from the village this afternoon. We've a fine grade again this year—clear and rich as cream. I thought I might spin some of it."

Emmalyn rather hoped that Bea might find the idea appealing as well, for she could do with a little company. Alas, the maid frowned. "Spinning?" she asked hesitantly. "At this hour, milady?"

At the young woman's look of desperation, Emmalyn relented with a soft sigh. "Don't fret, Bea, I won't insist on your help this time. But will you bring some candles to me there so that I might work a while?"

"Of course, milady," the maid replied, hiding none of her relief at having escaped the task. With a quick curtsy, Bea hastened off to carry out the request.

The women's solar, a veritable haven of books and textiles and peaceful ambience, was situated on the second floor of the tower, at the opposite end of the keep from the great hall. If she shut the thick oak door, Emmalyn knew she could close herself off from the rumble of conversation emanating from the large banquet room. But after igniting a small rushlight from the flame of a torch burning in the corridor, she left the solar door open a crack to await Bea's return. In the dim, flickering illumination of the sconced torchlight, she set about gathering the tools she would need to spin the wool.

And it was fine wool, she thought with pride as she plunged her fingers into the basket of soft creamy fluff. She could hardly wait to see what the harvest would yield at market this year. Fallonmour would be well stocked and healthy for two winters if her estimations were correct. Pleased to be holding the tangible results of her dreams to strengthen Fallonmour on increased wool production, Emmalyn grew anxious to work some of the fleece.

Where was Bea with those candles? Emmalyn thought she remembered tucking some away for safekeeping on one of the shelves that lined the west wall of the solar. She dragged a ladder from the corner of the room and climbed up, stretching as she reached for the supply. Her fingers closed around several cool wax columns just as footsteps neared the solar. "Never mind, Bea, I found some myself."

" 'Tis not the girl, my lady."

At the sound of Sir Cabal's deep voice, Emmalyn startled and nearly lost her balance. Only the knight's strong hands now encircling her waist kept her upright on the ladder while her candles clattered to the floor and rolled to the four corners of the room.

"I've got you," he said from behind her. "Are you all right?"

Still clutching the ladder in tight fists, Emmalyn did not turn to face him. She could not, for then he would see the heat suffusing her cheeks at the sensation of his strong fingers pressed against her. Shaken, not only from the near fall but also from her strange reaction to his touch, she could only stand there mutely, her lungs refusing to draw air.

"Are you all right, my lady?" he repeated, sounding a bit more concerned.

"Yes," she said at last. "I am fine."

Cabal's hands lingered at her waist a heartbeat longer than was seemly, as if he were testing the feel of her in his grasp. Emmalyn stiffened, sensing the strength and power in each curved finger that rested atop the flimsy fabric of her gown. It had been a long time since a man touched her, even to catch her from a spill. Remembering her husband's hands on her, Emmalyn decided she did not like the sensation overmuch.

To her relief, Cabal's grip eased and he released her. "I didn't mean to frighten you."

" 'Tis all right," she muttered, scrambling down the ladder and past him to snatch up the first errant candle and then the next, wondering wildly what had just happened to her and why she should always feel so unlike herself in his presence. Flustered for his watching her, she bent to retrieve the last candle ... at the same time Cabal reached out to do the same. Their fingers brushed, an unanticipated, momentary contact that Emmalyn found entirely too warm, too exhilarating. She drew her hand back as if she had been burned.

"Please!" she gasped, bewildered and desperate. "I don't want your help—I don't need it!"

She could not raise her eyes to look at him after so irrational an outburst, nor could she summon the strength to come up from her knees on the floor. Breath hitching and shallow, face burning with embarrassment, Emmalyn sat unmoving, clutching the lot of broken candles to her bosom. She wanted nothing more than for Cabal to turn around in that next moment and leave the room. She prayed that he would say nothing, that he would simply abandon her to her solitude—now, and for the rest of his time at Fallonmour.

To her dismay, he remained standing beside her.

Worse, he ignored her anger altogether, placing his hand under her elbow and helping her to her feet. Without saying a word, he collected the candles from her grasp and set them aside, leaving Emmalyn with nothing to cling to, nothing at all between them. Her empty hands were trembling as she brought them down to her sides and fisted them in the thin fabric of her skirts. She felt a rush of panicked anticipation as Cabal came to stand before her, closer now, his intense gaze far too penetrating to be trusted.

"W-what are you doing?"

She had meant why had he come to the women's solar, but to her chagrin, the stammered question seemed more a terrified query about his present intentions. In large part, she had to admit that it was. Feeling much like a fly being lured into a spider's web, Emmalyn took a hesitant step backward.

Sir Cabal moved so subtly she was not even aware he had advanced until his broad chest loomed scant inches from her nose. With the back of his curled hand, he tipped her chin up, forcing her to meet his gaze. "Why do you fear me so?"

"I . . ."

She was about to deny that he frightened her, but the words would not come, and she knew that her inability to voice it could only further weaken his estimation of her. In truth, she was afraid of him, terrified, but for reasons he would never understand. Reasons she would never reveal. Speechless, Emmalyn could only shake her head feebly, staring up into those silver eyes made flinty in the dim torchlight.

"Do you think I have come here to hurt you, my lady?"

"N-no."

"No?" he echoed. "What, then? Ravish you, perhaps?"

Emmalyn swallowed hard, her eyes widening. "Please, my lord, do not—"

She tried to take a step backward and nearly stumbled. Cabal caught her, righted her with a gentle hand. "You're trembling," he said quietly.

She could scarcely breathe. "Please, don't touch me."

"No," he soothed, "not if you don't want me to." A long moment passed before his voice rasped like rough velvet in the near darkness. "Why are you so mistrustful? Did Garrett make you skittish around men? Was he inattentive, my lady? Unskilled in loving you?"

Emmalyn looked away, unable to deny it, yet desperate that he not unearth the shame of her marriage. "My lord, you go too far."

"Perhaps," he said, his reply devoid of apology or repentance. He reached out and swept an errant tendril of her hair behind her ear. Tilting her face up, he forced her to meet his hooded gaze. "But I'm not Garrett," he whispered.

Emmalyn could not answer. Heaven help her, she could scarcely summon her breath under the blaze of his compelling seductive stare.

"Mayhap you think me no better than he," Cabal suggested with a grim smile. "Mayhap you think me worse. Do you see me as some sort of villain, Lady Emmalyn? Perhaps much the same as this beast you so despise—this Blackheart?"

"Are you?" she asked breathlessly.

His lips quirked with wry amusement. "Some days," he whispered, letting his warm hard fingers skate along the slope of her cheek.

Emmalyn shivered with the subtle contact, thrilling to his caress in spite of the danger she felt at being so near this darkly enigmatic man, so vulnerable to him. So unwillingly aroused by him.

Perhaps it was the dim, watery light that made his face so handsome now, made the harsh cut of his mouth seem less cruel. Perhaps it was her own loneliness that made his touch seem so enticing, made this hardened warrior seem somehow tender.

It was madness, surely, that compelled Emmalyn to stay when every fiber of her being warned her to flee. Only madness would have allowed her to hold his gaze when it grew dark and heavy-lidded with hunger. Only madness would have allowed her to remain unmoving when his mouth began to descend slowly toward hers. . . .

"Beg pardon, milady. . . . I have your candles?"

Bea's uncertain voice in the doorway shattered the moment like a hammer on glass. Emmalyn broke from Cabal's spellbinding gaze as if physically torn from it, backing away from him in sheer astonishment at what she might have allowed to happen had they been left alone any longer. A kiss, an illicit embrace—Heaven help her, but she might have allowed him even more. . . .

His indecent stare remained fixed on her, full of awareness, potent with knowing, the embers of hunger still smoldering in his eyes. Their penetrating intensity stripped her bare, left her shaking. He knew she desired him. He knew that in that moment she had been his for the taking. Worse, she could tell that he knew she still was.

Emmalyn swallowed hard. She pressed her fingers to her lips, which, to her dismay, still burned for his kiss. Without acknowledging the maid or uttering a single word of excuse, she spun on her heel and ran, not daring to so much as stop for breath until she was safely inside her bedchamber with the lock bolt slammed home.

Chapter Seven

The mass to honor Fallonmour's fallen lord began at dawn that next day, and despite Cabal's curiosity to discern the extent of Lady Emmalyn's grief over her husband's death, after last night's encounter, he decided it best to keep his distance. Instead, he occupied himself with training exercises in the bailey, pleased to avoid the swarm of mourners now making their way out of the chapel.

Cabal sensed trouble brewing when he spied a group of Fallonmour's knights heading his way, all of them grinning smugly as they approached. Shuffling along at the center of the pack of men was a long-limbed commoner who looked utterly lost and more than a bit fretful of where he was being led.

"What goes, Taggart?" Cabal asked the knight at the fore, a giant of a man whose girth well exceeded his brawn.

"If I recall, ye said to us, bring any man from his field and ye'd make him a battle-worthy warrior, did ye not?"

Cabal saw the challenge glittering in the men's eyes and met it with like attitude. "I did."

"Well, then, here he is. Yer first peasant pupil, ready to be made a knight."

Chortling, the crowd of soldiers broke, and Cabal's eyes lit on the skinny lad in dirt-smeared tattered homespun. The young man swiped his felt cap from his head and, eyes downcast, began to nervously twist the scrap of moth-eaten wool in his trembling fists.

Taggart laughed, his voice filled with mirth. "Petey here is not the strongest man in Fallonmour's fields, I'll grant ye."

"Ain't too smart, either," added another knight, snickering.

The peasant glanced up nervously, looking from Cabal's face to the knights around him, clearly unable to understand a word of what they said. His throat bobbed. Then he went back to mangling his cap, his gaze trained on his mud-encrusted ragged shoes.

"Are you a planter, lad?" Cabal asked him in the common English tongue. "A mower, mayhap?"

"Cottar, milord."

Cabal nodded, not altogether displeased with what he had been dealt by Taggart and the men. As cottars were generally called upon for many hand tasks around the village and fields, perhaps this trainee would prove agile, if not stout-hearted. "How old are you, Pete?"

"Seventeen this past spring, milord."

Taggart cleared his throat over the brief exchange, evidently anticipating a challenge of his selection. "If I recall, lord, ye said naught about brains nor brawn—"

"No, I did not," Cabal agreed. "I said any man, Taggart."

"Mayhap ye spoke in haste," the big man suggested.

"On the contrary. In fact, give me a short while with Pete and I expect he will prove an excellent fighter. Easily better than you."

Several knights choked in obvious disbelief. Taggart himself looked too incensed with the insult to give any reply at all. He stood, fists clenched, his great head taking on an unhealthy purple hue, from the top of his freckled pate to his quivering corpulent jowls.

"Ye want a wager, Sir Cabal, then so be it," he said at last, his voice tight with insult. "Train yer lackey as best ye can, and at week's end, we will indeed see who's the better."

"Two days," Cabal amended.

Taggart gaped at him as if he were mad. "Two days to train that daubhead to wield a blade?"

"Two days to make him better than you."

"All right, then," the knight growled. "But mind, lord, when I fight, I fight to the finish."

Cabal shrugged, unfazed, and remained unblinking as Taggart and the others regrouped and shuffled on toward the keep for the morning meal. Taggart paused in the shade of the pentice and looked back. His expression was one of pure malice as he spit into the dirt, then, chuckling, continued on within the dark corridor. Only after the clink of spurs had disappeared into the yawning darkness of the stone walkway did Cabal face Pete anew. Though he did not want to admit it, Cabal felt fairly certain he was looking at a dead man.

The thought of losing this contest did not sit well. If he had only a short time to train Pete, he had better get started. Cabal reached down and drew his broadsword from its scabbard with a smooth, efficient swish of unsheathed steel. To his exasperation when he looked to Pete, he found the lad quaking in terror, his eyes screwed closed, chin pulled low into his shoulders as if he thought he might lose his head in the next heartbeat.

"Open your eyes," Cabal instructed the trembling young man as he came to stand before him.

Pete's head only shrunk lower into his chest. "Whatever I done, milord, I'm sorry!"

Cabal heaved a sigh of frustration. "For God's sake," he clipped in irritation, "just put out your hands, lad."

Nearly blubbering with fear now, Pete extended his shaky fists. "Have mercy, milord, I beg you!"

Cabal seized the lad's right wrist, pried open his hand, and slapped it around the hilt of the sword. "Take it," he ordered.

Pete opened his eyes, frowning in total confusion. "Milord?"

"Take my sword." He let go, and the heavy blade immediately slipped out of Pete's grasp and fell to the ground. "Now pick it up."

The peasant shook his head desperately. "Milord, I beg you, do not make me fight—"

"I said, pick it up, boy." Cabal's staccato command sent Pete to his knees in the dirt. With one palm under the hilt, the other flat under the blade, Pete rose and held the sword out to Cabal, presentation style. "How does it feel in your hands?"

"M-milord?"

"Can you raise it?"

Pete blinked at him as if he were engaged in some perverse brand of test he did not fully understand. "I—I've no wish to raise it against you, milord."

Cabal scowled. Already the lad's arms trembled under the strain of the heavy blade. Saints' blood, but it would take more than two days to condition Pete's body for such a weighty weapon, let alone teach him any sort of skills in handling it. Cabal raked his hand through his hair in frustration. . . . Then he remembered something.

"Don't move," he instructed Pete, turning and heading back into the keep, up to his chamber where he kept one of his few souvenirs from his time in Jerusalem.

This particular treasure—a deadly arc of polished infidel steel—was wrapped in a swatch of linen and hidden away under the mattress for safekeeping. The weapon gleamed with lethal beauty, unveiled for the first time since Cabal had arrived back on English soil. He only hoped young Pete would wield it with more good fortune than had its previous owner.

Cabal returned to the bailey, somewhat surprised and frankly encouraged to find that his pupil had not fled for the hills in his absence. He strode forward with the lighter blade in hand.

"Try this one instead."

As a test of the peasant's reflexes, Cabal tossed the blade at him. Without pausing to think, Pete reached out and caught the hilt cleanly in his fist. The curved Saracen sword seemed a good fit for the young man, and Pete seemed intrigued with the gleaming weapon—if he yet remained outwardly discomfited with the purpose of his having been given it.

While Pete held the blade before him in two hands, marveling at its deadly beauty, Cabal retrieved his own weapon from the ground. Without warning, he made to strike at the

lad. The clank of steel on steel reverberated in the bailey as
Pete brought his blade down to meet the blow. The peasant
looked more surprised than Cabal reckoned he was himself.

"Very good," he commended the lad. "Now look away
from the weapon. Keep your eyes trained on mine, Pete, and
let yourself feel where I will strike next."

"Milord, please—"

Another strike, and another solid deflection. Cabal swung
his blade at him, again and again, pleased that Pete was able
to block nearly every blow.

"Now you come at me, Pete."

The lad stared, befuddled, and made no move to raise his
weapon against Cabal. "Milord, please! I cannot!"

"Do it."

Pete swallowed hard, then gripped the blade in both
hands, switching his slight weight from foot to foot. "All
right," he said, "if I must."

He raised the sword and let it fall in a wild artless arc that
sliced the air with the hiss and song of sharp deadly steel.
Cabal met the blade with the flat of his own, the force knocking Pete's weapon from his grasp. Cabal advanced without
pause, his sword poised to strike, and was pleased to see
Pete scramble to retrieve his blade in time to deflect the
ensuing blow.

It had been delivered with a deliberately heavy hand, a
test of Pete's heartiness that did not yield the most
promising results. Pete stumbled out of the way of the blade
and fell on his behind in the dirt. He looked up at Cabal,
more confused than frightened.

"A-are you going to slay me now, milord?"

"No, Pete." Cabal sheathed his sword, then reached for
the lad's hand and pulled him to his feet. "I'm going to
make you a soldier."

"A soldier, milord? You mean this has naught to do with
the thiev—"

Pete clamped a hand over his mouth, but it was too late to
reclaim the slip. The peasant's face had already blanched a

terrified shade of white in the instant it took for Cabal to whirl him around.

"What thieving?" he demanded.

"N-naught, milord."

"Tell me, boy!"

"Oh, rot my fool tongue," Pete whined. "Martin will throttle me when he learns what I've done."

"Have you been stealing from this keep?" Cabal charged.

"Nay! Milord, I would never!"

"Who, then? This Martin fellow? I warn you, Pete, I'll brook no thievery or falsehoods in you."

"'Twas neither me nor Martin what done the stealing, milord. I swear it!" He grasped the hair at his temples and pulled, groaning miserably. "Arlo said no one was supposed to know. . . ."

Cabal seized the youth's shoulders, commanding his full attention. "I will have the whole story, Pete. Now."

By the time the morning meal had ended and the folk were returning to their duties, Cabal was alone once more in the bailey. He had managed to wring a wealth of disturbing news out of Pete, and with an agreement that he would return later for more instruction with the sword, Pete had gone back to the village to carry out his day's tasks. Cabal was glad he had already sent him off, for the garrison looked eager for more trouble as they spilled out of the keep and into the courtyard.

Whether meant to intimidate or impress, Cabal was uncertain, but he watched with amusement as Taggart and the other men commenced practice in the bailey. Immediately, Fallonmour's two dozen guards set about butchering an assortment of logs and tree stumps that littered the far side of the courtyard. From the midst of this chaotic maelstrom of grunts and oaths and flying wood chips, Miles sauntered over to where Cabal stood observing.

"I hear Taggart was up to no good this morn."

Cabal gave a nonchalant lift of his brows. "Evidently my

means of fortifying Fallonmour's garrison does not sit well
with him."

The two men watched as Pete's challenger paused his
exuberant cleaving to wipe his forehead. Sweat streamed
down the big knight's face and drenched the neck of his
tunic. Taggart's girth made his movements sluggish after
only a few more minutes of exertion, but he still managed to
heft his blade high in the air and, with a solid connection,
buried it in the top of a thick oak stump.

"I fear this challenge between Pete and Taggart is a
losing proposition, Sir Cabal," Miles said after some consideration. "If Pete loses the match, 'twill only make your
work with the others all the more difficult."

Cabal was about to ask the old captain if he had ever heard
the ancient tale of David and Goliath, but at that moment
Lady Emmalyn stepped out of the chapel and into the sun-
shine of the courtyard. She glanced at the exercising knights,
then met Cabal's gaze and quickly looked away. Her squared
shoulders and efficient gait invited no dalliances as she
headed purposefully in the direction of the stables.

Vaguely, Cabal registered that Taggart had now abandoned his practice and was making his way toward him. He
said something, no doubt a jest of some sort, but Cabal paid
little attention, watching as Lady Emmalyn led a gray palfrey from the stables, then mounted and departed in the
direction of the village.

Beside him, Miles chuckled. "What say you, Sir Cabal?"

Cabal looked back at the two men, hiding none of his
sudden lack of interest.

"I say," Taggart repeated, "if I had gone to Palestine,
mayhap Richard would have reclaimed the Sepulchre for
Christendom and not lost it in shame to Saladin's heathen
forces."

"Mayhap," Cabal replied with a negligent shrug. "I must
admit, you have demonstrated excellent maneuvers here,
Taggart, truly excellent."

The big knight beamed smugly. Miles seemed pleased as

well, though his sage expression told Cabal that he was suspicious of such an easily won compliment. Cabal grinned, then clapped Taggart on the shoulder. "Though I expect the real trick would have been in convincing the infidels to stand still long enough for you to hack them down."

Taggart sputtered an oath behind him, but Cabal ignored it, already crossing the bailey and on to more appealing pursuits.

Relieved to be done with the mass and eager to immerse herself in responsibility, Emmalyn rode down to the village and immediately made her way into the fleece barn. There, the reeve and his family were already at work cleaning and baling the sheared wool. While Martin and his wife, Lucille, spread and rolled the fleece, their daughter, young Lucy—unmarried and made a mother just last month—sat on a narrow bench with a basket of washed wool at her feet. Her new babe lay swaddled in a blanket beside her in the hay.

"The three of you are certainly at this early," Emmalyn remarked lightly after greeting them all. She patted one of the many bundles of baled fleece that had been stacked along the wall of the small shed, satisfied with the solid weight of it. "Martin, I thought we agreed yesterday that I would help you with the wool."

"Aye, milady, but you were at chapel, and I thought it prudent to get to the task right off, so we can have it all finished and put away before vespers this eve. No sense leaving it lay about in here any longer, I reckon."

Martin seemed nervous in some way, suddenly anxious over the safekeeping of the wool, but Emmalyn shrugged it off, noticing instead how his young daughter could scarcely keep her eyes open to do her work. Her little son had begun to fuss, yet Lucy's chin dipped to her chest in sleep.

"Martin, how can you make this poor girl work when 'tis clear she's exhausted?"

The reeve looked over his shoulder to where his daughter

was now awake but struggling to stay so. "She's well enough, milady. Young Lucy won't complain over a bit of work."

"No, she won't, Martin, but look at the poor thing. She should be at home, resting. She's nearly faint with fatigue."

Emmalyn took up a seat next to Lucy and grasped her hand. The reeve's daughter was a sweet girl, just ten and six, the same age Emmalyn had been when she married Garrett. Perhaps for that reason Emmalyn had taken a keen and ongoing interest in the maid's welfare. "How much sleep did your babe give you last eve, Lucy?"

The girl shrugged weakly and shook her head. "Please, milady, I'm fine. Papa is right; I don't mind the work."

"Well, neither do I," Emmalyn answered. "Tend your child instead, Lucy. I think he's getting hungry."

As the girl moved to scoop up her fretting babe, Emmalyn pulled the basket of wool from between Lucy's feet and placed it at her own. Though the shepherds had bathed the sheep in the stream and brushed them before they were sheared, there were still burrs and other impurities that had to be taken from the fleece by hand. It was a tedious but necessary task if they wanted to get the best price at market. Unavoidable as well, would be the final step, more unpleasant than this. For once the fleece was picked clean, it would be soaked and scrubbed in a mixture of urine and water to break up the residue of natural oils present from the sheep's skin.

Intent to do her part, Emmalyn reached into the basket and pulled out a portion of the wool, spreading it out across her lap, stretching and pulling the length to expose the burrs and bugs and straw yet embedded in the fleece. Beside her, Young Lucy unlaced her tunic to bare her breast, then set about feeding her infant son.

Emmalyn watched her longingly, doubtful that she might ever have the chance to hold a child of her own. Her heart ached for the babe she had wanted so badly, the infant she had so tragically lost to a miscarriage. How she missed the precious little girl who would now have been toddling about the castle, babbling the charming nonsense of a three-year-old. Emmalyn's pregnancy had been the one bright spot in her marriage; the loss had left a deep wound that would never fully heal.

Grappling with painful memories and careless of what she was doing, Emmalyn was pricked by a burr as she spread her palm over the wool in her lap. She cried out in surprise more than discomfort and immediately began to pick the barbed cluster from her fingertip.

"Oh, milady!" Lucy wailed, denying her baby further sustenance to come to Emmalyn's aid. She pulled her tunic together and placed her son back on his bed of hay. "Milady, please, I should be doing this work, not you."

"Mind your son, Lucy. I'm fine," Emmalyn replied, her voice raw and more clipped than she had intended. The girl reached out for the wool anyway. "I said, I will do it."

At her lady's sharp tone, the young mother broke down in a fit of uncontrollable tears.

"Oh, Lucy, I'm sorry," Emmalyn soothed, feeling terrible for her actions. "I'm not upset with you. I shouldn't have snapped like that."

From across the barn, the reeve's wife clucked and abandoned her work to go to her sobbing daughter's side. "Pray, forgive her, milady," she said. " 'Tis naught of your doing. This girl has been a bundle of emotions these past several months. Last eve she bawled for hours over a ruined pottage."

Sympathetic and contrite, Emmalyn smiled, grasping Lucy's callused hand and giving it a gentle squeeze. "She is tired. Lucille, why don't you take your daughter back to her cottage and let her and the babe get some rest? I'll help Martin with the rest of the work here."

The reeve's wife nodded, then scooped up the swaddled infant and assisted her sniffling daughter out of the woolshed. Martin muttered an apology for his family as Emmalyn carried an armful of freshly cleaned fleece to him. He took it without looking at her and bunched it together with several other prepared fleeces, decidedly less talkative than she had always known him to be.

"Is anything amiss, Martin?"

"Amiss, milady?" He held her gaze for no longer than a heartbeat then shook his head and went back to his task.

"If you're worried over young Lucy and the welfare of her babe, I can assure you that no matter what happens, I will see that they always have a place here at Fallonmour."

"My thanks, milady, but nay, I don't fret over that. Never that. You've always been more than generous with me and my kin." He tied a length of twine around the bundle and hefted it over his shoulder, then picked up another that had already been secured. "By your leave, milady, I'll start taking these down to the storehouse now."

"Of course," Emmalyn answered.

When he departed, she picked up another tie and attempted to wrap it around several combed fleeces. Emmalyn struggled with the bulk of the wool, trying unsuccessfully to gather the twine closed for the girth of the fleece it held. From behind her, strong fingers wrapped around her hand.

"Allow me."

Emmalyn startled, nearly backing into Cabal's solid chest. Her senses filled at once with the mingled fragrances of musky wool, sweet hay, leather, and man. Immediately, she withdrew her hand from beneath his and ducked out of the circle of his arm.

"I thought you were training the men."

"So I was, my lady, but they have stopped for refreshment. In the meanwhile, I had hoped you would indulge me in a tour of Fallonmour's borders."

Remembering last night's encounter, Emmalyn broke his unsettling eye contact. Not even the morning's mass had been sobering enough to keep her thoughts from straying to wicked imaginings of Cabal's kiss. She had looked for him in the chapel, perversely hoping to see him there, shamefully disappointed that she had not. Dieu, but she could not allow this man such control over her thoughts and feelings. He would only use it to hurt her in the end.

Turning away from him, she retrieved an uncombed

shearing from the basket. "Perhaps Sir Miles would oblige you," she said at last. "I'm not much in the frame of mind for a lengthy ride, my lord, and as you can see I am elsewise occupied. . . ."

"Do you despise all men, Lady Emmalyn, or just me?"

If the wry humor in his voice was to be trusted, he had meant it not so much as a question but as a jest. A challenge. Taken by surprise at his candor, Emmalyn shook her head in polite denial, then shrugged. "I do not despise you, my lord. In truth, I don't even know you. 'Twould be unfair to pass judgment—"

He laughed at that, a hearty guffaw that compelled her to turn and face him. "Unfair," he said, "but true, nevertheless."

"I don't see why it should matter how I feel about you, my lord. Sir Miles captained my garrison for many years and he never required me to think one way or another about him."

Cabal's smile was a devilish curl of his lips. "You wound me, madam, if you mean to have me think that you see me in the same light as you see Miles: a paunched complacent graybeard."

"No . . ." she admitted quietly.

"No. Perhaps not, after last night." Looking at him, Emmalyn did not so much as blink, nor did she react to his answering chuckle. "You know, my lady, we do not have to be adversaries."

"Is that what we are, sir?"

His broad smile widened. "A simple ride, Lady Emmalyn, is all I ask. You and I both know that old Miles hasn't likely ventured beyond the castle gates in more than a fortnight. If I am to keep watch over this demesne, I would know the breadth of what it encompasses. I can think of no better person at this keep to show me than you."

Emmalyn started to decline, uneager to be alone with him and somewhat rattled by her body's unwilling reaction whenever he was near. She shook her head, denial at the very tip of her tongue, when Martin appeared in the open doorway of the woolshed. He glanced at the imposing knight, then at her, and backed out of the threshold.

"Beg pardon, milady. I meant no intrusion."

"Martin, 'tis all right," Emmalyn called. "Come in."

"Aye, Martin, come. Your lady and I would have a word with you."

Emmalyn turned to Sir Cabal, frowning, and reverted to her own Norman French. "You speak their language."

"Does that surprise you?"

"No," she denied quickly, "'tis just that Garrett would never deign . . ."

At her side, Sir Cabal smiled. Another reminder that he and her former husband were dissimilar in many ways. Another reminder of how little she knew about this man who had been ordered into her life.

"M-milady?" Martin stammered, looking increasingly nervous the longer he remained in the knight's company.

"You are the reeve?" Sir Cabal queried.

"Aye, milord."

"Show us to the granary, then, Martin. Your lady will have an accounting of the barley."

Emmalyn frowned in confusion. "I checked on the stores just yesterday afternoon, Sir Cabal. I don't see the point in making another account this morning."

"I suspect Martin grasps my point well enough," the knight replied cryptically.

"I don't understand," she said. "What are you talking about?" When the reeve would not lift his gaze from the ground, Emmalyn's heart began to hammer a tattoo of budding alarm. "Martin, have you something to tell me about the barley store?"

The reeve at last looked up, his face a sagging mask of contrition. "Milady, there was a robbery last eve. . . ."

"A robbery?" she echoed. "Fie! No wonder you've been acting strangely this morn. Was anyone hurt? What did we lose, Martin?"

"No one was hurt, milady. The thieves took just a bit of barley and two suckling piglets—"

"This time," Sir Cabal broke in. "Last month 'twas a cask of ale and six hens, was it not, Martin?" When the reeve made no response, the big knight pressed further. "And before that, you lost a peck of turnips and a sack of milled flour."

Sensing the peasant's rising fear, Emmalyn rushed to the defense. "You are badgering this man without cause, my lord. Fallonmour has lost none of these things and certainly not to repeated thievery. If we had, I assure you, I would have been the first to know. Besides, had our stores been robbed, do you not reckon those items would have come up missing in the keep's accountings? Arlo reported nothing missing."

Sir Cabal's eyes were on Martin. "Tell her."

"Er, m-milady," the reeve stammered, "I'm afraid 'tis true."

"How can it be? I reviewed the records myself, Martin. I saw these items with mine own eyes. How could I count grains and chickens that you now say were not there?"

"If you had looked to the village stores, milady, you would have seen the losses."

She cocked her head at him. "What are you saying?"

"They have been replenishing Fallonmour's stores with goods from their own supply, my lady," Sir Cabal explained evenly. "Turnips from the peasants' field, flour and ale from the village barrels, hens from their own stock."

"I don't understand. Martin, how long has this been going on?"

The reeve let out a shaky expulsion of breath, his voice equally tremulous. "Now and again since about the first thaw, milady."

Three months! A quarter year, and all that time she had been completely unaware. Sir Cabal, by contrast, had been at Fallonmour only one day, and it seemed he already knew more than she did about her own affairs. Emmalyn realized right away that her anger had less to do with a bit of stolen food than it did with her having been caught off guard and embarrassed in front of the dark imposing warrior.

Though she tried to curb her emotions, the sting of humiliation made her voice tight. "Why did you keep this from me, Martin? Did you not think I had a right to know?"

"Apologies, milady. We wanted to tell you, but Arlo advised us not to. He said you were not to be troubled with it."

"Doubtless he had reasons of his own for keeping the news from you," Sir Cabal said darkly. He pinned Martin with a chiding glance. "Thieving is thieving, man, be it grain or something more. It cannot be tolerated."

"And it won't be," Emmalyn added quickly, interceding before the knight saw fit to take it upon himself and mete out punishment to the poor reeve. "I expect to be informed immediately if these brigands return, Martin, do you understand? In the meanwhile, take from Fallonmour's stores whatever was lost to the thieves and return it to the village. I will not have my people going hungry out of charity for me."

"As you wish, milady," Martin replied.

Emmalyn watched him dash off, dreading the prospect of having to face Sir Cabal again after such a humiliating discovery. "How did you come to know about this?" she asked him.

"I have pledged my service to protecting this keep. It is my duty to know these things . . . and set them to rights."

Garrett would have laughed aloud to know she had been made a fool by Arlo's withholding news of the thieving and, as well, the villeins' apparent lack of confidence in her ability to manage the problem. He would have thought it laughable, and then his humor would have just as swiftly turned to anger. But there was no trace of smug amusement in Sir Cabal's voice and no mockery in his features when Emmalyn finally blinked up at him to measure the meaning of his comment. His handsome face showed no disdain, only frank sincerity, gentle regard. To her bewilderment, Emmalyn found she had no idea what to make of him.

He puzzled her further with a polite sweep of his arm. "Shall we tour the boundaries now, my lady?"

Chapter Eight

Cabal rode beside Lady Emmalyn on the tread-worn path from the village, his black destrier nearly dwarfing the palfrey she guided gently along the perimeter of the fields. Peasants working their rows and furlongs paused to hail her with warm greetings as she passed, devotion shining plainly in their smiles and in their exuberant boasts of the crops' anticipated yields.

Lady Emmalyn met this fond regard with like affection. Speaking to them in their common English tongue, she offered generous praises for their efforts, addressing many of the serfs by name and inquiring after new babies and family members taken ill. Cabal observed her guileless interaction with the folk, struck by the genuine interest she demonstrated.

Once out among her people and deep within her lands, she seemed to have all but forgotten his presence, which seemed to disturb her so continually. Out here Lady Emmalyn laughed easily, smiled often. Out here she was carefree and radiant, imbued with a clear passion for the land and its folk.

Watching her now, talking so easily with the field hands and helpfully informing the hayward about a bit of broken hedge, Cabal had to tamp down a queer nudge of guilt that gnawed at him, knowing that she would one day be taken from a place she so obviously loved. He did not want to ponder her future, no more than he endeavored to give thought to his own, but to his profound irritation, he could not keep the thoughts and questions from entering his mind.

How would she fare in the probable future Richard would choose for her as the wife of one of his rich vassals? What would happen to her spirit once it was caged in a distant fortress, bound in expensive silk gowns, and tethered to the stuffy expectations of a nobleman's bride? Would she buck, or would she break?

As if she sensed his dark speculation, Lady Emmalyn glanced over and met his gaze. Her smile dimmed instantly. A light shake of her reins set her mount off at an easy gait, following the outskirts of the fields and past the sweeping meadowlands. She pointed out landmarks and property lines to Cabal along the way, taking great care, it seemed, to keep the pride from her voice now that it was just the two of them once more.

But as they paused on a small rise that looked out over the rolling hills and far off to the horizon, her expression belied the truth, and her eyes could not conceal the depth of her love for her home.

"I can't imagine life outside these boundaries," she said quietly, almost to herself.

Cabal was at a loss for how to respond. He stared ahead at nothing, waiting out the lengthening silence. From the corner of his eye, he saw her dash away an errant tear. He steeled himself to her distress; he could not comfort her. It was not his place, and anything he said to try to set her mind at ease would only be a lie.

"This demesne is now more home to me than the place of my birth," she whispered. "I can close my eyes and see clearly every hill and dale, the patterns of the fields, the orderly grid-work of the hedges and furlongs. Without thinking, I can conjure the smells of the orchards and the sweet, earthy pleasure of sheared fleece and fertile soil." She gave a sad little laugh. "I don't expect you to understand."

But Cabal did understand, he thought grimly. His home had long been the battlefield, its sights and sounds and smells as much a part of him as Fallonmour clearly was to Emmalyn. When he breathed deeply, even now, his lungs

filled with the pungent scents of smoke and steel and blood.
He swallowed and tasted the grit of warfare in the back of
his throat. Behind his closed eyelids he saw mounds of
rubble, acres of destruction . . . an endless sea of death. He
expected he always would.

He had long ago convinced himself that he did not care.

"My husband lived here nearly all his life, and he never
truly appreciated Fallonmour," Lady Emmalyn remarked
distantly. "I suppose he craved action, much like yourself.
When the call went out for men to join the Crusade, Garrett
was eager to go. He could not stop talking of all the wealth
and glory to be had on campaign."

"He found neither in Palestine."

She paused, evidently hearing the harsh grate of his
voice. Turning, she regarded him with a wary glance. "You
knew my husband, Sir Cabal?"

There was an edge of suspicion, or perhaps it was fear, in
her hesitant query. "Garrett was one of King Richard's officers," Cabal told her with a casual shrug. "We were in the
same regiment; we fought together for nearly two years."

"Two years," she echoed, glancing away quickly, her
voice soft, guarded. "Then you and he must have been well
acquainted."

"Well acquainted, but we were not friends, if that is your
meaning, my lady."

Her fine brow pinched. "I don't think Garrett had any
friends."

"Not even in his lady wife?"

Clearly put off by his intimation, Emmalyn stiffened suddenly. She looked down at the reins in her hands, her dark
lashes shuttering whatever emotion had begun to surface in
her eyes. "I do not think my marriage is any concern of
yours, my lord."

It wasn't, but Cabal needed to know—for more than one
reason. He was well out of bounds in asking, to be sure, but
the question had been plaguing him since he first laid eyes

on Garrett's beautiful young widow. He had to know. "Did you love him?"

Her tiny hand had tightened on the reins of her mount, gripping them now like a lifeline. She hiked up her chin, but Cabal could see the wariness in her expression, the threatened look in her eyes. "Garrett was my husband, Sir Cabal. I honored him in all ways as his wife—"

"That is not what I asked."

Lady Emmalyn's stare went from cornered to outraged, but she said nothing to defend her vows. Instead, she faced him with more tenacity than the boldest of his soldiers ever had, holding his piercing gaze where seasoned warriors had been known to wilt quickly. She was a passionate woman, so fierce in her love for the place that was her home, and in her devotion to her folk. Inexplicably, Cabal felt compelled to know if Garrett, too, had enjoyed any measure of her affection.

"Did you weep for your husband in chapel this morn, my lady?"

"How dare you ask such things!"

"Did you?"

She scoffed, but her jaw quivered slightly. "Am I to assume, sirrah, that the king has charged you with prying into my marriage in addition to your commandeering my home?"

"If I ask you, madam, 'tis because I want to know." Cabal studied her closer now, seeing a fissure begin to appear in her stoic demeanor. "Garrett had your hand, my lady, but did he have your heart?"

He could not read the emotion that haunted her gaze in that next instant. She shook her head nearly imperceptibly; her lips compressed tightly as if to bite back her reply. "You have no right to ask me anything!" A slap of the reins set her palfrey off at a hard gallop, fast delivering her away from Cabal, following the perimeter of the fruit orchards.

He watched her flee along the path, knowing it would be wise to simply let her go. Best to leave her alone. Probing her on such personal matters was bad enough; he did not need to further entangle himself now by chasing after her. And for what? To apologize? To offer sympathy? God knew he had precious little experience with either.

He had nearly made up his mind to let her be when she turned off the safety of the track and plunged into the orchard, vanishing from his sight. Cabal rose in his stirrups as if to follow her with his eyes, but it was no use. She was gone, concealed by the dense trees. God's wounds, what recklessness was it for her to venture into the grove alone when she had just learned of thieves loose in the area?

With a growled oath of frustration, Cabal hauled on his mount's reins and wheeled the steed around. He kicked the destrier into action, riding for the orchard at an urgent thunderous gait.

The black shot between the neat rows of apple trees like an arrow, speeding Cabal deep into the cool shade of the forest, fast on Lady Emmalyn's heels. She was several yards ahead in the same row, now guiding her palfrey at a careful trot—until she sensed Cabal's approach from behind. She glanced over her shoulder and saw him bearing down on her. Her eyes flew wide open.

"Leave me alone!" she cried.

She turned to the fore and slapped her palfrey into a frenzied gallop. Cabal gritted his teeth, swearing under his breath. He spurred his mount, leaning forward in the saddle, listening to the relentless pounding of his horse's heavy hooves, determined to close the distance before she roused every thief and brigand in the area.

Lady Emmalyn was less than a furlong from his grasp when she suddenly drew back on the reins and leaped from the palfrey's saddle. She cast a wild glance at Cabal, then disappeared into the next row of trees. "Go away!" she shouted, her desperation carrying her deeper into the grove.

Cabal yanked his destrier to a halt and threw himself to the ground. "Damnation, lady—come back!"

He ducked under a low bough and took off after her,

following the blond streamers of her unbound hair as she navigated the grove of apple trees, cutting first to her left and then back to her right a few yards later. With his eye trained on her, anticipating the next angle of her blind flight, Cabal closed in. He ran harder, gaining on her.

She glanced behind her a mere instant before she veered to the left—plowing directly into the solid wall of Cabal's chest. He closed his arms around her, catching her neatly in his grasp. She bucked against his firm hold, twisting around and trying to pry herself free.

"Let go!" she cried. "Please, just leave me alone!"

"I've been sent to guard you, my lady," Cabal growled beside her ear. "I reckon the king would be most displeased to learn that I had let you run off and get your pretty throat slashed by the brigands who've been robbing your village stores."

"I can take care of myself," she muttered, making a forward lunge and straining against his grasp to no avail. "For pity's sake!" she gasped, breath hitching. "Will you afford me no peace at all?"

There was an edge of panic in her voice that made Cabal still. He loosened his grip on her but did not release her fully, gently guiding her around to face him instead. Moisture swam in her eyes; her cheeks were bright and stained with tears.

God's wounds, she was crying.

For Garrett? Cabal felt a stab of remorse for his part in driving her to this current emotional state. Worse, he weathered a hearty lash of jealousy for the bastard who had been born noble enough to make this proud passionate lady his wife and then been fool enough to leave her for campaign.

Seeing Lady Emmalyn standing there in his shadow, trying to harness her distress, inspired Cabal to do the unthinkable. He, Blackheart—the scourge of Palestine, who never made excuses for his actions—apologized. "My lady, I am sorry. I had no idea."

"No," she said miserably. "You have no idea, my lord."

She drew out of his arms and swept away her tears. "I do not weep now because I mourn my husband, Sir Cabal. If I cry, 'tis out of shame. I cry because I do not grieve for Garrett's death . . . because I did not love him."

A perverse sense of relief flooded Cabal to hear her say the words, although it was clear they weighed heavy on her conscience. "You are hardly the first noblewoman to feel no affection for the man who was made her husband."

She gave a slow shake of her head. "You do not understand," she whispered. "I entered my marriage fully prepared to love Garrett. But he was a hard man. I confess, I came to loathe him. For so long I yearned only to be free of him." Soberly, she glanced at Cabal and met his gaze. "Many times I wished him dead, and now—"

"You had nothing to do with his death, my lady."

"How can you be so certain?" she asked, desperation and guilt dimming the vibrant hue of her eyes. "How can you be certain that God is not punishing me for wanting out of my marriage? Perhaps in wishing Garrett gone I have only visited worse troubles on Fallonmour and the people I care about. I promised the folk here a better life. I promised them peace. They trusted my word and I have failed them."

"Garrett died because of his own careless actions, my lady, not because you wished it. And as for Fallonmour and its folk, you are relieved of the responsibility. 'Tis the king's to contend with now and, for the moment, mine as well. You needn't fret over it anymore, my lady."

"I needn't fret?" she choked, her sadness evaporating swiftly under the blaze of resurging anger. "Do you think 'tis so easy that I should turn off my feelings or ignore the concern I have for my people simply because the king has decreed it so? How black-and-white everything must be to your way of thinking, Sir Cabal. You have no idea what it is to have no say in your future."

"Do I not?"

"You are a man," she said, hurling the statement at him

like an accusation. "You at least have the freedom to choose your own destiny."

Cabal's answering chuckle was brittle, catching in his throat. "I have not known choices since I was a lad of fourteen," he replied, surprising himself that he would think on that pivotal day, let alone bring it to light before her now. But it was too late to call it back; Emmalyn was blinking up at him in quiet confusion, her gentle, questioning expression like a balm, drawing poison from a wound.

Cabal was not at all sure he wanted to be healed.

You are beyond mending, his ruthless conscience mocked in the next instant, coaxing him back to the dark safety of festering hatred and long-buried heartache. Venturing out into the light would only get him burned, and he had never let anyone step one foot into his bleak past. Nor would he, least of all this lady.

"What happened when you were fourteen?"

Lady Emmalyn's soft voice curled itself around him, and Cabal was struck at how hard it was to resist her soothing pull. He forced a casual shrug. " 'Twas the year I was sent to London for training in the royal garrison," he said, distilling the bitter truth to its most basic fact in an effort to dissuade her from further exploration of the topic.

Even now, another fourteen years away from the night that had forever changed his life—the night that had robbed him of all he had and made him what he was today—Cabal still felt the hot coil of rage burning deep in his gut.

Fourteen years ago, his mother had been assaulted by a nobleman before a crowded hall. The highborn lord grew enraged that a common entertainer would refuse him, and he struck her. She hit her head on the hard stone wall and never drew another breath. To add insult, her assailant then reached down and stole the only item of value she possessed: a ring of tooled silver wrapped around a large gemstone the color of smoky steel. The ring had been a gift from Cabal's unnamed sire, a token his mother had believed would keep her safe from harm.

Fourteen years ago, Cabal had stayed behind when the troupe of jongleurs and dancers left the castle, hiding himself away in a dark corner of the keep, numb with grief, trembling in fear, waiting until everyone had either departed or taken to their pallets. Then, in the dead of night, he crept into the lord's chamber and murdered him in cold blood.

"You fostered at the palace as a child, my lord?" Lady Emmalyn prompted, her light inquiry nearly successful in tugging his morbid thoughts back to the present.

But Cabal could not keep the memories at bay. "I fostered there, yes," he answered. "More or less." His reply was sardonic, wry for the recollection of the rigorous exercises and mental conditioning that turned a hurting young boy into an emotionless, lethally efficient warrior.

Fortune had smiled on Cabal fourteen years ago—or perhaps it had sneered—for when King Henry heard of the common lad who had slain an enemy of the realm, he sent for the boy. Cabal could still see the spark of intrigue in the aging king's eyes when he was ushered into the cavernous royal chambers in London. He could still hear the note of interest in King Henry's voice when he learned Cabal's name. Could still feel the steady, questioning regard of the king's eyes when he spied the ring Cabal had since fastened to a leather cord he had tied around his neck.

For fourteen years, he had worn the ring like a badge, drawing on it first for comfort and then for strength. Even now its cold weight against his heart centered him. It grounded him, kept him focused. Helped him stay true to his training when he might be tempted to feel. Every moment of every day, that thick knot of silver and coal-dark stone reminded him who he was, what he always would be.

Blackheart.

"No one has choices," he said abruptly, his voice so quiet, he had to wonder if he had actually uttered the words.

But Lady Emmalyn was frowning up at him, looking nigh as astonished as he felt. "I do not understand. Do you not want to be a knight, Sir Cabal?"

He laughed at that, a sharp cynical bark that made her flinch. "What does it matter what I might want? Who would care?" he whispered, deliberately crowding her, leaning in when she began to draw back. "Do you, Lady Emmalyn?"

"What do you mean?" she asked on a shaky breath of air. She backed away from him, a subtle half step that edged her closer to the wall of trees at her back. Her dusky lips parted as she stared up at him, all guileless beauty and feminine promise. "W-what is it you want?"

He was fairly certain she knew. After all, he had done little to conceal his desire for her since his arrival at Fallonmour. More than anything now, he wanted to taste that pert rose-colored mouth. He wanted to lose himself in the moment, lose himself in Emmalyn's kiss. Lose himself in the bliss of her body.

She could make him forget his past—forget himself—if only for a few exquisite moments. God help him, he wanted nothing more than to claim every sweet ounce of her passion and fill her with his own. He wanted to take her. He knew he could have her . . . but he could never keep her.

He decided he damned well didn't care.

Without another word, Cabal bent his head down and pressed his lips to hers.

Emmalyn's breath left her on a soul-shattering tremor the instant their mouths met. The slim trunk of an apple tree at her back was all that kept her upright when Cabal's sensual lips closed over hers. He was bewitching her, this man she should despise. This imposing warrior whom she had every reason to fear was instead seducing her, stripping her of her will and leaving her powerless to resist him. In his arms, inexplicably, she was anything but afraid.

She might have been wholly lost in his spell if not for the sudden flight of a flock of birds overhead. They shot out from the treetops and departed the grove in a flurry of upset leaves and beating wings. Then Emmalyn's ear was drawn to a small noise nearby.

Cabal had heard it, too. He drew back slightly and stilled, putting a finger to his lips in warning to keep silent. He cocked his head and listened, as she did, to their now still surroundings. Emmalyn's heart was racing, her lips yet tingling from Cabal's brief kiss, but he seemed unaffected. All warrior once more, he took a step away from her, his hand closing around the hilt of his sword.

From within the bushes at their left came a rustle of movement again, drawing ever closer. A twig snapped and then another, marking the clumsy gait as that of a two-legged interloper and not some harmless woodland creature.

Cabal launched into action as the sounds grew louder, his sword singing from its scabbard before Emmalyn had a chance to draw a frightened breath. Protectively, he pushed her behind him. "Who's there?" he demanded. "Give voice to yourself."

No one answered, but the rustling footsteps grew closer to where they stood. Without a word, a thin figure took shape in the bracken, coming forward. Cabal started to advance for the kill, but Emmalyn grasped his arm. "Wait," she whispered.

A filthy wild-haired boy of about six summers stepped into view then, munching an apple in utter contented bliss— until his eyes lit on the two of them. One look at the gleaming readied sword and his half-eaten fruit tumbled to the ground. His mouth dropped open in silent terror and he pivoted, about to flee, but Cabal was faster. He lunged forward and grabbed him by the collar of his tattered dirt-stained tunic.

The rotting material gave under the knight's firm grasp, tearing at the shoulder and nearly freeing the lad to make his escape. He bucked and twisted, a confusion of skinny arms and legs, and thrashing overlong hair, but Sir Cabal held fast, hastily shoving his sword back into its scabbard with his free hand while he held the youthful intruder tight in the other. He caught the lad by the shoulders, trapping him solidly in his arms despite the boy's desperate squirming.

"Have a care, my lord," Emmalyn cautioned. "Can't you see he's terrified?"

"As well he should be." Cabal's answer was as gruff as his handling of the boy. "What manner of simpleton are you, lad, that you don't answer a command to give voice? I might have cleaved you in two."

The child ignored the knight's anger and made another feeble attempt to escape his grasp while Emmalyn came around for a closer look at the child. She had to cover her mouth with her hand to stifle her gasp of pity. The poor creature reeked of neglect, from his unwashed skin and filthy clothing to the frail skeleton of his trembling frame.

"He is not one of Fallonmour's folk," she observed, having never seen him before and certain that none of her people would ever so mistreat their children.

"A thief's whelp, then." Sir Cabal's voice was hard with intolerance. "No longer satisfied to steal under the veil of night, are you, lad?"

"He's a child, my lord. A hungry child, from the looks of him." Emmalyn crouched down before the poor creature, ignoring Cabal's growl that she keep a wary distance.

"What's your name?" she asked the boy, brushing a stringy lock of brown hair from his eyes. She tried again, this time in English, and though he seemed to register the words, he did not answer, merely stared at her with a wild-eyed look of desperation. "'Tis all right," she assured him, in case he did indeed understand. "We mean you no harm."

She hooked the length of hair behind his right ear and drew in her breath, wincing in sympathy. At his temple and riding high on his sallow cheek was an angry, fist-sized red bruise. There were more marks, uglier than the first, on his neck and about his shoulders. "Good lord," Emmalyn breathed, heartsick. "This child has been beaten horribly."

Feeling an instant maternal urge to comfort this mistreated waif, she reached out to touch his face. The boy flinched, recoiling before beginning his struggles anew. He thrashed frantically, like a desperate rabbit caught in a snare, and

Emmalyn feared that he would hurt himself further should he not gain release from the knight's firm hold.

"Let him go, my lor—"

She started to rise as she said it, and suddenly, without warning, the boy kicked out. His rough-shod foot struck her squarely in the shin and knocked her off balance.

With a growl, Cabal pinioned his captive under one arm and grasped at the air with the other as if he meant to catch her. On her behind in the grass, Emmalyn waved him off, shaking her head. She was in no pain beyond the sting of a rising bruise on her leg, but she nearly thought Cabal intended to crush the lad for the affront.

"Beg the lady's pardon, boy!" he commanded in a voice that made even Emmalyn jump. He gave him an angry shake. "Beg it, you disrespectful son of a cur!"

The child was panting now, his small chest heaving in fright, but still he said nothing. Not even an outcry for the certain bite of Sir Cabal's strong fingers pressing into his shoulders, a fact that Emmalyn attributed more to the boy's pride than an inability to voice his pain. She looked into his deep brown eyes and saw the spark of intelligence within, a wiliness that had likely saved him from many a tangle. Would that he had been cunning enough to elude whomever the brute was that had delivered his horrible bruises.

Emmalyn could not bear to contribute to his troubles by detaining him any longer. "Release him, please," she commanded Cabal.

Immediately, the knight's grip on the boy became less punishing, if nonetheless sure. "Are you certain, my lady? If he has caused you harm . . ."

"No," she insisted. "I'm in no great discomfort, and you yourself tried to warn me away from getting near him. This boy is frightened beyond reason. He only did what instinct commanded him to do. Please, Cabal, just let him go."

"I should have him take me to the rest of his kind instead. 'Twould be a swift end to the thieving."

When the boy began thrashing in earnest, Emmalyn knew

her suspicions were sound. He heard and he understood; he merely chose to keep his silence. "My lord," she implored Cabal, placing her hand on his forearm. "Please, let him go."

The very moment Cabal released his grasp, the boy slipped out of his arms and broke for the shelter of the bracken. At the edge of the thicket he hesitated, glancing backward as if he expected them to give chase, then plunged into the greenery and vanished, nothing more than a retreating flurry of snapping twigs and swishing branches.

Sir Cabal was at Emmalyn's side in the next instant, assisting her to her feet. "Are you all right, my lady?"

"Yes," she said, smoothing down the rough skirt of her wool tunic. "I'm fine."

She met his gaze and felt her cheeks flame for what might have transpired between them before the boy's stumbling into their path. "I think it best if we head back to the castle now, my lord."

"Of course," he agreed, his eyes having lost none of their indecent smolder under the glint of steely battle-readiness. "I'll see you back to the keep, then set the garrison to ridding the area of the boy and his thieving kin."

"No," Emmalyn countered, loath to think of causing any greater harm. "They are only stealing food, my lord. I do not think it necessary to drive them off."

He shot her a dubious look. "You have a kind heart for those less fortunate than you, my lady. Mayhap too kind, for wariness of these vagabonds might keep you farther from danger."

"I would rather help them if I could."

"By allowing them to steal from your stores and orchards?" He shook his head, chuckling as if he thought her a soft-hearted fool. It was a mantle Emmalyn had worn too often for Garrett to accept it easily now.

"You would have them go hungry instead?" she challenged, somewhat piqued that he could be so apathetic when it came to the poor. "I'll not have them starve while Fallonmour's trees bear so much fruit it lies rotting on the ground or goes to waste in our stores."

"The brand of help you prescribe will only corrupt them further, my lady. And I warrant it can bring naught but trouble to yourself and this keep. I have no intention of letting that happen."

"Regardless of what I think is best?"

He did not answer her challenge, merely let her stand there fuming in his shadow for a long moment. "I will return you to the castle now, my lady."

Perhaps she needed a stern reminder that this man was not her ally but her keeper. Emmalyn stared into his hard gray eyes, forever grateful that she had not been fool enough to let herself become just another of his conquests. But the realization of precisely how close she had come to surrendering to him a few moments before haunted her as she followed him back in stony silence to their mounts.

Mother Mary, but even though she fought it, her mouth yearned for another taste of his kiss. Her body yet sang with the memory of his touch. Heaven help her, but despite her fears, despite her anger at him and all he stood for, some foolish part of her wanted him still.

Chapter Nine

Pete crouched low, ankle-deep in the muddy filth of the back bailey, his arms spread wide. The noontide sun beat down on him relentlessly, adding heat to the sweat of his exertion, but the soldier-in-training did not seem to notice. He blew a hank of hair out of his eyes and pushed up the loose sleeves of his tunic, preparing himself for another round of battle. Positioned several paces before him, his opponent snorted, meeting Pete's determination with an unruffled beady-eyed stare.

"Come on, ye wretched son of a swine," Pete goaded. "Let's see if ye can get past me this time!"

With a growl, Pete lunged.

The fat little piglet squealed and darted right, and for the umpteenth time in the last hour, Pete executed a fruitless frontal dive into the slick stinking mud. He lay there facedown and slammed his fist into the muck, swearing a vivid oath before he rose up on his knees and wiped the dirt from his face. On the other side of the enclosure, the piglet had begun to root along the base of the fence, munching blissfully on the few blades of grass that poked in between the slats.

Pete surged to his feet. With a murderous roar, he ran slipping and sliding across the width of the sty, bounding toward the piglet once more. Another rushing charge, another failed capture. Angered now beyond reason, Pete gave chase, circling the small fenced-in area like a mud-encrusted madman while the little pig oinked merrily, zigzagging and dodging its way out of Pete's flailing grasp.

Cabal watched the contest from the other side of the fence, careful to betray none of his doubts as Pete picked himself up off the ground yet again and launched into a further unavailing attack. The pitiful sequence repeated until, at last, huffing from exhaustion, Pete threw up his hands in surrender and dragged himself toward Cabal. At the opposite corner of the pen, his chubby pink opponent trumpeted his victory with a round of ebullient snorts.

"Milord, I beg ye, please give me the infidel blade so I can be done with this exercise once and for all."

Wincing under the foul stench that wafted off Pete's person, Cabal held out his hand to prevent him from coming too close. "The idea is not to slay the piglet, Pete, but to catch it."

Pete scowled petulantly. "At the moment, I would rather gut the accursed squealer." He mopped his brow with his soiled sleeve, then spluttered to expel some of the grit and mud from his mouth. "Milord, what I know about warring and knighting is not much, but I don't see how I am to learn anything from spending the day chasing after that stupid beastling."

"Ah, Pete, you will never be a knight if you maintain a defeatist attitude. And I warrant that piglet has exhibited far greater intelligence this past hour than you have."

Pete looked crushed.

"I'm not saying that you aren't smart," Cabal assured him. "I'm saying that you must learn to fight smart. That piglet is just a simple barnyard beast, surely no better a thinker than you. You are more intelligent and you're ten times his size, yet you were the one who surrendered. Do you know why?"

"I got tired," Pete muttered defensively.

"Precisely. And now you know the secret to winning most any battle, Pete."

He grunted in confusion, scratching his forehead. "The secret, milord?"

"Do you think 'tis always the strongest man who wins a fight?" Cabal asked. "Do you think 'tis the man possessing the greatest skill with a blade who always proves the champion?" When Pete looked pressed for an answer, Cabal shook his head. "Endurance, lad; that's the secret. You have to be able to pace yourself while you strive to tire your opponent. You have to be faster on your feet, anticipate his every move, and be ready to counter it, even before he strikes."

Dubiously, Pete asked, "How?"

"The piglet had only his instincts with which to elude you," Cabal pointed out. "He didn't have to see you to know you were coming; he could sense it. He could tell which way you were going to attack from the way you held your body, the way you shifted your weight when you were standing before him."

"Mean ye, milord, that if I can learn to think like that little pig, I can be a good knight one day?"

"Well, instinct alone is no match for good training," Cabal advised him. "But a truly great knight appreciates the value of both and will take care to hone his skills in equal measure."

Pete glanced back to the grazing piglet. "May I try again, milord? I think I can do better now."

"Give it your best."

Pete stripped off his soiled tunic and tossed it to the ground, stalking toward the far edge of the pen. The piglet, munching on a clump of twigs and muddy grass, raised his head, velvety ears twitching in awareness of the returning intruder. This time, Pete's steps became more calculated the closer he got to his quarry. He loomed before the piglet, completely still. Then, without warning, he surged forward.

Pete's arms closed around empty air, while his curly-tailed prey ambled off with an exasperated oink.

"What are ye training here, Sir Cabal, a soldier or a swineherd?"

Taggart's gibe was answered by the taunting laughter of four other Fallonmour knights walking along at his side. Cabal turned to face the approaching men, trying not to grimace when he heard Pete take another graceless spill in the pigsty.

"What do you want, Taggart?"

"Why, nothin', lord. We heard ye was out here with Petey, and we was curious to see yer schooling put to action, is all."

"Oh?" Cabal gave a sardonic lift of his brows. "In that case, stay as long as you like. Mayhap you'll learn something."

One of the men at Taggart's side choked back a guffaw; the others looked too stunned to utter a sound. For his part, Taggart seemed shocked as well, reddening to a shade of anger nearly as vivid as his scarlet tunic. "All I mean to learn is how loudly I can make yer peasant warrior scream before I skewer him on my blade come two days hence."

As if to punctuate Taggart's threat, a great complaining squeal rang in the pigsty, followed by Pete's exuberant shout of victory. "I did it! Milord, I got him!"

Cabal broke from the knight's slivered regard and glanced over his shoulder to the pigpen. Covered from head to toe in mud and dung, and grinning like an addle-pated farmhand, Pete stood in the center of the mire, clutching the squirming piglet by its hind legs and proudly holding it up for all to see. "Milord, did you see? I did it! I caught the wily little bastard!"

At Cabal's side, Taggart chuckled humorlessly. "Don't let us keep ye, lord. Yer swineherd awaits." With a chortle, he nodded to his companions and the group moved off, back toward the practice yard of the front bailey.

Cabal watched the men saunter away, vaguely aware that Pete had released his quarry and now jogged across the pen to his side. "Is something amiss, milord? Have I displeased ye in some way?"

"No. 'Twas good work out there, Pete. I knew you could do it."

Evidently, Pete could tell that his mentor's thoughts were yet on the retreating knights. "What did Taggart want?"

"Trouble," Cabal answered. "And trouble we'll give him,

in due time. What say you that we take our training elsewhere now, where we can work uninterrupted with the
swords?"

Pete nodded enthusiastically, sending little clumps of dried
mud flying from his hair.

"I think a bath in the river should be the first order of
business for you," Cabal told him as he led the malodorous
youth out of the bailey.

After seeing that his pupil took a long, cleansing swim,
Cabal brought Pete into the woods to train privately and to
practice his pivoting and offense skills among the tight
ranks of the saplings in the forest. The two men worked at
sparring all afternoon and, before either of them had realized it, right on past the supper hour.

Finally, as the sun was beginning to set, Cabal sent Pete
back to the village while he himself returned to the keep. He
passed the entrance of the hall, noting that the great room
had been cleared of the meal some time ago, the floor
already swept in preparation for the castle folk to take their
pallets for the night. Of a mind to do likewise, Cabal climbed
the stairwell at the heart of the castle, pausing at the top of
the first flight to let a maid by with her burden of blankets
and bolsters. She gave him a shy smile as she passed,
heading down to the great hall. Cabal turned to continue his
ascent when a sound caught his ear.

From the direction of the women's solar at the end of the
snaking corridor came the intermittent clatter of wooden
spindles and the soft muted voices of ladies conversing.
Though part of him was drawn toward the scene, if only to
see Emmalyn again, Cabal reined in the urge. He had gone
too far in the orchard that morning; he had likely been too
assuming, too harsh.

To seek the lady out now would only worsen her regard
for him and further jeopardize his duty to the king. His first
concern should be the protection of Fallonmour, an issue
made all the more serious for the reports of village plun-
dering. Bad enough that he and his sorry retinue of guards

would have to face Hugh de Wardeaux in a short time; the presence of vagabond thieves was an added nuisance he did not need.

No more than he needed to be distracted by thoughts of bedding the lovely Lady Emmalyn.

And so, instead, Cabal bypassed the solar and took the stairwell up to his chamber, where he hoped to find a few hours of much-needed rest.

Emmalyn's foot tapped under her skirts, keeping anxious time with the steady spin of her winding distaff rod. She had spent the past hour or more in the candlelit solar with Nurse and two of the castle maids, the four women busily spinning the baskets of finished wool she had brought up from the village the day before. Handling the combed fleece and seeing the spindles grow fat with fine yarn usually gave Emmalyn great pleasure, but try as she might, this evening she found it difficult to keep her mind on the work. Thoughts of the time spent that morning alone with Sir Cabal kept flooding in. Unwilling memories of their orchard interlude made her listen with more interest than was seemly to the young maids' excited talk of the upcoming St. John's Eve celebration and the prospect of festival-time romance.

The young women talked of stolen kisses and midsummer magic, of finding true love under the cloak of darkness and indulging in wild unbridled dancing around the blaze of a village bonfire. Both of them speculated on how many babes would be born the following spring, and to whom. Even Bertie seemed to find the gossipy chatter irresistible.

"Tell me, girls," the old nurse said with a twinkle in her eye, "which of the young village men do you hope to charm around the festival blazes come St. John's Eve?"

They both laughed as if they had already discussed that very thing. "Leave the village boys to someone else," Bea giggled. "There's but one man I hope to find alone at the fireside this year."

"Aye, but you can be sure that he won't be alone if I have anything to say about it!" laughed the other maid.

"Sir Cabal is more man than any around here," chortled Bea. "Mayhap we should share him!"

Nurse and the two maids dissolved into lively banter that took little time to wear on Emmalyn's nerves. Finally, she could take the incessant chatter no longer and decided to continue her work on the morrow. With instructions to the maids to finish up and douse the candles when they were through, Emmalyn departed the solar and began the short winding trek upstairs. Halfway there, impulse seized her and she decided to check on Sir Cabal, if only to assure herself that he was in the keep and not terrorizing misfortunate peasants, as he seemed so intent to do.

Each step seemed to take an eternity, giving Emmalyn plenty of time to question the wisdom of going to his chamber at so late an hour. But if she needed further reasons to justify seeking him out, she reckoned she had many. It would be well within her rights to inquire after his progress with her garrison that day, and as well to question his findings regarding the security of the keep. There would be no reason whatsoever for him to misconstrue her purpose in addressing him now.

Still, having reached the top of the stairwell at last, she paused. With nervous hands, she brushed the flecks of wool fibers from her kirtle, smoothing the deep blue skirts and feeling something of a fool, bedecked as she was in such rich attire. Not that she had worn the fine silk gown for his approval; she had simply tired of her drab homespun and thought a change was in order. And what she felt when Cabal did not attend the evening meal was not disappointment, surely, but rather mild curiosity. No more than a rightful interest in the welfare of what was still her demesne.

Nothing more than that.

Steeling herself with those flimsy convictions, Emmalyn pivoted left and walked down the corridor toward Cabal's chamber. His door was open just enough to let a thin column of candlelight slice through the darkness of the hallway.

Emmalyn followed that flickering bit of golden warmth, her hands down at her sides, buried in the voluminous folds of her skirts, nervously fisting and flexing them the closer she drew to his room.

The toe of her embroidered slipper had just broken the shaft of light on the floor when she heard it . . .

A woman's soft laugh.

She recognized the throaty feminine purr without looking, yet something compelled her to peer into the room. She braved only a quick glance, no longer than a heartbeat, but it was enough to paint a vivid picture of the scene within.

Pretty flame-haired Jane, who had often been a favorite pastime of Garrett's, had now caught the eye of Sir Cabal. The handsome knight was seated on the edge of the bed, half-undressed. His tanned broad chest was bare and gilded deep bronze in the candle glow, his dark head bowed in pleasure. Behind him, Jane was on her knees, her large breasts nearly spilling out of her unlaced bodice as she massaged his neck and shoulders with skilled wanton hands. In that instant, she had whispered something in Cabal's ear that made him chuckle, a low growl of amusement, which to Emmalyn's way of thinking, could only belie the wickedness of the maid's suggestion.

Disgusted with herself for bearing witness, and not wanting to consider what might next transpire in the dimly lit chamber, Emmalyn backed away from the door in utter silence. She did not fault Jane for her wantonness; in fact, when Garrett had been the object of her interest, Emmalyn had been almost grateful for the maid's lusty inclinations. Now, however, she burned with indignation.

It should not matter to her how Cabal chose to spend his nights—or with whom—but strangely, she realized that somehow, it did matter. It mattered to her that this man who, with one glance of his steady silvery gaze, could make her feel beautiful and vital should so easily develop interest in another woman. It mattered that he had said he wanted her, that he would kiss her and then so quickly take one of her

rough maids to his bed. It mattered that she had so hoped to
discover that he was different than other men. Different than
Garrett, better somehow. It mattered that she had almost
been fool enough to believe it.

Almost.

Emmalyn fled upstairs to the solitude of her own chamber.
There, in the chill and lonely darkness, she stripped out of her
kirtle and shoved it back into her clothing chest. Angry, frustrated, and in utter disbelief to think that she could be the least
bit jealous, she climbed into bed and stared up at the rafters,
listening as a steady rain began to patter outside. She lay there
in the miserable quiet for some long hours, cursing her
foolish heart and praying that her appeal to remove Sir Cabal
would reach the queen posthaste.

Chapter Ten

It was just past sunrise when Cabal returned to the castle from an early-morning search of the demesne. He and Sir Miles had taken a handful of the other knights out to comb the area for signs of the thieves, patrolling the fields and watching the woods and borders for evidence of trouble. They had found nothing to lead them to the brigands, but Cabal still considered the exercise a success, for it had taken him out of the keep well before Lady Emmalyn roused to break her fast.

In truth, he had called the predawn retinue together as a means of avoiding her, even for a short time. His thoughts still clung to his disrupted encounter with her in the grove, and the fitful night's sleep he suffered last eve had done little for his mood. He shouted an order for the garrison to commence the day's practice, then dismounted and walked his destrier to the stables.

Thomas, the man who tended the keep's horses, arrived a moment later carrying two buckets of water in from the bailey well. "Good morrow, milord," he called amiably, though his usual easy stride was hampered today by the lingering moisture in the air and the obvious ache of aging bones.

He shuffled into the stable, nearly losing his footing when his boot dislodged a loose stone from the earthen floor. Seeing him falter, Cabal threw his mount's saddle over the stall and loped to Thomas's side, taking up the elder man's burden.

"Thank ye, milord," the stable master said, pressing a fist into the small of his back. "Ach, I was fine with the first few buckets, but these last two felt as though they weighed ten stone a piece."

Cabal dismissed Thomas's gratitude with an impatient shrug, then dispensed the water to the horses that had yet to be tended. Meanwhile, the stable master ambled to the last stall and began brushing down a very pregnant bay mare.

"God's bones," Cabal said, coming to stand next to the animal. "That poor beast looks near to bursting."

Thomas frowned. "Aye, she does at that. But, pray, don't let milady hear ye say so. She's worried enough over Minerva and her overdue royal foal."

"Royal?"

The stable master nodded. "This foal has the blood of a royal stallion in him—a fine black Iberian. The dowager queen herself gifted milady with the breeding last summer when she and her traveling party came to stay at Fallonmour."

Cabal's curiosity stirred. "They are acquainted, Lady Emmalyn and the queen?"

Thomas nodded. "Milady's grandmother was a maid in Queen Eleanor's court in Poitou," he told him proudly. "Her Majesty has been known to tarry at Fallonmour on occasion when her business and travels bring her to the region."

"Indeed?" Cabal remarked. "I was not aware that the lady was so well connected."

"Aye, though would that she had not been," Thomas muttered. "Then she might have been spared the attentions of men like Lord Garrett."

Cabal pivoted his head to stare at him. "What know you of the matter, Thomas?"

"Ye will forgive me, Sir Cabal, if I speak against the man who was my master?" asked the old manservant. Cabal inclined his head in vague permission. "Lord Garrett never did have a care for anyone, save himself," Thomas explained. "His father took part in one of the rebellions waged against King Henry by his barons some years ago. Fearing he would suffer for his father's poor politics, Lord Garrett conspired with his brother, Hugh, to turn their sire in as a traitor to the crown."

"Jesu," Cabal hissed, having never known the bond between father and son yet unable to imagine such a villainous breach.

"Their treachery gained them scorn and met with only meager success," Thomas continued. "In exchange for their father's head, Lord Garrett and Hugh were allowed to keep but two of his many holdings: Fallonmour and Wardeaux."

"I take it Garrett expected to rebuild his demesne through his marriage to Lady Emmalyn?" Cabal suggested.

"Nay," Thomas replied. "Milady's family was not wealthy. Her father held a small manor near Lincolnshire. Though he was a simple farmer, he was respected in noble circles, as was her well-bred mother. Lord Garrett had designs to wed an heiress, but the queen decided against the match. Instead, she offered him the hand of Lady Emmalyn, who was scarcely sixteen when her father lay on his deathbed, eager that she should marry before he was gone."

"He had no wish to wed her?"

Thomas shook his head. "Nay, and I fear she bore the brunt of his anger for having been forced into the arrangement. Lord Garrett could be a cruel man, Sir Cabal, vicious in the things he would say. But not even he could spoil milady's kindness. Oh, she kept up a brave front for all of us, and thankfully, he spent a good deal of his time away. Still, 'twas no real secret the private hell she must have endured."

Cabal swore under his breath, wishing for what had not been the first time that Garrett of Fallonmour had suffered more in his final moments. Would that he could conjure him back now, he would wrap his hands around the bastard's throat and slowly choke the despicable life right out of him.

"She said nothing of this to me," Cabal grumbled, irritated with himself for being so brash with her since his arrival.

"Milady is a proud woman, Sir Cabal," Thomas said quietly.

"And I reckon I have likely said too much as it is. She would be sorely displeased to know that I have been discussing such personal matters with—"

The stable master broke off abruptly, and Cabal felt fairly confident that he had nearly just been called "the enemy."

"I mean only that I do not wish to dishonor milady further by relaying details of something she so clearly meant to keep private, Sir Cabal."

He shrugged and gave Thomas an understanding nod. "No offense taken," he told him.

The old manservant smiled, then set down the brush he had been using on the bay mare. "By yer leave, milord? I've got to piss of a sudden, and if I don't use the bucket for the wool wash, I warrant the sheepherders' wives will call for my head."

Idly, Cabal waved Thomas off, hardly noticing his departure. Instead, he reached out and stroked the mare's neck, moving farther into the stall and following the line of her strong back with his palm. The matron nickered, swishing her tail as Cabal skimmed his hand over the enormous bulge of her midsection. Beneath the thick brown hide he could feel the steady beat of a new life, and he swallowed an unexpected chuckle of awe.

From the low-slung entryway of the stable, soft footsteps padded forth, drawing his attention. "Is there any change this morn, Thom— Oh, 'tis you."

Lady Emmalyn walked farther inside, halting next to her mare's stall. She scowled at Cabal as if his tending the bay were a violation of considerable degree. "Where is Thomas?"

"Gone for necessary matters," Cabal replied, coming from within the berth to move toward her. "He should be back shortly."

She gave him a scornful, disapproving look. "Then I shall return later." As she pivoted to leave, the mare whinnied and began to shift in her stall. Lady Emmalyn hesitated, coming back to gentle the beast with her soft touch. "Is Minerva all right?" she asked Cabal.

"Her foal is growing restless, and anxious to greet his world," he said, finding it impossible not to be somewhat charmed by the lady's obvious devotion to the animal. "Give me your hand," he instructed.

She slanted him a dubious look, but he gave her no time to withdraw. Instead, he grasped Emmalyn's fingers and led her into the berth with him. Holding the confused gaze she directed up at him, Cabal pressed her palm to the outward rise of Minerva's distended belly, keeping it there, his hand placed lightly over the top of hers.

They felt the ripple of movement at the same time.

"Oh my!" Emmalyn exclaimed.

Her swell of unbridled girlish laughter made Cabal's insides squeeze peculiarly, made his body warm all over. He felt a smile reach up from inside him when she turned to look at him, her eyes wide with wonder. He did not remove his hand from atop hers, allowing himself the time to enjoy the moment, for enjoy it he did. Too damned much for his own peace of mind.

"There's another kick!" she said breathlessly, looking back to Minerva when a second movement traveled under the glossy hide of the matron's midsection. " 'Tis sure to be a strong healthy babe, is it not, my lord?"

Cabal nodded, struck by the need for reassurance he heard so plainly in her voice. "I reckon it will be," he said. "After all, he's got the blood of a royal champion running in his veins." She turned her head to him then, frowning inquisitively. "Thomas told me something of your acquaintance with the queen, my lady."

Her hand slid out from under his. "I do not appreciate your gossiping about me with my folk, Sir Cabal."

She stepped away and left him standing there, putting added space between them by striding to where a bucket of red apples sat on the floor. Reaching into it, she took her time choosing the brightest one, as if to delay facing him.

Cabal came out behind her, leaning his shoulder against the supporting beam of the stall. Her wariness was evident in the rigid line of her back, in the utter quiet that had come over her. "I am not your enemy, my lady. You could have told me about Garrett. You could have told me how he treated you."

She turned around without answering and came to stand before Minerva, refusing to look Cabal in the eye. "When last I checked, Sir Cabal, you had been sent here by the king as Fallonmour's guardian, not my confessor."

"You still do not trust me," he remarked, stung somehow, and astonished to realize that he should actually want her esteem.

In place of a polite denial, Emmalyn withdrew a dagger from its sheath on her leather girdle and cleaved the apple in two. She held a crisp wedge out to the horse and pivoted her head to level a scathing glare on Cabal. "I trust people for their deeds, my lord, not their words."

In that instant, paying no mind to the beast's foraging muzzle, Emmalyn might have lost more than what was left of her apple if not for Cabal's swift action. He rushed forward to grasp her hand protectively in his own, pulling it away from the horse's snapping teeth. The dagger and pieces of fruit tumbled to the stable floor.

"Please," Lady Emmalyn said, stealing her hand from his as if his touch had burned her. "She would not have hurt me."

"Neither will I."

Cabal was unsure where the pledge came from, but looking into her innocent upturned face, he was certain he had meant it. She swallowed hard, her gaze entwined with his in the long heartbeats of silence that followed his whispered promise. He saw doubt flash in her eyes. She took a quick breath as he moved closer to her. "I am not looking for a lover, Sir Cabal," she said quietly, her voice tremulous. "I don't need your protection. Nor do I need you about all the time, forever unsettling and confusing me."

Cabal could not harness the pleased grin that tugged at his mouth. "Is that what I do, Emmalyn? Unsettle you? Confuse you?"

"W-what I mean to say is that I am quite capable of looking after myself," she stammered, then bent to retrieve the fallen dagger and apple before moving away from him several paces, putting the mare's big head between them.

"I have no doubt on that score, my lady. But what if I were to tell you that you intrigue me somehow? That I am finding I simply like being in your company?"

She blinked at him as if surprised, as if she thought he might have said it in jest. Then she scoffed. "I would daresay 'tis more to your liking to enjoy whatever lady you happen to find yourself in the company of, my lord."

"Indeed?" he said, puzzled by her retort and wondering what the devil he might have done to warrant such deep scorn.

"If 'tis an easy conquest you seek, my lord, or merely a means of relieving your boredom during your stay here, I warrant you will find better luck elsewhere. No doubt you already have."

She had no sooner muttered the sarcastic remark when a gravelly voice invaded the stables. Humming a tuneless song, Thomas returned inside. The old man entered and hailed the two of them with a smile and a nod but busied himself near the doorway as if understanding their conversation was not meant for his ears.

Lady Emmalyn glanced at the stable master, then brushed at her dark woolen skirts with nervous hands. "If you will excuse me, Sir Cabal, I would have a word with Thomas about Minerva's delivery before going on to my daily duties."

"I would like to know what you meant just now, my lady."

She pivoted to leave. "'Tis of no consequence, I assure you."

Cabal took care to keep his voice low but could not refrain from grasping her arm to delay her flight. "Emmalyn, if I have done something to upset you, I want to know."

Finally, and, he suspected, only because he was giving her little choice, she relented. "If 'tis such a great puzzle to you, then I suggest you ask Jane, my lord. You seem to enjoy her counsel."

With that, she left him, striding across the length of the stable to where Thomas stood. Cabal could only stare after her, bewildered. Jane, did she say? It took a moment before he was able to place the woman's name, so taken aback was he by the lady's brittle outburst. When he did place it and then pieced together that Lady Emmalyn must have heard of the maid's visit to his chamber—or worse, witnessed it for herself—he started to chuckle low under his breath.

God's bones, but she was jealous! And for no good cause, truth be told, though she did not seem interested in giving him the chance to explain what had happened last evening.

Cabal had been eager only to stretch out his fatigued body and sleep when the soft rap had sounded on his chamber door. Against all reason, he had been hoping his late-night visitor might have been Lady Emmalyn. But, of course, it was not, and his hope had given way to disappointment when his eyes lit upon the lady's young maid, Jane, standing at the threshold. She wore a coy smile and an unlaced bodice that showed off her ample cleavage and a wedge of supple white shoulder where the worn fabric slipped down her arm on one side. But more appealing to Cabal, as he recalled it now, had been the small tray of bread and cheese and the tankard of ale the red-tressed maid had brought him.

"I thought ye might be hungry," she had said, and without bothering to wait for an invitation, she had entered his chamber.

Cabal had made short work of the food and drink, and was too tired to object when Jane climbed onto the bed behind him and busied herself with his shoulders, kneading his tension away with skilled, sure hands. He knew of Jane; he and the other Crusaders had heard often of her prowess and erotic appetites from Garrett, so it had come as no surprise to Cabal when she suggested he take her as his mistress while he was at Fallonmour.

What had surprised him was his lack of interest in the woman. At first he had found her lusty banter amusing, had even let her kiss him when she grasped his chin and descended on his mouth. But he had found that her lips were too willing; her slick, probing tongue roused no more than a primal flicker of desire, and the provocative words she murmured against his mouth were far too practiced to stir him to arousal. His body longed for the artless touch and cool regard of a stubborn, serious-minded young widow who would likely never have him. And so, Cabal had turned Jane out of his chamber with nary a pause for second thought.

A hungered part of him, too long denied, had since been ruing that decision. That is, until this very moment. Now, seeing Lady Emmalyn's reaction to the thought of his having taken another woman to his bed, Cabal knew that try as she might to deny it, he affected her. Now her apparent disgust with him this morning had merit. Jealousy he could understand. More than understand it, Cabal was duly flattered by the lady's scorn.

Emmalyn shot him an incensed scowl as she quit the stable, and instead of irritating him, as it rightly should have, he found it buoyed his spirits as nothing else could.

Chapter Eleven

Pete was waiting in the practice yard, pacing to and fro, ready to begin the day's training when Cabal swaggered out of the stables a few moments later. Upon seeing his mentor's approach, the youth dashed forth and met him halfway. "Milord, what's troubling Lady Emmalyn? When I told her I was looking for you, she said, 'Can no one at this keep exist a single moment without that man?' Then she stormed past me, all red in the face and scowling."

"Did she, now?"

"Aye, she did." Pete stared up at him, likely confused by his apparent nonchalance. He leaned in closer, dropping his voice low, as if the friendly, man-to-man advice he was about to impart warranted a confidential delivery. "Best you beware, milord, and keep your distance from her for a time. She seems in a rare, awful mood this morn."

Cabal's grin widened. "Yes, she does, Pete. A rare, awful mood." He clapped the youth on the shoulder. "So, are you ready to begin your exercises?"

Together, the two men girded for practice, Cabal with his broadsword and Pete with the Saracen blade. Today, Pete donned Cabal's tunic of chain mail, giving him a measure of added protection should he take a blow. However, seeing the lad in action made the precaution seem almost unneeded, for his extensive training of the day before had made him a master of the parry and dodge. Pete's long limbs and raw agility served him well this morn; he danced nimbly out of Cabal's path each time he charged, and where

114

he could not twist or duck away from danger, he stood his ground, deflecting every strike with the flat of strong Saracen steel.

But for all his defensive aplomb, it was clear that Pete was loath to land a blow of his own, a reluctance that would bode ill for his chances, indeed, when he met with Taggart on the morrow.

"Swing as if you mean to hit me," Cabal ordered, concealing none of his frustration.

"Milord, please! I cannot!"

"And damn it, Pete, stop calling me milord. When you're in combat, you cannot afford to give a thought to your opponent's rank or who he may be off the field. In battle, 'tis but man against man," Cabal advised him. "Come now, start the match anew."

A few more feeble bouts left Cabal thoroughly irritated and wishing he had simply taken Taggart and the entire garrison on himself, rather than trifling with this folly. The challenge was becoming little more than a tax on his patience.

"God's blood, lad!" he cursed when Pete pulled his last thrust before connecting. He lowered his sword and walked forward to confer with his pupil. "Is there nothing that sets your soul on fire? Nothing you can think of that's worth fighting for?"

Eyes downcast, Pete considered the dusty toe of his boot. "Fallonmour and Lady Emmalyn?" he ventured after a thoughtful moment. "I warrant both are well worth fighting for, milord."

Cabal shook his head. " 'Tis not a trick question, Pete. I want to know what matters to you. You've got to feel it in your gut—something you would kill for." Pete bit his lip in contemplation. "Have you never wanted something you couldn't have, lad?"

"Aye," the young man murmured, "I reckon so." Meekly, he lifted his eyes and met Cabal's expectant gaze. "Lucinda."

"Lucinda? Ah, a woman, of course! The cause of countless wars and bloodshed." Cabal might have made light of the cottar's infatuation, but it was clear from the florid color of Pete's cheeks that the young man was besotted with the maid. "Tell me about this Lucinda, then. Who is she?"

"She's from the village, milord. Martin's daughter."

"Martin the reeve?"

"Aye, the same. He'd kill me if he knew how I felt about Lucy, though it hardly matters. She doesn't even know I exist."

Cabal chuckled, suddenly lighting on a way to stoke Pete into action. "Well, I've not seen the girl, but more's the pity should she liken her father in any way. I reckon she can't be much to look at, your Lucinda."

Pete swiveled his head toward Cabal as if he had just blasphemed. "Lucy is beautiful, milord!"

"So beautiful she won't give you a second glance, then— is that more the problem?"

"Nay." Pete sighed, wearing a forlorn pitiful scowl. "'Tis worse than that. She pines for another, a faithless cur from a neighboring village."

"Ah, unrequited love," Cabal remarked idly. "How tragic."

By now Pete's eyes had grown intense and bright with feeling. "The tragedy is that she was left to bear and raise his child after the louse returned to his wife."

The lad's tender underbelly revealed, Cabal pressed on, edging the sharp blade of cynicism a bit deeper now. "You have designs on a peasant wench who's saddled with another man's bastard? Saints' balls, Pete! Even a sorry whelp like you could do better than that."

The youth's reply was schooled but all the more tight for its restraint. "You will pardon my saying so, milord, but you misjudge her. Lucinda is sweet and kind and mild."

"Oh, I don't doubt that one bit," Cabal said, chuckling as he moved in for the kill. "In fact, Pete, I'd wager I could find at least a dozen other men who would attest to much the same thing when it comes to your Lucinda. She is sweet and kind and mild . . . and oh so willing to spread her creamy thi—"

Without preamble, Pete raised his sword and struck to Cabal's left. The angry clank of steel on steel reverberated in the courtyard as Cabal deflected the blow a startling mere hair's breadth from serious contact. He lifted a brow at Pete in surprise, but the young man's eyes continued to blaze. "You misjudge her," he repeated tersely.

Ah, now they were getting somewhere, Cabal thought with satisfaction. He repositioned himself and delivered an offensive counterattack, grinning when Pete blocked it and came at him again. "She must be quite a prize, after all, Pete. Mayhap I should see about her myself. Perhaps you would oblige me in an introduction when we finish here? As you say, she is disinclined to notice you, but mayhap I could make her forget the cur who so grievously wronged her."

It was a jest, but the young man seemed lacking any humor when it came to the matter of his lovely Lucinda. He snarled and advanced on Cabal, striking hard and with a singular determination worthy of even the most seasoned tournament competitor. After several minutes of what Cabal assumed was mock—if ardent—combat, he called a stop to the practice.

"This is what I was looking for," he told Pete, giving his mop of hair a good-natured tousle. "This is the sort of focus you need to call upon in battle."

Pete looked at him, panting and thoroughly confused. "Milord?"

"You've got the heart of a knight after all. It just took some prodding to bring it out."

"I don't understand. You foxed me into fighting you, milord?"

"Nay, Pete, you foxed yourself. Just like every warrior must learn to do each time he goes onto the field. Can you do that?"

Pete shrugged. "I—I reckon so, milord."

While not the most confident of rejoinders, it would have to suffice, for at that very moment, Taggart and the other knights came out of the keep and caught sight of the suspended training. "What's this?" Taggart called with a chuckle as he strode toward them and placed himself between Pete and Cabal. "No piglets to spar with today?"

His meaty fist came down on Pete's shoulder as if in well-meant greeting, but it contained all the force of a smithy's iron hammer. The combined weight of the chain mail tunic and Pete's total unpreparedness for the blow sent him to the ground like a sack of grain dropped off the back of a cart. He lay in the dust, prone and coughing, sprawled at the big knight's feet. "Clean them off while you're down there . . . *peasant*."

Though Taggart's heavy Norman accent blurred the mouthful of English words, his implied malice rang unmistakably clear. Soundlessly, and with abject solicitude, Pete made to dab at the large boot with the edge of his sleeve.

"Don't do it," Cabal growled. "He's no better than you, Pete. Come up off the ground."

While Pete rose up, then slowly dragged himself to his knees, Taggart's anger refocused, centering on Cabal. "No better, did you say? *No better?*"

As his voice climbed with outrage, castle folk abandoned their tasks, the crowd assembling in the bailey growing several rows deep. From the corner of his eye, Cabal saw the reeve push to the fore of the gathering, and then, at his side a moment later, were two women: a rotund matron of middle age and a slender pretty young maid holding a swaddled infant. Without a doubt, this had to be Pete's beloved Lucinda, now present to witness his humiliation before the entire keep. Cabal swore softly under his breath.

In the quiet moments that passed, Taggart's mood turned darkly belligerent. "Surely, Sir Cabal, you don't mean to say that this filthy, stinking, lowborn cottar, who wouldn't know his prick from a pick-spur, is in any way my equal."

Cabal clamped his jaw tight and bit back the reply so quickly coming to his tongue. It would be easy to level Taggart right there on the spot and be done with this risky match of peasant against knight. Cabal considered what this day might cost him—verily, what it might cost Pete—and cursed his want to take the big knight down a notch.

Beside him, Pete dropped his chin, his downcast face doing nothing to hide his defeat. The rest of the onlookers—Martin, his wife, Lucinda, and dozens more—each wore morose expressions of concern. More than concern, their faces reflected their humiliation, for in degrading Pete for his lowly station in life, Taggart degraded them all. Even Cabal felt his gut twist with a coil of rage, a bone-deep reaction to oppression that he thought he had long ago learned to control.

Taggart's ensuing bark of laughter called for full attention. "My equal, indeed! Why, there's not a body present this morn who'd agree that this peasant vermin is good enough even to wipe my noble arse." His narrowed gaze panned the crowd, arrogantly inviting defiance. *"Is there?"*

"No," Cabal replied, countering the man's irate bellow with a calm that belied none of his own enmity. "And your point is well taken, Taggart. I misspoke myself when I compared the two of you. Pete is not your equal . . ."

"Damn right he's not," the knight interjected.

". . . he's your better."

The bailey echoed, first with a wave of stunned whispers as Cabal's challenge swept the crowd, then with an answering ebb of endless foreboding silence. Pete's knees began to knock, but to his credit, he remained standing upright and spoke none of the fear that showed in his face. Cabal suspected the lad was entirely unaware that his hand had since curled around the hilt of the Saracen sword, a reflexive anticipation of pending conflict. Whether he knew it or not, this simple cottar did indeed have the heart of a warrior.

For his part, Taggart seemed oblivious of Pete's substance, so distracted was he by his wounded pride. He glared at Cabal, turning three shades of purple while a muscle jerked in his jaw. His thick lips quivered with the incomplete forming of what surely would have been a string of vile threats and curses, if only he'd had the ability to rein in his futile voice-robbing rage. That inability counted chief among Taggart's weaknesses; Cabal could only pray the behemoth suffered more than bloated pride alone.

"Pete's a better man," he said, deciding then and there to throw a bit more fat into the fire, "but what's more, I wager he's also a better fighter."

"We shall see about that on the morrow," Taggart snarled.

"Why don't we see about it now?"

Taggart's was not the only head that swung around to stare disbelievingly at Cabal. Pete, the other knights, and Sir Miles as well, who had hence moved to the front of the retinue's ranks, all gaped slack-jawed upon hearing the challenge issued in such a public forum. The old captain shot Cabal a sober look of doubt, then shook his head slowly as if to caution against the idea.

"Very well," Taggart agreed. "Now it is."

With a cocksure chuckle, he turned away and drew his broadsword, making a great show of cleaving the air as the group of knights backed off, creating a circle in which the two men would spar. Pete grabbed at Cabal's sleeve, his voice a strangled, desperate whisper. "But, milord, I'm not ready!"

"You're as ready as you would be come the morn. I see no reason to put this off any longer."

"But if I lose—"

Cabal did not afford him the chance to finish the grim thought. "There is a lovely young lady standing at the front of the crowd who seems hopeful that you will not."

Frowning in confusion, Pete followed Cabal's gesture, glancing to where Lucinda stood on tiptoe, peeking over her father's shoulder, her pretty lower lip caught between her teeth, her eyes fixed on Pete and bright with optimistic anticipation. When she saw Pete look her way, she flushed shyly and gave him a wobbly smile. "Saints preserve me," he whispered fervently. " 'Tis Lucy!"

Cabal feigned a measure of bland disinterest. "Is it? Well, it seems to me that she has noticed you after all. A shame her first impression had to be that of a bullied peasant lad knocked facedown in the dust. More's the pity, should it also be her last."

"It won't be," Pete averred. "I'll show you, milord. I can do this."

"Don't show me, lad. Show her." Cabal then gestured to the crowd of onlookers. "Show all of them."

Pete nodded, and within moments the courtyard filled with the sounds of competitive combat: the rhythmic clank of steel on steel, the gasps and lauds of the spectators, and, soon enough, the huffing and panting of Pete's overweight, over-confident opponent. Taggart spent himself early, making wide sweeps of his blade and trying to keep up with Pete's agile feet as the latter danced around the circle of the courtyard.

Like the piglet he had chased about the morning before, Pete kept Taggart ever on the move, hopping from side to side and intermittently jabbing his blade with the speed that seemed to come so naturally to him. Pete kept his eyes trained on Taggart's gaze, anticipating his every action and countering it with surprising effectiveness.

Cabal was almost certain Pete had the match well in hand when he saw the lad lunge and stumble. Taggart wasted no time in seizing the opportunity. Drawing his arms high, he cleaved the air in a wild downward arc. Pete twisted where he had fallen, having just enough space to turn his sword flat to deflect the ensuing blow. But the heavy Norman steel proved too much.

Taggart's weapon sparked against Pete's Saracen blade, jolting the curved sword cleanly out of his grasp. A collective gasp washed over the crowd of onlookers. Taggart's chuckle echoed with malicious satisfaction. He shot a smug glance over his shoulder to Cabal. "Do ye remember what we said, Crusader?" he taunted.

Cabal swore under his breath, a hair's breadth from dashing in to take Pete's place against Taggart. To do so would spell the young man's supreme humiliation, but as well, it might be the only way to spare him from a public skewering.

"We said to the finish!" shouted Taggart, brandishing his weapon high above his head.

An instant later, his feet shot out from under him, and with a great *oof*, the big knight crashed to the ground. A heap of dust rose to conceal the sparring circle, plunging the entire bailey into stunned watchful silence. Cabal himself had hardly been aware of what hit Taggart until he saw Pete scramble up from where he had rolled, knocking Taggart off balance. He vaulted to his feet and retrieved his weapon. In a trice, he was standing over the other man, blade poised for the kill at Taggart's throat.

Cabal's half-chuckled disbelieving oath was swallowed up in the next instant by the spectators' thunderous roar of approval. The bailey rang with victory shouts and a wild gale of applause.

"To the finish," Taggart grumbled from where he lay pinioned beneath Pete's sword. The peasant took a step back, relaxing his stance and bringing his blade down to his side. "Damnation," Taggart fumed, his voice rising. "We said to the finish, peasant! Now finish it!"

Instead, Pete reached down and held out his hand—an offer of peace. Taggart glared at him as if the young man had just thrown mud in his eye. With a huff of outrage, the big knight got to his feet, ignoring the gesture. He grabbed up his lost weapon and slammed it into its sheath, then spat onto the ground and stormed out of the ring.

The crowd parted to let him pass; then they closed in on their new hero, applauding Pete's skill. But Pete seemed oblivious of their praise. He dashed to Cabal's side, breathless, his eyes bright with pride.

"I did it! Can you credit it, milord? I actually did it!"

"You did a fine job, Pete," Cabal told him, slapping him

on the shoulder. "But I can't credit why you would want to jabber on about it to me when you could be wooing the fair Lucinda. She's been waiting very patiently for you to notice her, I suspect."

Pete looked over his shoulder in her direction, then grinned back at Cabal. "You knew she was there all along, didn't you, milord? You made me fight Taggart today because you wanted her to see me do it."

Cabal shook his head in denial and gave a mild shrug.

"Aye," Pete insisted. "You did this for me."

"No. You did it all yourself."

Pete was evidently unwilling to let his appreciation go unsaid. He grasped Cabal's hand. "Milord, thank you. I am indebted."

"God's bones, begone with you already," Cabal said with mock gruffness. "A lady that fetching isn't likely to wait all day for a homely scruff like you—be you the day's proud victor or nay."

With a beaming smile, Pete sheathed his sword, then loped across the bailey. Congratulations were called to him as he went; even the reeve gave a kindly nod of acknowledgment for Pete's victory. Though Martin did not look overly pleased to see his daughter eyeing Pete's purposeful gait with such shy feminine regard, he seemed too engrossed in his conversation with Sir Miles to interfere. A moment later, the two men approached Cabal.

"There has been another thieving in the village," Sir Miles informed him. "A short while ago, a group of brigands broke into the mill. Old Jack, the village miller, was dragged into the field and beaten something terrible. He did manage to see which direction of the forest the thieves fled."

"Then why are we dallying here, men?" Cabal said to the group of them. " 'Tis time we root these vermin out."

Stalking across the bailey with Sir Miles and the reeve in his wake, Cabal shouted for a handful of guards to bear arms and saddle up. Eagerly, half of the small garrison complied, falling in behind Cabal. On his way to the stables, he approached the spot where Pete stood charming a smile from both Lucinda and her babe. "Come, Pete," he said as he passed. "You've got business to attend now. Lucinda will wait for your return."

She nodded her assurance, and as Pete dashed off on his mentor's heels, she called after him, "Be careful!"

Cabal found Taggart, alone, brooding in the shade of the stables and nursing his wounds with a skin of wine. The big knight looked up as the men sauntered toward the outbuilding, the group of them alive with the excitement of a possible confrontation after so long a period of inactivity. While the others filed in to retrieve their mounts, Cabal paused at the doorway. "You'd be a benefit to me down there as well, Taggart."

He did not wait for the knight's reply, but he was well pleased to see that when the party had assembled in the courtyard, mounted up and ready to ride, Taggart was indeed among them. His besting evidently put aside for the moment, Taggart wore a look of eager anticipation, the same as the others.

"To the woods, men!" Cabal shouted, and led the group out of the gates at a thunderous gallop.

Emmalyn's rash, emotional outburst in the stable some hours before had haunted her for the remainder of the morning and long past noontide. The truth was, she still burned when she thought of Cabal with Jane. Seeing how easily he was winning over the rest of her folk only made her anger harder to control. To say nothing of her fears.

Risking her heart was one thing, but her first duty was to her folk and to the welfare of Fallonmour. She could not afford to let her own desires and foolish emotions cloud her focus with regard to her responsibilities.

In an effort to keep her thoughts schooled around that notion, she busied herself with tasks about the castle and in the gardens, supervising the sweeping of the rushes and, at present, collecting herbs alongside Nurse for the evening's supper. Anything to avoid thinking about what a fool she had made of herself with Cabal.

She had made a point of keeping Jane in sight most of the day as well, occupying her with various duties and trying not to take overmuch glee in her decision to send the young maid out with the urine buckets to volunteer her aid to the shepherds' wives in the washing of the wool for market.

"'Twas hardly Christian to take such petty revenge against her, let alone delight in it," she told Bertie when the old nurse started to titter over the idea. However, whether it was becoming Christian behavior or nay, before long, both women were engulfed in delicious laughter.

Emmalyn was the first to collect herself. "I reckon we've enough fennel and rosemary in this basket to season three hams," she told Bertie. "Will you take it up to Cook for me? I think I'll linger a moment and see about the roses. I've been meaning to bring some in for a few days now; 'twould be a pity to let them spoil on the briar."

Bertie said nothing to remind Emmalyn of how long it had been since she had taken interest in her flower garden, but the knowledge was there in the elder woman's eyes: a soft expression and a gentle nod that said she understood. For her own reasons, Emmalyn needed a bit of time alone. Only after she could no longer hear the soft rustle of Bertie's skirts or the heavy pad of her feet on the walkway did Emmalyn rise and begin the short trek to the fragrant enclosure that had at one time given her such great joy.

Now, and for too long, the garden had been home to painful memories, sad reminders of a young bride's hopes for a small piece of happiness . . . and the precious gift she had lost. It seemed somehow important to Emmalyn now, that in light of Garrett's death—more, as a testament to her hope for her future—that she take steps to reclaim this piece of her broken heart.

Entering the manicured alcove, Emmalyn passed by the neat beds of varied colorful flowers as if in a trance. She paid no mind to the small fish pool, nor the bench nearby, formed of packed earth and covered in plush thickly grown grass. Not even the fruit trees, filled with singing birds, distracted her from venturing toward the most forsaken corner of the garden.

There, like a grim sentinel, it stood: a glorious briar of bloodred roses, planted to celebrate the pending birth of a babe that never had the chance to draw its first breath. Now it was little more than a pretty grave marker, a tribute made all the more poignant for its defiant strength in spite of prolonged neglect. Guilt pricked Emmalyn's eyes as she approached, and by the time she dropped to her knees in the soft moss bed that blanketed the corner, she was weeping.

"I'm sorry I couldn't protect you," she whispered brokenly, "I'm so sorry."

Letting her tears fall freely, Emmalyn pulled the dead leaves from within the twining branches and plucked the weeds from around the base of the briar. As she wept, a soft breeze traversed the garden, sifting through the shade trees and climbing vines, carrying with it the mingled scents of fragrant greenery and lush, summer blooms. The gentle air was a soothing balm to Emmalyn in her solitude, a coaxing caress that assured her it was all right to feel, that there was no shame in hurting.

Her pain seeping out of her, Emmalyn scarcely heard the rustle some short space behind her. She bit her lip, listening, but heard nothing. Still, she could not dismiss the sensation that she was no longer alone in the garden. The fine hairs on the back of her neck confirmed the notion, prickling a warning.

"Is someone there?" Dashing the tears from her cheeks, Emmalyn swiveled her head to look over her shoulder. "Bertie, is that you? Jane?"

When no one answered after a long moment, Emmalyn came to her feet and brushed the dirt and twigs from her skirts. Perhaps it had been just the breeze playing tricks with her ears, she decided. Listening closely to her surroundings nonetheless, she withdrew her dagger and set about collecting an assortment of flowers to bring into the keep. Then she heard a noise once more, this time a definite footstep several paces behind her. She whirled around, dagger in hand, prepared to defend herself.

Stepping forward, she scanned the area. There were no signs of danger or intruders in the empty space that greeted her, but at her feet she discovered something queer, indeed. On the ground lay a scattering of daisy tops, arranged in a pattern that formed a crude heart. Looking at the sweet, childlike design, Emmalyn's fright of the moment before rushed out of her on a breath of surprise . . . and wonder.

"Who—" A movement caught by the corner of her eye cut short her questioning whisper. Behind a bush near the entrance of the gardens stood the waif from the orchard. "Oh! 'Tis you," Emmalyn said, sheathing her blade and advancing subtly lest she scare him away. "You're so very quiet, I'm afraid I didn't see you there."

Whether it was her familiarity that drew him from the thicket or if he was instead avoiding being trapped there, the boy slowly came out. The poor child was in desperate need of care and feeding, his appearance having worsened from the first time she had seen him. He looked hungry and long overdue for a bath, his face and clothes covered in filth and grime. Her heart ached to take care of him.

"Did you leave those pretty flowers for me?"

At first she did not think he was going to respond, but then he nodded. His guarded, inquisitive brown gaze did not leave her face for a moment as he emerged fully and came to stand before the garden gate, his every lean muscle poised for instantaneous flight.

"Thank you," Emmalyn said, taking another step forward and trying to reassure him with a smile. "I like them very much."

He moved back slightly, then stopped, cocking his head as he peered hard at her. From his questioning expression, Emmalyn realized she must look a fright with her tear-stained face and puffy eyes. "Y-you . . . crying?" he stammered, startling her with the sound of his voice, revealed at last.

"You can speak," she gasped, and before she realized what she was doing, she took a step toward him. Like a grazing deer caught by the hayward, the boy leaped over the gate to safety. He stood on the other side, clutching the wooden barrier now put between them.

This close, Emmalyn could see that he had been beaten again; his bruises were fresher than those he had worn when she saw him last, and what she had assumed was dirt caked at the corner of his mouth was in fact dried blood. Seeing him again, Emmalyn was not sure which was the stronger urge: her need to comfort this neglected soul or her want to mete like punishment on whoever was responsible for his current condition. "Please don't be frightened. I would never do anything to hurt you. I promise."

He did not look entirely trustful of that fact, but neither did he move when she took another step forward and reached out her hand. "Come with me to the castle," she coaxed. "If you're hungry, I've got ham inside, and unless I miss my guess, I smell a sweet honey cake baking in the kitchens. I'm sure I could convince the cook to let you have a piece while it's warm. Would you like that?"

His eyes brightened and he started to nod, but then, as if suddenly thinking better of it, he shrank away from the gate and took two hasty steps backward.

"Don't go," Emmalyn said. "You don't have to go back there."

With one final, lingering glance, the boy turned on his heel and bolted out of sight.

Chapter Twelve

Fallonmour's knights filed into the great hall for supper that evening, riding a wave of boisterous, masculine bravado. The commotion surrounding their arrival drew Emmalyn's attention away from her talk with Bertie at the high table, and her eyes fell instantly on Cabal. He strode along at the crest of the bustling swell of guards, appearing for all the world like a just-returned conquering hero. Emmalyn frowned. His black hair was windblown and tousled, his chiseled cheeks ruddy and shadowed with a day's growth of stubble. One of the men said something to him that made him laugh—an unchecked, baritone rumble of amusement—and Emmalyn was stunned to realize that she had never heard anything quite so appealing.

She struggled to remain unaffected by the grace in his confident swagger as he led the knights across the rush-strewn floor. She pretended not to notice the way his muscles coiled and flexed with each step he took, or how, for wholly different reasons, his very presence in the room commanded the attention of both man and woman alike. An uncontrollable, surreptitious glance about the hall proved that Jane was not yet arrived for the evening meal. Equally uncontrollable, if not more distressing to Emmalyn's way of thinking, was the satisfaction that bit of knowledge brought.

She watched over the rim of her goblet without drinking as Cabal made his way to the dais. He looked up at her, evidently sensing her regard, and something almost tangible passed between them in that moment: a jolt of awareness, a beat of invitation. A promise of pleasures as yet untold.

Flushing with the very notion, Emmalyn disentangled her gaze from his as the handsome Crusader abandoned his throng of eager disciples and now came striding across the length of the hall to stand before her. "Good even, my lady. Nurse."

Though he greeted them both with equal courtesy, his smile centered on Emmalyn alone. He seated himself beside her as if he belonged there, leaning back in the chair and accepting a cup of wine from the page serving the dais. He smelled of woodsmoke and leather and time spent out of doors, and it was all Emmalyn could do not to lean closer and breathe him in. She drank what was left of her wine, wondering if it would be possible to pass the entire meal without speaking to him.

She nearly succeeded in doing just that, for even though they shared the same trencher, they ate in silence throughout the first course of roasted ham and long into the second, a lighter fare of fish stew and boiled vegetables. It was not until the pages came to clear for the third course, an assortment of cheeses and fruits, that Sir Cabal broke the quiet. "I would have wagered my eyeteeth that Cook had a honey cake in the oven this afternoon." He shrugged and gave her an easy smile. "Mayhap 'twas merely wishful thinking."

Emmalyn stared at him. "No, it wasn't. That is, he did. I had Cook set the cake aside for me. On the morrow, I'm going to take it down to the . . . village." A partial truth, that. She did not think he would approve of her plan to bring it to the woods in the hopes of finding the boy again, and for some reason, she was loath to invite his scorn. "If you like, I could send someone to fetch a piece for you," she suggested.

He held up his hand, shaking his head. "'Tis not necessary. I am contentedly stuffed as it is, my lady. Besides, I wouldn't want to take anything away from the miller; I reckon he, more than I, is deserving of your special consideration."

Whatever did old Jack have to do with anything? Emmalyn wondered. She tilted her head at Cabal, brow pinched in confusion.

"The miller, my lady. I trust that cake is meant for him, is it not? In reward for his actions in leading us to the brigands this afternoon?"

"The brigands?" Emmalyn echoed. "I don't understand. What has Jack done?"

"If not for him, I doubt very much that the men and I would have been able to locate the thieves' camp. Thanks to his keen eye, I believe we may have finally put a stop to the filching."

Suddenly, Emmalyn's heart began to pound with dread. She thought of the little boy, so shy and mistreated. She closed her eyes and saw his bruised face, his frail torso, skinny limbs. Her promise made to him in the garden, that she would never hurt him, came back to her like the cruelest jest, and all at once a cold knot started to form in her stomach.

"What do you mean, put a stop to it?" she asked, her voice thready. "What have you done?" Emmalyn could scarcely think for the deafening rage of her pulse thrumming in her temples. She swallowed past the bile that threatened to rise in her throat. "Did you . . . kill them?"

"No," he said lightly, reaching for his tankard. "The camp was empty when we came upon it." She thought he might have sounded disappointed, and felt a new anger stoke to life within her. "We did confiscate some of their belongings," he continued after quaffing a mouthful of wine. "The rest we burned."

Emmalyn gasped, recoiling and thoroughly appalled. "Good Lord! Is that why you're all so smug tonight? Because you drove off a group of starving defenseless misfortunates?"

"Not so defenseless as it turns out," he murmured, but Emmalyn was not about to listen to another word. Her concerns focused wholly on the boy she had befriended and now inadvertently betrayed, she shoved her chair back and stormed off the dais, heedless of the sea of confusion she left in her wake.

She was out of the keep and halfway across the dusk-filled bailey when Cabal caught her by the arm. "Where are you going?"

"To find him!"

She wrenched herself free and started off again, this time at a more urgent pace. Three long-legged strides carried Cabal past her. He stopped in front of her, grasping her firmly by the upper arms. "Who, Emmalyn? It's nearly dark outside and I just told you there are thieves yet on the loose. Who is it you would be willing to risk your life and limb to run to at this hour?"

"I am concerned for the boy," she informed him tightly.

He did not respond; indeed, at first he did not even seem to recall the pitifully abused urchin they had encountered together on their ride around Fallonmour's borders. "Evidently the sight of a neglected child makes very little impression on you, my lord."

"I remember the boy," he said at last. " 'Tis your continued regard for him that puzzles me. What care you about a thief's lowly whelp, my lady? Particularly one who sought to cause you harm the first opportunity he had."

"He was frightened that day in the orchard; 'tis the only reason he lashed out. When I saw him this afternoon, he was sweet and very shy—"

"You saw him again today? Where?"

"In the flower garden near the castle." His scowl darkened and she hastened to explain further. "I was cutting roses for my chamber when I found him hiding amongst the bushes. He left me some daisies."

Cabal looked at her as if she were a toddler who had just been playing with a venomous serpent. "You were by yourself with him, and you didn't call a guard to apprehend him?"

If she was not quite so outraged, Emmalyn might have laughed at his overcautious reaction. "He's not a criminal, my lord, just a young boy in need of care and kindness."

"You could have been killed." He swore vividly and raked a hand through his hair. "How can you be sure he was alone? How do you know that he was not bait, meant to lure you from the safety of the castle? God's wounds, my lady, are you truly that naive?"

"Are you truly that unfeeling?" she countered. "That boy is an innocent mistreated child. You saw as much yourself, or have you forgotten how he was covered in ugly bruises? Today his condition was even worse."

Cabal regarded her dubiously. "How do you know those marks were not earned in the getting of stolen goods? Can you be so certain that they weren't delivered in defense of an attack—mayhap the very one made on the old miller today?"

Emmalyn shook her head. "He's naught but a shy, neglected little boy, not a monster, as you would have me believe. And I'm not going to listen to this for another moment when I should be out trying to find him and bring him back where I can make sure he's safe from further harm."

"Leave him to his own kind, my lady. That's where he belongs. Don't tempt him with promises of a better life that can never really be his."

"How can you say that? How can you possibly know what's best for that child?"

"I know because I have—" He broke off then, as if his anger had devoured the rest of what he meant to say. A deep exhalation seemed to steady him enough to meet her gaze once more and continue. "I know, because I have seen their kind before. Given the chance, I warrant that boy and any one of his kin would be more inclined to lace open your pretty throat than they would be to thank you for your noble charity."

Cabal's gray eyes were steely in the gathering darkness; not a bit of mercy or understanding softened the hard gaze staring down at Emmalyn. The dim glow from a lantern hanging outside the stable reflected on the planes of his

face, making his features appear all the more harsh and
unyielding. Perhaps it was the diminishing light that let her
see him so clearly now for what he was: a dark, uncaring
warrior. A man of swift violence, his heart blackened by
savagery, and utterly devoid of remorse. Not so very different than Garrett.

No, she thought with a keen, dawning sense of regret; he
was not so different from him at all.

"You think I was wrong to destroy their camp, do you,
my lady? You must think it an excessive retaliation for a bit
of harmless pilfering. Or do you rather believe it was naught
but an act of heartless barbarism?"

Emmalyn did not have a chance to voice her reply. He
grasped her by the hand, his strong fingers wrapping around
her wrist and pulling her in tow as he crossed the bailey with
long, purposeful strides. "I don't appreciate being strong-
armed in this manner," she said through gritted teeth, experi-
encing more than a little trepidation at seeing him behave so
boldly with her. "Where are you taking me?"

He was not inclined to tell her, evidently. He grabbed the
lantern from its iron hook as they passed the stable, and with
the wobbly flame lighting a dim path, he stalked with
Emmalyn past the smithy's alcove and toward the armory,
an outbuilding used to house the garrison's shields and
heavier weapons in times of peace. Somehow, she doubted
that in bringing her there at such a brisk pace, Cabal intended
anything of a peaceful nature.

She was about to take further issue with his treatment of
her when they neared the last armor stall and he released
her. Emmalyn rubbed her wrist, admittedly more in nervous
anticipation than out of any inflicted pain, and watched as
he set the lantern down on a wooden shelf behind them.
Before she realized what he was about, he grasped her
shoulders in his hands and pulled her in front of him, facing
her toward a heap of helmets, knives, and crossbows.

"Look," he instructed tightly, his heated breath rasping
at her ear. "This is what I found at their campsite. Does

it appear to you that these miscreants would have been happy for long with stealing just a bit of barley and a few chickens?"

Emmalyn sagged against his solid chest, her anger and fear leaking out on a heavy ragged sigh. She shook her head, staring at the jumbled cache of confiscated weapons. He turned her around in his arms then, his touch calmer but nonetheless firm. When she would have looked away from him, he brought her gaze back with a gentle lift of her chin. " 'Twas food they took thus far, but what might have been next? A beast or two? A village woman? Where would you have had me stop it, Emmalyn?"

"I—I don't know," she whispered, shaking her head. "I didn't know. . . ."

Embarrassed that she could have been so wrong—about the thieves, certainly, but also, as it again appeared, wrong to doubt him—Emmalyn grew very silent. He would ridicule her now; he had every right. Were Garrett here, he would assert he'd had the right to beat her for such incompetence and reckless poor judgment. Would Cabal feel likewise?

She edged away from him, a cautious half-step backward that she took nearly without forethought. Through the wavering glow of lantern light, she kept her focus trained on his eyes, knowing all too well that it was there she would first see a portent of the rage to come. But what she saw in his dark-fringed gaze was nothing like the reproach and loathing she had so often seen glittering in her husband's eyes. She was nearly tempted to call Cabal's steady regard affectionate, but then, out of the corner of her eye, she saw his hand rising up out of the darkness beside her, and she nearly jumped out of her skin.

Eyes squeezed shut, chin tucked against her shoulder in protective reflex, Emmalyn did not dare so much as breathe.

Cabal swore softly. "How is it you are willing to trust the motives of common thieves yet recoil from me as if I would strike you?"

Unable to answer, neither could Emmalyn look at him,

desperate that if he did not already know the depth of her
shame, he would not plainly see it now swimming in her
eyes. He reached out when she drew a shaky breath and
brought her close once more, tipping her chin up until she
was forced to meet his eyes. She trembled as Cabal's hard
warm knuckles skated down the slope of her cheek with
aching tenderness. "What are you so afraid of, Emmalyn?
Do you truly think I would ever mean to hurt you?"

Emmalyn was unsure what she thought anymore, unsure
she could trust her feelings. In that moment, though her conscience warned her to be wary, she wanted nothing better
than to revel in Cabal's touch. She wanted to remain there in
the semi-darkness, studying every plane and angle of his
handsome face until she could picture him in her mind whenever she closed her eyes. She wanted him to press his mouth
to hers and kiss her with the same desire as he had likely
kissed Jane the night before. She wanted to feel like a
woman—innocent and earthy, protected and powerful—and
knew deep in her soul that this was the man who could take
her to those heights.

She wanted to believe that there was something honorable in this dangerous man, this man who had made his
living through violence and destruction. And that was verily
the greatest folly in her line of thinking.

Reminding herself of who and what he was, Emmalyn
pulled out of Cabal's embrace. "I think I've seen quite
enough in here, my lord. You have proven your point about
the thieves, and now I would like to return to the keep—"

"Are you going to run from me each time we end up
alone, Emmalyn? What are you afraid might happen?"

His challenge rooted her feet where she stood, two paces
from him. Meeting his serious probing gaze, she crossed her
arms one over the other and rubbed off a chill that wasn't
there. "I'm not afraid."

"Yes, my lady, you are. You may not be afraid to stand
up for yourself and what you believe in nor, from what I've

seen, are you afraid of hard work and responsibility. But you, dear lady, are very much afraid of me."

"If I am afraid, then so are you, my lord. Afraid there might be one woman walking the earth who hasn't fallen the fool to your charms."

He acknowledged the barb with a casual lift of one black brow. "Indeed?"

"Yes," she averred, suddenly feeling that she was gaining ground. "Why else would you insist on pursuing me when you could have any one of the maids in this keep?"

"Simply put, I don't want any of them."

"Or is it rather that you have already sampled and tired of them all?"

"I think you know better than that, Emmalyn."

"I don't know any such thing. I don't know anything about you."

He pursed his lips, a wry sound escaping his throat. "Yet you are very willing to think the worst of me."

"I was wrong to doubt your decision this afternoon and I have told you as much—"

"That's not what I'm referring to, Emmalyn. I'm referring to your thoughts regarding me and that maid of yours. . . . What was her name?"

"Jane," Emmalyn supplied reluctantly.

"Yes," he said, smiling now. "Jane."

Emmalyn frowned. "I admit I had no right to say what I did in the stable this morn. I assure you, my lord, it makes no difference to me whom you should choose to spend your time with."

Those silver eyes bore into her. "Regardless of what you might have heard, I did not take her to my bed."

"But I saw you—" Too late, she bit back the horrible admission. "Please don't feel you have to deny anything to me. 'Tis none of my concern."

He leaned toward her and spoke slowly, as if she were a dull child. "I did not make love to Jane."

"You didn't?"

He shook his head and Emmalyn cursed the wave of relief that flooded her senses. "She came to me with food and drink," he said, "and, truth be told, an offer I likely would have taken at one time. But I turned her away. Do you know why, Emmalyn?"

She did not know if she shook her head or even if she managed to stammer an answer, for in that next moment, his mouth was descending on hers, brushing her lips with an aching sweetness that swept all conscious thought from her mind.

Cabal commanded her mouth as he did everything else: expertly, with easy confidence and gentle mastery. Without her being aware, he freed her hair from the confines of her wimple, startling her with the sensual feel of his fingers wading through the heavy tresses to caress her scalp. He kissed her reverently, passionately, as if he were a long-thirsting man at last fallen upon a well of fresh clear water. Emmalyn went pliant in his arms and let him drink her in.

She did not know what to do with her hands at first. Hesitantly, she let them relax until they fell gently against his arms. She skimmed up their hard, muscular length, tentatively resting her palms on his broad shoulders. Her fingers found the soft hair at his nape and she twined them into the glossy waves, marveling at how he could be such an abundance of both steel and silk. He made a noise in the back of his throat that sounded like a growl and drew her up against his chest, breaking their kiss to look down at her, his gaze heavy lidded and tender in the lantern light.

Neither one of them said a word. All Emmalyn could hear was her frantic heartbeat, pounding in the silence of the armory. Her shallow breaths mingled with his. She wondered if he would want to make her his lover, right there where they stood.

She wondered if she would have the strength of will to stop him. . . .

Distantly, she began to hear noises in the bailey. Voices coming from one of the outbuildings. The haste of leather-shod footsteps on the path leading from the stables to the castle. Then a shout. "Milady, are you out here?"

Emmalyn looked up at Cabal, now desperate. How could they explain their presence together in the unseemly quiet of a darkened outbuilding? How could she explain her kiss-swollen lips and her disheveled hair? No explanations would be necessary, she reasoned, for it would be clear to all what had transpired—indeed, what might have further transpired had they been given any longer to consider it.

A long beat passed before Cabal answered the page's hail. "In the armory, Jason."

The lad entered the building but remained at the threshold, peering inside. "Milady, Thomas sent me to fetch you. He says he needs you in the stables."

"Minerva?" Emmalyn guessed, feeling her heart suddenly gladden despite the discomfiture of her present situation.

"Aye, milady. 'Tis about the mare." Though the near darkness concealed the lad's expression, nothing could mask his concern. "Thomas says to come at once, milady."

Chapter Thirteen

With Cabal following behind her, Emmalyn raced to the stables, her heart clenched in fear for the fate of her beloved mare. At the threshold, the silence within the humid outbuilding nearly stole her breath away. Twin candles, halfburnt on the iron holders affixed to Minerva's stall, provided only the dimmest light to guide her to where Thomas's voice cooed in low, soothing tones.

The old stable master knelt beside the mare, mopping the sweat from her neck with a square of damp linen. When Emmalyn's feet crunched in the soft hay of the stall, Minerva's eyes rolled in her direction. The matron bay nickered, lifting her head. She made an effort to rise up, but Thomas held her down with a tender hand placed on the horse's shoulder.

"Something is not right," Emmalyn said, noting the fatigue on Thomas's face.

"She broke water a quarter of an hour ago, milady." He shook his head. "This foal hasn't got much time left if Minnie won't push him out."

"Why won't she push?" Emmalyn asked. "What is wrong with her?"

Thomas shrugged hopelessly. " 'Tis her first birth, so it could be any number of things. Mayhap she's distressed. Could be the foal is too big, or not right in some way."

"Oh, Thomas, you don't think it's gone already. . . ."

"Nay, 'tis alive and warm, and Minnie's body will sustain it for a short while."

"Is the foal misaligned?" Cabal had brought the lantern, Emmalyn noticed; he set it down where it would give off more light in the stall and stood beside her.

Thomas shook his head as he answered the big knight's question. "When last I checked, the forelegs were positioned as they should be. 'Tis as if Minerva has simply refused to deliver." He looked to Emmalyn in concern. "I'm sorry, milady, but to delay much longer might well cost us the both of them."

A jolt of panic racked Emmalyn. "Oh, Thomas! Can't you help her? Can't you pull the foal free?"

"I have already tried, milady. Without Minerva's help, I will only cause more damage in forcing the birth."

"Well, we have to do something!"

Emmalyn's desperation was answered by Cabal's voice, deep and calm with gentle command. "My lady, the mare has been watching you since we arrived. Even still she listens for your voice. Go to her, talk to her. Perhaps she has been waiting all this time for you."

Emmalyn looked to Thomas for his opinion. "You don't think—"

"Do as he says, milady," Thomas encouraged. "She trusts me well enough, but that stubborn beast loves you beyond measure. Go to her; it can only help."

Emmalyn approached Minerva with care not to frighten her and knelt beside her in the hay. She spread her skirt out and lifted the bay's head onto the soft wool, stroking her muzzle. "Minnie, what's the matter with you?" she whispered soothingly. "Have you been waiting for me, you willful beast? Did you remember my promise to be here with you? Well, I am here now, Minnie. You've got a beautiful baby just waiting to be born. 'Tis time to be done with this."

The mare did indeed seem responsive to the sound of Emmalyn's voice, so she kept talking, kept encouraging. At last, to her delighted surprise, with the next contraction, Minerva began to push. Thomas called out that the foal was starting to show, and Emmalyn sent a thankful prayer heavenward. When she opened her eyes, she found Cabal watching her from outside the stall, and wholly caught up in the moment, she returned his smile.

The sputtering candlelight played strange tricks with his penetrating gaze. It could not hide the desire still blazing in those compelling silver depths, but the reflection of the soft flames seemed also to give the peculiar and tempting illusion that there was something more profound yet kindling in his gaze. She did not dare wonder what it might be. She glanced away; then Thomas's voice dragged her attention back to the task at hand.

"The foal's forelegs and muzzle are passed, milady."

Exercising expedient, meticulous care, he cut away the membrane from around the newborn's head so it could breathe on its own. Relieved beyond measure, Emmalyn whispered gentling praises to Minerva as she stroked the mare's head and mane. Just three more waves of contractions and at last the foal was delivered.

Healthy and strong, Minerva's glossy black colt was a stunning combination of both his parents: the proud features and strong carriage of his royal sire, and the gentle eyes and bright white blaze that marked him as his mother's offspring.

"Isn't he the most beautiful thing you've ever seen?" Emmalyn breathed in a whisper of pure amazement, nearly moved to tears while Thomas rubbed the babe down with a dry sheet of toweling.

Just moments into his strange new world and the colt was already testing his awkward legs: first his front legs, then several unsuccessful attempts to lift his hind quarters. He trembled and shook, collapsed a few times, but then, with a burst of determination that would surely mark his noble future, the black rose up on all fours.

Emmalyn did not trifle with an attempt to contain her giggle of delighted awe. Even Cabal, chuckling at his place outside the stall, seemed moved by the colt's stouthearted resolve. The soft, reverent oath he whispered spoke volumes for the effect this experience had on him; indeed, Emmalyn reckoned, it spoke for all of them.

For several glorious minutes, time ceased to exist and the stable pulsed with the wonderment of precious, newly given life. The soft glow of candlelight, the sweet earthy smells of straw and linen and birth, the throaty sounds of the colt's curious grunts and rasping breathing as he became accustomed to his new world. Emmalyn had never experienced anything so remarkable, so incredibly inspiring. She might have stayed there all night, rooted to that very spot, if not for Cabal's quiet warning.

" 'Tis not over yet," he said, his voice low with concern. "Look to the mare."

Minerva still lay on her side, panting softly, her eyes glazed with moisture. The bulge in her belly had lessened, but it retained a queer fullness that did not bode well. She gave a small moan and closed her eyes as a deep shudder racked her exhausted, sweat-soaked body.

"Oh, mercy!" Emmalyn gasped. "What's wrong with her?"

"She's delivering a second foal," Cabal said, his voice grim as he stepped into the stall.

"Twins?" Emmalyn asked in utter astonishment. "I have never heard of such a thing!"

" 'Tis rare," Cabal told her, "but it happens."

He knelt down near Minerva and placed his hand on her midsection while Thomas rushed over from where he had been tending the colt. A contraction seized the mare, but she hardly responded to the pain, save to lift her head and lay it back down with a groan. Cabal glanced to Emmalyn, his gaze solemn.

"This beast is too tired to go on," said the stable master, confirming Emmalyn's worst fear. "We may well have to choose between either Minerva or her second foal, milady."

"No!" Emmalyn leaned forward and embraced her mare's strong neck, heartbroken to think of losing her and at the same time determined to do whatever she must to save the unborn foal. "We must help her somehow."

"Milady, even if we deliver the twin, it could be sickly or damaged in some way. Minerva will likely be unable to care for the both of them."

"We have to try." She looked imploringly to Cabal when Thomas's sober expression gave her little hope.

He held her gaze without saying a word, the emotion in his cool gray eyes unreadable, even at this close range. Emmalyn waited for him to shrug off her plea for help, not really expecting the cynical warrior to have a care for her feelings or for the fate of one humble beast.

"Please," she mouthed silently.

Cabal scowled faintly; then he turned to the stable master. "How can I help, Thomas?"

Emmalyn caressed Minerva's forehead and watched, warmed and wholly grateful, as Cabal went around to where Thomas stood assessing the mare's condition with a dubious eye. "'Twill be all right now, Minnie," she whispered, trusting inexplicably that what she said was true.

Thomas gave Cabal instructions for how to assist him in easing the foal from Minerva's taxed and uncooperative body. The babe would have to be guided out gently with the mare's contractions, a painstaking process that Thomas warned was all but certain to fail. Emmalyn prayed against the odds while the two men worked in concert, anticipating the proper time and then applying subtle pressure to position and guide the foal forth.

"Can you see it yet?" Emmalyn asked hopefully, stroking Minnie's damp face and neck.

"Aye," Thomas answered. "'Tis coming, but we will need more toweling." Emmalyn started to get up, but the stable master held her back with a small shake of his head. "I'll go, milady. Minerva needs you to remain with her."

He left the outbuilding, ambling into the night and leaving Emmalyn alone with Cabal. "Thank you," she whispered when he looked up and caught her watching him, his answering grin warming her from the inside out.

Another spasm racked Minerva in the next instant, more severe than the ones that had come before. Emmalyn pressed her cheek to the mare's neck, cooing soft assurances even though Cabal's expression had suddenly become grave. " 'Tis coming breech," he said, the words falling like daggers in the humid pall of the stable. He swore, stripping off his tunic and tossing it aside.

Emmalyn held her breath as Cabal leaned in, attempting to turn the foal around. A sheen of sweat had broken out on his brow. He hissed a frustrated oath, his face schooled into an expression of utter determination, his eyes filled with genuine concern. He spoke to Minerva as he worked, issuing coaxing assurances that she could do this, that she must help her foal, that everything would be all right.

Emmalyn could scarcely believe what she was witnessing. Cabal was not sitting there in the dank stall in the middle of the night, sweating and swearing, striving to save a helpless beast and her unborn babe because Emmalyn had asked him to. He was doing it for himself. He was doing this because despite his harsh exterior and professed lack of interest . . . he cared.

She had never seen anything quite so heroic.

Emmalyn stared at him as if noticing him fully for the first time—the cold destroyer turned bringer of life. She watched him being so gentle with Minerva, so respectful, and she knew without the slightest inkling of doubt that he would succeed tonight. Minnie and her unborn foal were safe in Cabal's strong hands; in that moment, Emmalyn trusted him implicitly.

Thomas came back, huffing from his trek to fetch more cloths. When he saw what Cabal was presently contending with, he sucked in his breath and threw the heap of linens to the ground.

" 'Tis all right," Cabal assured him. "I've nearly gotten it turned about now."

Neither Emmalyn nor Thomas dared utter one sound in the tense moments that followed. Minerva made a couple more efforts to expel her misaligned babe, and then, with one last push, it was over. Cabal drew back, holding the small chestnut filly tenderly in his arms.

"Thank heaven!" Emmalyn gasped, relieved that the worst danger was behind them.

But she could not allow herself to truly rejoice until Thomas and Cabal had made sure the foal was breathing and healthy. She soothed Minerva, mopping her neck and face with a dry cloth while the two men cleaned and rubbed down the new foal. Their vigorous massaging roused the filly's lungs to fill for the first time, but she was weak and made no effort to stand.

"She will need special care," Thomas warned gently, turning to Emmalyn. "Even then, she may not be strong enough to survive. . . ."

"She will," Emmalyn whispered fiercely, believing it with all her heart. "She only needed the chance."

Cabal was smiling at her as he scooped the foal into his arms. He carried it over to a nest of blankets that Thomas had fashioned in the corner of the stall and deposited it carefully onto the soft bedding. While the stable master commenced tending Minerva and her two babes, Emmalyn rose to gather the soiled linens and give him space enough to work. Cabal had since washed and was now putting his tunic back on.

"There is much here yet to be done," he said, coming to stand beside her. "Perhaps I should see you back to the keep now, my lady."

Emmalyn started to protest, wanting to remain near Minerva until she could be certain the mare and her new family would be all right, but she was also exhausted. She would likely be of little use to Thomas tonight, and the last thing she wanted was to be in his way.

"If you wish, milady, I will send for you should there be any change for the worse," he offered.

Emmalyn nodded. With a final awestruck look at the

horses, she turned and walked with Cabal out into the summer night air.

"How incredible," she said when they were halfway across the moonlit bailey. "Twin foals! Have you ever seen anything like it, Cabal?"

"No," he replied. "It was . . . extraordinary."

"Yes, it was. Extraordinary."

"Having seen this with mine own eyes," he continued, his voice quiet and reflective, "I can only imagine that the birth of a child must seem all the more divine—it must seem something akin to a miracle, I reckon."

Remembering her own lost babe, Emmalyn's step faltered; she swallowed the lump of sorrow that lodged itself instantly in her throat.

"Did I say something wrong?"

"N-no." She pressed her lips together and shook her head, uncertain whom she needed to assure more: him or herself. "You are right, my lord. The birth of a child is indeed a divine miraculous event."

Was her keen regret evident in her voice? she wondered, feeling the tears well in her eyes. She purposely said nothing more, praying as they neared the entry to the castle that she could make it safely into her chamber before she made a fool of herself by weeping before him. But at her side, Cabal's steps slowed until he stood unmoving. His hand brushed hers, a gentle request that she pause.

"Emmalyn, what is wrong?" he asked softly.

Though the urge to flee for solitude was strong, strangely, she found that some part of her wanted to stay with Cabal. Some aching part of her yearned for his comfort. Woodenly, Emmalyn turned to face him. He opened his arms to her, and she stepped into his embrace, pressing her tear-soaked cheek against the warmth of his solid chest.

Because he said nothing, because he did not pressure her or seem impatient with her weeping, Emmalyn was moved to explain. No matter how much it hurt to remember and to say the words.

"There was to be a babe," she whispered brokenly. "More than anything in this world, I yearned for my child. I didn't care about the things I did not have in my marriage, or the things I would never be; all I wanted was to love my baby and be a good mother. I didn't get the chance."

"Ah, Emmalyn. Sweeting, I'm sorry." Cabal's voice was thick, his breath warm in her unbound hair.

She took a strengthening breath, and before regret robbed her of her voice altogether, she said, "Three months before my baby would have been born, I . . . I suffered a miscarriage. She was all I had. She was all my hopes, all my love, and I lost her. I was granted the blessing of her precious little life, and I failed her."

Cabal held her tighter, his strong arms wrapped around her tenderly, keeping her safe. Shielding her from hurting alone.

"I became pregnant the year before Garrett left on Crusade," she heard herself say quietly. "I thought the baby would surely please him, for he had said often how much he wanted an heir. Of course, knowing my husband's lack of use for females, my prayers each morning, noon, and night were filled with wishes for a boy child. I bargained with God that I would endeavor to be the best wife, that I would curb my willfulness and give Garrett no reasons to punish me, if only He would deliver me a healthy son."

"Jesu. Emmalyn, you deserved so much better," Cabal whispered, pressing a soft kiss in her hair.

"Garrett had gone off for several days of hunting with some influential young lords from the London court," she continued, swallowing around a sob. "I had been sick the day he left and was still bedridden when he arrived home early, with two of the men accompanying him for an extended stay at Fallonmour. When Garrett saw me resting in the middle of the day, he called me lazy, ordering me to get up and make myself presentable to greet his guests. He threw one of my court gowns at me and told me to rouge my cheeks and cover my hair before I came downstairs."

"Bastard," Cabal hissed, holding Emmalyn closer and caressing her back with a warm, gentle hand.

"I'm sure I must have looked dreadful," she said vacantly. "The gown no longer fit because of the babe, and I could scarcely hold my brush, let alone braid and cover my hair. But I dragged myself to the stairwell and tried to act as if nothing was wrong because that's what Garrett expected me to do. I blacked out, and when I awoke two days later, Bertie told me I had fallen down the stairs. My babe was gone." Emmalyn had to take a fortifying breath to tell him the rest, the part that hurt most of all, the cruelty that she would never forgive. "Afterward, when Garrett next saw me, he chided me for my grief. He said he didn't want to see me crying over it anymore. . . . After all, 'twas just a smallish, useless baby girl."

"Emmalyn, I'm sorry," Cabal whispered. "I'm sorry if I made you think on it now. I didn't know."

"No," she said, drawing out of his embrace slightly. Already a bit of her pain was beginning to ebb. "I need to remember. And I'm glad I told you. It helps."

He caressed her cheek with aching tenderness, wiping away the last of her tears, his eyes soft in the moonlight. "You are not to blame for the loss of your child, my lady. You could not have seen misfortune coming, let alone protect her from it. No more than you by yourself can be expected to protect Fallonmour and its folk from Hugh de Wardeaux."

Emmalyn nodded weakly. "But these people are my family now, all of them. Perhaps where I could not protect my daughter, I have tried to make life better for everyone here," she said, realizing the connection for the first time.

"And now the boy from the orchard as well?"

"He is just a child, my lord. A child in need of love and care. It breaks my heart to think he might be hurt and I could help him. If only I could see him to a safe place."

She could see the doubt in Cabal's eyes, even in the dark

gloom of the bailey. But he did not deny her. "If it pleases you, I will ride out on the morrow to search for him."

Emmalyn smiled at him fondly, her sadness nearly replaced by the warmth of her gratitude toward Cabal. Wrapping her arms around his neck, she clung to him in an impulsive wholehearted embrace. "Thank you," she said, placing a quick kiss on the soft skin below his ear.

As she released him and began to withdraw, Cabal's arms came down around her back. He held her there, pressed against the length of him, looking at her upturned face as if he debated whether to kiss her. As if he were weighing the prospect of picking up where they had left off in the armory. But he only smiled and brushed a wisp of hair from her brow.

"It has been a long evening," he told her as his grip relaxed. "Perhaps I should bid you good night."

"Yes," she whispered, stepping out of the circle of his arms even though she would have gladly remained there, content to have him hold her beneath the watery moon for the rest of the eve. "Until tomorrow, my lord." Then she turned and quit the bailey before he could see how much she longed to stay.

Cabal watched her go, feeling a potent mixture of relief and regret. Relief because he knew that only Emmalyn's leaving would have kept him from sweeping her into his arms and carrying her into his chamber, where he would make love to her, slow and sweet, until morning. Regret, because it was what he so keenly wanted to do.

He did not try to deceive himself that when he heard the longing and despair in her voice over the loss of her babe, he had not entertained a brief and all-too-pleasant fantasy of siring a child for her. But never would he beget a bastard. If he could manage to maintain no other scrap of honor during his time on this earth, here was one thing at which he was determined not to fail.

In truth, it troubled him to think how much he needed to be with her, how much he longed for her. It frightened him to think how much she was coming to mean to him after just a handful of days. How strong would his feelings be once the king finally relieved him of his duties at Fallonmour? God's blood, what if Richard never returned?

Cabal had to shake himself mentally to keep from harboring the unwilling treasonous hope that circumstances might keep him at Fallonmour indefinitely.

If he were clever, he would be hoping for the king's immediate release instead, praying for the orders that would send him back to the battlefield. Back to the things he knew. Back where he belonged, before it was too late.

Before he came to care any more about Emmalyn and her folk.

Already he was finding himself getting involved at Fallonmour in ways he could hardly fathom, let alone afford. Forgetting his keen interest in the lovely widow, Cabal had also become entangled in several other areas that were none of his concern: from his unwitting hand in matching Pete with Lucinda, to endeavoring to deliver a sickly foal that might have been better off dead, and now his promise to Emmalyn to ride out in search of a thief's whelp and deliver him into the keep.

Anyone who had known Cabal a few short months ago— anyone who had known him by his well-deserved *nom de guerre*—would think he had gone mad. In truth, mayhap he had.

Hearing the guards on the tower changing watch, Cabal decided some fresh air and a reminder of his duty to the king and Fallonmour might be just the things he needed to clear his head. He entered the keep and climbed first the spiraling stairs, then the wooden ladder, up to the tower roof. The five guards on post bade him good eventide when he appeared; Sir Miles gave a nod of greeting and stepped forward to meet him.

"How did the smithy fare today on the making of the lances and crossbow bolts?" Cabal asked, walking with the grizzled knight to the edge of the parapet to overlook the darkened hills and plains. "I trust he is making good progress."

"Smith reported thirty lances done, and in the morn he starts on the bolts," Miles answered. "We should have enough to supply the weapons we had already, as well as those taken from the thieves' camp this afternoon."

"Excellent. Our soldier candidates from the village will need those arms." He advised Sir Miles that they would start training the lot of them in earnest with crossbows at first light. "The lances will have their purpose," he added, "but I reckon we could better use bowmen when Hugh comes to call. They will be our only hope should the dispute escalate into an armed conflict."

"And you think it will?" Miles asked.

Meeting the old captain's concerned frown, Cabal answered, "I think it will depend on what Hugh sees when he arrives . . . or, rather, what he thinks he sees."

Chapter Fourteen

Cabal was disturbed, but not entirely surprised, to see Emmalyn already in the stables early that next morn when he and the two knights he had enlisted to ride with him on the search for the boy arrived to saddle their mounts. What did surprise him was that the lady appeared fully intent upon accompanying them; her gray palfrey was outfitted for the trek and standing ready in its stall.

"Good morrow, my lady," Cabal murmured, walking past her to tend his destrier.

She returned his greeting and the other men's, then walked with Cabal and watched as he saddled the black. "I've been up for hours already," she confessed cheerily. " 'Twas all I could do to wait 'til morn so I could rise and see about Minerva and her babes." When he deliberately neglected to inquire after the animals, she said, "They fare well. Would you like to see them for a moment before we depart?"

"We, my lady?" he asked, though it was hardly necessary to feign confusion over her intentions.

"Yes, we. I pray you haven't changed your mind about riding out to search for the young boy."

"I have not changed my mind, but I did not say I would bring you with me," he told her as he tightened and cinched the girth on his saddle. He stood and faced her. "Nor am I about to bring you."

"But I want to go," she protested tightly, taking care to keep the argument between the two of them. "I mean to be there should you locate the child."

Cabal shook his head. "The men and I can manage the task well enough. You will only be in the way."

If her expression was any indication, that remark did not win him any favor, nor did it gain him any ground. There was a stubborn set to her jaw now that had not been there before; he tried hard not to be charmed by it.

"That boy trusts me," she insisted. "Do you honestly think he would be willing to come to any of you—particularly if he witnessed yesterday's destruction?" Her chin climbed higher. "I'm going with you."

"I would make better progress without having to worry all the while over your whereabouts and the safety of your person."

She seemed to take that as a further challenge, fixing him with an uncompromising stare. "I am not entirely defenseless, my lord, nor am I careless enough to walk headlong into danger. Certainly you can give me that much credit."

Cabal groaned, sensing that he was quickly getting nowhere. "I don't suppose you would stay behind regardless of what I said on the matter, would you?" One slender brow lifted, an acknowledgment of the looming impasse. Relenting, Cabal slanted her a wearied look. "You will ride by my side at all times and never venture from the path for any reason. If we should find him, I will have your word that you will not go near him—no matter his apparent condition—unless I determine it is safe for you to do so."

"Agreed." Her smile was wry but subtly triumphant. "If there is nothing else, my lord . . ."

There was, indeed, although he would not allow himself to say as much. He wanted to tell her to don a wimple so he did not have to be tempted with the desire to unbraid her mass of fine golden hair. He wanted to tell her to refrain from smiling at him or otherwise giving him cause to think that if he kissed her she might not push him away, as she very well should. He wanted to tell her how unwise it was to put herself in his company again when he wanted her so badly, he had lain awake most of the night burning for her, trying unsuccessfully to convince himself that he could resist her.

He wanted to tell her all those things and more, but instead, jaw clamped tight, hands fisted around the reins of his destrier, he followed Emmalyn out into the dawning morn, then rode beside her out of the bailey and under the shadows of Fallonmour's massive fortress gates.

Two hours of looking for the boy had yielded nothing more promising than a pile of rotting apple cores and some childish carvings cut into the trunk of an old ash tree. The two knights from Fallonmour's garrison had since broken off to follow the southern edge of the orchard while Cabal and Emmalyn traveled the north. Despite dismal results, Emmalyn seemed loath to abandon the search, no matter how long it took. She interpreted each meager find as encouragement that the boy could not be far. Cabal could only ride along dubiously, his eye trained to spot every movement, his ear tuned to every sound.

Although concern for Emmalyn's safety had been his foremost disagreement with her coming along on the search—to say nothing of the temptation she presented—part of it, too, had been a want for time alone. A need for space and solitude in which to think. Now that he was many yards away from the castle with Emmalyn at his side, Cabal realized anew how pleasing her company was.

Though he fought the feeling, it gladdened his heart to look over and see her face. He was content to listen to her voice, telling him the status of the various fields as they passed them, and sharing with him her hopes to gain a good profit on the wool she would sell at market next week.

Their search carried them deeper into the orchard, to where a stream cut through the heart of the grove. Knowing the lady would not admit her fatigue until she dropped from her palfrey of exhaustion, Cabal suggested they rest awhile and water the horses. He swung down from his mount, then went to Emmalyn's side and helped her to the ground.

"All this talk of crops and trading must serve only to bore you," she said as she smoothed her skirts. "Forgive me if I try your patience with such matters."

He gave her a wry smile. "You must think my interests can stretch no farther than the bailey and the battlefield, my lady."

She looked stunned. "Do they?"

Without answering, he took a rolled-up blanket from behind his mount's saddle and handed it to her before leading both horses to the water's edge. Emmalyn had seated herself upon the large square of wool that she had spread on the grassy embankment and was staring at him inquisitively as he made his way back from the stream.

"Who are you, my lord?" Her verdant gaze was probing. "Who are you really, Cabal?"

Now it was his turn to look stunned. But he schooled his expression to one of casual amusement as he approached, reaching up to pluck a small blossom from a flowering branch above her head. "You know who I am, my lady," he answered wryly. "I've told you. I am a simple knight, sworn in service to the king."

"I know that's what you have told me, my lord, but watching you these past couple of days, I don't quite believe it. And I suspect you are anything but simple."

His answering chuckle sounded forced, even to him. "Pray, don't look too closely, madam. You may not like what you see." Leaning down, he tucked the tiny white flower behind her ear, then took his place beside her on the blanket, resting his elbows on his up-drawn knees.

"Would you like me to tell you what I see?" she asked softly.

It was the very last thing he wanted her to do, but for some reason that he could not comprehend, he was unable to tell her so. Mutely, feeling as though he were balanced on the edge of a chasm that was about to swallow him whole, Cabal turned his head and met her guileless gaze. He stared hard, torn between wanting her to see the depths of his darkness and wanting to shelter her forever from such a terrible truth.

Unflinching, she offered him a tender smile. "I see a man of honor," she said, shocking him with her earnestness. "I see a man who wants the world to believe he is uncaring and cold but who instead feels deeply. You tell me you are merely a simple knight, my lord, but I see a noble, complicated man. I see a man who has so much to give. You could be anything you want to be, Cabal."

There was a time, not so very long ago, that Cabal would have scoffed to hear such lofty nonsense bestowed on his questionable character. Strangely, however, now he found nothing humorous in the notion at all. Rather, it struck him as profoundly sad. And pathetic, when he acknowledged just how much he wanted to believe that he could ever be more than what he was. That he could ever be the sort of man Emmalyn thought she saw in him after only a handful of days.

He could not stop himself from reaching out to trace the slope of her cheek. Cocking a brow, he endeavored to sound casual, vaguely amused. "You think you have me all figured out, do you, my lady?"

"No," she answered, smiling. "There is much about you that remains a mystery to me. This ring, for instance." Before he realized what she was doing, Emmalyn had reached out and hooked her finger under the leather cord at his neck, pulling the dark amulet out of his tunic. Teasing playfully, she asked, "Is this the badge of a lover's conquest or a broken heart, my lord?"

She startled when Cabal snatched the ring out of her hand. "It belonged to my mother," he told her gruffly. "She's dead."

"I—I'm sorry," she stammered, shrinking away from him. "I didn't know. I did not mean to pry."

He shook his head, staring down at the damning black stone, his humorless chuckle no more than a wry exhalation amid the silence of the grove. When he spoke, his voice was sharp, cutting. "You don't have the slightest idea who I am, Emmalyn."

He got up off the blanket and paced away from her, suddenly feeling stifled by her kindness and needing the distance. He was not aware she had followed until he heard her feet pad softly behind him in the grass. "Then tell me who you are. Please, I would like to know."

That brave gentle plea shocked him. He pivoted his head and stared at her, infuriated with her for not sensing the danger in him, for not being afraid to look the beast in the eye. "Are you sure that's what you want, my lady?"

She swallowed hard, perhaps sensing the threat in his voice after all, but her intrepid gaze did not waver.

"Where would you like me to start?" he asked harshly. "With an account of my misbegotten birth, mayhap? Do you want to hear how my mother, a dancer entertaining at the palace, was summoned to one of the royal chambers and taken in the dark by a highborn lord who planted his bastard in her belly and didn't even bother to give her his name? Do you want to hear how when she warned him that the seed would take, he merely laughed, telling her that if she bore his whelp she should call it Cabal?"

He tore himself from Emmalyn's steady regard, unable to endure the sympathy he saw glistening in her eyes. "Mayhap you want to hear how he then insulted her by paying her with this ring—a token she should have shoved down his noble throat but instead treasured because it was the only thing of value she had ever possessed. Perhaps you would rather hear how some years later, when I was fourteen, my mother died at the hand of a drunken lord who thought her too common for such an exotic bauble."

He hardly recognized his own voice now, it sounded so wooden to him, so brittle. Cold talons of memory dragged him back through time, speeding him to the night when a boy was lost forever to darkness and a soulless destroyer named Blackheart was born in his place. "Shall I tell you how I stole into that man's chamber in the middle of the night and cut his throat to steal it back, my lady?"

Emmalyn gasped, recoiling from him now, horrified, as he had fully intended. So why, then, did Cabal feel so sick inside to know that he was succeeding? Steeling himself to the idea, he pushed on before he lost any further resolve.

"Surely you haven't heard enough already," he challenged. "I haven't yet told you how the king took me into his garrison after that night, where I was schooled in war and killing. You haven't heard how I excelled in my training. How eager I was to be tested in combat. How quickly I came to be feared and despised for my lethal skills. Shall I hazard a guess as to how many men I've slaughtered in service to the crown, Emmalyn?"

"Stop it," she whispered fiercely, her breath catching in her throat.

"Perhaps you'd rather hear about the many villages I've decimated for God and country," he said, ignoring her distress. "Perhaps I should tell you how by the time I left, the streets ran ankle-deep with blood and the air hung heavy with smoke and the screams of the dead and dying. Perhaps then you would have a better idea of who—and what—I am."

She stared at him as if she had been physically struck, her backward steps carrying her an arm's length away from him. "Please, my lord . . . stop."

"Do you still think you see something noble in me, Emmalyn? Do you truly believe I could be more than what I am?" He shook his head, grinning, full of self-mockery. "There's nothing complicated about me or what I do. I'm a warrior, my lady. A destroyer. I don't want to be anything else. I wouldn't know how. Don't fool yourself into thinking you see something more."

He had frightened her; he could see it in the fine lines that bracketed her mouth, in the slight quiver of her jaw. She might have turned and ran in that next instant, perhaps fled him for good, but the jangle of approaching horses and the muffled protests of a young child drew her attention over her shoulder.

Fallonmour's two knights rode into the small clearing, one of them holding before him the struggling bedraggled quarry they had been dispatched to find and retrieve. Lady Emmalyn rushed forth to meet her guards. "Be careful with him," she ordered the men. "He's just a helpless little boy."

"I am not helpless!" the lad shouted. His high-pitched cry and frantic squirming began to unsettle the knight's destrier. "Unhand me, ye great smelly oaf!"

"'Tis all right," Lady Emmalyn soothed, her voice gentle, but tremulous from the distress of her argument with Cabal. "No one is going to hurt you," she told the boy. "Will you tell me your name?"

His wary gaze strayed toward her and he swallowed. "Wat."

"Wat? As in Walter?" He nodded. "Well, I've been eager to meet you, Wat. My name is Emmalyn."

Cabal had brought the horses from the stream and was halfway up the embankment with them when he saw her reach for the lad, blatantly ignoring his earlier warning to keep her distance. Emmalyn's touch and easy demeanor seemed to calm the boy, and he could almost imagine the affectionate smile she must have bestowed on him in that next instant. A caring smile that would likely never warm Cabal again. He reminded himself that he did not care, that it was better this way.

"Where are your thieving parents, lad?" he demanded as he approached the search party.

Emmalyn shot him a seething look over her shoulder and took up her mount's reins. Keeping his gaze rooted on her, the boy answered shakily, "My papa was killed 'fore I was born, and my mama gone away."

"And the rest of your kind?" Cabal prompted. "Where are they?"

"G-gone," Wat said. "They all ran off after they got found out and our camp got burned."

Cabal could feel Emmalyn's reproach permeate to where

he stood beside her. "You've been left all by yourself?" she asked. When the boy nodded, she said, "I'm afraid I can't let you live out here in my orchard anymore, Wat. 'Tis no safe place for a child. How would you like to come and stay in my castle instead?"

Wat's dirty little face brightened instantly. Without waiting for agreement or even sparing Cabal so much as a glance to gauge his thoughts on the matter, Emmalyn stepped into her stirrup and mounted her palfrey. "Let's go, then," she said to the two knights, and with a shake of her reins, she led the party out of the orchard and back to the keep as if in her mind Cabal no longer existed.

Chapter Fifteen

Two days later, Emmalyn was still reeling from her unexpected and disturbing confrontation with Cabal in the orchard. She had managed to say nary a word to him since, purposely avoiding his dark presence whenever possible and lamenting the fact that she could not simply wish him away from Fallonmour entirely. She had received some promise on that score: a letter had arrived yesterday morn from her sister in Lincolnshire. Knowing the trade fair would bring Emmalyn to town for market, Josette had invited her to stay for a few days and visit.

Emmalyn could scarcely believe her good fortune when she read that Josette would be hosting a grand feast at which Queen Eleanor was expected to be in attendance. In the day since the letter had arrived, Emmalyn had read that same passage over at least a dozen times to assure herself it was real. She would gain an audience with the queen after all, whether or not her appeal regarding Fallonmour's status had reached London yet. And there was nothing Cabal could do to stop her.

To occupy her mind with other things, she had taken little Wat under her wing. Now the lad was hardly recognizable as the sullen mistrusting waif Emmalyn had first encountered. Multiple scrubbings, a haircut, and fresh clothing helped contribute to his transformation, but Emmalyn suspected that more than any physical considerations, it was his easy absorption into castle life that brought him from his initial state of withdrawal. Once she had seen that his neglected belly was filled, and that he had gotten a couple nights of much-needed sleep in the hall with the rest of the folk, Emmalyn had taken the boy aside and given him a duty to tend to.

"In and around a castle, everyone has responsibilities," she told him now as she walked with him to the stables. "You could train as a page, but my hands are full enough with those I already have. What I don't have is someone to help Thomas with the new foals."

Wat's brown eyes brightened; it was no mistake that Emmalyn had chosen this position for him. She had seen how awed and excited the boy was when he first saw Minerva and her twins, and she had already discussed with Thomas the possibility of his taking Wat in as his assistant. Unable to contain his excitement, Wat scampered into the stables several paces ahead of Emmalyn and dashed to Minerva's stall.

"Easy, son," Thomas warned when the sudden rush of activity upset the horses.

Wat settled immediately and apologized, standing at Minnie's berth in complete wonder as Emmalyn drew up behind him. The chestnut foal stood on spindly legs, nursing ardently at her mother's teat while her glossy jet brother walked over to investigate his visitors. The black colt sniffed at Wat's outstretched hand, then paused regally to let the boy and Emmalyn stroke him, as if he knew he was a creature born to be admired.

"They are doing very well, milady," Thomas said. "I did not think the filly would survive, but she is hale and getting stronger every day. The time is coming that you should name the both of them, I reckon."

"Yes," Emmalyn agreed, her heart gladdening with the news that Minerva's family was healthy and thriving. Fulfilling, too, was the knowledge that she had been able to help young Wat. The boy looked up at her, beaming, so happy in his new surroundings. "How would you like to name the foals, Wat?"

"Me?" He blinked at her, stunned, as if he had just been handed a crown and scepter. "Do you mean it, my lady?"

She nodded and he threw his arms around her in a fervent embrace. But she was nearly forgotten a scant instant later, Wat turning his attention toward the weighty responsibility he had just been granted. He began testing worthy names for the black first, excitedly whispering and then discarding them in rapid succession.

"That ought to keep him out of trouble for a while," Thomas murmured wryly.

Emmalyn smiled, sharing his humor, but their gaiety was short-lived. From outside, high atop the castle tower, came the wailing blast of a horn: a guard on the morning watch, heralding the arrival of visitors. Before Emmalyn reached the stable door to inquire after who had come, one of her men-at-arms appeared at the threshold.

"There's a riding party on the approach to the castle, milady."

With those words, a dark and swelling unease rose in her breast, squeezing her lungs as it engulfed and swallowed up her joy of the moment before. "Do they bear colors?"

The guardsman nodded. "A black boar rampant on a gold field, milady."

"Hugh."

Her fears confirmed, Emmalyn's breath rushed out of her on a shaky sigh. She could take no comfort in the grim face that greeted her an instant later, either. Dressed in mail from his morning's exercise, Cabal strode past the group of them at the doorway, entering the stables with sober purpose.

Emmalyn turned, ignoring her unease and following after him as he stalked to his destrier and began to saddle it. "Hugh is here?" she asked nervously.

"He is, my lady."

She was not sure what caused the greater swell of panic in her throat: de Wardeaux's dreaded arrival or Cabal's continuing cool detachment toward her. Girding herself for both, she demanded, "What do you mean to do?"

Cabal faced her at last, walking his battle-readied destrier out of the stall. "I mean to hold this property for the king and send Hugh on his way."

Emmalyn watched him lead the stallion out of the stable, trepidation gnawing at her to think that he was going out there alone. She did not want to worry for Cabal, but she could not quell the tremor of concern that gripped her when she thought of him facing off with Hugh. "Help me saddle my horse, Thomas," she ordered once Cabal had stepped into the courtyard and out of earshot.

"But, milady—"

"Do it, Thomas. And please, we must hurry."

They worked in haste to outfit the gray palfrey, and within moments, Emmalyn was riding out into the courtyard, toward the closing portcullis of Fallonmour's massive gates.

"Wait!" she called to the guards in the gatehouse as she approached. They looked down at her in confusion but held the grate up for her to pass.

Sir Cabal was less accommodating. "Jesu! What are you doing, Emmalyn?" he bellowed when she brought her mount to a halt beside his on the other side of the wall. "Get back inside!"

She shook her head. "This is my battle as much as it is yours. I have every right to face Hugh alongside you."

"Have you gone mad, woman? You're in danger out here!"

"No more than you, my lord," she answered resolutely, squaring her shoulders. "I am staying."

Though it was cool in the shadow of Fallonmour's soaring curtain wall, Emmalyn knew the shiver that coursed through her had nothing at all to do with the chill morning air. Grasping her mount's reins with fingers made damp from anxiety, she looked out to the group of armed riders now assembling at the crest of the south hill.

They were a company of nearly a dozen men on warhorses, garbed in long surcoats the striking gold of de Wardeaux's crest. Sunlight glinted off their fine chain mail

armor and their polished steel helms as they cantered into
position and formed a line. At the center of this row of
guards, between two pennon-bearing knights and riding a
massive white charger, was Hugh himself.

Emmalyn swallowed past a knot of cold unease. "He's
come with armed men."

The fact that Cabal said nothing and, as well, that his face
showed no trace of surprise, told Emmalyn that he had
expected this. She supposed she had been anticipating much
the same, although it did not make her any more prepared to
confront the situation now. Looking at the row of assembled
guardsmen, ready to attack Fallonmour on Hugh's command,
Emmalyn felt anything but bold.

She could do nothing but watch, and wait, as Hugh called
an order to his company of soldiers and they brought their
lances to upright position, the gleaming, deadly tips pointing skyward. Then he and another man broke from the
crowd and cantered forward, down the hill, and up the sloping motte toward the castle. As her brother-by-marriage
neared, Emmalyn's nervousness turned to mounting fear.
"What if Hugh orders a forced entry?"

"He won't."

"But how can you be certain?" she asked, an edge of
panic in her voice now.

"Stay calm, Emmalyn," Cabal warned. "You do not want
him to scent your apprehension. If Hugh has any sense, he will
not risk a confrontation when he is so plainly outnumbered."

"Outnumbered?" Emmalyn echoed in a tight whisper. "I
count fifteen soldiers behind him and all of them look armed
to the teeth. Fallonmour has but some two score knights; the
thought of a few extra men will pose no great concern to
Hugh and his trained army."

Cabal leaned toward her then. "Look behind you, my
lady, to the walls."

Emmalyn pivoted in her saddle and glanced up to the
ramparts of Fallonmour's towering curtain wall. There,
perched high above them, stood a line of thirty men-at-

arms—mayhap more, too many for her to discern their precise number. Each of them was armed with either crossbow or lance, and every man stood alert and poised for action. "But how—"

"Turn back to the fore, Emmalyn, and mask your surprise. Hugh is watching us closely as he comes."

The Wardeaux standard, a black boar rampant on a gold field, emblazoned the large, flat-topped shield and snapping silk pennon of Hugh's armed escort. His stamp of position and authority was made clear by his every uniformed guardsman, but as if he meant to leave no room for doubt, Hugh himself was outfitted in a black surcoat that bore his heraldic emblem affixed to the chest. It was a bold display of status, one usually reserved for the pomp and parade of the tournaments . . . or war.

By contrast, in her drab wool gown and leather boots, Emmalyn felt shabby and common, which she was certain had been Hugh's intention in arriving so richly appointed. Beside her, Cabal's horse stirred, and Emmalyn glanced at its stoic rider. If he took note of Hugh's militaristic bravura, Cabal seemed wholly unimpressed. His eyes were flinty and narrowed, calculating; his face was an emotionless mask. He rested his right hand on the pommel of his sword while his left gripped the black's reins.

Though garbed in a tunic of unpolished chain mail and somber hose, sullied in places from the morning's practice, Cabal's utter lack of vanity only made him look all the more fearsome. This was the king's most capable warrior at Emmalyn's side; he could be mistaken for nothing less. Determined to stand proud beside him, she lifted her chin and straightened in her saddle, prepared to face Hugh unflinchingly, no matter if she trembled within and without.

Hugh had aged since Emmalyn last saw him. His dark hair, trimmed to an impeccably fashionable length, was now silvered at the temples where it had once been a glorious mane of flawless dark brown. His beard showed similar signs of untimely aging, the neatly combed whiskers speckled gray beyond his years. Hugh's blue eyes had never been youthful, nor were they now, slivered and hard with suspicion as he slowed his mount to an arrogant trot and drew up before Emmalyn and Cabal.

"Greetings, my sister," he fairly hissed, an arrogant twist to his mouth. Hugh had never addressed her in such a familiar way while Garrett was alive, and Emmalyn knew it was now meant more as a reminder that since they were kin in the eyes of the law, in all ways that mattered, her rights fell second to his. "I would offer you a kiss of condolence, but it appears you've wasted little time in mourning my dear, departed brother."

Emmalyn steeled herself, trying not to let Hugh's scathing sarcasm provoke her. Nor would she allow him to intimidate her. "Somehow, I doubt the purpose of your journey has aught to do with sympathy," she said. "Be it for your brother or for me."

"No, lady," Hugh admitted easily. "I did not come out of sympathy. But I did come out of concern. Concern for what was my brother's and what now is mine."

"Not yours, de Wardeaux," Cabal interjected in a low growl. "Fallonmour belongs to the king, Richard of England."

Hugh slanted him a derisive assessing look. "You must be the Crusader turned guard dog that Arlo mentioned. When he came to me with the report of my brother's death—and indeed, the more troublesome news of Fallonmour's pending dispensation by the crown—I confess, I accused him of exaggeration." Hugh's gaze swept the battlements then, a pointed assertion that Fallonmour's defensive measures had not gone unnoticed. "Unless you mean to tell me you have assembled here outside the gates to provide me with a personal welcome within, it would seem that Arlo's claims were true, after all."

"You'll find no welcome here, de Wardeaux. Take your men and be gone."

Hugh chuckled. "Just like that, you think I will abandon my claim on this place?"

"The king commands that you do," Cabal replied. "Your claim on Fallonmour is void."

"Have you not heard, sirrah? Your king is imprisoned," Hugh challenged glibly. " 'Tis his command that is void. I mean to have what is mine."

"Do you threaten treason, de Wardeaux?"

"No threats; I am merely telling you the way it is. The only thing that has kept me from outright seizing Fallonmour before was the fact that my brother was yet alive. Now that he is not, I have no intention of surrendering my claim on this holding—particularly not to the pawn of a powerless king." Hugh's focus shifted to Emmalyn then, a cutting glare of contempt. "It will take far more than a piece of paper to make me step aside."

Next to her, Emmalyn saw the nearly imperceptible movement of Cabal's hand, tightening around his sword. His voice was lethally calm. "I am fully prepared to meet you with force, de Wardeaux."

"Are you, cur? Are you then also prepared to meet Prince John with force? Because I warn you, to challenge me in this is to challenge him."

"Hugh, please," Emmalyn interjected, knowing that what he said was likely true, and loath to see the situation escalate. "Do not turn this into a battle. You will only hurt Fallonmour in the end. You will only hurt the folk if you try to take the place by force."

Hugh's malicious glance slid to her. "Would that you had thought of that before you allowed this guard of Richard's to insult me with his presence. You should have come to me, Emmalyn. I would have helped you." He smiled thinly. "I might still. All it would take is a word from you now. I reckon you could persuade your garrison to side with me today and the matter can be settled quickly."

She knew what he was suggesting, of course. Side with him, and between his guards and hers, Hugh would see Cabal ejected on the spot . . . or worse. Emmalyn hesitated, expecting Cabal to challenge the affront, to say something in his own defense. At the very least, she expected him to try to influence her against Hugh's intimation of alliance. But he remained silent, stoic and unmoving, refusing to so much as look at her, as if his fate at that moment rested on her shoulders alone.

Perhaps after what he said to her in the orchard—after pushing her away as he had—Cabal thought she would be glad to accept Hugh's offer now. Glancing at his hard expression, she wondered if he might have wanted her to do just that!

"What say you, Emmalyn?" Hugh prompted. " 'Tis not a difficult decision, after all. Do you side with me in this, or do you invite my wrath on Fallonmour?"

A tiny voice reminded her that whether she admitted Hugh within the gates today in the hopes of avoiding bloodshed or later sought the queen's help in maintaining Fallonmour on her own, she was in fact defying her king's command. To say nothing of betraying Cabal. But she would not do it like this. To trust Hugh now was to reach for the hand of the devil himself.

Forcing herself to hold his chilling gaze, Emmalyn said, "I believe you heard Sir Cabal well enough, Hugh. You will find no welcome here today. Nor ever, so long as I am lady of this manor."

His answering chortle was more a sharp bark of disbelief, but his eyes blazed with naked fury. "Garrett never did have much flattering to say about you, Emmalyn—least of all the strength of your wit. Now I see he was right."

Emmalyn ignored the barb, though it stung just the same. "You know my position in this, Hugh. Now I will thank you to remove yourself from these lands."

"You'll what?" Hugh started to laugh in earnest, looking to his armed companion in mocking humor. The knight beside him joined in chuckling amusement, but his eyes flicked upward to the soldiers poised to beset them at the first indication. "You expect I will leave simply because you request it?"

"The lady asked you to leave," Cabal interjected, permitting his restless mount to advance a pace. "I suggest you do."

"Rather protective of the grasping little wench, aren't you, man? Arrived here less than a week ago and already sniffing around her skirts, I suspect."

Hugh's horse sidled, bringing him a bit too close to Emmalyn for her comfort, but she hardly had a chance to fret. Cabal moved in a blur, bringing his mount up beside Hugh as he drew a dagger from his baldric. Hugh's guard reached for his sword, too late.

"Come no closer," Cabal warned the knight, the sharp tip of his knife pressing into the tender skin of Hugh's cheek. The soldier glared, but it was a futile threat; he would make no untoward move while his lord was at the killing end of an enemy blade. "The both of you will make haste to leave in peace. Now."

Hugh's defeated nod was long in coming and scarcely perceptible. When Cabal slowly withdrew his attack, Emmalyn saw that a bright red line had begun to trickle down Hugh's face and into the edge of his neat beard. He reached up and wiped at the blood, glaring in outrage as he withdrew his hand and his gaze lit on his stained fingers. It was more an insult than injury, but Hugh bore murder in his eyes, all of it directed at Cabal. "I will not forget this day. You have just made yourself an enemy, knave."

Hugh spat at the ground where Cabal's mount stood, then growled to his guard to return to the retinue. He threw a chilling smile at Emmalyn before wheeling his charger about and giving it an angry jab in the sides. The white steed thundered off at a hard gallop, and within moments both Hugh and his armed escort had rejoined the company on the south hill. When the band of Wardeaux knights began to disperse and retreat, a shout rang out from high atop the battlements at Emmalyn's back.

It was a victory cry, she realized, feeling a mixture of startlement and pride as the jubilant clamor traveled the line of guards and climbed heavenward in a great roar. Somehow they had managed to send Hugh away—she, Cabal, and the garrison Arlo had once called pitiful. Though she was rattled from the confrontation, and well aware that there would be another to come, never had Emmalyn's heart felt so unencumbered.

But when she looked to Cabal, she could not help noticing the firm set of his jaw or the way his narrowed warrior's eyes remained rooted on Hugh and his men, watching in cautious silence until they were completely out of sight.

Chapter Sixteen

For the rest of that day and well into the next, all of Fallonmour—castle, courtyard, cottage, and croft—buzzed with the retelling of their lady's valiant stand against Hugh de Wardeaux. Cabal could go nowhere without being pressed by someone to recount the details of his own clash with Hugh, forced time and again to dispel the rumors that he had laced open the baron's throat, then sent him off with his noble tail tucked between his legs. The truth was hardly that dramatic, but the folk seemed disinclined to see it that way. He, Lady Emmalyn, and indeed, the entire garrison, had been lauded heroes of the day, the people's enthusiasm made all the more fervent for the preparations of the St. John's Eve festival taking place that very night.

While the castle servants and village folk had been granted the feast day for themselves, Cabal had set the garrison to practicing in the yard. The men had taken to the task with very little grumbling and a visibly new sense of purpose. The old guards were puffed up and boasting of their faded reminiscences of past battle glories, while the squires and trainees were imbued with the brand of buoyant cockiness that every soldier feels before he is faced with the gravity of killing another man, or watching in horror as his own guts spill out of him onto the battlefield.

Only Sir Miles seemed to share Cabal's unspoken understanding of what a future confrontation with Hugh would mean—for Fallonmour, certainly, but more to the point, for Lady Emmalyn. The old captain wore a sympathetic expression as he ambled over to where Cabal stood in the far corner of the bailey, mopping his brow on his sleeve after a vigorous bout of exercise with sword and pell. For the past hour, Cabal had been taking out his frustrations on the tall wooden practice post, leaving it scarred with angry hack marks and deep-cut grooves where his blade had bitten into it countless times.

"I am glad you were so fast to turn me down this morn when I offered to spar with you," Sir Miles said, handing him a clean dry towel. "You nearly cleaved that pell in half; I shudder to think what you might have done to my brittle old bones, given the chance."

Cabal smiled despite the weight of his thoughts. In truth, he welcomed the diversion. Accepting the swatch of fresh linen with a grateful nod, Cabal dried his sweat-dampened hair and neck. "My apologies if I was curt with you this morn, Miles. I wasn't in much of a mind for company."

From across the courtyard, a ruckus drew Cabal's attention. Two pages had taken notice at the same time of his break in practice, and now, a brief but frantic scuffle was under way as both boys lunged for a pitcher of ale, each clearly determined to be the one to serve him. The older boy proved the faster, leaving the younger to sulk as he hastened over with refreshments. Cabal's murmured thanks might have been a blessing from the dragon slayer, Saint George himself, based on the awed expression of the lad when he heard it.

"You're gaining quite a reputation," Sir Miles remarked after the page had strutted back to where his companion sat brooding. "Fallonmour's own champion is what they're calling you about the castle and in the village. From the looks of your progress here this morn, I'd say it appears you are taking the role a bit too seriously, my lord. You're not planning to take on Hugh and his army single-handedly, are you?"

Cabal shot the captain a quelling look. "You know as well as I do, Miles, that what we did yesterday amounted to a great deal of nothing. What Hugh saw was naught but a mirage, just as we had planned. Had he gotten any closer to the walls, or worse, had he decided to put us to the challenge then and there, I doubt very much that we could have held him off, even if we did outnumber him more than two to one." Cabal shook his head, feeling the start of a headache pulse to life in his temples. " 'Tis going to take more than a few dozen scarecrows to hold this keep when it comes under siege from Hugh."

"We've got at least another seven days before de Wardeaux can possibly return," the captain argued, "not counting the time it will take him to assemble reinforcements. That leaves us plenty of room to prepare. Consider how far the men have come in just the short time you've been here."

"Not far enough."

"If yesterday's confrontation did nothing else, my lord, it bonded those men like mortar. Look at them." Sir Miles gestured to the practice yard, where the clash of swords and lances rang, along with shouts of encouragement and good-humored gibes.

The line between knight and peasant soldier had blurred considerably, to where at a distance, it was difficult to tell one from the other. Even Taggart had begun to cooperate with the rest of the men. The big knight had paused in his sparring to show one of the new soldiers the proper way to hold his weapon before continuing to demonstrate to three rapt trainees the side-to-side finesse employed when fending off more than one opponent.

"They are working together now," the captain said, "helping each other. Today they are a unit. Given another week's time, I warrant they will be an army."

Cabal chuckled. "When did it come to pass that you actually started believing in this plan, Miles?"

He seemed to consider for a moment. "I suppose when I saw how much you wanted to believe in it. Those men respect you, as I do. They trust you to lead them; 'tis on you to trust that they will not disappoint you."

Smiling, Miles reached up and placed his hand on Cabal's shoulder the way a father might do to a favored son. The unexpected contact and, indeed, the fond regard, took Cabal wholly aback, both felt so foreign to him. Fear he had earned easily enough from the time he could first raise his fists to fight, but never had he known anything akin to the warmth of a father's pride, to say nothing of another man's respect.

Stunned, he found he had no idea how to react. Something inside his chest felt squeezed and unfettered at the same time, the weight of some unknown yet compelling emotion pressing down on him until he could scarcely gather his breath. He didn't want to know this feeling; he wasn't sure he deserved it, and he certainly didn't need the responsibility of trying to uphold it. With a gruff murmured excuse to Sir Miles that he needed some cool water for the ache in his temples, Cabal left the training yard to search out the bailey well.

The boy, Wat, was there when Cabal rounded the corner. He was struggling with the winch, trying without success to bring a full bucket of water back up the long distance of the well. Cabal hung back, watching quietly and reluctant to get involved. That is, until it appeared he would be waiting for his turn most of the afternoon did he not intervene. The third time Wat lost his grip on the handle and the bucket splashed back down into the water far below, Cabal cleared his throat.

"You're going about that all wrong." Wat startled upon hearing his voice and whirled around, red in the face and panting, clearly frustrated. He said nothing but gave Cabal a wide berth as he strode up beside him at the well. "The way you're standing there, before the winch instead of to the side of it, means you must work harder to bring the bucket up."

"'Tis how Thomas does it sometimes. I seen him."

"Well, Thomas is stronger than you are. You need to put your body weight into it. Stand here." Hesitantly, his brown eyes watching Cabal with guarded uncertainty, Wat inched forward to the place indicated. "Now grab ahold of the handle with both hands."

"But this is how the maids do it," Wat protested.

" 'Tis how you will do it, too, until you grow muscles enough to do it some other way. Now lean in as you turn the crank, and when you bring it forward, pull back using your weight as leverage." Though clearly disgruntled to have to employ such an unmanly method to carry out his task, Wat did as Cabal instructed, and in little time at all, he found success.

"Much more efficient, was it not?" Cabal asked when the bucket cleared the top of the well. "Now fill your pail and go, so that someone else might have use of the water today."

Without a further care for the boy or how he had just dismissed him, Cabal watched idly as Wat transferred the water from the bucket at the well to the one he had brought from the stables. He returned the former in silence, then quietly walked away. Absorbed in his own thoughts, Cabal assumed Wat had left the area entirely until he heard the child's voice behind him, a miserable, strangled-sounding croak.

"Why do you hate me, Sir Cabal?"

For a moment Cabal did not move. Then, slowly, he turned to face the boy. God's truth, he felt like the worst sort of clod when he saw the hurt in Wat's eyes. He was small for his age—a number Cabal guessed to be somewhere near seven or eight—and he was painfully thin, wan, like the beggarly children of the foulest city slums. Wat's bruises were fading since he had come to Fallonmour, and Emmalyn had seen to it that he was clothed and groomed as fine as any of her castle pages. But underneath all of that, he was still a scared insecure child, and from the first time he had seen him, Cabal had behaved no better than the most careless of noble brutes.

Without waiting for an answer or a chance to be further abused, Wat turned to head back for the stables.

"Wait," Cabal called after him before he could scurry off.

"How old are you, Wat?" The boy's brows crashed together and he shrugged. "You don't know?"

"No, sir."

"Do you reckon you're old enough to ride a horse?"

"Don't know, sir. I never done it 'fore."

"Never?" Cabal scowled faintly, considering. "Well, if you can bring my mount to me before I change my mind, mayhap I'll take you out and teach you today."

The instant the words were out of Cabal's mouth, Wat dashed off as on winged feet, sloshing water out of his pail in his haste and excitement to reach the stables. Cabal turned back to draw the bucket out of the well and started washing up, feeling a bit better for his offer to Wat. He supposed he owed the boy this small benevolence. For that matter, he supposed he owed it to himself.

A day of festival also meant a day without the castle folk about to tend to their duties. With the servants off preparing to celebrate Midsummer's Eve in the village, Emmalyn was able to enjoy an uncustomary quiet within the keep. There were none but she and Bertie to shake out the sheets and do the mending, and Emmalyn found the solitude a comfort. She had been aware of the garrison training in the yard for most of the morning, but the bailey had been empty now for some hours, save for the occasional changing of the guards stationed on the wall walk. Soon dusk would begin to creep over the land, giving rise to the sounds of revelry from the village below.

Already she could hear the rumble of laughter and men's voices carrying on the breeze as they prepared the bonfires that would light the night sky and fill the air with the heady aromas of woodsmoke and seasoned roasting meat. As she did each St. John's Eve, Emmalyn had given the villeins enough mutton and venison to feed them all twice over, along with several casks of red wine and ale.

But while the peasants would feast like lords, she herself made do with a light supper of cold meat and cheese, a meal she shared with Bertie in the women's solar. The sounds of festival churning outside, the old nurse had set aside the wool she had been spinning and went to the open window.

"Oh! Look, milady," she said on a laugh when Emmalyn made no immediate move to join her. "The men have just brought the wheel to the top of the south hill. Come quickly, milady, else you'll miss the turn of the solstice."

Emmalyn sighed and put her work down, crossing the room to stand beside Bertie at the window, even though the annual tradition taking place outside was quite familiar to her. The men of the village had set an old cart wheel ablaze and let it roll down the steepest hill. This not only marked the start of the night's festivities but also depicted the coming change of seasons, for it was on this day that the sun reached its highest point in the sky. Like the burning wheel now descending downhill, so would the hours of daylight diminish as the summer gave way to autumn.

"Time goes by so quickly," Emmalyn reflected aloud, her voice scarcely audible amid the raucous din traveling up the distance from the village as the wheel reached the crowd at the bottom of the south hill. "'Tis hard to believe that tomorrow begins the hay harvesting already."

"Aye, 'tis hard to believe," Bertie agreed. "But that is tomorrow's worry, milady, not today's. Today you should follow your people's example and make yourself merry. Your troubles will be waiting for you in the morn, whether or not you stay up here brooding over them. Come with me to the celebration, child. 'Twould do your heart good."

Although it was hard to argue with Bertie's logic, and the offer to join the festivities was tempting, Emmalyn shook her head. She could not remember the last time she had attended one of the villeins' feast days. For her to go now, when she was yet being hailed by the folk for her stand against Hugh, would only make her the center of unwanted, and certainly undeserved, attention. "This is their celebration, Bertie, not mine. And please do not feel that you have to tarry about keeping me company when you really want to be outside with everyone else. Go on and enjoy yourself."

Bertie gave her a frustrated look but argued no further. She finished the rest of her wine and put away her spinning, then, on Emmalyn's reassurance, quit the chamber. Emmalyn remained at the window, listening as the woman's footsteps grew more distant in the corridor. Bertie would change into one of her better kirtles, Emmalyn knew, and she would spend the evening dancing around the bonfires and singing with the common folk as if she were a girl younger than Emmalyn's own twenty years.

In truth, Emmalyn envied her folk that freedom, harboring a sudden want to be carefree and devoid of her responsibilities, even if just for a few hours. But thoughts of the confrontation with Hugh, as well as worries for what the future held, kept her heart heavy. Weighing on her, too, was the knowledge that if the queen entertained her request, Cabal would soon be removed from Fallonmour . . . perhaps removed from her life forever.

No matter how hard she tried to convince herself that it was what she wanted—that it was what she needed to do, for herself and for Fallonmour—Emmalyn found little joy in the idea of Cabal's imminent absence. As it was, she had missed him terribly these past days. His determined aloofness tore at her deeply, but she could not bring herself to risk his rejection by seeking him out.

Heavy with regret, Emmalyn was about to retire to her bedchamber when the rhythmic pounding of a nearing horse's hooves drew her attention to the window. Below, in the dusk-filled bailey, she saw Cabal, just returning to the keep. Seated before him on the destrier, and looking more spirited than she had yet known him to be, was little Wat. Emmalyn hid herself behind the stone embrasure and watched in curious silence as Cabal dismounted, then swept the boy off the saddle and set him on the ground.

At first she wondered if Cabal had taken Wat out to search for his kin, but the boy seemed too animated for such a sober task. Wat chattered so fast, it was impossible for her to discern a word of what he said. His excitement was unmistakable, however, as was his adoration for Cabal. Clutching a small object in his hands, Wat followed along like an eager pup while Cabal walked his mount toward the stables. Emmalyn waited for the knight to rebuff him, to brush him aside with the same impatience he had shown the boy from the day he had first seen him.

She watched, waiting for Wat's certain dismissal, but it did not come. Instead, the both of them disappeared into the stables with the black steed and a few moments later reemerged looking like easy—if oddly mismatched—companions.

Just then Bertie came out of the castle and into Emmalyn's view. The russet samite gown she wore was at least a decade out of fashion but still fit her well. Emmalyn could tell from the elderly maid's sashaying steps that she felt feminine and pretty, despite the age of her person and her garment. Cabal crossed his arms over his chest and gave a low whistle of appreciation, a move that Wat promptly adopted for his own. Bertie cooed with delight at all of the attention, dropping into a clumsy curtsy before her two admirers.

"And who might this fair maiden be?" Cabal teased.

Frowning, Wat tugged on the hem of the knight's tunic. "'Tis Nurse, my lord! Can you not see?"

While Emmalyn bit back her amusement, Cabal hunkered down to Wat's level, still smiling at Bertie. "Why, by the Rood, lad, so 'tis. Is she not the loveliest damsel you've seen all day?"

Wat nodded enthusiastically, clearly willing to agree to anything the knight suggested. In the next breath, he rushed to Bertie's side and grasped her hand. "Sir Cabal learned me to ride a horse today an' I only fell off two times! He says someday mayhap I will ride good as him, an' look Nurse, see what he made me?"

Wat held out the prize he had been cradling, a chunk of

wood carved in the shape of an animal. "Oh my!" Bertie
gasped as he waggled it before her, mimicking a beastly roar.

" 'Tis a lion," the boy explained. "Sir Cabal seen a real
one on Crusade."

"Did he, now?"

Wat nodded. " 'Twas a magic lion that disappeared right
out of its cage!"

"Really," Nurse drawled, slanting Cabal a dubious look.
"Well, mayhap Sir Cabal will regale us all with his tale
about this disappearing magical lion as we sit around the
bonfire tonight, do you suppose?"

Wat turned to look up at Cabal with wide, adoring eyes.
"Will you, my lord?"

"Mayhap," he answered with a mild shrug.

The boy beamed, seemingly oblivious of the knight's
reluctance. "I can't wait to show Lady Emmalyn!" he told
Nurse excitedly. "Has she already left for the festival?"

"No, Wat. I'm afraid she won't be going," Bertie said on
a sigh. "Milady is tired this eve and resting in her chambers.
However, I'm certain she would love to see your prize in the
morn."

Wat pouted, shoulders sagging. His obvious disappointment tugged at Emmalyn's heart, as did the notion that
Cabal had given the boy such a sweet and surprising token
of regard.

"No need to be so glum, child. You do have me!" Bertie
grabbed up Wat's small hand. "Now, come along. These old
legs of mine are itching to dance!"

"Sir Cabal!" Wat called over his shoulder as Bertie set off
with him at a jaunty pace. "My lord, come with us, please!"

As if he sensed her watching them, Cabal looked up to
where Emmalyn stood at the window. The casement shadows
and the gloom of the chamber surely concealed her from
view, but she felt the weight of his keen regard like a warm
coaxing caress. She backed away, deeper into the darkness,
afraid to trust what she saw in his soulful silver eyes.

Wat called to him again, and with a final lingering glance

at the tower keep, Cabal loped off to join the boy and Nurse. Together, the trio crossed the wide bailey, Bertie and Cabal on either side of Wat while he skipped along between them. Somewhat wistfully, Emmalyn watched them go, feeling lonely before they had even disappeared through the gates and out of her view.

More than anything, in that moment she wanted to be a part of the gaiety. She wanted to see for herself Bertie dancing about the bonfires with Wat. She wanted to hear firsthand about Cabal's adventures with exotic creatures in exotic lands. But she knew he would be different knowing she was there. He would be on guard, mayhap even push her away as he had in the orchard. She did not think she could bear his rejection again. If only there was a means for her to become invisible, like the magical lion Cabal purported to have seen.

And then she realized there was a way.

Excitedly, Emmalyn quit the solar and hastened upstairs to her chamber. She rummaged through her clothing chest until she found the item she sought and slipped it over her bliaut. The long summer mantle was dark as night itself and covered her from neck to foot in voluminous folds; her face and hair would be well concealed within the deep hood. Cloaked in her own brand of midsummer magic, Emmalyn waited for darkness to descend outside; then she left the castle and headed down to the village.

Chapter Seventeen

The sights and sounds of festival set Emmalyn's heart racing as she tread down the path that led from the castle to the village below. The guards on post at the keep had offered her escort, but she refused them with assurances that the walk was not so very long and the fires would light the way for her. If she had worried that an armed attendant might draw attention to her arrival, she realized soon enough that she need not have bothered with that particular concern. There was far too much activity going on about the village and plains for anyone to take notice of a cloaked figure come to join the countless other folk in attendance at the feast day celebration.

Bonfires glowed from the center of the village, and on nearly every surrounding rise. The flames crackled and undulated as they leaped high into the blackness of the night sky. Music and singing filled the air, along with the laughter of dancers spinning circles around the many crowded blazes. A group of young boys broke from the perimeter of one of the fires, each of them brandishing a burning torch. They ran past Emmalyn as if she weren't there, yelling at the tops of their lungs as they set off on a mission to drive away mischievous dragons that might be tempted to poison village wells during the revelry.

As the boys zigzagged hither and yon with their brands, Emmalyn was able to discern the dark silhouettes of couples heading into the woods together. Some did not even trifle to conceal themselves in the thicket; their passions consumed them so much, they embraced and kissed wherever they happened to be standing—in the fields and pathways or pressed against village outbuildings.

Safely obscured in the shadows, Emmalyn walked along the fringes of the gathering, drawn toward the aromas of roasting venison and freshly baked bread. She got a portion of both from the men tending the cook fires, then sat down on a thick log that was being used as a makeshift bench. At her left, two little girls were playing with their food and giggling over the antics of the village boys and other fanciful nonsense. Emmalyn munched idly, so engrossed in her meal and eavesdropping that she almost didn't notice the tall broad-shouldered man who took up the empty space at her other side.

"How many times has that old nurse dragged ye out to dance with her this eve, Sir Cabal?" someone asked from across the circle of folk partaking of the viands.

"Too many to count. I vow she means to make an old man of me before the night is out."

His velvety voice rumbling directly beside her sent a shiver of awareness skating up Emmalyn's spine. She shrank deeper into her cloak, eating in silence while Cabal gnawed on a mutton shank and conversed easily with the people.

Watching their rapt faces as they all vied for his attention, it struck Emmalyn how easily they had come to adore and depend on Cabal in the short time he had been there. This gruff warrior, who professed his lack of interest for farm and folk so vehemently, was a part of Fallonmour now, whether he liked it or not. They would miss him. Indeed, so would she.

Emmalyn felt a sudden prick of guilt, knowing that soon she would travel to Lincolnshire and meet with the queen to discuss the tenancy of Fallonmour and Cabal's removal. Strange that what had once seemed like the very thing she wanted most for herself and for Fallonmour was now beginning to feel more like a deep betrayal: insidious and underhanded. But how ridiculous that she should feel thus when he seemed so anxious to be delivered of her, Emmalyn reasoned, shaking her head as if to physically deny the thought before she allowed it to linger for another moment in her mind.

"Ah, you see?" Cabal startled her as he placed his hand at her back and addressed his growing audience, evidently unaware that it was she seated beside him. "Here is one maid who does not want to listen to a tiresome soldier's story this eve."

"But, Sir Cabal, you promised!" Wat complained as he entered the area and plopped down at the knight's feet. "We want to hear 'bout the lion!"

A roar of approval traveled the crowd and brought more folk to the fireside. It was not often that country people got to hear firsthand accounts of the wild, dangerous beasts lurking beyond their island home. Within moments the area was surrounded by a sea of eager faces, among them common folk, knights, Sir Miles, Bertie, and even Father Bryce. Children seemed to materialize from out of everywhere, weaving their way between adults standing shoulder-to-shoulder to get places up front, nearest they could to Cabal.

He chuckled as the ranks tightened around the fireside. "Can't a man eat his supper in peace?" he groused.

"If I had to sing for my sup," the reeve's wife said on a laugh as she laid down her lute, "then you, sir knight, can pay for yours with a tale of derring-do."

Assenting shouts went up from those gathered. Wat beamed at Cabal as if the knight were a treasure that belonged to him alone. "Tell us 'bout the lion, my lord," he pleaded, holding out the carving Cabal had made for him.

"Another time, lad."

He tried to resume eating, but the crowd's interest had been piqued beyond escaping. "Did ye slay the beast on Crusade, Sir Cabal? Ye must tell us the tale, milord!"

"'Twas a magic lion, and Sir Cabal touched it with his bare hands!" Wat exclaimed, his eager interjection causing the children, and many of the adults as well, to gasp in wonder.

Cabal cleared his throat. "Well," he said, setting aside his meal, "I cannot attest that the lion was enchanted, but I reckon there was magic in the air, for 'twas on this very eve one year ago that the giant cat strayed quite calmly into our camp."

Emmalyn listened, breathless and beguiled like the rest of the folk, while Cabal told how the company of English soldiers had netted the lion, imprisoning him in one of the caged carts used for transporting prisoners and hostages of the Cross.

"The king was due back at our camp that next morn, and the men thought it a fitting tribute to gift Coeur de Lion with a royal captive of his own. The king of beasts for the king of England, they said."

Emmalyn could hear the bite of sarcasm edging Cabal's voice, but for their part, the folk seemed oblivious, most of them whispering lauds for King Richard's reputed bravery and murmuring their approval of the prize. They were all too caught up in the tale to notice the subtle tightening of Cabal's jaw or the distant look that had crept into his eyes.

"Was he a vicious creature, Sir Cabal?" one of the knights asked eagerly. "A ferocious man-eater?"

"I expect he was, in his time. But as regal as this beast might have been, he was old and tired. No doubt that was the only reason we were able to capture him as we did," Cabal said. "We kept him caged in the center of the camp while we took our evening meal around the cook fire. All that time, the lion just sat there, watching us, his noble head erect, his eyes intense and glowing iridescent in the firelight.

"Some hours later, when we were all full of wine and growing bored with each other's company, one of the men got up, deciding he wanted to hear the great beast roar. He went to the cage and drew his sword, dragging it along the bars and jabbing it within to goad the lion into striking out."

"Did it work, my lord?" Wat asked on a gasp. "Did he strike at the man?"

"No, he did not," Cabal answered thoughtfully. "The lion

moved out of the way of the blade, retreating to the corners of its cell, but the soldier would not cease provoking him. Before long, more men joined the first, all of them shouting and banging their swords on the cage. Through it all, the beast remained quiet. Passive.

"He was bleeding from a cut on his flank, panting and anxious, but he did not strike out." Cabal's voice had grown reflective, almost haunted. "He could have easily killed any one of those men; they were all getting careless and too close to the bars to be safe, but the lion did not seem interested in shedding their blood, not even to spare his own."

One of the men scoffed from the perimeter of the gathering. "Not much of a man-killer after all, was he, 'lord?"

Cabal shook his head. "There could be no disputing his dignity, but the beast's fighting days were long over. When he provided no sport, the men soon grew tired of the game. Someone suggested they let the king have the honor of slaying the beast himself when he arrived at the camp the next morn and the others quickly agreed. 'Twas the consensus that the lion's head would make a better prize than would the sorry creature itself."

Her stomach coiled with sympathy and dread, Emmalyn wanted to ask if that was truly what had come to pass, if King Richard was actually given the beast to kill in cold blood. In the next heartbeat, someone else voiced the question for her.

"Ah, I reckon that is where the magic comes in," Cabal replied. "For while the camp slept that night, something remarkable and unexplained took place. That next morning we awoke to find the cage locked but empty. The lion had vanished without a single trace."

A flurry of questions came from the crowd. "Were there no tracks left outside, Sir Cabal? And what about the cage? Had he smashed his way out through the bars?"

"There were no pawprints to be found," Cabal answered. "The cage was wholly intact and the gaoler's keys were yet strung about his neck, same as they had been when he fell asleep that night."

A murmur of awe traveled through the group. Then someone asked, "Was the king angry that his gift had gotten away?"

Cabal chuckled. "When he heard the tale of the lion's easy capture and then its subsequent disappearance from within a locked cage, the king laughed. He thought it a jest. Either that, he said, or a mass illusion, which he blamed on the desert heat and too much potent Saracen wine." Cabal scanned the circle of listeners, an enigmatic, playful glimmer creeping into his eyes. Then he shrugged. "Who is to say, in truth? Perhaps that's all it was after all."

"Oh," chorused many in the crowd, clearly suspecting they had been duped into believing a yarn. Some started to walk away, joking and laughing good-naturedly about having played the fool for Cabal and his tall tale.

After the crowd had dispersed, Wat gazed up, frowning on the verge of disappointment. "Do you believe there was a lion, Sir Cabal? Was he real?"

"Do you believe he was real?" Cabal countered gently.

Wat looked down at the carved lion in his hands, turning it about and tracing the etched mane with his fingertip. "Aye," he answered after some consideration. "I do think he was real, an' I believe he was magical, too."

Cabal ruffled the lad's hair. "Then I reckon that's all that matters."

Smiling, his eyes full of admiration, Wat nodded. Some of the boys from the village called out to him then, asking him to come with them to find the St. John's fern. He jumped to his feet and ran after them, leaving Cabal and Emmalyn nearly alone at the fire. Only a handful of stragglers remained, and they seemed more interested in second helpings of food than they did in Cabal and the petite cloaked figure at his side.

"I believe that lion was real, too," Emmalyn said softly, moved by his story and compelled to bridge the gap of silence that had separated them the past few days. "I believe it was real, but I don't believe the beast was enchanted. I think you were the magic behind its escape, my lord."

His dark brows knit into a frown, Cabal leaned toward her, peering intensely as if he meant to see inside her hood. "Emmalyn?" he whispered harshly, but she could hear the warm note of surprise in his voice. "God's blood, woman, have you been sitting here the whole time? Where is your escort?"

Emmalyn shrugged, pleased despite good reason to have him speaking to her again, even if only to scold her. "I had no need of an escort," she told him. "I am disguised in this cloak; so far as anyone here is concerned, I am merely one of the folk. No different than any other woman in attendance this eve."

He cursed under his breath. " 'Tis my worry exactly. Has it escaped your notice how filled the woods and shadowed corners are with couplings this eve? What is to stop any one of these drunken swains from mistaking you for a willing peasant girl and scooping you up to have his way with you?" He shook his head, clearly exasperated. "You should not be out here alone."

"I'm not alone anymore," she said, smiling shakily.

A group of men brought out another cask of wine, rolling it past them to replace the last. When the swelling crowd began to press in for more drink, Cabal grasped Emmalyn's hand and led her away from the boisterous inebriated throng. They walked together along the outskirts of the gathering, pausing near the bonfire, where a circle of folk danced merrily around the blaze.

With music, laughter, and the warm glow of firelight surrounding them, Emmalyn glanced at Cabal. "Why did you let them think your story about the lion was merely a jest, my lord? Why did you not tell them 'twas you who spared the lion and gave him his freedom?"

"You seem very certain that was how it happened," he said almost mockingly.

"I am certain. 'Twas you who freed him."

He stared at her for a long moment, neither admitting nor denying it, then returned his attention to the dancers. Emmalyn did likewise, her eye immediately drawn to Pete, the cottar from the village, linked arm in arm and laughing with pretty young Lucy, the reeve's unwed daughter. The pair were quite obviously enamored of each other, their hearts entwined as surely as their gazes. Here was one more example of Cabal's compassion, Emmalyn thought fondly, Pete and Lucy's matching being another kindness for which the dark knight at her side would take no credit.

The longer she knew him, the more Cabal seemed two distinct people to her: the hardened warrior, with his cold logic and steely sense of duty, and the enigmatic guarded man beneath the chain mail. The man he seemed to keep hidden away from everyone, so intent on denying his existence to her . . . denying it even to him-self. It was that man she had missed keenly these past few days, the man she had been able to see only in fleeting glimpses, as she had the night Minerva's foals were born and then again this evening, entertaining her folk with tales of daring and adventure.

It was that man she was coming to care for deeply.

"I have been wanting to thank you for your help the other day with Hugh," she said softly, searching for common ground, a way to clear the air between them. "What you have done with Fallonmour's garrison is remarkable."

She had not expected him to scoff. Nor did she expect the sudden, hard set of his jaw, the unforgiving twist of his mouth. "I did nothing," he said crisply. "What you saw was much the same thing Hugh did: a mirage. Don't make the mistake of believing an illusion, Emmalyn."

"I believe in you," she whispered, pained to hear the bite of self-mockery in his voice. "You are not an illusion."

"No?" he shot back harshly. "I thought we covered this matter in some detail the other day, my lady."

He walked past her, heading away from the bonfire's warming light and into the shadowy fringes of the gathering.

Emmalyn turned and followed, uncertain that he would want her yet determined that he not retreat alone into the darkness of whatever continued to haunt him.

"Why do you prefer to believe you are a bad person, Cabal? Why can you not admit that if you have demons—if you have done things you regret—there is still much that is good inside you?" He paused but would not face her. "I have seen your compassion, my lord. I have felt it. I know you care. I know you are capable of goodness and mercy, as with the lion you encountered on campaign. So why do you continually seek to deny it?"

He chuckled, tipping his head back to stare up at the star-filled sky. "You want me to admit to freeing that beast, do you, my lady?"

"Yes."

"Very well, I freed him," he said flatly. Then he turned to look at her, and instead of feeling relieved by his admission, Emmalyn felt strangely chilled. "After everyone had fallen asleep drunk or exhausted, I stole into the gaoler's tent and took the key. I set that haggard beast free and swept away his trail, Emmalyn, but I was also the one who saw him caged. I was the one who provoked him, who drew his blood simply because I could. 'Twas my idea to give him to the king, my suggestion that Richard be given the chance to slay the beast."

Emmalyn's heart grew a little heavier in her breast to hear him confess his part in the lion's capture, to hear the blurred edge of remorse in his voice. "But then you set him free," she said, a gentle reminder that despite his initial intent, his humanity had still won out over his darkness.

She wanted so badly to reach out to him then, to caress away the tension in his stern jaw, to chase the hauntedness from his eyes with a kind touch, with understanding. She wanted to hold him, inexplicably needing to soothe him. Wishing beyond all logic that she had the power to bring him out of his seclusion. Knowing that he alone could do the same for her.

"Why did you come down here tonight, Emmalyn?" he asked brusquely, an element of impatience in his voice. "Why are you standing here with me in the dark when you must know you are but a hair's breadth away from being pulled into my arms? What are you looking for?"

"N-nothing," she stammered, certain he would see through the lie. "I only wanted to be a part of the festival."

"Disguised and lurking about like a ghost?" he scoffed, but his gaze was anything but cool. "I warn you, my lady, you are getting in over your head."

Emmalyn swallowed hard, unable to break his potent gaze, watching the faint flickers of firelight reflect in his smoldering eyes. The village chapel stood behind him, deep shadows stretching out like veils of night-black velvet: soft, inviting. Emmalyn said nothing when Cabal reached out and caught her hands. He stepped back into the darkness of the alcove, pulling her along with precious little effort.

Once ensconced in the seclusion of the tiny church, he reached up and swept back the hood of her mantle, his rough, battle-scarred hands smoothing first over her hair, then tenderly following the slope of her cheek and jawline. His voice was a deep rasp that she responded to almost as surely as his touch. "Have you missed me, Emmalyn?"

"Yes," she breathed.

He smiled. "I have been wanting you more than ever these past few days."

In truth, Emmalyn felt much the same. For days—since the night in the armory—against all prudent reason, she had yearned to be with him again, to feel his strong hands weaving into her unbound hair, to see his dark-fringed eyes hooded with passion and smoldering for want of her. Heaven help her, but she had longed to breathe in his heady scent once more, to hear his heartbeat pound in time with hers. To taste his kiss . . .

As if sensing her need, Cabal dipped his head and claimed her mouth with his. A low growl rumbled at the back of his throat as their lips met; his palm cupped the back of her head and brought her closer, deeper into his embrace, deeper into his kiss. Tentatively, Emmalyn parted her lips, allowing his tongue to spar with hers, thrilling to feel its tender invasion. His breath rasped out of him on a harsh oath when Emmalyn reached up to twine her fingers in his hair, bringing him closer, kissing him fully.

He tasted of wine and something ever more intoxicating: a potent, wild desire that felt too bold for its tether and ready to snap. But if she feared that knowledge, even a little bit, it was soon engulfed by her body's growing answer to Cabal's touch.

With a sensuality that threatened to be her undoing, Cabal dragged her against the solid length of him as his kiss deepened, one hand splayed at her back while the other caressed her hair, her cheek, the sensitive skin of her neck. Vaguely, Emmalyn felt her mantle slip off her shoulders and down her arms. It pooled at her feet in an audible crush of soft fabric upon the ground. Cabal's hands were heavy and warm as he smoothed them down her arms, his strong fingers coarse and rasping atop the sleeves of her gown.

He broke their kiss only to press his lips against the hollow at the base of her throat, his tongue like a wisp of warm, raw silk, so smooth and sensual that Emmalyn gasped at the pleasurable sensation of it, her head arcing back as of its own accord, granting him freedom to roam further.

And, Heaven help her, he did just that.

He bent into her, his arm at her back, holding her steady against him as his lips swept every inch of sensitized flesh bared above the scooped neckline of her bodice. His breath was hot and fevered—shaky, shallow, much like her own. His stubbled growth of whiskers abraded her tender skin like the subtle scrape of a cat's tongue, an exquisite contrast to the moist softness of his hungry roving kisses.

Emmalyn thought he might have murmured her name, but she couldn't be sure above the mesmerizing din of distant music and pounding drums. She clung to him, feeling his heart beat a wild tattoo beneath her palms, knowing she was slipping farther and farther away from herself . . . edging dangerously closer to what she yearned to be with him.

All thought and reason fled when he cupped her breast through the fabric of her gown, kneading the swell of flesh that so ached for his touch. Emmalyn sucked in her breath, thankful for the chapel's stone wall at her back—the only thing keeping her standing as Cabal traced the shape of her body with his hands, skating past her ribs and over the swell of her hips. He grasped her bottom, squeezing her, wringing a mewling, desperate cry from somewhere deep inside of her as he nestled his mouth at the curve of her neck, his lips warm, the soft nip of his teeth startlingly erotic. "God help me, Emmalyn," he murmured on a harsh breath against her ear. "I've never wanted anyone the way I want you. Never."

He drew back slightly, his gaze searching hers in the semi-darkness a moment before he bent and captured her mouth anew. His kiss was not the same tender taking that it had been the first time; now it was raw with passion, deeply sensual, hungry. Emmalyn melted into his embrace, parting her lips to him, taking him in, letting him pull her against the hard plane of his chest, her abdomen pressed to the steely ridge of his groin.

He wanted her; she could feel the evidence of his desire pressing insistently into her hip as he dragged her closer, enveloping her in his strong arms while he kissed her nearly senseless. He wanted her. It was more than any other man had ever felt for her, and that alone should have pleased her. He wanted her, but she wanted more. Deep in her heart, she wanted Cabal to love her.

The way she was coming to love him.

Emmalyn felt her legs go weak beneath her as the realization struck her, stunning her as much as it terrified her. Dear Lord, it could not be. How had she let this happen? She could not be in love with this man! Bracing her hands on his shoulders, Emmalyn tore herself away from Cabal's kiss, panic mounting within her breast.

"What is it?" he asked huskily. "What's wrong?"

At first she could only manage to shake her head. "This is a mistake," she gasped. "I can't do this. I'm sorry, I just cannot—"

"I'm not going to hurt you, Emmalyn. Trust me . . ." He pressed his lips to hers once more, his seductive kiss making her senses reel.

"I'm sorry," she whispered on a broken intake of breath. "I can't. I'm so sorry."

Without further explanation, she ducked out of his arms and left him standing there alone in the dark, before he had the chance to respond. Before he could stop her flight with gentle hands or a tender promise that she would surely be too weak-hearted to doubt.

Chapter Eighteen

Cabal cursed softly as he bent to pick up Emmalyn's forgotten cloak. His pulse was still thrumming in his ears, his body still heavy with want of her, and remained thus long moments after she had fled his arms. What had gotten into him that he would think to make love to her here, in the midst of a village festival, sheltered from view by nothing more than a few feet of shadow? He had behaved like a beast, so blind with passion that he had afforded her no more consideration than a randy peasant lad would give a common wench.

He did not think it likely that he had imagined the desire he felt stirring within her as he kissed her; her response seemed to echo his own hunger. But there could be no doubting the fear in her eyes when she pulled out of his embrace and stared up at him, her lips trembling as she shook her head, horrified. He wished he could deny the look of utter desperation he witnessed on her face before she had backed away from him and bolted headlong into the night.

Cabal was certain he would be the last person she would wish to see right now, but he could not simply let her run off like this. Pride be damned, he had to make sure she was all right. He had to apologize at the very least. With her mantle draped over his arm and his lust coming to heel at last, Cabal rounded the chapel wall and stepped back into the teeming crowd of revelers.

He scanned the mass of people, moving among them impatiently and biting off a frustrated oath when it seemed

Emmalyn was nowhere to be found. She could not be difficult at all to spy without her shapeless concealing cloak. Her crown of glossy white-gold hair and her fine silk gown should act as a veritable beacon among the crush of unwashed bodies clad in homespun milling about everywhere he looked. He stood in the center of the throng, wanting to yell out her name yet knowing he could not. He would not cause her that added humiliation before all of her folk.

Agitated, and with a queer sense of dread niggling his every instinct, Cabal searched the hundreds of dirty faces once more, crushing Emmalyn's mantle in his fist as his initial prickling feelings of dread began to further gnaw at him, becoming with every passing moment something closer to a wary mounting alarm.

Damnation, where could she be?

Emmalyn skirted the ongoing celebration, scarcely able to resist the urge to run. Her head was spinning from the jumble of festival noises and the barrage of her confusing feelings. Having no cloak to hide her flushed cheeks or her kiss-swollen lips, she hoped to avoid the discomfiture of prying eyes by keeping to the shadows along the backs of the village outbuildings, walking briskly toward the path that would lead her back up to the castle.

She had made an utter fool of herself with Cabal this evening, first by sneaking out to be near him, and then, even worse, by encouraging him physically—only to flee without excuse an instant later like a skittish untried maiden. Chagrined anew by her behavior, Emmalyn tucked her head down and rushed on, past the rows of cottages and furlongs, beyond the village grain stores.

The sound of muffled voices in the vicinity of the woolshed caught her ear, momentarily distracting her from her own inner turmoil and giving her something more productive— though not much less troubling—to consider. Who would be tending the fleece at this hour, let alone during festival? she wondered as she neared the barn. She wanted to think that it was merely a band of village boys left unsupervised and getting into mischief, but the closer she got to the outbuilding, the better she knew that the voices did not belong to children. And inside there was far more under way than just a bit of harmless mischief.

Emmalyn stood in the partially open doorway, watching as four men rummaged around in the unlit shed, gathering up the rolls of precious fleece that had yet to be sacked for market. Several rolls had been corded together with thick twine, making neat packs, each manageable enough to be carried off and stolen. Outraged beyond reason, Emmalyn stormed inside. "What do you think you are doing in here? Get out this instant!"

The men all turned to stare at her in the dark. A couple of them merely chortled, but the largest of the four strode toward her. "Well, well. What have we here?"

"Get out, all of you, before I have you thrown out."

That garnered more amusement from the trio, but the one approaching Emmalyn leered with malicious interest. "My, but ye're a fine pretty bit of fleece. Come around for a tupping, did you?"

His companions chortled, but Emmalyn could see that the one who said it was not laughing. She ignored the intimidation and took a step backward, trying to gauge the distance between herself and the entrance to the shed. "You men have no right to be in here," she said with all the authority she could muster.

"My, she is a comely little stray," one of the brigands said, the band of them all moving forward now like a pack of wolves surrounding a helpless lamb. They closed in, their tight ranks forcing her away from the center of the barn and toward a shadowy corner that would afford no easy escape.

"Stealing is a hangable offense. . . ." she warned shakily.

"Not when we been hired to do it, sweetling. And anyway, who's here to stop us? You?"

"What do you mean you've been hired?" Emmalyn demanded in confusion.

"Clive," warned one of the thieves. "Arlo said naught about hurting anyone. Let's leave her be."

"She's seen us," the big man shot back. "And now you've gone and told the wench who we work for."

Emmalyn had a man on either side of her. The menacing giant named Clive accosted her from the front while the last thief followed closely at his back, pulling a length of twine from the coil in his hands. "Th-there are forty men-at-arms in the village tonight," Emmalyn stammered. "All I have to do is yell and they would all be here in an instant. Any one of them would be quite able to stop your thieving permanently."

The big man chuckled. "Forty men-at-arms you say, and not a one guarding the wool. I reckon they're all too drunk or too busy rutting themselves senseless to come around, even if they could hear you scream over the din outside."

Emmalyn's heart sank a little when she realized that he was right. Who would hear her above the music and laughter of the crowded village and plains? Who could discern a cry of alarm among all the other voices raised in celebration?

"Go ahead and scream if you want to," Clive said, a nasty twist to his mouth. "I likc it when my tups bleat a little. Makes things interesting."

And Emmalyn did scream.

She cried for help at the top of her lungs, only to be silenced a moment later by the crushing weight of her attacker's filthy body as he lunged for her, capturing her in a hard, bruising embrace. She thrashed wildly, twisting herself around so that her back was against him, all the while struggling to break out of his arms and biting at his hand when he reached up to clamp it over her mouth. Frantic and desperate to get away, she kept screaming under the viselike grip of his palm on her face, even if the sounds rang louder in her head than anywhere else.

She stomped and bucked, using any means of defense at her disposal. With her heel, she kicked backward and jammed her foot into her assailant's unprotected shin. He barked a curse and shoved her forward, right into the waiting

clutches of another brigand standing at the ready. Laughing
with the sport of it all, the ruffians took turns pushing her
around from one man to the next until their gang leader
stalked toward her once more, fuming with anger. Panting,
locked in the steely grip of one of the thieves, Emmalyn
could only stare at Clive as he came to stand before her,
glaring his hatred through narrowed cold eyes.

"Take the bitch over there and tie her up," he ordered the
others with a harsh jerk of his head. "She's mine first. The
rest of ye can have what's left of her when I'm through."
Then he laughed wickedly. "Providin' there's aught left to
be had, that is."

As she was dragged toward the corner of the barn and
thrown down on one of the solidly packed sacks of wool,
Emmalyn felt as if she were somehow removed from the
scene. As if it were happening to someone else, somewhere
outside her conscious understanding. One man held her
down while another worked to secure her arms with a rough
abrading length of twine. She was only vaguely aware of
her chief assailant standing behind the others, where he
fought with the ties of his chausses.

She felt cool air hit her legs and kicked wildly as one of
the men tried to ruck up her skirts with groping, impatient
hands. Though the stink of the thief's decayed mouth told
her that he had his lips pressed almost against her ear when
he warned her to cooperate or face the consequences, his
voice sounded slowed, muffled, as if it had come from a
great distance away. It was shock, she realized dazedly. She
was becoming too shocked and panicked to make sense of
her surroundings, let alone wrest herself free from this
abhorrent imminent harm. Before the struggle could leak
out of her entirely, Emmalyn gathered her strength and
made a last effort to buck the men away from her.

Her cry of "Nooo!" seemed to echo up into the rafters of
the barn, rallying her for one more brief futile moment
before she was silenced with a harsh slap across her cheek.
The blow stunned her, so much so that she almost did not

hear the angry order issued for someone to bar the shed door closed. Her vision swimming, she watched as the blurry silhouette of one of the three spectators standing over her suddenly disappeared to carry out the command. There was a splintering crash nary a moment later, too powerful to be the slamming shut of any door.

And she had no idea what to make of the terrible, animal-like roar that followed in the next heartbeat.

A ruckus stirred up in the barn, a swift and confusing hail of queer noises, all of them completely foreign to Emmalyn's ears: the sharp grate of metal against what she was certain had to be flesh; voices raised in anger and surprise, then dissolving into some strange liquid gurgle; and, undercurrent to it all, a deep, vicious snarling.

Though it was surely happening in mere moments, to Emmalyn the events seemed to elongate, dragging out in surrealistic sequence for some untold time. Above her, the last man holding her down moved off to confront the ruckus behind him.

The instant he got to his feet, Emmalyn scrambled aside, wanting to run but having strength enough only to cower on the other side of the huge wool sack, hoping to remain hidden from whatever danger had just been unleashed on the thieves in the barn. Shielding her eyes, she waited in terror, trying to blot out the awful sounds of the violence taking place a few paces from where she sat trembling. She heard a gruff voice bite off an oath, followed by a sharp cry, then the sickening crack of breaking bones.

The barn fell into an instant utter silence, save for her own hitching sobs . . . and the rasping breath of the sole survivor of the carnage. Footsteps approached her hiding place, but she could not bear to open her eyes and face this new menace. Shaking, sobbing, the rope bindings cutting into her wrists, she waited for fate's merciless decree.

"Emmalyn." The deep voice was an instant balm to her rattled nerves, the sound of her name beginning to clear away some of the haze that had settled over her senses. "Emmalyn, say something. Are you all right? Did they hurt you?"

Slowly, afraid to trust her ears, she looked up and opened her eyes, blinking into the darkness. She knew the figure of the man standing before her the way she knew her own shadow. "Cabal," she gasped, dragging herself off the ground and allowing him to catch her in his solid embrace. "Oh, Cabal! They were trying to steal the wool! They said Arlo hired them, just as you thought. I only meant to stop them but they—" she could not finish, choking on a sob as he cut away her bindings and threw them aside. "Oh, Cabal! I was so frightened!"

He shushed her with gentle, soothing words as he pulled her away from him. His tunic was covered in dark sticky stains. Even his face—the kind, handsome face she loved so much—was splattered with a metallic-smelling slickness. "You're bleeding," she said with mounting alarm, all thoughts for her own state of harm vanishing under a sudden crush of concern for him. She reached up to wipe at the ugly wetness that marred his cheek. "Oh, God, you're bleeding!"

"No," he murmured, catching her hand in his. He shook his head, pressing her fingers to his lips. "No, Emmalyn, I'm not bleeding."

"You are," she insisted, shakily. "I can see it. 'Tis all over you!"

"No, not my blood. Theirs, not mine."

And then her gaze was drawn behind him, to the four dead bodies lying scattered and broken on the barn floor. One man had fallen on a bale of wool; the stark contrast of his black-dark blood and the fluffy white fleece making Emmalyn fully conscious of her surroundings. Her stomach threatened to revolt when her mind finally began to acknowledge the awful events that had just transpired—to say nothing of what she might have been made to endure.

As if she needed further clarification of the night's shocking atrocities, a group of villeins appeared in the open doorway to the barn, their torches throwing light within and

illuminating the grim scene in vivid color. Sir Miles rushed
to the fore of the small clutch of folk, drawing in his breath
when his eyes lit on the both of them.

"Lady Emmalyn! Sir Cabal! What happened in here?"

The captain was followed by a flurry of fretful questions,
everyone inquiring at once after their lady's welfare and the
meaning of the bloody havoc wreaked in the barn. "The
thieves decided to come back, evidently," Cabal answered
with utter calm, totally in command of the situation. "Everything is all right now. Your lady is safe, and I warrant there
will be no more trouble from these brigands."

Emmalyn was grateful that he chose not to divulge the
circumstances of her humiliating attack, grateful as well for
the protective shelter of his arm as he wrapped it around her
shoulders and led her out of the corner of the barn and
toward the door. He seemed to take care to walk beside her,
matching her steps, his body blocking her further view of
the damage he had wrought on the robbers.

Once outside, he turned to Sir Miles. "Have you seen Wat
about?"

"He was at the cook fire with some of the other lads just a
moment ago."

"Good. Keep him away from here; 'tis bad enough he
will have to be told what happened. I don't want him to see
it for himself." Miles nodded and Cabal continued. "Make
sure the shed is put back in order yet tonight, and tell the
reeve to have the rest of the wool sacked for market first
thing in the morn. I'm going to see Lady Emmalyn back to
the castle."

Chapter Nineteen

The castle and surrounding courtyard stood quiet when Cabal escorted Emmalyn through the barbican gates, she leaning heavily on his strong arm. Only the few guards who had remained on watch were there to see their lady's ashen face as she trod weakly into the bailey alongside the bloodied, grim knight. He met their concern with the same calm he had shown the rest of the folk, wasting no time on explanations, his focus centered wholly on Emmalyn's current welfare and seeing after her comfort.

"Bring Lady Emmalyn a cup of wine," he told a maid who had come out of the hall when they entered the keep. "Heat a bowl of water for her as well, and deliver it to her chamber at once."

The maid stared for a moment at his ruined clothing, clearly unsure what to make of his frightful appearance, but without a word, she bobbed her head and dashed off to carry out the order. His arm gentle and steadying against Emmalyn's back, Cabal guided her to the stairwell.

"Thank you," she said, turning toward her tender protector. She was scarcely able to resist the urge to lovingly cradle his grizzled cheek in her palm. Instead she wrapped her arms one over the other and tried to fight off a chill that permeated her bone-deep. "It hardly seems enough merely to tell you how grateful I am that you were there," she told him, her thready voice belying her inner shakenness.

" 'Tis more than enough for me, my lady."

"No." Emmalyn shook her head, indebted beyond explanation and unwilling to let him discount this further act of valor performed on her behalf. "You risked your life for me tonight. I don't know what would have happened if you hadn't come when you did."

But she did know, she realized, her chest still constricted with fear at the thought of the horrors she had been spared. An involuntary shudder coursed through her, and from the corners of her eyes, her vision began to cloud over. She braced her fingers against her temples and tried to blink away the queer and spreading haziness.

"Come," Cabal prodded gently. "Let us get you above-stairs, my lady. You need to lie down and rest awhile."

Emmalyn started to protest his further care, but as she moved to take the first step, her legs suddenly began to buckle beneath her. Before she knew it, Cabal had swept her up into his arms.

"Cabal, please," Emmalyn said on a weak breath. "You do not have to do this for me." But she clung to his strength just the same, needing him despite her desire to be sound and able on her own. Wrapping her arms around the warm solid column of his neck, she nestled her cheek against his shoulder as he carried her easily up the stairs and into her chamber.

The room was dark, save for the distant glow of the village bonfires and a pale wash of moonlight coming in through the open window. Cabal crossed the floor, bringing Emmalyn to her bed and setting her softly upon the mattress. Using the flint that lay on a table at her bedside, he lit a tallow candle, then reached around her to plump the feather bolsters at her back.

"Is that better?" he asked as he loosened the coverlet and brought it up over her body, securing her within the warm woolen cocoon. Emmalyn nodded. "You're still shaking," he said, his voice edged with concern and something less easy to discern.

When the maid came in a moment later bearing the wine and basin of water that Cabal had ordered, he directed her to set them down beside him, then dismissed the girl with idly murmured thanks while he brought the cup to Emmalyn's lips and bade her drink of it. The wine warmed and soothed her almost immediately, though no more than Cabal's continued gentle treatment.

Emmalyn watched him tend her in the wavering light of the single candle, astonished at the compassion she saw etched in his features, the tender care evident in this warrior's every touch and movement. He dipped the swatch of linen into the water and wrung it out, gingerly applying its warmth to her brow. Emmalyn studied his face, noting the gentleness in his eyes, the sympathy softening the blunt line of his mouth.

His hands were still stained from the confrontation with the robbers; his face marred with blood and bruises, streaked with sweat and grime. If she had not seen it with her own eyes, it would have been difficult to believe him capable of the swift violence she had witnessed this eve. He had seemed so chillingly efficient with the brigands, so detached from himself. Four men dead at the end of his blade and he left standing among them with nary a scrape nor any reaction whatsoever to the deed. The hauntedness she had seen in his eyes then in the barn was yet evident in his gaze, though even that was dissipating the longer he sat at her side.

Emmalyn looked up at him—this fighting man that she was somehow falling in love with—wanting so badly to understand him. That his life had been spent in violence should have repelled her, and in some small way it verily did, but more than any fear or revulsion she held for what he might have done in his past, Emmalyn found she was instead compelled to know him better. She needed to know what he was feeling, where he had been. Hesitantly, she asked, "Have you . . . killed many men?"

At first he didn't answer. He dabbed at her abrasions, then met her gaze as if he had to force himself to do so. "More than I care to remember."

"And it does not bother you?"

He exhaled sharply, not quite a sigh but rather a harsh bitter-sounding laugh. "It used to, I suppose, a long time ago. I've seen too much death and killing to give it much thought anymore." His expression became stony. "What bothers me is that you had to see it. Would that I could cleanse it from your memory."

Her heart squeezing with affection, Emmalyn tried to adopt a light tone, hoping to ease some of the somberness she saw in him. "Do you think it now your responsibility to shield me from every unpleasant facet of life, my lord?"

"There are times, my lady, when I want nothing more in this world than to do just that."

The intensity of both his voice and his gaze nearly swept all the breath from her lungs. Emmalyn stared at him unblinking, unable to say a word, unable to look away. She was afraid to suppose what he may have meant, unwilling to hope that she might have come to mean something to him in their short time together. She parted her lips, nearly at the brink of confessing the breadth of her own confusing, steadily growing feelings for him, when the heavy pound of approaching footsteps sounded on the plank flooring outside the chamber door.

The oak panel swung wide as Bertie rushed in, frantic and clearly having not given a thought to pause and first announce herself. "Milady! Oh, my dear, dear child! I just heard what happened in the village! I hadn't even been aware that you had come down to the festival! Are you all right? Were you hurt? Can I do anything for you? . . ." The nurse's panic-stricken voice faded off to nothingness as her wild eyes settled on the knight perched at Emmalyn's bedside.

"'Tis all right, Bertie. I am fine." Emmalyn was surprised she was able to find her voice, let alone make it sound so calm. "My nerves are a bit rattled, but I am for the most part unharmed, thanks to Cabal. He came to my aid with the brigands and has since been personally seeing to my welfare. Quite admirably, at that."

Cabal cleared his throat and made to rise. "Perhaps now that your maid is here, you would be more comfortable if I left you in her care."

"No." Emmalyn's answer was swift, her hand reaching out as if of its own accord to catch his fingers before he could leave her side. "Please, stay," she said, softer this time, lest she belie her desperation to be near him longer, even if it should be for just a little while more.

He looked surprised at her request, and perhaps a bit reluctant to oblige, but he nodded and remained standing beside her.

"As you will, milady," Bertie said, glancing at the two of them for a long moment.

Once the door had closed behind the maid's retreating figure, Cabal turned back to regard Emmalyn with intense searching eyes. "Why would you want me to stay with you any longer after all that has occurred this eve? Indeed, after all that has occurred since I came here."

"Because," she answered simply, "I feel safe with you."

He took his place on the edge of the bed once more, but a long moment passed before he spoke. "This was my fault."

"No," Emmalyn whispered, shaking her head. "How could you possibly be to blame for any of this? You saved my life."

"Only after my actions put it in jeopardy." His voice was bitter as he retrieved the cloth and pressed it gingerly to her brow. "If I hadn't been such a . . . *beast* . . . down there at the festival, you would have had no reason to run off alone."

"I ran because I was frightened," she admitted quietly.

When he cursed under his breath and hung his head, Emmalyn reached for his hand, the gesture drawing his gaze back to her. Something about his present apparent vulnerability lent her a measure of strength. She did not want him to hurt or blame himself, even if it meant exposing a bit of her fragile heart to him now. "I was not frightened of you, Cabal, but of myself. I was afraid of the way you make me feel."

For a beat that stretched into an eternity, he stared at her, saying nothing. "And now?"

"I am still afraid."

At her breathless confession, Cabal smiled wistfully as if weathering some inner untold pain. "I could never hurt you," he said, his intense whisper sounding so like a fervent lover's vow. A vow that Emmalyn wanted more than anything to believe.

He leaned forward then, reaching out to cup her face in his palm. As he did so, the candlelight played over his dark skin and spilled between his fingers, illuminating the blood-stains and abrasions that riddled his hand. He saw the grim reminder of the night's events at much the same time Emmalyn did. He swore an angry guttural oath, and instead of touching her as she so wanted him to do, he abruptly drew his hand away, attempting to conceal it from her further view.

But Emmalyn stretched her arm out to him, tenderly placing her hand over his. She rose up off the mattress and retrieved the damp cloth from beside the washbasin, then uncurled his tight fist. With gentle strokes, she wiped the ugly stains from his fingers, swept clean his callused palm. "You've done so much for me this eve," she told him softly, "'tis only fair that I tend to you in return, my lord."

She could feel his eyes on her as she carefully washed his other hand. When he spoke, his voice was heavy, reflective. "In Palestine, my hands were so bloody at the end of each day, no amount of scrubbing would make them clean. So often I think that's all they are good for, even now . . . killing, destruction."

"No. You mustn't think that, Cabal. Not when you have done so much good around here. Not when you have done so much for me. Don't believe yourself a monster. I don't believe it."

His answering chuckle caught in the back of his throat, a strained, grating sound. "No? Mayhap you would be less inclined to defend me if you knew everything I have done. . . ."

"It does not matter," she whispered, reaching out and

grasping his thick, strong fingers, curling her hand around his. She brought his palm to her lips and pressed a kiss against the roughened skin at its center. "I don't care if you have killed a thousand men in battle. None of that matters to me. Not now."

He stared at their entwined fingers, scowling. A queerly distant look washed over his features, hardening the line of his jaw. "Emmalyn, if I spend another moment in this chamber with you, I will not want to leave at all."

There was an edge of warning in his tightly reined voice, but Emmalyn felt not even the smallest tremor of apprehension for what she was about to invite. Wordlessly, she rinsed out the cloth and brought it up to his face, using the pretense of washing away the grime of battle as an excuse to touch him. Her gaze locked on his, she stroked the linen swatch down the sharp slope of his stubbled cheek, then skimmed it across his broad furrowed brow, scarcely able to breathe for the smoldering look in his eyes.

Cabal's own breath leaked out of him on a harsh groan when Emmalyn let her hand caress the other side of his face, her touch lingering against his skin. "Please, Emmalyn," he growled. "Tell me to go."

But she would tell him no such thing. Instead, with trembling fingers, she set aside her cloth and quietly took his hand, bringing it to her mouth, pausing to kiss his bruised abraded knuckles. He watched her through hooded eyes, his jaw clenched, as she then placed his hand over her breast in silent invitation. Her heart was racing under the weight of his warm palm, pounding with anticipation and longing for this gentle warrior at her side.

From some distant corner of her mind she heard the warning that this was far more dangerous than anything she had ever known with Garrett. If she was wrong about Cabal, wrong to entrust him with this gift of herself, her soul would never recover, but she did not care. All she knew—all that mattered—was this moment. All she needed was this night. All she wanted was Cabal. She would take whatever he was able to give her, and if her heart broke for her folly in these next few hours, then so be it.

"Are you sure this is what you want?" he asked, his voice gravelly, constricted. "After everything that has happened tonight—"

"After everything that's happened, I just want to feel safe. . . ."

"With me?"

Emmalyn nodded once, squeezing his hand beneath hers. "I haven't been with a man since—" She broke off, wincing in light of painful memories, suddenly reminded of her woeful relations with Garrett. "It has been a long time," she confessed, "and I'm afraid I'm not a very skilled lover."

Smiling, Cabal leaned forward to brush a wisp of hair from her brow. "It has been a long time for me as well, my lady." He bent down, pressing his lips to hers in a chaste gentle kiss, even though his eyes fairly smoldered, heavy-lidded and dark with passion's fire. His fingers shook as he traced the line of her jaw. "God's bones, what you do to me, Emmalyn. I become like a fumbling lovesick youth whenever I'm near you. I've never known this desire."

He kissed her again, this time leaning into her as if he could not stop himself from claiming more of her, his warm hand plunging through her unbound hair and spanning the back of her neck as he brought her up into his embrace. "Tell me you feel the same, Emmalyn. That you have never wanted anyone like this," he whispered against her lips, his breath warm and sensual, growing more fevered as he explored the corner of her mouth, the curve of her jaw, the pulse point at the base of her neck. "Tell me you have never known this passion before."

"Never," she gasped when his mouth pressed against the sensitive skin below her ear. Dear God, but it seemed she had been waiting an eternity to feel his arms around her again, to know once more the pleasure of his kiss. "I have never known this, Cabal. Only with you."

He growled and caught her earlobe between his teeth, the

gentle nip wringing an odd, strangled little cry from some-where deep inside of her. She drove her fingers into the thick glossy waves of his hair, caressing the back of his head in almost mindless wonder as his mouth traveled down the column of her neck and then teased the hollow at the bend of her shoulder. And then his lips were just above the neckline of her bodice, tasting her tender skin. Torturing her with sweet, intoxicating kisses.

Her breasts ached for his touch. And as though he knew this about her body already, Cabal cupped one fleshy mound in his hand, kneading it over the fabric of her gown. Emma-lyn sucked in her breath, tipping her head back when his mouth began to rove lower, into the cleft of her bosom. She moaned his name, and he caught the mewling cry in his mouth, cap-turing her lips in a fervent, hungered kiss as he pressed her down into the feathered cushion of the bolster.

Emmalyn surrendered to the breadth of his passion, sub-mitting to the erotic penetration of his tongue, taking him into her, accepting the ardent mating of their mouths as she anticipated the imminent joining of their bodies. Inside, she was on fire, melting like wax left out under the blaze of a hot summer sun. Needing something solid to cling to, she slid her hands down the rough silk fabric that covered his back, feeling the tightly corded muscles jump and flex under her fingertips, marveling at his body's sheer power. Its graceful masculine strength.

"I need to feel your hands on me, Emmalyn," he rasped, pulling away from her to tear off his sullied tunic and throw it to the floor. He knelt at her side on the mattress, his strong thighs parted, the full measure of his arousal straining against the fabric of his hose. Cabal's eyes were dark and beseeching as he gazed down on her in watchful silence, his broad shoulders and bared torso magnificent in the wavering candlelight. It seemed strange to consider this formidable battle-hardened warrior beautiful, but beautiful he was, in the most primal, essential meaning of the word.

Moved by the sight of him like Eve gazing upon Adam,

Emmalyn reached for Cabal. She rose up onto her knees, smoothing her palms over the warm, solid musculature of his chest, reveling in the dual sensations of the soft bristle of hairs tickling her fingertips and the heavy thrumming of his heart, pounding beneath her hands. This close she could see the various scars and faint protrusions that riddled his dark skin, old battle wounds and broken bones that had not healed quite right.

The notion of him being wounded, inflicted with any one of these injuries, tore at a place deep in her heart. It made her want to protect him, made her wish she could take away every one of his past pains and shield him from any further harm. Seeing the evidence on his body of the numerous times he might have died in battle—realizing that she might have lost him even before he came so unexpectedly into her life—made Emmalyn all the more certain that she loved this man, body, heart, and soul.

Reverently gliding her hands around to his back, she bent forward and placed a lingering kiss at the base of his neck, letting her tongue graze over the salty-sweet surface of his skin, savoring every inch of him. He moaned deep at the back of his throat, bringing his hands up around her as if he meant to hold her in place, but Emmalyn had no intention of leaving off so soon. Languidly, she followed the thick line of his shoulder with her mouth, learning from his earlier example, tasting him as he had done to her.

And she went a bit farther than he had, catching the bud of his nipple with her lips, sucking it boldly into her mouth, drawing the tight pebble between her teeth.

Cabal's hissed oath was sharp and vivid. "Emmalyn," he grated, repeating her name again as he drew her away from him, his expression tight with a control that seemed at the very precipice of breaking loose. "If I don't touch you now—all of you—I swear I'll go mad with wanting. Let me see you, Emmalyn, let me feel your skin against mine. . . ."

"Yes," she gasped.

With frantic, shaking hands, he gathered up her skirts and

freed her of her gown, pulling it over her head and idly dropping it in a heap on the floor next to his discarded tunic. Then he simply gazed at her for a long, silent moment. A moment during which it took all of Emmalyn's strength of will to remain uncovered for him, naked.

Vulnerable.

The urge to douse the candle and plunge the room into comfortable darkness was nearly overwhelming, the light made tolerable only by the look of pure reverence shining in Cabal's eyes. "We can go as slowly as you wish," he told her, as if sensing her sudden trepidation. He chuckled softly and offered her a wry smile. "Don't think it will be at all easy for me to hold back my need for you, my lovely lady, but you have my vow. I will be as patient as you want me to be. And I'll stop at any time, if you wish it."

"I'm not going to stop you," Emmalyn whispered.

She watched, half in curious anticipation, half in rampant desire, as Cabal backed off the mattress and shed his hose and braies. If she thought him beautiful before, the sight of him fully nude was nothing less than awe-inspiring. Every inch of him was firm and delineated with solid muscle, from his broad shoulders and chest to his slim waist and hips. His thighs were spread apart slightly; his penis jutted out from a thatch of darkness, heavy and erect, the member every bit as formidable and majestic as the man himself.

For once, Emmalyn was glad she was not an untried virgin, for the notion of this man coming into her bed would have surely made her swoon. As it was, her stomach fluttered queerly, her insides feeling coiled with some elusive, unfamiliar hunger. Something warm and unsettling began to stir in her loins, quickening her breath as Cabal returned to his place on the bed.

Kneeling before her, his eyes trained on hers, he kissed her. Not the fevered way he had claimed her mouth before, but slowly now, maddeningly languid. He moved farther into her, pulling her body up against the warm length of him as his tongue slipped past her lips in a soulful erotic questing.

Emmalyn felt the rigid line of his erection, hot and pulsing at her abdomen, felt the faint slick moistness of his mounting desire as he rubbed shamelessly against her. That moistness was echoed within her own body, a rapturous stirring that started deep inside her and spread lower, enflaming her with a longing for him that ached to be sated.

Though she was no stranger to the act of coupling, never had Emmalyn craved it before. She had never touched a man intimately, never thought she could find such pleasure in opening herself to a man's attentions. While Garrett had taken her virtue and despoiled her fragile trust, somehow with Cabal she felt reborn. His reverent kisses and careful caresses made her feel pure, untainted, cleansed of the fear and shame she had borne throughout her marriage. The fact that he asked nothing of her—that he took no more than she would give, allowing her to set their pace tonight—moved Emmalyn.

It emboldened her.

She broke their kiss and sat back to gaze upon his body, running her hands along the same path her eyes took: across the solid line of his shoulders, down the rigid planes of his chest and stomach . . . then lower still. When her fingertips waded into the dense patch of hair below his navel, brushing against the hard silk of his arousal, Cabal sucked in his breath. It hissed out of him an instant later as Emmalyn tentatively wrapped her fingers around the width of him, feeling his thick shaft surge tighter in her light grasp, astonished at the heat and strength she dared hold only briefly in her hand.

He ground out her name between clenched teeth, little more than an inarticulate growl, as she released him and skimmed her hands back up the sides of his rib cage. He cupped her breasts, bending forward to kiss first one, then the other, hungrily laving her sensitive nipples, pulling them into his mouth, swirling his tongue around the hardened peaks until Emmalyn wanted to scream with the delicious agony of it all.

She was vaguely aware of his hand sliding down around her bottom, clutching it tightly. Emmalyn could scarcely breathe; his fingers were so very close to the moist, burning cleft at the juncture of her thighs. His grip on her loosened and in the next heady instant, he touched her there. Slid his finger nearly inside of her, just enough to make her certain she wanted more. Emmalyn's whimper twined around his reverent oath, their breathing harsh and matched in time by a shared pure need for each other.

"I want you," he whispered savagely, seeking out and finding the slick swollen bud of her desire. His touch was light, spellbinding, and all too fleeting. "God, Emmalyn, I must have more of you."

He pressed her down to the mattress, their lips joining in a deep sensual kiss. Emmalyn expected that he would simply enter her then, poised above her as he was, his legs between her open thighs, his sex heavy and warm against her woman's mound. He had given her untold pleasures already this evening, bestowing on her more attentive consideration than her husband had ever thought to show her in the dismal hours she lay beneath him in their marriage bed.

Though she secretly yearned for something more from Cabal, Emmalyn was prepared for the night to end with the swift culmination of their mating. It was his turn to take full measure of his own satisfaction; she would be his willing vessel. She moved her hips against him in an effort to convey her readiness, feeling a rush of sweet exultation when the blunt head of his manhood pushed into the wet sheath of her womb.

A tremor rocked him and he groaned, pressing his forehead into the bolster above Emmalyn's shoulder. A gentle thrust of his hips filled her with the full length of him, wringing a soulful sigh from Emmalyn as she felt her body expand to accept his, felt her flesh wrap tightly around him. He moved slowly inside of her, driving forward and withdrawing, all the while kissing her, his shoulders quaking under her palms and instantly covered in a sheen of sweat.

Emmalyn was soon lost to his seductive rhythm, riding along with him on a wave of sensations she had never known before. Pleasure, desire, satisfaction, hunger—they all combined, spiraling around and around, emanating from the burning core of what had to be her soul, a place that Cabal touched with every masterful stroke of his body.

But soon something powerful overcame her, and she found she was no longer content to simply drift along with him. She needed more, had to quench an elusive thirst with a tonic she felt certain only Cabal could provide.

"Please," she gasped, unsure what she wanted from him yet meeting his thrusts and clinging to him as if her very life depended on it. She felt poised at the pinnacle of a wide, churning chasm, wavering unsteadily at the brink. Torn between a want to fling herself in head over heels and the knowledge that there would be no coming back from the fall. If she let herself plunge into the swelling abyss with him, she would never be the same.

"Cabal," she whispered, her heart nudging her closer to the dangerous edge of ecstasy's turbulent waters. "Please, Cabal. Take all of me now. Make me yours. . . ."

With a strangled roar that belied the depth of his hunger, Cabal gathered her close to his chest, bringing her torso up off the bed as he drove into her, rocking his hips in an urgent rhythm that nearly stole Emmalyn's breath away.

Something was building inside of her with every fevered stroke of Cabal's body. Something frighteningly strong, a great wave sweeping toward her, about to wash her far off shore. The alluring power of it stunned her, commanded her senses like nothing she had ever known. She could not look away from it, could only cling to Cabal like a lifeline as the shimmering wave hurtled toward her. It shattered against her in the next heartbeat, showering her from the inside out with glittering droplets of pure, exquisite pleasure. Tremor after tremor rippled deliciously through her body and down into her limbs.

Only then did Cabal resume his own rhythm, holding her

tight as he pumped into her without restraint, the sheer urgency of his lovemaking overwhelming her. Humbling her. He had waited to take his own pleasure until she was fully sated. That realization only made her want to give him more of herself now, despite her exhaustion. She moved against him, aiding the depth of his thrusts, whispering his name when hearing it seemed to heighten his arousal.

He drove deeper, harder, until with a strangled shout, he withdrew—a mere instant before his own release seized him, wracking his body with a series of savage tremors that brought him down on top of her. Holding her tight, he nuzzled his mouth against her neck, his chest resonating with the heavy beat of his heart, the labored rasp of his breathing.

"You're mine, Emmalyn," he whispered roughly beside her ear. "Tonight and forever, no matter what. Only mine."

"Yes . . . oh, God, yes," she answered, on the verge of weeping and terrified for how true she knew her pledge to be.

Chapter Twenty

The following day, with a supply cart packed full of wool sacks and foodstuffs to bring to market, Emmalyn, Cabal, a driver, and three mounted guardsmen set out for the Lincolnshire trade fair. Emmalyn had seemed troubled throughout breakfast, even suggesting at one point that they cancel the trip to market, or at the very least postpone it. She seemed loath to leave Fallonmour, even though she had been eager all week for the chance to trade her wool at Lincolnshire. It was not until Cabal reminded her of the garrison's need for weapons and arms that she relented at last and ordered the traveling party to assemble.

The journey took the better part of the day, carrying them leagues away from the pleasant tranquillity of Fallonmour and, by dusk, into the heart of a bustling city. The tradesmen were closing their stalls for the day, but hundreds of people yet milled about the streets and alleyways, some hawking wares, some their bodies; raggedy children begged all comers for food or coin while still other folk meandered aimlessly through the crowds of dispersing nobles and pilgrim travelers on legs made clumsy from overmuch ale and wine.

It seemed to Cabal some untold ages since he had last been around the press and stink of mass humanity. The fact that it had been little more than a week shocked him. The memory of his lovemaking with Emmalyn last night lingered with potent clarity in his mind, and in his body as well. It had been damned hard to remove himself from her bedchamber as the night waned into dawn, but they had agreed it would be best if the castle folk were not made privy to the intimate nature of their relationship.

Although to anyone with half a mind to pay attention, Cabal supposed that discerning their attraction to each other would not be too terribly difficult a feat to manage. While Emmalyn had trouble holding his gaze for any length of time beyond a heartbeat, Cabal could scarcely take his eyes off her.

She had bewitched him, this gentle, noble young woman. Not with the many endless facets of her stunning beauty, nor was it with the shattering purity of the passion she had shown him last night. Emmalyn of Fallonmour enchanted him without trying. With every glance and gesture, every word that passed her lips, Cabal slipped a bit deeper under her spell. He did not know what one more night in her bed would do to him, but he was more than willing to find out.

Providing the stretch of time before they would return to Fallonmour didn't kill him first.

Cabal was still brooding in frustrated impatience over his want to sweep Emmalyn off her horse and kiss her senseless when two of the guards returned from their quest to find shelter for the riding party in one of the many Lincolnshire inns.

"What did you find, James?" the lady asked. "Did you meet with any success?"

"Aye, m'lady, we found a place at the far end of town. 'Tis not the best quarters, I'm afraid, but most of the inns and hostels are already full. There must be something bringing people to town this week, aside from the market."

She nodded, seemingly unsurprised. "Then I reckon we should make haste ourselves and get settled without further delay."

When they reached the end of the street and stood in front of what was to be their evening's accommodations, Cabal cursed under his breath. "This is no bloody inn, man," he growled to the guard.

" 'Tis all there was in the city to be had, Sir Cabal."

"Then look harder. I won't have the lady stay here."

" 'Tis all right, really," Emmalyn said, laying her hand upon his arm and then drawing it back as if to catch the slip before anyone else spied it. "This will serve us just fine, my lord. We'll only be here for one night."

The inn, a low-slung structure of black rotting wood and moldy thatch, seemed more suitable for the whores and drunkards loitering outside the door than it did for a woman of Emmalyn's class and gentility. But she said nothing to betray her discomfort, riding along with her party to the back of the establishment, where they secured their mounts and gathered what they would need for their stay. They left the trade cart under the watch of the driver and one guard— plenty of security for the duration of the evening, for the wool sacks were enormous and far too heavy to be carried off now that they were packed full and sewn shut.

While Emmalyn strode past the curious onlookers and into the building with the other two guards at her side, Cabal hung back, assessing the scurvy assemblage of patrons while the lady made arrangements to pay their night's rent. He soon became aware of her distress over something the proprietor had told her.

"They have only one room left," she said when Cabal stepped up close behind her.

"One room is fine, my lady. I would not advise your lodging alone in this hovel."

"But to share quarters with three men . . . 'twould hardly be seemly."

He did not point out that no one in this place paid any mind to seemly behavior or propriety. "James and Albert can sleep outside in the hallway to guard the door." The knights nodded agreeably. "As for me, I shall sleep within, on the floor."

The innkeeper snorted and pointed them toward their room. Without a care for what her guards or the others in the hostel might think, Cabal took Emmalyn's arm and led her slowly down the dark hallway, surreptitiously revealing the hilt of his sword and making sure that if any of the other men had designs on the lady, they would know that he stood in their way.

The room could hardly be called such. It was a cramped little alcove that reeked of urine, stale smoke, and recent sex. The door would provide little use as a barrier against entry: It lurched at an odd angle, supported by only one leather hinge at the top of the battered oak panel. An old straw mattress lay rumpled in the corner of the small space; a moth-eaten blanket had been bunched up and evidently used for a pillow by the last tenant.

Cabal turned to Emmalyn, ready to scoop her up and deliver her away bodily from the filth of the place. "There must be a better alternative than this."

She shook her head, frowning at the darkness that awaited her. "There is nowhere else," she said remotely. " 'Tis fine for one night. Really, I will be all right here. We'll just have to make do."

"As you wish," he acquiesced reluctantly. He retrieved a candle from his pack and lit it, cursing the idea the moment the light traveled into each revolting corner and crevice of the cramped space. Gruffly, he sent one of the men out to get a blanket from the cart. The large square of wool was clean and worked well to create a makeshift pallet for Emmalyn. Cabal's satchel would serve as her pillow.

"Thank you," she told him as she removed her boots and settled in fully clothed. When the guards had been posted outside the door and Cabal had positioned himself against the wall at her side, sitting on the packed earth with nothing to cushion his body, Emmalyn rose up, frowning. "That cannot be a very comfortable place to rest."

A crash of pottery sounded from the main area of the inn, followed by a woman's sharp scream. "I do not expect to rest here much at all," he told her. "But you should try. Close your eyes, Emmalyn. I'll watch over you."

Slowly, she resumed her place on the pallet, curled toward where he sat, her eyes half-open and watching him in quiet contemplation. "I missed you after you left last eve."

He turned to look at her and could not keep from echoing her warm smile. "It was very hard to leave you," he admitted. "I came back to your door twice before anyone stirred within the keep. Both times I had my hand on the latch, ready to push it open and come inside."

"I would not have turned you away."

"I know, my lady. And that is the very reason I chose not to enter. 'Twould only make things more difficult for you, should your entire keep know that you have taken me as your lover so soon after learning of your widowhood."

She broke his gaze and toyed with the edge of the blanket. "Would it shock you if I said I do not care what people think? What if I told you that it does not matter to me who should find out about us?"

Cabal smiled, humbled by her frank admission but unable to accept such selfless consideration. "And how will you feel when King Richard is returned to England and you are sent away to marry one of his vassals?"

"The king may command my future, but he cannot command my heart," she whispered fiercely. "Until he's returned, I am free to live much as I wish. For now, I am free to . . . to be with whomever I choose."

Cabal did not miss the hitch in her voice, the sudden amendment of what she might have said on emotional impulse. Had she nearly said she loved him? The idea pained him more than it elated him, for if she did feel something for him, those feelings belonged to another man . . . the man she thought him to be. The man he could never hope to be.

For long moments he looked at the beautiful trusting face of Garrett's wife, remembering her sweet innocence of the night before, the velvet warmth of her touch. Wondering what he had done to warrant the pure affection he saw shimmering in her eyes. Thinking how he did not deserve any of the bliss he felt in being with her. How he would never have known it had it not been for Garrett's death. . . .

"Have I said something wrong, Cabal? You seem a thousand miles away."

"Just thinking," he said, but in truth, his thoughts were very distant. More than a thousand miles away, in Palestine. Farther even than that.

The base sounds of sex and drunken fighting in the streets and beyond their room carried Cabal back to what felt like a thousand years ago, back to his childhood. In fact, the longer he remained in the hovel, the less it bothered him. It merely served to remind him of nearly every night he had spent as a child traveling from town to town, keep to keep, with his mother and her troupe of entertainers. The presence of sex and violence had been as much a part of his childhood as eating and sleeping. But it was because of Emmalyn that he felt embarrassment now. Knowing that she was awake and listening made him sick with disgust and eager to speed her away from the ugliness of it.

" 'Tis late," he whispered, hearing the harsh grate of emotion in his voice. Hoping the dark would make the place more tolerable for her, he leaned over and blew out the candle. "Try to sleep now, my lady."

Her small hand reached out from under the blanket and curled around his fingers, warm and tender. So very sweet. " 'Twill help, I think, if I can feel you there beside me," she whispered.

For a moment all he could do was sit in silence, feeling her trace his knuckles with her soft fingertips. "After my mother died and I was first sent to live in London," he heard himself say quietly in the dark, "I used to tell myself stories when I could not sleep."

"What kind of stories?"

He shrugged, trying to recall what had fed his child's mind all those years ago. "All sorts, I suppose. Mostly boyish fantasies of slaying dragons and wooing beautiful princesses. Foolish tales, anything to pass the hours till dawn." A memory came back to him then, and before he could stop himself, he was telling her about it. "The tale I liked best was something my mother said King Henry had once told at a great feast she attended. 'Twas about a brave knight named Sir Lancelot."

"Arthur's champion," Emmalyn supplied eagerly.

"You know this story?"

"Some of it, yes. But I would have you tell me what you remember of the tale."

She snuggled deeper into her makeshift pallet, and Cabal began to tell her what he remembered of the life of the great white knight. He told her how Lancelot was rescued from abandonment as a young child and raised by the mystical Lady of the Lake. How he became the king's most trusted knight—Arthur's closest friend and the boldest champion of the realm. He told her the most troubling part of the story, too, of the noble hero's darkest hour, when he betrayed the king's trust and fell madly in love with the fair queen Guinevere.

As a boy, when honor and duty had meant something to Cabal, he had never understood how a few stolen moments with a beautiful woman could have caused a man like Lancelot to betray his friend. How love could make a man forsake his responsibility to his king and country. But feeling Emmalyn's fingers entwined with his, hearing her soft sighs as sleep reached out to claim her, he finally knew how Lancelot had fallen.

Cabal had not betrayed a friend to be with Emmalyn, but every moment he spent with her—every hour that brought him closer to telling her how much she was coming to mean to him—enmeshed him deeper in an impossible situation. Entangled him further in a seemingly inextricable deception.

He should have told her in the very beginning of the full circumstances surrounding Garrett's death. At the least, he should have made sure she knew before she had taken him to her bed. Now the situation was swiftly escalating out of his control.

Now he suspected he was falling in love with her, and he was not sure he could bear the thought of one day losing her. From some cruel corner of his mind, his conscience warned that he would never truly have her—God knew he did not deserve her—so long as he chose to keep the truth from her.

"Emmalyn?" he whispered haltingly. She did not respond, but her steady breathing told him that she had drifted into a peaceful slumber. Taking some measure of comfort in her restfulness, Cabal lay on his back on the cold hard floor and stared up at the shadowy rafters until morning at last began to break through the cracks in the shuttered window.

As soon as they finished their trading that day and returned home to Fallonmour, he would tell her everything.

Chapter Twenty-one

Cabal woke Emmalyn early and with a noticeable sense of urgency. He had already sent the two guards out to rouse the driver and the watchman, insisting that they get a start on the day's trading right away so they could be done with it and be off by midafternoon. He seemed troubled somehow, and very anxious to be back at Fallonmour. A feeling that Emmalyn shared.

The night spent in the hostel was among the worst she had ever endured, but despite the despicable accommodations, she refused to risk a visit to Josette's castle, a move that might well put her in the company of the queen. It seemed strange to her, how determined she had once been to be rid of Cabal. Now, seeing his handsome face smile upon her as he helped her gather their things to leave, Emmalyn could hardly imagine life without him.

Nor would she, until she was faced with the cold reality of the king's decision.

Emmalyn craved a bath to wash away the day's travel and the mustiness of the night's stay in the horrid little room, but she did not so much as entertain the notion of obtaining an acceptable tub of water from the innkeeper. Instead, covering her nose in the edge of her sleeve and trying to ignore the many slumbering filthy bodies littering the corridor and great room, she trudged along with Cabal out into the alleyway to meet the others.

The streets of Lincolnshire were already crowded with people come to trade. Great throngs of finely dressed nobles paused at the silk merchants' and spice traders' stalls, sifting through the bolts of lush fabrics and sampling the varied herbs imported from the East. The cacophony of heated conversations and gay laughter mixed with the complaining of penned livestock, filling the air with a near-deafening racket. Fresh fruits and vegetables perfumed the small spaces they occupied, but nothing could mask the stench of tanning hides emanating from the leather worker's shop at the end of town.

Emmalyn and her party ambled past the rows of foul stalls, following another cart laden with wool sacks to the area where the fleece merchants had assembled. The trade went quickly and in their favor, netting far more silver than Emmalyn had anticipated.

"The finest quality he had seen all week," she said to Cabal as she returned from the transaction, buoyed by the trade, jingling her fat purse and unable to keep from beaming with pride. She gave a few coins to her three men-at-arms and granted them leave to break their fast with instructions to bring back some bread and ale for the journey home.

"Don't be too boastful about your wealth, my lady," Cabal advised her when she drew near him, grinning even as his eyes scanned the crowd in wary observance. "Wag that purse around any longer and you are liable to lose it as quickly as you filled it. This town is swimming with cutthroats and vagabonds."

He was likely right, of course, and seeing his expression grow more stormy the longer they lingered in the market, Emmalyn became increasingly eager to be gone from Lincolnshire. "I have only a few items that I must buy while we are here: salt and candle wax and perhaps a skein of silk thread for embroidery," she said as the two of them rode along behind the empty wool cart. "It should take no more than an hour to purchase them and obtain the arms you wanted for the garrison. Then we can be off."

Her assurances seemed to afford him little comfort. With his watchful eye trained on the crowd now filling the narrow streets, Cabal told her, "I believe we passed a bowmaker and an armorer at the head of the avenue. Wait here with the cart and driver, my lady, and I will get whatever we need."

" 'Twould go all the faster if we split up," Emmalyn offered, dismounting to follow behind him as he paid a groom to brush and feed their horses while he traded. "I shall fetch the household goods while you see to the garrison's supplies."

Cabal scowled down at her in complete disagreement, but before he could argue that they should remain together, Emmalyn opened her purse and poured out a portion of the coins for herself. She tucked them into her satchel, then handed him the pouch containing the bulk of her trade. "So you will not worry that I will be robbed, you may take this. I will meet you here in one hour."

"My lady, I do not think—"

Pretending she did not see Cabal's dubious expression, Emmalyn stepped into the street. "Your trade will surely take longer than mine," she told him. "I shall wait for you over there, in the shade of the abbey wall."

Emmalyn afforded him no further dispute. She headed off in the opposite direction that she had sent Cabal, turning only to assure herself that he was not stubbornly following her despite her wishes. Spying his dark head moving above the others flowing up the street, she smiled. While she was anxious to leave and she did indeed have items to purchase at market, her boon at the wool trader's stall had put her in a generous mood. She wanted to find something nice for Cabal, something special, and she wanted her purchase to be a surprise.

As she walked briskly up the alleyway, various silk dealers and perfumers called for her to come peruse their wares. Emmalyn ignored them all. With swift steps and a light heart, she hastened instead toward the snaking corridor of the artisans' row.

Cabal found the armorers' shops easily enough. Situated where the avenue widened and spread toward the massive city gates, the many stalls were crammed with weapons of varying quality and purpose. Maces, swords, daggers, and battle-axes stood on display with crossbows and lances, while outside, the booths were surrounded by similarly diverse packs of mercenaries and knights-errant. Some were clearly the younger sons of noblemen, out to seek their fortunes in the city, while still others were gray and hard-eyed, seasoned warriors who appeared more interested in their drink than in obtaining employment from any of the wandering barons and wealthy landowners.

Among these dozens of fighting men were the wholly unsavory types: the cutpurses and murderers who frequently followed itinerant soldiers, too shiftless to make a living off their own sweat. Like vultures, they hung about at the periphery of the workingmen, begging for money or ale and greedy to make off with whatever scraps and refuse they could find.

Cabal clutched Emmalyn's coin purse a little tighter in his fist and strode through the crowds, up to the front of the line of merchants' stalls. He passed the shieldmaker's booth but paused briefly at another to watch a smithy craft a finely tooled sword on his forge. A nobleman haggled with a merchant over a similar blade, scoffing at the handsome price the man wanted for the piece before walking off to another shop. His customer lost to him, the seller turned to Cabal.

"Twelve deniers for a blade that will serve you well in this life, sir, and thereafter serve your sons and their sons after them. What say you? Twelve deniers for an heirloom. 'Tis a bargain at twice that price, sir." Cabal touched the smooth length of polished engraved steel, fingering the scrollwork and markings that decorated the gleaming blade. "'Tis inscribed in Latin, my lord. Read it for yourself and tell me if the verse would not be a testament to your line's courage and honor."

Cabal shrugged, looking at the indecipherable markings and suddenly losing interest in the exchange. "'Tis a fine weapon, but I'm not in the market for a sword today." He started to walk away.

"Might you be for ten deniers, sir? Perhaps eight, then?"

Cabal shook his head, chuckling as he left the booth and

headed to the armorer's stall to conduct his business and be done with it. In little time at all, he had procured a dozen crossbows and a supply of two hundred bolts, six longbows, and shields enough for half of the new garrison.

"I'll have a cart sent around to pick up the lot within the half hour," he told the armorer as he paid him the agreed-upon amount. He turned to leave the booth and nearly trampled a filthy wretch who stood too close, directly behind him. The beggar blinked up at him through long-unwashed stringy brown hair, his eyes bleary and ringed with dark circles. A lice-infested beard covered most of his face. Blocking Cabal's path, he thrust a grimy palm out at him.

"Spare a sou, lord?"

" 'Tis not mine to give you."

He stepped aside but the man followed, having evidently heard some of Cabal's transaction with the merchant. "Come now, lord, have a care for those less fortunate than yerself. I've been out of work for nearly three months now. Surely ye can spare a bit of yer coin for a returned Crusader. God would smile fondly on ye, were ye to bless me with, say, half a sou? Just to fill my belly for the night."

Fill it with ale, no doubt, Cabal thought, smelling the rank vapors on the beggar's tongue. "There's a man two stalls down calling to hire twenty lances today. As you claim to be a returning soldier, why don't you go and ask him for work instead of begging for coin?"

Cabal brushed past him and started to walk away, but stopped when he heard the man curse behind him. "Jesu! I do not believe my eyes! Can it be?"

Hearing the unmistakable note of recognition in the man's voice, Cabal's stomach suddenly lurched; a cold wash of sweat broke out on the back of his neck.

"Blackheart, is that ye?"

Rannulf. Cabal knew without turning around that the dirty beggar could be none other than his comrade from Palestine. The very same soldier who had been present in Garrett's tent that fateful night in September of last year. The one person who, whether Rannulf knew it or not, held the power now to destroy Cabal.

Hoping his expression was one of cool dispassion, Cabal faced him. "I think you've got the wrong man, friend. Mayhap too much ale has impaired your eyesight."

"Nay," Rannulf said, shaking his head. "Nay, 'tis ye all right. Do ye not recognize me, Blackheart? 'Tis me, Rannulf! God's bones, but I know ye remember me!"

"Sorry, no. I'm certain I have never seen you before." Eager to be rid of him, Cabal hoped the easy boon of a handful of coins would send Rannulf away. He opened the purse and dug around for a sum large enough to keep the mercenary mindlessly drunk for the better part of the day. "Here. Take this and be gone. 'Tis more than you asked for."

Rannulf took the offered coin, but it only seemed to put the glimmer of greed in his red-rimmed eyes. "Why do ye refuse to acknowledge me? Ye know who I am, Blackheart, just as I know ye."

"Get out of my way, drunkard, before I decide to move you myself."

The mercenary scowled. "Ye say you don't know me? Why, then, are ye suddenly moved to give me five sous to send me away?"

"Do you need more?"

The question caught in Cabal's throat, betraying the stifling press of panic closing in on him. He was trapped in a conversation he would pay anything to avoid. He knew it, and so did Rannulf. The mercenary grinned, a nearly toothless mockery of good humor.

"Ye've certainly done well for yourself, Blackheart. Half the men in our regiment came home to starve and scrape out a living on a land bled dry to pay a king's ransom. But look at ye. Fine silk clothing, well-shod feet, a purse nearly fat enough to choke an earl."

Cabal cleared his throat. "I have neither the time nor the interest to stand about arguing with you, man. You've got your coin, now take it and get out of my sight."

"Why, Blackheart, ye look as if someone has just tramped over yer grave. What are ye so afraid of?" The mercenary chuckled, rubbing two of his silver pieces together. "More to the point, what are ye willing to give me to keep my silence?"

The threat was more than Cabal could bear. He drew his dagger and flew at Rannulf, pressing the lethal edge up against the mercenary's neck. "I said, you are mistaken," he bit off tightly. "You do not know me. Don't force me to convince you."

He eased off and left Rannulf coughing and sputtering behind him. Shaking from the confrontation, his mind spinning to calculate the many possible ramifications, Cabal stalked away, praying as he had never prayed before that his implied warning would be taken seriously. Now more than ever it was imperative that he get Emmalyn out of this place and back to Fallonmour. Before she learned the entire ugly truth, and this damnable situation blew up in his face.

Emmalyn left the goldsmith's stall, dejected. She had hoped to find something unique for Cabal among the expensive trinkets and bejeweled items for sale at the market, but nothing caught her eye. Nothing seemed quite special enough. She turned back up the street in lethargic disappointment.

From within one of the stalls she passed along the way, a merchant called to her. " 'Tis far too lovely a day to look so sullen, my lady. Mayhap I have something for sale here that might cheer you."

Emmalyn smiled at the kind-faced old man and started to shake her head. Then she saw his vast array of leather-bound tomes and beautifully crafted tablets. Ever fond of reading and learning, she found herself drifting over to the bookseller's stall with little reluctance, willing to browse, if only for an indulgent moment or two.

"What do you like to read, child?"

"Everything," she answered, marveling over the intricately tooled leather binding that covered an illuminated manuscript of the Book of Psalms. Beside it was a text on herbs, the pages painted with illustrations depicting various plants and trees and spelling out their many healing qualities. "These are beautiful volumes, all of them."

"Ah, you see?" He clapped his hands together in apparent delight. "I told you I would have something here to cheer you. Which of these might you like to take away with you this morning, dear girl?"

Emmalyn laughed at how the twinkle in the old man's eye had gone so swiftly from kindness to commerce. "'Tis tempting, I assure you. But I am not looking for anything for myself today. I was hoping to find a gift for my . . . for my friend."

"And what better gift than a book?" enthused the old man. "A wise choice, my lady. Something for your friend to enjoy time and time again."

Regarding him wryly from under her lashes, Emmalyn quipped, "You, sir, are attempting to charm me out of my money."

He chuckled good-naturedly and came off his stool to stand before her. His movements were careful, halting with a pronounced stiffness of the joints, and when he selected a slim volume out of one of the stacks and presented it to her, his gnarled thin-skinned hands shook with the tremors of advancing age. "Mayhap your friend likes flowers, my lady? This is a lovely text devoted to pleasure gardens. I obtained it last summer while I was visiting on the Continent. I've whiled away many an hour perusing this book. In all honesty, I would miss it dearly; however, I reckon it would please me more to let you have it today for ten sous."

Emmalyn shook her head gently. "Thank you, but no. I don't think my friend would be much interested in flowers or gardens. Although he does enjoy tales of travel and adventure," she added, recalling Cabal's fondness for both subjects.

"Does he, now?" the bookseller asked, his rheumy eyes lighting up, but whether it was from Emmalyn's casual admission that her friend was a man or the merchant's anticipation of a pending sale, she could not be certain. "Travel and adventure, travel and adventure," he mumbled to himself as he turned and thoughtfully scanned his inventory.

Having gathered an assortment of texts, he came back to where she stood. One by one, he went through them, extolling their individual merits and listing their varying prices. Although each was lovely in its own right, none moved her enough to retrieve her coin.

"What is that one over there?" She pointed to a handsome volume that had been uncovered when the seller brought her the other books to consider. Rich enameling and precious gold leaf adorned the top of the deeply carved tooling on its leather cover, twinkling in the morning sunlight.

"Ah," the old man sighed. "You have fine taste, indeed, my lady. That is a history book, copied from a text commissioned by the first King Henry some twoscore and ten years ago. 'Tis the most exquisite—and the most costly—item in my collection."

"May I see it?"

"Of course."

His step growing more spry by the moment, the bookseller retrieved the ornate volume and presented it to her. Awed by its beauty, Emmalyn admired the cover in breathless wonder before opening it to the text within. " 'Tis about the kings of England," she mused. Carefully, she turned the crisp parchment pages, pausing to admire some of the colorful illustrations and exquisitely scribed passages.

" 'Tis an historic account primarily, but you will find 'tis also filled with tales of adventure, my lady." He flipped the pages and spread the book open for her at a certain section, gesturing to a painting of a handsome golden-haired monarch. "The great king, Arthur, was among the most daring rulers who ever lived. Why, I warrant the stories of his times alone are well worth the price."

"King Arthur, did you say?" Emmalyn's heart soared. Could there be any more perfect gift for Cabal? "I must have this book. Please, how much is it, sir?"

"As I cautioned you, my lady, it does not come cheaply.

I'm afraid that a book of this quality and import could sell for no less than a livre. . . ."

Dieu! She could buy the finest-bred ram and ewe at market with that much silver. Nevertheless, she poured out her coins, hoping she had enough. She counted out her money, aware that the old man was adding up the sum right along with her.

"I only have a marc and three sous," she said. For a fleeting moment, she considered trying to find Cabal to retrieve her purse, but if she wanted to surprise him with the book, the transaction would have to take place now. "I do not have nearly enough."

The bookseller stared down at her handful of coins, stroking his chin. He looked about as disappointed as Emmalyn felt, pursing his lips and letting out a weighty sigh. Then he gently closed the book and tucked it under his arm. She was almost tempted to grab the tome away from him when he abruptly turned and carried it to the other side of his stall, delivering it far out of her reach. His back to her, he took a length of fabric from a shelf beside him and wrapped it around the precious volume, perhaps to place it in safekeeping for another customer, one who could pay him what it was worth.

Feeling worse now than if she had never seen the book, Emmalyn put her money away. "Thank you for your time, sir," she said as she started to leave the booth.

"Just a moment, my lady," the bookseller called.

She looked over her shoulder and frowned in confusion. In his quaking hands was the book, swathed in linen and tied securely with a length of twine. The old man held it out to her, smiling warmly. "Today is my last day at market, you see. This eve I shall have to pack up all of these heavy books and carry them back home with me to London. I reckon I would rather lessen my burden and know that I made a lovely lady happy this morn. Will you take this book for a marc and three sous, my lady?"

"Yes!" Emmalyn cried, spilling her coins in her haste to surrender them to him. She scrambled to catch them all and placed the sum in his pale wrinkled palm. "Thank you so much! 'Tis more than kind of you to offer."

Chuckling, he pocketed the money and gave her the book. "I only hope your friend enjoys your gift as much as I have enjoyed meeting you, my lady."

Emmalyn clutched the prize to her bosom, her heart nigh to bursting with gratitude and joy. "He will be very pleased, I'm sure. And I will treasure your generosity always."

With an elated wave of good-bye, she left her new friend and hurried back up the street, anxious to meet Cabal and start home. She could hardly wait to give him her present. Her head was so filled with joy and pleasant ruminations over how he would react to an entire book devoted to his childhood heroes, she almost did not hear someone calling her name.

From the vicinity of a silk trader's stall, the hail came again—a dulcet female voice rising over the hubbub of the crowd. "Emmalyn! Emmalyn, for Heaven's sake, please wait!"

Unable to escape the inevitable encounter, Emmalyn turned to greet the young noblewoman. From the clutch of drably garbed people crowding the streets emerged Lady Josette of Beaucourt, a vision of wealth and style—from the top of her gossamer-veiled brunette head to the hem of her flowing kirtle of rich forest green silk. She rushed forth and embraced Emmalyn, pressing a quick kiss of greeting to each side of her face.

"I wasn't sure I would see you," Josette said breathlessly. "Did you receive my letter, Emmie?"

"I did, yes." Emmalyn nodded, smiling fondly to see her sister, even if she had hoped to leave Lincolnshire unnoticed.

"Well, I do hope you had planned to come visit me while you were in town, and not slip in and out without a word, as it seems you fully intended to do," Josette scolded lightly, sounding years older than her two and twenty summers. "When did you arrive?"

"Yesterday," Emmalyn said, "but I'm afraid I cannot delay

overlong; in fact, I'm off to meet my traveling party now. We depart for Fallonmour later today."

Josette gave her a perfect pout. "So soon? You must stay a while with Stephan and me at Beaucourt, Emmie! Queen Eleanor herself is in the shire and expected to attend our feast on the morrow's eve. Pray, tell me you will stay! It has been so long since I've last seen you."

"I'm sorry, I cannot," Emmalyn said, wishing she could spend some time with her sister yet knowing that her first obligation was to Fallonmour. She gave Josette's hand a gentle squeeze. "I'm afraid I have lingered overlong as it is. I should well be on my way."

"Then at the very least, I shall walk with you and say good-bye as you leave," Josette offered brightly. A snap of her slender fingers brought two of her maids scurrying to her side. "Besides, I want to show you what I purchased today."

Nodding, Emmalyn linked arms with her sister, and they started back up the street, heading toward the abbey, where Cabal had likely been waiting for some time already.

Behind the two sisters, following in their wake at a deferential but protective distance, were Josette's maids and several men-at-arms come from her entourage. A long-limbed page rushed forth from the group, carrying a portable awning of sorts. It was evidently his foremost duty to see that his lady's fair skin did not burn in the midmorning sun, for he trotted along at Josette's side like a puppy, his every attention fixed on keeping her head covered in shadow.

Emmalyn walked beside her sister, feeling rather like a peasant next to the queen. Yet for all her pomp and grandiosity, Josette remained sweet as an angel and entirely unfazed by the flurry of attentive activity—to say nothing of the number of people—that her going to market seemed to require.

"Aside from spending far too much on Stephan's favorite spices," Josette confided in Emmalyn as they strolled the avenue, "I indulged terribly and bought three large bolts of sendal, imported from Sicily. Emmalyn, you'll simply not believe the colors to be had this year! There is scarlet, of course, and various shades of blues and greens, but the most exciting find by far—and, indeed, the most costly—was the violet. Can you imagine? Oh, would that Mother were still alive. How she would have adored a gown of purple silk!"

"Yes, she would have," Emmalyn agreed.

Their mother had passed away peacefully some years before at the ripe old age of twoscore and seven. Thinking on her now made Emmalyn reflect, a bit sadly, on family and life. She had long missed her mother's counsel but took some comfort in the fact that she had her sister beside her now. Before she could stop herself, Emmalyn had blurted out the circumstances of her recent widowhood and the pending dispensation of Fallonmour.

"Oh, Emmie, I'm so sorry!" Josette grasped Emmalyn's hands and brought them tightly to her chest. "I know that yours and Garrett's was not an ideal match, but how awful this must be for you, so recently widowed. And here I am, prattling on about silks and gowns and spices. You must think me terribly insensitive."

"No," Emmalyn soothed, patting her hand. "I don't think so at all. You could not have known."

It seemed she was always calming Josette, from the time they were children. Emmalyn's sister had been a sunny child, the elder, but highly emotional and quick to burst into tears over the slightest worry. Having grown up coddled and protected, Josette could have easily become a spoiled shrew, but instead she had blossomed into a lovely delicate flower whom no one begrudged for her fragility, even now.

"Whatever will you do, Emmie? Is there aught that Stephan and I can help you with? Do you need anything at all?"

"No," Emmalyn said, shaking her head. "Really, I am managing well enough, Josette. Please don't fret over me."

"Don't fret? I can't imagine what I would do if I should ever lose Stephan. Oh, Emmie, you must feel so terribly alone."

"I was long used to being on my own, even before," she admitted gently. "And I am not entirely alone now. The king sent one of his finest men to watch over my safety and that of

Fallonmour. Sir Cabal has been a great help to me and the rest of the folk since his arrival. He is . . . a very special man."

Josette's brow creased slightly. "Special . . . ? Perhaps I should meet this man, Emmie."

Emmalyn felt a blush creep into her cheeks at her sister's knowing tone. "There he is now," she said, spying Cabal as he paced along the outside wall of the abbey.

The closer they got, she could see that he was agitated about something, wearing a track into the earth where his boots had tread back and forth apparently countless times. He looked up as they approached and began to hasten forward, only to stop short a moment later when his gaze lit on Josette and her entourage.

"I am sorry if I kept you waiting overlong," Emmalyn said as the group of them drew closer. He greeted her with a polite nod, saying nothing as the group of them approached. Emmalyn had never seen so much stress in his features. Cabal's mouth was a tight line, his eyes warily assessing the approaching clutch of guards, his forehead creased with a frown. "Josette, Lady Beaucourt," Emmalyn announced, gesturing to her sister, "meet Sir Cabal."

"Good day, sir."

Josette bestowed on him one of her guileless dazzling smiles, but Cabal seemed wholly unaffected. He offered a perfunctory greeting, then stared at Emmalyn as if he wanted to pull her aside and scold her for her tardiness. Instead, he handed her the coin purse and cleared his throat. "The armorer is holding our supplies, my lady. All we need do is retrieve them and we can be on our way."

"I have been trying to convince my sister that she should stay and visit with me, Sir Cabal," Josette interjected with a sly look in Emmalyn's direction. "She seems to think that she cannot afford so much as a night or two away from Fallonmour. I tried to tempt her days ago with an invitation to attend a grand feast I am hosting at Beaucourt, but not even the promise of the queen's attendance has been enough to persuade Emmalyn to come. Perhaps you can convince her that a short visit away from Fallonmour's worries will do her good, Sir Cabal."

Cabal looked from Josette to Emmalyn. "I was not aware that my lady had kin in Lincolnshire," he said, eyeing Emmalyn suspiciously. "Nor did I know that Queen Eleanor was expected in the area."

"I would have told you—" Emmalyn began, but he cut her off with a stony gaze.

"Perhaps we should stay, my lady."

"Y-you think we should?"

"At the very least, I reckon we should take this opportunity to make the queen aware of our recent trouble with Hugh de Wardeaux."

"Then you will come?" Josette asked excitedly, oblivious of the cold undercurrent in Cabal's voice. She did not wait for confirmation before hurriedly instructing some of her servants to hasten ahead to Beaucourt with the news of her sister's arrival.

While Josette issued orders for chambers to be prepared and refreshments to be assembled, Emmalyn slid a guilty glance toward Cabal. His agitation had only increased with this development, and most of it seemed centered on her now.

"I'll send the cart around to pick up the garrison's supplies," he said. "One of the guards will need to be dispatched to Fallonmour to deliver word of our delay."

"Of course," Emmalyn replied.

He handed her the coin purse and stalked away to make the necessary arrangements. Emmalyn watched him disappear into the street, troubled by his cool tone and brusque departure.

She nearly followed him to try to explain about Josette's letter and her want to avoid the queen after she had sent her appeal for help, but just then, from somewhere along the crowd loitering in the shadows of the abbey walls, a beggar rushed forth. He caught Emmalyn by the arm, startling her with the unexpected contact. "Spare a denier or two for a returned Crusader, milady?"

Josette gasped, one pale hand fluttering to her breast. Her men-at-arms advanced on the accoster, but Emmalyn held them back with a quick shake of her head. " 'Tis all right," she said.

"Please, milady," the beggar croaked, his breath reeking of ale and sorely neglected hygiene. "I've been out of work for some three months now—can't recall when I had my last meal. . . ."

"Emmalyn, really, we must be on our way," Josette called, looking utterly appalled at the filthy vagabond clutching her sister's arm.

The dark ragged hand on her sleeve bothered Emmalyn beyond reason, perhaps because it reminded her how fortunate she was to be healthy and well-fed in a time when many were starving in England. Feeling generous because of her boon at the fleece market today—and guilty for her indulgence over her own purchases and those of her sister—Emmalyn dug through her purse and deposited half a sou in the beggar's hand.

"Thank ye kindly, milady. 'Tis most generous." He grinned up at her as his fingers closed around her coins. "If it please ye, I should like to offer up a special prayer for ye this eve in chapel. Will ye tell me, madam, what be the name of God's own angel who delivered me from the pain of hunger today?"

"Emmalyn," she answered somewhat uneasily, finding herself increasingly eager to be away from this man. "Lady Emmalyn of Fallonmour."

It was difficult to see the subtle lift of his brows through the grime and unruly mop of hair that covered his face, but the reaction of surprise had not gone unnoticed. His eyes lit with a peculiar questioning light, the beggar bowed his head and began to back off into the crowd. "My thanks," he said, offering her a queerly disturbing smile. "God be with ye . . . *Lady Fallonmour*."

Chapter Twenty-two

In the day that passed since the trade fair, Cabal had not been able to see Emmalyn alone, much less find a private moment in which to speak to her. From the time they had arrived at the expansive Beaucourt Castle, Lady Josette had managed to keep her sister occupied and never out of her reach. She had sequestered her all day in the ladies' chambers and then cocooned her at last night's meal within a circle of noble guests and attendants. Cabal, meanwhile, had been left alone to brood with his troubling thoughts, alternating between what Emmalyn might decide to say to the queen when she arrived that evening and the more pressing concern sparked by Rannulf's appearance in the market yesterday.

For what had not been the first time, Cabal regretted that he hadn't simply done away with the potential threat right there in the center of the market. It would have been easy enough. The brigand had accosted him on a public street. Many had witnessed Cabal's sizable trade at the armorer's booth; who was to gainsay him that this beggar had seen the transaction, too, and then demanded some of the coin for himself? Who would doubt that he had posed a danger to Cabal's life as well as his purse?

Cabal's dagger had been poised to kill; it would have been no trouble at all to drag the razor-sharp blade across Rannulf's throat and claim the act self-defense, that he was only protecting his lady's hard-won coin from a desperate thief. Who there would have questioned him? Indeed, who would have cared?

Blackheart, Rannulf had called him in the street. What a jest the name was coming to seem to Cabal now! Blackheart would have laced Rannulf open simply for daring to call him thus in a public setting. Blackheart would have immediately recognized the threat that Rannulf posed and eliminated it—without hesitation or afterthought. Blackheart would have no cause to waste time cursing his mistake and dreading what his inaction might one day cost him with Emmalyn.

Being kept away from her was making him mad with impatience. He needed to see her, touch her, assure himself that she cared for him. Perhaps he needed to assure himself that he was not the same person Rannulf had known in Palestine. His time at Fallonmour had changed him. With Emmalyn, he was a better person. With Emmalyn, he had hope.

Deciding then and there that he would wait no longer to see her, Cabal strode into the castle with solitary purpose. He passed the furious activity in the hall, dodging the scurrying maids who rushed hither and yon with buckets of wash water and brooms. On the stairwell leading to the guest chambers, a troop of a dozen servants filed past him carrying fresh linens and newly made feather bolsters. The corridors on the second and third floors rang with the excited chatter of maids and attendants, everyone flitting about in nervous haste over the preparations being made for the evening's grand reception and a pending royal visitation.

Perhaps Cabal should have been anxious himself to think that he might catch a glimpse of the venerable queen Eleanor in a few short hours, but the only person he wanted to see at the moment was hidden away from him behind a thick oak door. He stood outside Emmalyn's chamber and waited for two serving women to pass by before he knocked. What greeted him was a vision of loveliness that verily left him speechless.

"Cabal!" Emmalyn exclaimed, her green eyes wide with surprise. "I thought you were the tailor come to finish my gown for the feast tonight. What are you doing here?"

She was garbed in a flowing kirtle of lustrous violet silk, the color of which he had seen only on nature's palette before. Thin ribbons of the same exquisite fabric had been adorned with small glass beads and woven into her plaited hair, the heavy blond coils gathered atop her head like a shining crown of purple and gold. When he could only stare at her in awe, Emmalyn grasped his hand and brought him into the chamber, pushing the door closed behind them.

"Josette insisted I should have something fine to wear at this evening's feast. Do you like it?" she asked, twirling before him and then looking up uncertainly. " 'Tis not quite finished; the tailor still has to sew on the edging and fit me with a veil and girdle. . . ."

Cabal could not see where the gown or the woman in it needed any improvements. The silk bodice fit Emmalyn's delicate figure like sheer perfection: clinging to the rise of her bosom and the artful shape of her shoulders and arms; following the curve of her tiny waist and the gentle flare of her hips the very way he wanted to follow her form now with his hands. The long, sweeping skirts fell to the floor in soft folds, emphasizing the graceful length of her legs. The toe of one intricately embroidered slipper peeked out from under the hem.

"You look . . . enchanting," he told her, struck beyond words.

She beamed, placing a quick kiss on his cheek. "I am glad you came to see me. I've missed you. I cannot wait for us to be back home at Fallonmour."

He flicked one of the tiny beads in her hair, watching it twinkle in the morning sunlight. "Yes, I can very well see why you would wish to be away from all of this," he quipped. "Would that your sister's tailor had outfitted you in sackcloth instead, my lady. I am loath to consider the sort of torture I will be forced to endure tonight, watching you bedazzle every man in the hall."

She soothed his sullenness with a brilliant smile, wrapping her arms around his torso and gazing up at him wide-eyed. "Why, Sir Cabal, I do not believe my ears! You are jealous!"

He was, although the idea did not thrill him half as much as it seemed to please her. He had no right to feel possessive of Emmalyn. No right to want to keep her barred in this room where he alone could admire her. Here, where she would see only him and have no time at all for the countless fancy lords who would surely vie for the beautiful young widow's attention at the gala this eve.

Would one of them be the man Richard would eventually choose for her husband?

Damnation, how the notion of her being wed to another burned him now. What he felt when he thought about her being sent to marry someone else surpassed jealousy. It nigh consumed him. Knowing it was only a matter of time before he would be dispatched to another mission, likely never to see her again, was as though a piece of him were being torn slowly from his chest. He was not sure he could bear it.

What was this desperate, aching feeling she stirred in him?

Looking down into Emmalyn's clear, warm gaze, Cabal felt some of his lingering petulant mood begin to melt away. She was his in the only way it mattered; the truth was there, if he could trust his eyes that what he saw reflected in her face was real. Although at the moment, he would rather feel her need for him, know it was as strong as what he felt for her.

Pulling her closer, he kissed her, letting his mouth cover hers, tasting the sweetness of mint on her breath as she opened her lips to him. His need jolted through him, hot as a flame, rocking him to the core. He tore away from her kiss, his body tense with hunger and quickening with desire. He trembled with the force of it. "God, Emmalyn, what is it you have done to me? I can hardly stand to be away from you."

"We'll be home tomorrow eve," she whispered, bringing his hand to her mouth and pressing her lips to his palm. "Everything will be as it has been. 'Twill be better than before."

But Cabal did not want to wait, not when every passing moment brought him that much closer to Emmalyn's learning the truth about the man he was. Being away from her was pure anguish when he thought he might lose her sooner than later.

He stared down at her in hungry silence, feeling a growl curl up from somewhere deep in his belly as she traced a line of kisses from the center of his palm to the tips of his fingers.

"It pleases me to think you are missing me," she whispered, her breath warm and moist against his skin. With her eyes trained on his, she slid her tongue around the callused pad of his index finger, then slipped it into her mouth, sucking it. Her gaze was innocent, uncertain, but her satin kiss was hot and deliciously brazen. Cabal's body went as rigid as granite.

"Emmalyn," he rasped, scarcely able to think straight, "you are playing with fire. I want you too much to abide being toyed with now."

To his anguished delight, she ignored his warning. She drew away from him, her lips glistening with moisture. "I don't want to wait another moment," she whispered. "I need you to love me, Cabal."

"I do." He said it fiercely, reverently, startling himself with the depth of pure feeling that swelled inside him with the voicing of that admission. He hated himself to think how unfair it was to tell her that when he still withheld a truth that might turn her against him forever. "God help me, Emmalyn," he said, too weak to risk losing her now, "loving you is all I want to do."

"Then show me, my lord. Show me now."

Powerless to deny her, Cabal bent forward, capturing her mouth in a fervent claiming, a soulful kiss, filled with all the passion and anguish that clashed within him in the heat of that moment. She said she needed him to love her, but he had never known a need so strong as the one he felt for Emmalyn. He had never yearned for love, never wanted to be loved as he did now.

"Please, make love to me," she whispered brokenly, shud-
dering against him as he let his lips trail down the curve of
her neck.

He reached around and unlaced her gown, parting the soft
fabric and letting his hands roam over the silky pleasure of
Emmalyn's delicate back. Cabal slid the lush gown over her
shoulders and let it pool at her feet, baring her and drinking
in her beauty like a priceless artifact revealed for the first
time. Slowly, he lowered his head, cupping the soft under-
side of her breast and bringing it up to his mouth. She
moaned softly as he caught the dusky nipple between his
teeth, coaxing the sugar-sweet pearl to a hardened peak
before turning his attention to its perfect twin.

He felt Emmalyn grapple with his tunic, her hands fisting in the fabric at his back, clutching and pulling at it
with almost mindless effort as she arched further into his
embrace, opening herself to his tender assault. Sharing her
frustration for the offending linen barrier, Cabal stripped the
tunic off and thrust it away. His sigh mingled with hers
when the bare flesh of their torsos met and pressed so deliciously together.

He wanted to go slowly, to savor every beat and nuance
of the moment, but his desire proved an urgent and commanding force to be reckoned with. All it took for him to
shed his hose and braies was the feel of Emmalyn's fingers
brushing tentatively at his waist, the subtle lift of her hips
against his hardened groin. Naked, his desire now unleashed,
Cabal's appetite for her was overwhelming.

With a hungered growl, he moved out of her embrace,
ignoring her little mewl of protest as he slowly lowered himself before her, raining kisses from her shoulder to her breast,
past her stomach and lower, to the tender ridge of her hip and
the thatch of silky golden curls at the juncture of her thighs.
Her breathless gasp as he opened her for his kiss nearly
unstrung him on the spot. The sweet, musky essence of her
body's perfume lured him in like a siren's song, the first heady

taste of her sending a bolt of lust coursing like fire through his veins.

She went rigid when he stroked his tongue around the swollen pebble secreted at the crest of her dewy folds, then seemed to slowly melt in his arms as he held her against him, gentling her with his mouth. Never had he heard a more enchanting sound than the soft cry that escaped her as her body began to quicken, her thighs trembling in his hands as he brought her to a frenzied climax, laving her with a savage tenderness that left his own loins heavy and straining for release.

He rose and scooped her into his arms, carrying her to the bed. Gently, he laid her down on the mattress, easing her onto her back as he covered her body with his. "I did not want to rush," he whispered, a rasping, frustrated apology. "Emmalyn, I need to be inside you."

"Then come, my lord."

Her sweet reply, the gentle way she opened her legs for him, was like a balm to the many ancient abrasions on Cabal's heart. He moved his hips forward, entering her with a deep, careful thrust that sapped the breath from his lungs and left his limbs rigid, his body awash in a sheen of perspiration. Emmalyn's gasp of pleasure fanned his ear as he slowly buried himself to the hilt inside of her. Her body flexed around him, the sleek, soft walls of her sheath caressing him with every stroke and withdrawal, coaxing him toward the edge of his teetering control.

Cabal's hope to prolong the moment shattered when Emmalyn started to move in time with him. "Give me all of you," she commanded breathlessly, arching up to meet his thrusts and urging him deeper with the heat of her kisses and the insistent pull of her hands at his back.

Before long, he was lost, overcome by desire and eager for release from the coil of pressure mounting in his loins. He clutched the coverlet above her head, rocking faster, harder, rejoicing in the look of erotic bliss that came over her as she bit back a whimpering cry and tensed beneath him, caught in the throes of ecstasy. Cabal followed her there in the next instant, shouting her name like a reverent curse as his climax seized him and his seed pumped, swift and hot, recklessly, into the haven of her womb. He trembled, feeling his essence fill her—this one last vestige of control, lost to him.

He had no idea how sweet being the vanquished could be.

They lay there, entwined and panting, for some long moments. Emmalyn embraced him, smoothing her hands over his sweat-sheened back, her heart thudding in time with his. He heard her breath hitch slightly; then he felt a small tremor begin to ripple in her chest. Praying he hadn't hurt her in some way, Cabal rose up on his elbows to peer down at her.

Emmalyn was laughing.

Cabal scowled. "I can't say that I expected this reaction," he drawled, finding it hard to feel wounded when her cheeks were still flushed from arousal, her eyes yet heavy-lidded and dusky with the embers of smoldering passion. "What do you find so amusing, my lady?"

She reached for the disheveled braid that had been coiled so neatly atop her head when Cabal arrived. The ribbons and beads hung in complete disarray now, a good number of the tiny glass orbs dripping off as she unfastened the skewed mass of blond tangles and let it fall down around her shoulders. "I spent most of the morning trying to force my hair into this absurd style," she said wearily. "I wager Josette would be positively scandalized to see it now."

"Ah, damn, Emmalyn. I'm sorry." Cabal rose up on his knees to assess the damage. Her hair was in a shambles and her beautiful gown lay in a heap on the floor. "'Twas selfish of me to come up here like this. Let me help you fix it."

He reached for what was left of the braid, but Emmalyn sat up and placed her hand over his, shaking her head gently. "I don't want to fix it, Cabal. It didn't suit me anyway. And I am very glad you came up here." She smiled at him, a sultry, kiss-swollen grin of pure sated pleasure. "I have something for you."

She scooted off the bed and crossed the room to pick up a small bundle that rested atop a clothing chest. Returning to the bed, she held the package out to him.

"What is it?"

" 'Tis a surprise. I found it at the market yesterday. I wanted to save it until we returned to Fallonmour, but it pleases me more to give it to you now." The affection he saw shining in her eyes both elated and wrenched him. He did not know what to say.

"Open it," Emmalyn instructed eagerly, climbing up onto the mattress and inching closer to him as if she meant to unwrap the gift herself should he hesitate any longer.

Gingerly, Cabal loosened the twine that held the linen wrapping together. He swept aside the fabric and stared dumbfounded at the exquisite object that had been inside. It was a book, a costly-looking volume, ornately bound and heavy with countless gilded pages. Intricate scrollwork covered the top of the tome, the leather deeply tooled with twisting vines and a large rose in its center, the petals spread wide, carved with such care, they appeared almost real.

Though his pride urged him to stop there, he was compelled to open the cover and peer inside. He turned past the first few pages, marveling at the many colors and illustrations contained within. Speechless with wonder and profound humility, he closed the book and set it aside.

"You do not like it?" Emmalyn asked, her voice edged with disappointment.

"No, I like it very much. In fact, 'tis the most beautiful gift I have ever received." He turned toward her and cupped her cheek in his palm. "I shall treasure it always. Thank you."

Frowning, she pulled away from him slightly. "If you like it, what is wrong?"

A soft, humorless chuckle escaped him, surely betraying the depth of his discomfiture. "Emmalyn, I'm a soldier, not a scholar. I've had no use for letters. I don't read."

"Then I shall teach you," she said gently. She reached around him and brought the book onto her lap, opening it to the inside cover. "We can start with the inscription I wrote for you last night."

Her slender finger following along on the page, she began to read the words she had written for him. *"To Cabal, champion of my heart. None of these great men can compare to the hero I have found in you."*

Wholly moved, he let the words soak in for a long while. Then he leaned in and kissed her. "Emmalyn," he said, hardly able to summon his voice he was so touched. "My sweet, dearest lady. I do not deserve such kind affection. You cannot know how much this gift means to me."

"Would you like to hear one of the tales now?" she asked, clearly overjoyed that her present pleased him. "I can read you something about King Arthur."

"Truly?" Cabal asked, his interest piqued. "The great king is mentioned in this book?"

"Indeed, his life is the most detailed account of all."

Cabal leaned back on the bed while Emmalyn stretched out beside him and flipped through the colorful pages. After some searching, she settled on a passage and began to recite the story of how King Arthur came to love and wed his enchanting Guinevere.

It did not take more than a few moments of lying next to her for Cabal to lose himself in the sound of Emmalyn's voice, no longer hearing what she read but transfixed by the movements of her lips as she formed beautiful words out of the jumble of confusion he saw scattered on the pages spread open before her. He could not resist reaching out to touch the delicate shell of her ear.

"That tickles," she protested on a soft gasp of laughter. "Now you have made me lose my place."

"I would be only too pleased to help you find it again, my lady."

Playfully, he moved closer to her, pulling her hand toward his lap and attempting to push the book aside, but Emmalyn held fast. She shot him a look of mock exasperation. "Never you mind, sir. Here is where I left off."

Ignoring his throaty growl, she continued on with the story. Cabal pretended to listen a little while longer, but mischief soon got the best of him once more, and he began to toy with the wispy hairs at Emmalyn's neck, blowing them softly and watching in sheer amusement as her skin prickled with gooseflesh. Each time she shivered, his body coiled a bit tighter, edging his self-control closer and closer to the point of breaking.

"My lady," he teased, tracing his finger down the length of her bare arm, "as you insist on reading to me about romance, I feel it only fair to warn you that my thoughts are becoming less chivalrous by the moment. It would not take much to persuade me to bar the door and hold you captive in this chamber, ravishing you for the remainder of the day and well into the night."

She slanted him a coy smile. " 'Tis tempting, but I don't think my sister or the queen would find that very sociable behavior on either of our parts. Perhaps I had better see if I can find something less . . . stimulating?" Giggling, she skipped forward in the book. "Ah, here is an account of King Arthur on the hunt. Do you think that talk of boars and hounds will pose any manner of problems for us, my lord?"

"My lady, I reckon you could read to me about the cleaning of the garderobe and I would still want to ravish you." His quip drew a gasp of shock from Emmalyn before she dissolved with him into a burst of delicious laughter. "Read on, if you will," he told her. "I will strive to control myself."

He closed his eyes and listened as Emmalyn recited a story about one day when King Arthur and his knights set off on a quest to hunt an exiled king-turned-boar. The wily Twrch Trwyth possessed between his bristly swine's ears the special instruments needed to slay an enemy of the realm. It was up to Arthur and his men to outsmart their foe and see the deed done. "The king had brought with him on this most important quest his favorite hunting dog," Emmalyn read, "and this faithful hound was named . . ."

When her voice trailed off suddenly, Cabal opened his eyes. "Pray tell me you do not mean to stop just when the tale was getting interesting."

She did not laugh at his mild jest. Her brow was pinched into a frown, and it seemed to be something of a struggle for her to hold his gaze. "'Tis getting late," she said quietly as she rose up from the bed. "May we finish this another time? We will have plenty of opportunity for reading together once we return to Fallonmour."

"Is anything wrong?"

"No," she answered quickly. Too quickly. Her smile seemed forced. "Nothing is wrong. 'Tis just that I have much yet to do before the queen arrives. Josette may need my help, and I still need to see the tailor about my gown."

She was making excuses, already off the bed and crossing to the door, ready to grant him his leave. Confused by her queer change of mood, Cabal retrieved his clothing and dressed. She would hardly look at him. Tying the laces on his hose, he glanced down at the book, which lay open still to the tale of Arthur on the hunt.

"May I take this with me?" he asked, watching her expression closely. He saw sympathy there, and something else. Something elusive that softened the line of her mouth so that it made her look on the verge of tears.

"Of course you may take it," she answered gently. "'Tis yours, Cabal."

He picked up the book, inserting his finger between the pages to hold the place as he then closed the cover and tucked the thick volume under his arm.

"I hope you understand," she said as he crossed the room to where she waited. "Would that we could spend the rest of the day alone together. We will have plenty of time once we are home."

At his nod, she rose up on her toes and placed a kiss on his cheek. "I will look for you at supper this eve," she told him as if she thought that might reassure him.

She seemed strangely melancholy as he stepped out into

the hall and slowly closed the door between them. Cabal waited for a moment, staring at the cold oak barrier, wondering what he might have done or said—what she might have seen—that caused her to react so peculiarly. What might have made her so anxious to dismiss him. He had the niggling feeling that he would find the answer in the book she had given him.

Taking it into the garrison's quarters, Cabal pulled a chair up next to the hearth and opened to the section that described the king's hunt. The black hash marks on the parchment meant nothing to him at all, just a mass of indiscernible pen strokes framed by an elaborate colorful painting that stretched down the side of the page. An emblem of a snarling, rampant red hound engulfed the upper left corner of the page, its tail curling and looping around itself like a vine, sweeping down the full length of the margin. Beneath the beast, clutched in its hind feet, was a flared banner that beheld a single word. A word that looked somehow familiar to Cabal.

He ran his thumb over the scripted letters, staring at the beastly hound as if it might speak to him, tell him what had so troubled Emmalyn when she had been reading these passages. But the hound kept its secret; the page remained a cryptic puzzle even though Cabal knew the answer was surely there before his eyes. He scanned the page, searching for some clue or pattern that would make it come clear for him, but in the end the exercise served only to make him all the more frustrated with his own ignorance.

"God's blood," he swore as he slammed the book shut. How could he think to decipher a sea of words when he could not even read the simple inscription Emmalyn had penned for him? To prove it to himself, he lifted the ornate cover and turned to the place where she had written those kind, undeserving words about him. He could not read it, but he remembered every word as though she were speaking it to him again. *To Cabal, champion of my heart. None of these great men can compare . . .*

Suddenly, his temples started to pound. Something cold began to coil in his gut, and his heart thudded heavy and hard in his chest. Dread crept up his throat as he looked at the beginning of her inscription once more. He willed her voice to slow in his head, pausing to look closely at each word, praying he was wrong. *To . . . Cabal . . .*

Calmly, with a deliberation that rode a mere hair's breadth ahead of the emotional storm stirring to life inside him, Cabal turned back to the place in the book where Emmalyn had left off in her reading. Now the red hound did not seem so much snarling as he did sneering, his lips pulled back, teeth bared as if in mocking, derisive laughter. Cabal's eyes drifted down the page to the bottom of the painted illustration.

From somewhere distant, he heard Emmalyn's voice again, reciting the last line she had read to him, the words becoming clearer as his gaze settled on the banner clutched in the beast's clawed feet.

"And this faithful hound was named . . ."

Cabal.

That was why she had stopped reading, the reason she was acting so queerly. And it hadn't been sadness he saw in her eyes as she dismissed him from the room, he realized now, but pity. She felt sorry for him. Cabal stared at the single damning word written on the hound's scroll. It was his own name. No, he thought bitterly, not his name. A beast's name.

And the fact that Emmalyn had not told him—that she had let him take the book with him, certain that his ignorance would keep him from figuring it out, wounded him. He had trusted her, allowing her to get closer than anyone ever had, and she had betrayed him. The realization cut deeply. More deeply even than the pain of knowing he had been branded a fool for the whole of his miserable life. A bastard given a beast's name by a father he never knew. How his noble sire must have laughed over the richness of his jest.

Cabal struggled to hold back the rising swell of his anger. His throat had suddenly gone parched, burning with the acrid bile of his lifelong untold shame. Inside he was empty, bereft by the knowledge that Emmalyn knew of his shattering humiliation, too.

Was she laughing at his dishonor now, or was she weeping for the fool she had chosen as her champion and lover? Damnation, but how could he ever face her again with any measure of pride? How could he ever bear to hear his name upon her lips when each time it would remind him of his shame?

Grabbing an abandoned tankard of ale, Cabal quaffed what was left of its contents. The bitter draught soothed him for an instant, but he found that the promise of inebriation only left him thirsty for more. He did not want to feel this pain. Not here, not now. If he could not choke it down by force of will, he decided as he quit the garrison's quarters, then he would simply drown it.

Chapter Twenty-three

Emmalyn had not realized quite how nervous she was to see the queen until she found herself curtsying before Her Majesty in Beaucourt's solar that evening. The lavish antechamber had been set up as a royal receiving room in prelude to the grand feast, with the queen seated in an elaborate cushioned chair brought with her from London, her favorite court maids assembled behind her like a colorful perfumed backdrop of sophisticated finery. Josette, resplendent in her new gown of red sendal, stood to the queen's right, motioning the queue of waiting visitors in, one by one, to make their proper introductions.

Though Eleanor of Aquitaine, dowager queen of England, could be no less than seventy years old, no one in the room or in the corridor immediately outside seemed able to look away from her legendary noble visage. She was thinner than Emmalyn had recalled—doubtless fraught with worry for King Richard, her imprisoned, favored son—but Eleanor still exuded flawless grace and the natural regality that had earned the matriarch her esteemed reputation throughout all of Christendom.

"Rise, my dear," the queen bade Emmalyn, her once crystalline voice a trifle rusty for her years. "It has been some time since I have last seen you, almost a year if memory serves. Fare you well, Lady Emmalyn?"

"Yes, Your Majesty. I am honored that you would ask." Emmalyn rose but kept her head slightly bowed in deference to the great lady seated serenely before her.

"We received Fallonmour's generous ransom contribution for the king's return," the queen said evenly. "Your gift is well appreciated, by myself and on behalf of my son."

"I am pleased that I could help, Your Majesty." Emmalyn dipped into a slight curtsy, but her heart sank even lower with dread for what was certain to come next. If the queen had received her ransom portion, she had more than likely also received her letter of appeal regarding Fallonmour.

"Come, stand here beside me." Eleanor gestured regally with her left hand. "I would like to talk further, but there are still many yet to greet this eve."

Emmalyn did as requested, standing patiently—if somewhat apprehensively—aside while the line of visiting nobles continued forward, richly clothed lords and ladies dropping into deep obeisance in the presence of their queen. Eleanor met each one with a placid kindness that clearly dazzled all who felt the warmth of her regard. Only Emmalyn seemed to notice the smooth efficiency of the queen's conversations, the subtle care she seemed to take that no one be allowed to linger longer than another.

The queen kept the line moving quickly while still managing to make every comer feel that he or she was special among the crowd. More the capable politician than her now deceased husband, Henry II, or any of their princely sons, Eleanor knew how to finesse her subjects. Her beauty had won her the most acclaim in the days of her youth, but it was her wit and keen intelligence that marked her as a force to be reckoned with, even now. As if she sensed Emmalyn's thoughtful observation, the queen glanced sidelong at her and offered her a sly wink before turning back to greet the portly lord now struggling into a clumsy bow before her.

During the space between his departure and the arrival of the next guest in line, the queen inquired, "I understand that you have increased Fallonmour's wool production, Lady Emmalyn."

"Yes, Your Majesty," she answered hesitantly, hoping the queen would not consider the venture foolish, as Garrett and Arlo both had. " 'Twas done gradually," Emmalyn explained, "growing the flock over the past three years. We had to sacrifice several fields to grazing, but Fallonmour now earns twice as much revenue from our fleece as we do from our other crops combined."

Eleanor's mouth quirked in mild approval. "A daring endeavor, but obviously not without merit. You will have to tell me more about this, my dear. Perhaps you will convince me to consider much the same with my own estates."

The queen then turned the full measure of her charm onto a young baron and his wife, accepting their gift of a silver chalice with a gracious smile that left the lady weeping and overcome with emotion. As the couple departed, Eleanor whispered discreetly to her steward to see that the expensive gift was added to the king's ransom coffers. Countless more like offerings were made and similarly received over the course of the next hour.

Between the comings and goings of her visiting subjects, Queen Eleanor kept Emmalyn occupied with pleasant, if brief, conversation. She asked after Fallonmour and the welfare of its people, surprising Emmalyn with her remembrances by name of common folk such as Bertie and Father Bryce, inquiring about Minerva's pregnancy and beaming with genuine delight to hear that twin foals were delivered whole and hale.

Somehow, although she tried to measure carefully what she said, Emmalyn found that with every mention of Fallonmour, she kept coming back to Cabal. It was difficult to comment on any aspect of her life without also bringing up his name and the positive effects of his having arrived at Fallonmour.

She told the queen of their recent troubles with Hugh and Cabal's clever means of fending him off, praising his skill in turning her garrison into a feasible army. She told how he had protected her at the festival and then rid Fallonmour of the thieves Arlo had hired. She could not hide her admiration, and it did not take long for the sage old queen to reach that very conclusion.

"This hardly sounds like the same man you so convincingly requested I have removed from Fallonmour, my dear."

So her letter had reached London after all. Emmalyn swallowed hard, regretting more than ever her hasty appeal to the queen all those days ago. "I warrant he is not the same man, Your Majesty," she admitted. "That is to say, I have revised my opinion of him greatly . . . having come to know him better."

The queen waited for another guest to depart before sliding Emmalyn a knowing glance. "You have some manner of affection for this knight my son dispatched to guard Fallonmour, do you?"

Emmalyn inclined her head, embarrassed that she had been so careless as to make her feelings obvious and well aware that the queen was watching her closely now. "I had not intended—" she began, then broke off abruptly, not sure what to say about her feelings for Cabal. "I don't know what I would do without him, Your Majesty."

"So, it would seem that the king's judgment was sound in this particular matter at least, was it not?" the queen replied dryly.

"It was, Your Majesty. But I never meant to question or imply—"

" 'Tis all right, my dear. A crown and scepter do not absolve a person from making mistakes. I myself made one some years ago. A mistake in judgment that sentenced a sweet young girl to a marriage with a treacherous, wicked scoundrel."

Was she speaking of Garrett? Emmalyn tried not to gape at the queen, but she could not keep the surprise and confusion from her face. Had the queen regretted her decision to match her with Garrett? Emmalyn had not expected Her Majesty to have given the matter a second thought.

For a long while, Queen Eleanor said nothing at all. Then she held up her hand to halt the line of guests and turned to converse with Emmalyn in confidential tones. "You have never asked me for anything, my dear, not even when you could have. But now you request my involvement in a matter that may well pit my son against me. Granted, if he should disagree with my meddling, it will not be the first time we clash. Nor likely the last."

Emmalyn saw frank devotion in the queen's eyes, an appreciation for her strong son that softened the keen gaze of a woman long used to being in control in a man's world.

"While I would be tempted to help you based on my fond regard for your grandmother, as well as a desire to make right a mistake that cost you much unhappiness, I'm sure you would agree that neither affection nor regret are enough to warrant granting you a fief such as Fallonmour."

"Of course not, Your Majesty." Emmalyn nodded soberly. "I understand."

"Looking after an estate is no easy feat, my dear. 'Tis a task made all the more challenging for a woman—particularly a woman alone. Aside from tireless devotion, it also takes a special brand of wit, integrity, and sheer brazenness: all qualities I have seen amply demonstrated in you." Stunned, Emmalyn looked up. "Oh yes, my dear. I expect you are quite capable. In fact, you rather remind me of me."

The queen's mouth arched subtly over her own mild jest. Emmalyn, on the other hand, was astonished beyond words or humor. She stared at the queen, agape. "Your Majesty, I do not know what to say."

Queen Eleanor motioned for one of her servants. "Fetch the royal counsel and tell him to draft a writ granting Lady Emmalyn full tenancy of the northern holding called Fallonmour." She glanced at Emmalyn thoughtfully, then added, "Provide as well that she be removed of the obligation of remarriage, and be free to remain widowed until such time as she should decide to wed again."

The attendant bowed, then hastened off to carry out the queen's command.

"B-but, Your Majesty, I had only mentioned my concerns for Fallonmour in my letter. I did not expect—"

"I know you didn't, my dear. You have earned Fallonmour. This last favor I do simply because I want to."

Emmalyn curtsied low, placing a reverent kiss on the queen's cool, thin-skinned hand. "Thank you, Your Majesty. I am moved, and so very grateful for your kindness and consideration."

Eleanor seemed uncomfortable with the impulsive show of affection. She withdrew her hand and sat up a little straighter in her chair, but Emmalyn saw the warm curve of her mouth. "I will see that you are delivered the signed decree later this evening, my dear. Now, let us get through this reception and on to sup before we both swoon from hunger. Perhaps you will introduce me to Sir Cabal before we dine."

Emmalyn could scarcely contain her excitement. She resumed her position beside the queen, beaming with happiness and flooded with relief. Her heart soared with the knowledge that she and Cabal were now free to be together. More than anything, she wanted to race out of the room and tell him the news.

In truth, Cabal had been foremost on her mind since their encounter that morning; despite her current elation, she was still reeling from her discovery of the origin of his name, praying she could puzzle out a way that he might never find out. How devastated he would be to learn the depth of his father's cruelty. She had let him leave in confusion over her abruptness to dismiss him, but at the time, she had not known what else to do. Now she cursed herself for finding that book, cursed herself for letting him take it with him when he left her chamber.

How she longed to be home with him at Fallonmour, tucked away in their private corner of the world. All that stood between her and that goal now was a few hours more at Beaucourt. Hours that should go all the swifter for the queen's magnanimous decision.

Waiting for the last guest to depart the solar seemed to

take forever, but finally it was time to assemble for the feast in the great hall. Josette, her husband, and Emmalyn escorted the queen into the large banquet room, taking their places at the high table, Eleanor seated between the two sisters. As the guests vied for optimum positions below the dais, Emmalyn scanned the crowded hall, searching for Cabal among the throng.

"Do you see your guardsman yet, my dear?" inquired the queen.

Emmalyn started to shake her head, but then she spied him near the entryway, his dark hair and broad shoulders towering over the rest of the folk pouring inside. Just seeing him again set her heart racing in her bosom, made her eager to be near him. "There he is now, Your Majesty."

When Emmalyn might have popped out of her seat to wave him forward, Queen Eleanor slanted her a quelling glance. With the most casual nod, she motioned one of her waiting minions to her side. "Fetch the knight known as Sir Cabal and bid him come to the front of the hall. We would have him dine below the dais this evening."

The servant wended his way through the scores of people, hailing Cabal as he got close to the entryway where the knight stood. Emmalyn watched with a slight sense of confusion as the look on Cabal's face faded from one of casual disinterest to something dark and unsettling. His footsteps seemed heavier than usual, his gait somehow unsteady when he fell in behind the queen's attendant and made his way toward the front of the hall.

Proud of him in this moment and hoping that her pleasant regard would set him at ease, Emmalyn smiled at him as he approached. He did not reciprocate. Staring at her as if he meant to pierce her with his steely gaze, he trod up to the dais. An awkward moment passed in silence while Emmalyn—and indeed, everyone seated already at the high table and pretending to be elsewise occupied—waited for him to bow before the queen.

Cabal's back remained erect, his broody gaze rooted on

Emmalyn and burning with unreadable meaning. She laughed nervously and endeavored to introduce him, inclining her head as a cue for him to act with the proper respect. "Your Majesty, 'tis my great honor to present Fallonmour's esteemed defender, Sir Cabal."

His lips curved sardonically at Emmalyn's polite introduction, but he gave his full attention to the queen then, bowing as aptly as any had thus far that night. "A pleasure to meet you, Your Majesty," he murmured, the edges of his speech oddly blurred to Emmalyn's fine-tuned ear. She scented wine on his breath and realized in wild alarm that he had been drinking.

The queen was peering at him through slightly narrowed, assessing eyes, her expression studious, as if she might have recognized him from somewhere before. "I understand you served my son, the king, in the war against Saladin."

He gave an idle nod. "I did."

"Your faith and honor are to be commended, sir." Queen Eleanor bestowed on him a smile that would have charmed legions of soldiers, yet Cabal remained impassive. "Did you know that I myself took up the Cross for my king? My ladies and I traveled to Jerusalem during the second of the church's wars with the infidels. 'Twas many, many years ago, when I lived in France, but I still remember as though 'twere just yesterday the very instant we disembarked and I laid eyes on that veritable sea of desert sand. And as well," Eleanor added gently, "I recall how grateful I was to be home again."

"Indeed, Your Majesty."

Irked with Cabal's current reckless state and his seeming lack of appreciation for the queen's endeavor to engage him in pleasant conversation, Emmalyn eagerly broke in. "Not only did Sir Cabal serve King Richard on Crusade, Your Majesty, but he was also acquainted at one time with your husband, King Henry."

"Really," the queen inquired, her slender brows quirking in interest. "I thought there was something familiar about your face, Sir Cabal. Were your family members of the court, then? Perhaps I might know of your parents."

Cabal's startling bark of laughter was a mere shade away from insult. "No ... I do not think so, Your Majesty. My mother had met the king only briefly before, and my father ... well, my father was unknown to me. I'm afraid that Lady Emmalyn, in her enthusiasm, has made it seem more than it was—"

"The king arranged for Cabal to come to London when he was orphaned as a young boy," Emmalyn supplied, trying not to let his mordant, red-eyed countenance disturb her as she strived to patch his flagrant breach in decorum. " 'Twas at King Henry's own direction that Cabal was enlisted as a guard in the royal garrison, Your Majesty."

"How interesting," the queen remarked, her cunning gaze now fixed on Cabal's face in calculated appraisal. " 'Tis no small feat to have won my lord husband's favor in such a way. He was not known for his benevolence, particularly to those outside his circle. At times, not even to those within."

Eleanor was likely referring to her ten-year imprisonment, her internment—and subsequent release—ordered by Henry himself. It had been harsh punishment for the mother of his children, whom he accused of poisoning his sons against him. Emmalyn felt sorry for the queen for having that blemish among the memories of such an exalted life, but perhaps worse was the common knowledge of her husband's many affairs while Eleanor was removed. King Henry's purported by-blows were scattered across England and deep into the Continent.

On the heels of that thought, and for the first time, Emmalyn paused to consider the noble qualities of Cabal's features: his broad forehead and piercing gray eyes, his sharp cheekbones and patrician nose, his firm-set square jaw. She considered this bastard knight's proud carriage and regal bearing.

And now, she wondered. . . .

"Fascinating to make your acquaintance, Sir Cabal," the

queen said, breaking into Emmalyn's thoughts. "We have reserved a place of honor for you there at the front table. My manservant will show you to your seat for the meal."

Cabal executed a courtly bow, shooting a flat stare in Emmalyn's direction before following the queen's minion to the trestle table foremost below the dais. He had been seated facing directly across from Emmalyn, where he continued to stare darkly up at her—almost accusingly, she thought—as the feast commenced. He blatantly ignored the attempts his table mates made to introduce themselves, preferring instead, it seemed, to further pollute himself with wine.

Emmalyn cringed when he called a serving page over to fill his cup, then snatched the entire flagon away from the lad and kept it for himself. She prayed the queen had not taken notice of his surly behavior with her, and wondered why he would risk such continued recklessness when he knew how much this night could mean to them. Deciding to make the best of the distressing situation, Emmalyn strived to keep her mood light, trying to participate in the conversations at the high table and see that the queen was equally diverted.

Josette was a tremendous help in that endeavor, chattering brightly throughout the first three courses about one pleasantry or another, carrying the queen from topic to topic with consummate social adeptness. For once, Emmalyn was thankful for her sister's faultless charm. Emmalyn herself would have been no use; her attention kept drifting to Cabal, the seeming stranger seated before her. He stared hard into his tankard, shoulders sagging under the weight of whatever was pressing him into such broodiness, looking for all the world like this was the very last place he wanted to be. Like he was trapped.

Emmalyn was suddenly reminded of the story he told at Fallonmour's midsummer festival, about the old lion he had captured and caged on campaign. She recalled how Cabal had said the beast was tired and worn, yet fully capable of striking down any one of the men who goaded him from outside the cage if he so wished.

Cabal had that very look about him now.

Vaguely, unable to take her eyes off Cabal, Emmalyn listened to the conversations buzzing about the dais: To her right Josette's tinkling laughter rang like a dozen tiny bells, and to Emmalyn's left, seated some three chairs down from her at the high table, one of the visiting barons droned on about the sorry state of his demesne and how the peasants were getting beyond themselves with all their recent talk of rights and demands for fair treatment by the noble classes.

"I tell you, the serfs must be watched closely and controlled," the baron said in a low voice. "They are no better than animals, the lot of them. They would breed like vermin if we allowed it."

"Let them," one of the other men commented on a rich chuckle. "All the more able bodies to one day work your fields, Lord Spencer."

From there, the men's exchange soon dissolved into a light discussion of the Lincolnshire market and the various new imports to be found this season, Lord Spencer bemoaning the steady increase in prices for all things shipped from abroad. This evidently reminded another lord of a story he had heard about a villein gone to market for the first time. With a great deal of humor, the nobleman recounted how the peasant had entered the trade square leading a pack of donkeys, offending all with his commoner's stench and filthy appearance.

"This vile creature wandered by several shops," the young lord said jovially, "but when he happened upon the perfumer's stall, why, he fainted on the spot."

"Fainted?" someone repeated. "Doubtless the miscreant was diseased in some manner."

Several people at the high table offered further suggestions of what might have caused the peasant to swoon, but the nobleman telling the tale only gave a little chuckle and continued. "No one could puzzle out what had caused this

man to react so queerly. That is, until a lad of about five
summers—holding his nose for the stench rising off the
prostrate peasant—suggested that the unaccustomed, pleasing
smell of the merchant's perfumes might have shocked the
villein senseless."

"For pity's sake," one of the ladies exclaimed, aghast.

"Evidently the boy was correct," the young lord concluded,
to the tittering amusement of all who listened at the high
table. "The townsfolk brought the peasant back to his wits by
holding a shovel full of manure under his nose, then promptly
sent him on his way."

An answering wave of jocularity swept the dais, the light
mood echoed by the many swelling conversations and gen-
eral enjoyment of the others seated in the hall. By contrast,
Emmalyn and Cabal were each enveloped in a certain
apprehensive silence, neither of them participating in the
mealtime talk, both so clearly anxious for the night to end.

Emmalyn might not have even noticed that the high table
had been cleared and readied for another course had the
guests seated around her not gasped their pleasure at the
most recent delicacy presented to them. A large assortment
of fruit tarts and honey cakes covered a gleaming silver tray,
the varied colors and blended citrus-sweet aromas setting
even Emmalyn's mouth to watering.

"Fig tarts, Your Majesty," Josette announced as she gestured to the sampling of exotic fruit confections spread out
before the queen. "As well as glazed oranges, quince cakes,
and spiced pomegranates—all for your pleasure this evening."

"Such a lovely temptation, my dear. I believe I may have
to sample one of each," Eleanor declared to her hostess's
obvious delight.

Once the queen had taken her choice of the desserts, the
tray was then carried to each person at the high table. When
it got to Lord Spencer, the irritating baron three places
down, he reached out and greedily shoveled a handful of the
richest-looking treats onto his trencher.

"I vowed I'd never eat another fig after I returned home

from Palestine," he remarked, chuckling around a mouthful of the imported fruit. "I had a serving woman in Jerusalem who put the accursed things in every dish she prepared for me. I tell you, I nearly thought I would perish, I got so sick of eating them."

"You were on Crusade, then, Lord Spencer?" someone inquired.

"Aye, indeed I was. I spent two years in Palestine, pledged in service to God and my king." The baron's voice had taken on a self-important timbre, clearly meant to impress all within earshot. "'Twas a proud time for England, and a glorious adventure for all who rode on behalf of Christendom."

A muffled but derisive snort came from the direction of Cabal's table. Emmalyn glanced to him in warning, eternally thankful when one of the young lords spoke at nearly the same moment, inquiring after the baron's recollections of the Holy City. "Were the streets really paved with gold as I have heard, my lord?"

Lord Spencer chuckled. "I had heard much the same tales, lad, however, the only gold I saw was secreted within the many heathen temples. Nevertheless, I found Jerusalem to be a lovely city, indeed. I daresay 'twould have been a thoroughly enjoyable pilgrimage if not for the terrible heat and the crowds of beggars filling nearly every alleyway and public courtyard."

"Mayhap they would not have been so beggarly had the Crusaders not burned every grain store and field in their path."

At Cabal's muttered comment, Emmalyn held her breath, hoping that she was the only one at the high table who had noticed the brash remark. A silent prayer sent heavenward that the night would pass without further incident shattered an instant later when Lord Spencer asked, "Am I to assume that you were there as well, sir?"

"I was." Cabal's answer was a caustic growl as he rose from his seat at the trestle table. "I fought in Palestine nigh on three years, but I am trying to think what place you speak of that it could differ so from the Jerusalem I knew."

Emmalyn saw the hard lines of anger creep into his features, knew his smile was tight with malice. "Cabal, no," she whispered under her breath as he drained his cup and clumsily set it down on the table.

"No gold in the streets, you say? Indeed not, but then how could anyone be sure? Jerusalem's streets ran ankle-deep with Saracen blood on the day I marched through the city."

A pall of silence now cloaked the hall, everyone shocked with this unseemly interjection. Emmalyn wanted to beg Cabal to cease, but her voice was nowhere to be found. She could only stare at him, fearful of what he might say yet compelled to let him speak.

"While you noble officers remained leagues away from the fighting, gorging yourself on figs and sleeping on clean sheets with servants to see to your every need, the soldiers took to their pallets hungry each night but too sick from exposure to eat. We bedded down sometimes a dozen to a tent, all of us caked in sweat and blood. Most of us didn't dare sleep for fear that the rats or desert predators would come to feed if we chanced to close our eyes.

"What lingers best in my memory is a hot summer day in August of last year," Cabal said with chilling calm. "An assemblage on a hill outside the city of Acre, where the English forces had grouped together more than two thousand prisoners of the Cross, including their wives and children—"

"That is quite enough!" Lord Spencer barked, his corpulent cheeks turning an unhealthy shade of crimson. "You, sir, have had too much wine with your sup. I warrant there is no one here who wants to hear your drunken ramblings—least of all, your queen!"

But Eleanor said nothing. She sat in stoic silence as Cabal continued, his voice distant and hard with rage. "Like vicious animals, we slaughtered twenty-seven hundred innocent people on that hill."

"Oh, Stephan!" Josette cried. "Please, make him stop!" But even Josette's husband seemed too shocked for words, staring at Cabal in mute astonishment, as if the devil himself had come to dine in Beaucourt's hall.

"We cut them to pieces in a matter of moments," Cabal added woodenly, his haunted gaze now sliding to Emmalyn, who stood with her hand at her breast, shielding the ache in her heart. "When it was done," he continued, "a few stayed behind to sift through the bloody remains, looking for any gold or jewelry that the prisoners might have swallowed before we captured them." Cabal's chuckle was brittle, humorless. "Such a proud time for England, wouldn't you say?"

On the other side of the queen, Josette let out a little gasp and swooned, slumping daintily into her husband's arms. While the dais and the rest of the hall erupted into shocked exclamations, Emmalyn could only stare at this bitter, wounded man that she so loved, aching for his pain and wondering if she would ever know him fully.

"Oh, Cabal," she whispered, feeling hot tears leak from her eyes to stream down her cheeks. She reached out to him, ignoring the shocked gasps of the other guests—not even pausing to see if her compassion for him in this moment would anger the queen.

She said his name again and nearly jumped out of her skin at the sharp bark of sarcasm he spat back at her. "Don't call me that," he said harshly, his eyes blazing with anger and pain. "Don't ever call me that again."

He knew.

Oh, God, Emmalyn thought desperately, somehow he knew about his name. Cabal looked at her now, his eyes blazing with emotion, as if she had been the one to wound him. As if she had betrayed him. Heaven help her, but in not telling him about his name, in letting him puzzle it out on his own, mayhap she had betrayed him. Mayhap even more so than his negligent sire.

With a final scathing glance at her, Cabal turned abruptly

and quit the hall, storming past the sea of stunned faces in a veritable thunderhead of rage.

"Your Majesty," Emmalyn said, pivoting at last to face the stoic, unruffled expression of the queen. "I am . . . so sorry."

She did not wait for royal reprimand or pardon. Her heart breaking for Cabal's certain pain, Emmalyn stepped away from the high table and dashed off the dais. Scandalized whispers and aghast expressions of disbelief for what had just transpired before the queen and the other hundred guests followed her flight from the hall. Emmalyn paused for none of it, running out into the torchlit corridor and along the snaking hallway toward Cabal's retreating form.

Her frantic steps brought her up behind him, several paces from the arched entry of the pentice that led out to the bailey. "Cabal, wait! Please!"

He kept walking, more purposeful now, his hands fisted at his sides, his gait strong, angry, unrelenting. Emmalyn followed him through the dark, tunneled gateway of the pentice and out to the courtyard beyond the keep stairs. A steady rain had begun outside, casting big, heavy drops from the canopy of a starless night sky. Cabal stepped out into the midst of the deluge, intent, it seemed, on leaving her behind.

"Cabal, I know you are hurting, but please, talk to me!"

"Go away, Emmalyn," he called without turning around. His voice sounded strangled, thick with fury and emotion. "Leave me alone."

"Cabal, please wait."

"Go back inside, my lady. That's where you belong."

Emmalyn caught up with him and reached for his arm. "I belong with you, my lord. You are all that matters to me."

He swore, tearing himself out of her grasp and rejecting her declaration with a harsh, self-directed oath. "I'm a fraud, Emmalyn. God's blood, I'm worse than a fraud. I am nothing."

"No, you are not. Don't say that."

"What an idiot I've been," he scoffed. "Gone about all my life never knowing I'd been branded a fool!"

"Stop it," she croaked, on the verge of tears, she hurt so badly for him. "Don't say such things. Do not even think it."

He laughed suddenly, a terrible, pain-filled sound. "Come now, my lady. Don't you see the humor in this? I'm a god-damned walking jest!"

He reached into the neck of his tunic as he strode away from her, savagely working to rip something free. It took only an instant for Emmalyn to know what it was. "Cabal, don't," she said miserably as he whirled around, full of rage.

Ignoring her, he pitched his father's ring against the stone wall of the tower keep. It sparked high on the jagged bricks with the force of his anger, the sharp metallic *ping* as it hit the wall making Emmalyn flinch. It dropped to the ground then, swallowed up by a pool of muddy water.

"I'm sorry I didn't tell you," she said as he headed deeper into the rain. "I should have, but I didn't want to see you hurt. Please, Cabal, let me help you."

"I don't need anyone's help!" he barked, putting distance between them. "I'm not some misfortunate waif in need of your nurturing, Emmalyn, and I don't need your damned pity. Christ, all I need is to be left alone."

"No, you don't," she challenged stubbornly. "Being alone is the last thing you need. I think you've been alone far too long."

"Don't push me, Emmalyn," he warned sharply.

"No," she said, feeling her frustration claw at her. "You seem to be the one intent on pushing tonight, Cabal. In fact, I think at present you would push me away from you for good, given half a chance. That's what you were trying to do in the hall, was it not? You thought you could turn me against you with that horrific account of the prisoners' slaughter. Look at me, my lord. I am still here."

She saw his step falter and slow, but he was still walking away from her. Still intent on rejecting her love, the same as he rejected everyone else's affection.

"Don't you understand?" she cried, desperate to reach him. "You give your name honor, Cabal. The way you choose to live your life now gives it meaning. It doesn't matter what you have done in your past. It doesn't matter what you are called."

"It matters to me!"

"That's it, then?" she shouted when his angry strides carried him almost out of her sight. "You expect me to just let you walk away like this?"

He did not answer, and chasing him was only pushing him farther away. Emmalyn stopped where she stood, letting the rain drench her, feeling it soak her hair and ruin her gown. "Cabal," she called after him, "Cabal, I love you!"

He stopped and spun around to face her then, chuckling. "No, my lady. There you are wrong." How cold his voice was now, sharp as the edge of a blade. It lacerated her, but not nearly so terribly as did his hard eyes. "If you really want to know who's been sharing your bed these past days, ask those assembled in the hall. Ask the queen. They'll tell you who"—he scoffed suddenly—"they'll tell you *what* I really am."

Emmalyn stared into his bleak gaze through the pelting rain, recalling his detachment, his determined reluctance to get involved with her and her folk. She recalled how easily he had slain the robbers who attacked her, how coldly efficient he had been. Now she was beginning to understand his self-imposed solitude, his eagerness to push away anyone who threatened to get too close to him. He could not risk attachments. He could not risk feeling because of who he was, what he had been bred to be.

"Blackheart . . ." she breathed, feeling the epithet leak out of her, a barely audible gasp of air.

Cabal's mouth twisted into a ruthless half-smile. "Now tell me how much you love me, Emmalyn."

He turned on his heel and left her standing there, shaking, numb with shock as he stalked into the darkness, vanishing all at once behind the curtain of blinding rain. Emmalyn's tears mingled with the wetness that streamed down her cheeks and off her chin. She stood in the dark emptiness of the bailey, soaked by the swelling downpour, the weight of her drenched skirts making it hard to withstand the heavy burden of her heart.

She did love him. Heaven help her, but she had never loved anyone the way she loved this man. This fierce, formidable, frightened man who was so convinced he needed no one.

Emmalyn turned, forlorn, and headed back for the castle. A glint of metal reflected faintly out of the mud, catching her eye as she neared the towering wall: Cabal's discarded ring, all but concealed in the swirling, thickening mire. She bent down and retrieved it, clutching the knot of cold metal and stone to her bosom, the only piece of him she might ever be able to hold close again.

Chapter Twenty-four

Cabal was nursing a wicked headache by the time morning dawned that next day. He had spent the night outside—where, specifically, he could not recall. Never one to imbibe so carelessly, he was disgusted with himself to think back on his spectacle of the night before. Once he was conscious, finally able to peel his eyes open and drag himself back to the castle at Beaucourt, he was certain of only one thing: He had an apology to deliver.

He could not be sure how it would be received; he had behaved appallingly. The maid who granted him entry to the antechamber to await his requested audience gaped at him in utter shock when she opened the door and saw him standing there. He had freshened up a bit, but no doubt he still looked as awful as he felt. He took the seat the servant girl offered him and watched as she disappeared behind another door to inform her lady that a visitor had arrived.

Cabal waited the long moments it took for the maid's return; then, at her bidding, he followed her into the lush chamber on the other side of the wall.

"Sir Cabal," Queen Eleanor said as he dropped into a humble bow before her. "I trust you have not come this morn to regale me with more grisly accounts of your time on Crusade."

"No, Your Majesty," he replied, chagrined to hear her sardonic tone. "I have come to offer an apology for my actions last eve. I had no right to behave the way I did."

278

"No, you did not," she agreed mildly, then bade him rise to speak freely with her.

A pointed glance at her attendants sent the women out of the room, but two armed knights remained poised at either side of her cushioned chair. Bodyguards meant to protect the dowager from a possible madman, no doubt.

"Your Majesty, I have come to apologize and seek your pardon, but also to make a request."

Eleanor's brows arched. "This is becoming quite a sennight for requests of royal favors," she quipped supremely. She leaned back in her seat, a vaguely bored stance that she likely adopted for many a solicitous visit. "What is it you would seek this morning, Sir Cabal?"

"Granted, I have no right to appeal to you for anything," he began, surprised to realize just how nervous he was in the queen's presence. But it wasn't apprehension for the mother of his king that made his palms sweat now; it was the understanding of what his self-pitying, reckless negligence might have cost the woman he loved. "Your Majesty, my behavior at the feast last eve was reprehensible. I can think of nothing to say that would excuse it, but I beg you, do not allow my careless actions to reflect poorly on Lady Emmalyn. The blame—and Your Majesty's reproach—should rest squarely on me."

Queen Eleanor's eyes narrowed slightly; her chin lifted an almost imperceptible degree. "You have come to seek my benevolence on behalf of Lady Emmalyn?"

"I have, Your Majesty. I care not what should happen to me, but I need to know that she—that Lady Emmalyn—will not suffer your disapproval for her association with me."

"I see," said the queen. "Would it surprise you to know that I received a similar request some hours ago from her?"

"Your Majesty?" Cabal frowned, astonished.

"She came to me, asking that I hold her accountable for your unseemly outburst at supper. She endeavored to have me pardon you, Sir Cabal, for she felt that she was in some way responsible for contributing to your distress last eve."

Cabal bit back a curse. "No. 'Twas my fault, Your Majesty. She had nothing to do with it—"

Eleanor silenced him with a gentle shake of her head. "Leave us," she instructed the two guards who flanked her. They departed the chamber at once. The queen then regarded him with assessing, watchful eyes. "I know you," she said thoughtfully. "You are the knight known as Blackheart, are you not, Sir Cabal?"

Cursing the abominable reputation that seemed destined to follow him all his days, Cabal replied, "I am, Your Majesty."

She studied him in silence for a long moment, her expression unreadable, distantly reflective. "The king spoke highly of you on many occasions."

"King Richard is my liege," he answered without hesitation. "I would do anything for him."

"I do not doubt that, my lord," said the queen. "You have always been loyal to my son. But actually, I was speaking of my late husband, King Henry."

Cabal's confusion must have shown in his face, for Queen Eleanor offered him a placid smile. "I had already been exiled for some years when he had you brought to London, but I had friends who kept me abreast of the palace happenings in my absence. And I heard quite a bit about you, of course. The orphaned son of a dancing girl who'd once caught my husband's eye. Oh, she wasn't the first, nor by any means the last," Eleanor added wistfully when Cabal stared at her in frank astonishment. "When I heard about the ring you had in your possession—the black diamond that once belonged to Henry—I suspected his reasons for bringing you to London went deeper than the early recruitment of another knight for the royal garrison. Seeing you for myself would have obliterated any doubt, for there can be no mistaking your features."

"Y-Your Majesty," Cabal began, stammering for the first time in his life. "I don't understand. Why are you telling me this?"

Queen Eleanor smiled. "Because my husband has been dead many years now, and soon enough I will follow him. I tell you because I have long known of your loyalty to my son, and I am grateful. But most of all, I tell you this now because I think it will help you to know it." She fixed him with a wise, level gaze that seemed to look right through him. "Despite the infamy surrounding you, Sir Cabal, you are no Blackheart. I don't think you ever were. And I know that you have too much honor to go back to the life you once knew."

"War is what I do," Cabal said, clinging to safe ground. He felt too vulnerable after last night to consider any alternative to what was real to him, what was true. "There is nothing else for me. I know of no other way to live, Your Majesty."

"I think you do," Eleanor answered. "If 'twill help you find your way, perhaps I should tell you that Lady Emmalyn has been granted permission to remain on at Fallonmour for the rest of her days." Cabal's head snapped up, his chest swelling with elation. "She has also been awarded the right to choose whether or not she marries again, and to whom."

Cabal felt a bittersweet jolt on the tail of that news. She would never choose him now. Not after last night. Not after he told her the secret he was still keeping from her, a secret that gnawed at him even more than the revelation of his ignoble past. But it did not matter if she would have him or not. He owed her the truth, and he would delay no longer.

"Your Majesty, I thank you for everything you've given me today, but I must beg your leave. I have to speak to Lady Emmalyn at once."

"Then you'd best hurry, my lord. She and her party left Beaucourt immediately after she spoke with me this morn."

She had left without him? Although he well deserved it, a sudden panic bloomed in Cabal's heart. He had to reach her before his sins caught up with him.

Sparing the queen no more than the briefest of good-byes, Cabal flew out of the castle and away on the road that led back to Fallonmour, praying for a chance he likely did not deserve.

Emmalyn reached Fallonmour just before dusk that same evening. It pained her to leave Lincolnshire without Cabal, but he had been nowhere to be found that morning, and for all she knew, he had no intention of returning. The queen had assured her that she harbored no malice toward him and that he would meet with no reproach from the crown for the unseemly display in the hall. Seeing Emmalyn's distress, Josette was equally forgiving, offering her a much needed shoulder to cry on and sending her off with assurances that she was never too far away if Emmalyn ever needed anything.

Upon her arrival on Fallonmour's lands, Emmalyn felt a little of her sadness disappear, though nothing would ever wipe away the pain of loving—and losing—Cabal. She ordered the driver of the supply cart to distribute some of the goods in the village. The two Fallonmour knights who had remained with her in Lincolnshire stayed to help unload, while Emmalyn rode ahead on the winding path toward the castle.

Silhouetted by the blaze of the setting sun, a guard on the tower barbican heralded her approach with a short call of his horn. He turned away before Emmalyn could send him a friendly wave of greeting. The castle seemed quiet somehow. Expectant. In fact, the whole world seemed to be holding its breath as the heavy gates swung wide and the portcullis began its slow grind upward.

Something was wrong. She knew it as soon as she passed under the gatehouse and into the bailey. Leaving her no time to wonder, a troop of de Wardeaux guards rushed forth and dragged her from her mount. Emmalyn screamed as they captured her in a bruising prison of mail-covered arms. Her struggles were of little avail.

"Well, well, at last the lady returns," Hugh said as he emerged from out of the tower keep. "Where is your guardian, Emmalyn?"

"Gone," she said, thankful at least that Cabal's leaving her had spared him Hugh's evil intent.

But her heart faltered in that next instant, for high on the battlements a guard on the watch shouted, "There's a rider on the south hill, my lord. 'Tis the Crusader."

Hugh smiled thinly at Emmalyn. "Well, by all means, let's bid him welcome, shall we?"

Hauling Emmalyn out of view, Hugh ordered his guards to open the gates to Cabal. She heard the thunder of his destrier's hooves as he approached, riding at breakneck speed. Though she wanted to feel relief that he might have come for her after all, she could not allow him to walk into Hugh's trap. She shouted a warning, but it was too late.

Cabal rode under the gatehouse and was beset at once. The portcullis slammed shut at his back as an army of uniformed guards rushed forth to apprehend him. Thrusting Emmalyn aside for a bigger prize, the Wardeaux knights surrounded Cabal, their lances poiscd to kill.

"On your feet," one of the men snarled, jabbing the lethal point of his weapon up near Cabal's face.

He did as instructed, dismounting and standing peacefully before the wary guards as if he intended to put up no struggle at all. Almost as if this attack came as no real surprise to him. Indeed, from the dispassionate expression on his face, it would seem as if he had somehow been anticipating that he would be set upon by Hugh in this manner.

Panicked where Cabal remained calm, Emmalyn rushed into the knot of armed guards, clawing at them as if she could tear away their advancing assault. "Stop at once! This man has done nothing wrong! I order you to release him!"

"Emmalyn, stay back."

Cabal's cool command unsettled her almost as much as the bewildering situation that faced them now. "What is the meaning of this?" she shouted at Hugh. "Where is my garrison? I demand to know what is going on!"

"That is precisely what I would like to know," he answered. "What is going on?" He motioned to someone in the crowd, the gesture bringing forth a begrimed grinning vagabond who looked strangely familiar to Emmalyn. "Imagine my surprise when this man here came to see me at Wardeaux the other day, informing me that he had just brushed arms with my brother's murderer."

"Murderer?" Some of the wind rushed out of Emmalyn's lungs. "I don't understand."

"Neither did I, at first. My brother was killed on Crusade so far as I knew. That was the story we were delivered after all, was it not?"

"Yes. Garrett was killed on the last day of fighting in Palestine. The king's letter said as much." Emmalyn glanced at Cabal and felt a tremor of dread when he would not meet her gaze. "He died in a struggle with a Saracen prisoner. . . ."

"That is what you were told, Emmalyn. However, my lady, this man was there in Palestine, too. Rannulf is well acquainted with this man, Cabal—this Blackheart. Rannulf was there, Emmalyn, in the very tent where he saw this man standing over my brother's dead body, a bloodied dagger in his hand."

Though this image shocked her, Emmalyn shook it off. "Even were that true, it hardly proves Cabal's guilt. Indeed, it proves nothing at all."

"That fact alone, perhaps not," Hugh agreed. "But there is more to the story, isn't there, Blackheart?" When Cabal did not react to the goading in any way whatsoever, Hugh scowled and nodded to Rannulf. "Tell her what you told me."

"I was there," the filthy creature named Rannulf confirmed, his beady gaze sliding to Cabal. " 'Twas after a battle outside Arsouf. We were supping around the fire when Lord Garrett went to fetch one of the prisoners. She was making a fuss the whole way to his tent—"

"She?" Emmalyn asked, revulsion twisting a knot in her stomach.

Hugh gave an unconcerned shrug and indicated for Rannulf to continue. "Not long after Lord Garrett had taken the chit with him, Blackheart left the fire. He wasn't gone more than a quarter hour when I noticed the girl's screaming had stopped. I thought maybe I'd get me some of her, too, once Lord Garrett was through, so I headed to his tent. When I got there, I didn't see no girl, but there was Blackheart, standing over Lord Garrett's bloody body and looking cool as ye please."

"I do not see how that points to Cabal's guilt," Emmalyn interjected when Cabal said nothing in his own defense. "Perhaps the girl killed Garrett trying to protect herself. I certainly would not blame her in the least for her actions."

Rannulf chuckled. "At first, I expected 'twas the girl what killed Lord Garrett, too. But then I got to thinking. There was no blood on the rope that kept her bound in the tent. It was cut clean in two. And the dagger that killed Lord Garrett—the dagger that Blackheart took care to wipe off when I found him—was dripping with blood. It didn't seem right to me that this girl would free herself, then stop to kill Lord Garrett before running off."

"Indeed, Blackheart. Why would she do something like that?" Hugh asked Cabal, his eyes hard and narrowed.

"Well, I turned that puzzle over in my mind from the day I left Palestine," said Rannulf. "It didn't make a bit of sense until I saw Blackheart again, waving about a purse full of coin and garbed so fine, I didn't recognize him on first glance. He acted like he didn't know me, and that's when I was certain. I always knew he secretly lusted for what Lord Garrett had."

"Evidently, enough to kill him for it," Hugh added.

Emmalyn shook her head, despite the queer heaviness that was beginning to cloak her from within. "I don't believe that for a moment. Cabal was sent here on the king's command. He never wanted to be here."

"The king may have sent him, but he certainly has managed to settle in," Hugh said acidly. "Look at him, dressed in my brother's clothes, riding his mount. . . . Doubtless that's not all he's been riding since he's been here."

Emmalyn's cheeks flamed, but she refused to cower under Hugh's cutting sarcasm. "Cabal never wanted to be here," she averred, weathering the little tremor of regret she felt to realize how true that statement was. "Nor, I expect, does he wish to remain here now," she added sadly.

She looked from Hugh's smug countenance to the vagrant at his side. Suddenly the dirty face staring back at her gained a firm ground in her mind. Rannulf was the beggar from Lincolnshire market square. The man who had asked her for coin and then solicited her name . . . so he could pray for her, he had said. Instead it looked as if he had used her to falsely betray Cabal to Hugh. But why?

She could not care less why, she decided in the next heartbeat. She did not need to know what the man's motives were, nor did she plan to let Hugh scheme his way into Fallonmour by bringing harm to Cabal.

"As lady of this manor, I demand that your men release Sir Cabal at once, Hugh. I want all of you off my lands—take this vile creature and his lies with you."

"Have you failed to notice, my lady? Your garrison is gone. When they heard what this beast had done—indeed, what he might do to you if permitted to remain here—they were kind enough to let me and my guards in."

Emmalyn swallowed hard. "What have you done to them?"

"You'll find the sorry lot tucked safely away in the armory stockade." Hugh held up a large iron key like a prize. "I'm in command here, Emmalyn, not you."

"You're wrong, Hugh," she challenged. "And I don't need my garrison. I have something even stronger than the sword." Emmalyn reached into her saddle pouch and withdrew the royal proclamation. "I have a writ from the queen stating that Fallonmour is mine. You have no claim to it now, nor did you ever."

Hugh stared across the bailey at the sealed document Emmalyn held in her hand. Then he chuckled. "Well, my lady, this does make for an interesting dilemma. The queen has given you a writ for Fallonmour, and I have obtained a pledge for the same from Prince John."

"This castle and its holdings are held in trust for the king, not his scheming brother," she replied. "John has no right to assign it to anyone so long as Richard lives. Only the queen, as regent to the throne, has the jurisdiction to grant properties on the king's behalf. John's pledge is invalid next to mine. I command you now to free Cabal and take your leave."

Hugh laughed, but the humor in his eyes was black as night itself. "Even if I were inclined to leave Fallonmour—which, I can assure you, I am not—I would not do so without first bringing this murderer to justice. No court in the land would deny me that right." He jerked his head in command to his men. "Put him with the others in the stockade to await his punishment."

"No!" Emmalyn shouted, rushing forward as one guard retrieved the key from Hugh and the rest of the knights closed ranks on Cabal. "You have proved nothing here today, Hugh! All you have is this drunkard's word. You will never convince me that Cabal is guilty of this crime, and I will fight you to my last breath before I let you touch him!"

"My lady." Cabal's voice was so devoid of expression that Emmalyn could scarcely command herself to face him. Her heart thudded heavily and labored in her breast, each beat bringing her closer to a dread that wanted to choke the very life from her. "Emmalyn," he said gently, "what Rannulf said is true. I killed Garrett."

Chapter Twenty-five

In that moment, Emmalyn's entire world—indeed, every particle of her being—froze. She hardly registered Hugh's smug snort of victory, could scarcely feel his knights pushing her aside as they moved in to grab Cabal. All she could see were Cabal's eyes, his expression of profound regret as he stared at her over his shoulder while the guards led him away from the bailey. "I'm sorry," he told her quietly. "Emmalyn, I'm so sorry."

"Well," Hugh sneered from beside her, "I expect a confession voiced before a dozen men should be proof enough for anyone. Including the queen."

Dazed, Emmalyn looked to him and saw that he held a folded square of parchment in his hand, the wax seal jolting her back to clear-mindedness like a slap to the face. Heaven help her, but he had the queen's writ! She had been so numb, she did not even feel him steal it from her fingers.

Hugh's smile was pure evil as he tore the decree in half, then tore it again and again and again. He released it with a chuckle, grinning as the tiny scraps floated down around her feet like confetti on the breeze. "Your having trusted that conniver so thoroughly just shows once more why women are indeed the weaker vessels."

Hugh wagged a finger at one of his guards, motioning for him to come. The armed knight stood next to Emmalyn, ready to subdue her with force on Hugh's order. "Don't feel too badly for your foolishness in this, Emmalyn. All you need is a strong man to look after your interests. To that end, the prince and I have made some arrangements on your behalf. There is an aging earl in Wales who's got an urgent need for a new wife. He's lost his last three in childbirth, you see, and time is fleeting if he is to beget an heir. You've been consigned to wed him posthaste."

"Never," Emmalyn vowed. "Neither you nor the prince can force me to wed. The queen will never agree to this scheme."

Hugh stroked his jaw, seeming utterly amused with himself. "If it has slipped your mind, Emmalyn, the queen is an old woman. Mere steps away from her grave, God willing. She can try to curb John's maneuvers, but she cannot be all places at once. By the time she learns of your marriage, there will be nothing for her to do about it."

Emmalyn glared her contempt, perfectly willing to defy both Hugh and Prince John if need be. "I won't go."

"Go, you will, my lady, tomorrow morn. You'll be dispatched to Wales at first light to meet your groom. Right after you watch your murdering lover swing at the end of a noose for his crime."

"No!" Emmalyn screamed, horrified at Hugh's edict. The instant she moved to strike at him, the guard seized her arms, pinning her in a bruising grasp. "Hugh, no! I beg you, do not! Please, do not go through with this!"

"'Tis too late for begging, Emmalyn. The matter is settled. My man will take you for the eve to your chamber, where you may make whatever preparations you must for your journey on the morrow. I have already set your maids to packing your belongings."

"You won't get away with this, Hugh! Heaven help me, I won't let you get away with this!"

Hugh did not seem the least bit concerned. A jerk of his head sent his guard off at a lumbering pace, the big knight forcibly guiding Emmalyn out of the bailey. With each step, she felt her legs weakening beneath her, her heart squeezing at the thought of Cabal's death. Her stomach twisted in keen anguish when she realized that in a few short hours, she would be separated from him forever.

"Oh, and one more thing, Emmalyn," Hugh called after her with a gleeful little chuckle. "If you thought Garrett a strict husband, prepare yourself, for after a week under your betrothed's punishing rod, I warrant you will come to view my brother as a bloody saint."

The setting sun dipped below the curtain wall as she absorbed Hugh's grim prediction, the darkness of coming night descending over the bailey as surely as it was soon to settle over her future. Swallowing her fears, Emmalyn squared her shoulders and walked ahead of Hugh's guard, her head held high as she entered the castle.

Inside, the keep resounded with the boisterous clamoring of Hugh's army, the bulk of which, from all appearances, had converged on her hall like a swarm of locusts. As she and her escort neared the large banquet room on their way to the stairwell, Emmalyn counted upward of two score men lounging at her tables, devouring great helpings of food and wine while the kitchen maids scurried about in a panic, serving the men and trying to avoid their groping hands and randy inclinations.

If Hugh's knights seemed bent on bullying and gluttony, it seemed they had also been given free reign for destruction of her things. They had torn down most of the heirloom tapestries Emmalyn had brought with her from her parents' manor and hung about the hall for decoration. Her white table linens had been shredded or stained with spilled wine, and the rushes that covered the floor were littered with food scraps, bones, and broken pottery.

In the midst of all this deliberate negligence sat Arlo. Garrett's seneschal leaned back in his chair at the dais, his booted feet propped up on the high table, a half-eaten shank of mutton in his fist. Nell, one of the young castle maids, had just poured him a tankard of wine and was about to leave the dais when Arlo dropped his food suddenly and reached out to snag her by the trailing length of her long blond hair. The petite maid cried out, struggling as Arlo hauled her toward him, laughing.

He must have sensed Emmalyn's outrage all the way

from the corridor, for he stopped then and looked to her. "Ah, Lady Emmalyn," he hailed cheerily. "Welcome back."

The guard looming behind her gave Emmalyn a little push. Futile anger surged through every particle of her body as she was guided abovestairs to her chamber and shut inside. Bertie and the other maids gathered there fell upon Emmalyn the instant the door closed.

"Oh, milady!" Bertie cried, catching her in a fierce embrace. "We have been so worried! When Hugh arrived today with his soldiers, no one knew what to think!"

One of the other maids added, "They threw the men in the stockade and have been ordering us around like chattel ever since!"

"And why wouldn't they?" said another. "Fifty men armed to the teeth and the rest of us left with no choice but to do whatever they say."

"Aye, that's precisely de Wardeaux's style," Bertie said. "He and his kin have always taken great pride in bullying those left defenseless against them."

"Perhaps not so defenseless as he might like to think," Jane said with a sly smile. When the ladies turned expectant eyes on her, she told them, "I saw the kitchen maids put enough sweet bay in the guards' food to turn a horse's stomach inside out. In a couple of hours I wager they'll all be too sick to do so much as stand up."

Not even Emmalyn could stifle her gasp of astonishment over the prospect. To think that Hugh's brutish army might meet their match in a handful of simple maids who conspired to use the men's stomachs against them! She only hoped that Arlo's appetite would prove as plentiful as that of the other gluttons in the hall. It gave her considerable—if wicked—satisfaction to picture him suffering a night of gastric discomfort.

"Getting revenge on Hugh's guards might keep them from further tormenting us this eve," Bertie interjected in a low voice, "but what about Lady Emmalyn? None of this alters the fact that she will be sent away in the morn. We must figure a way to stop Hugh from going through with this."

"If only I hadn't let him get his hands on that royal decree," Emmalyn said, shaking her head in regret. "I should have known Hugh would find a way to make trouble here. I should have asked the queen to send an escort with us from Lincolnshire."

"There is no time to fret over such things, milady. We must figure a way to get you out of the castle and someplace safe. Hugh cannot be allowed to succeed in sending you off to wed that Welsh beast."

"Before I worry about that, Bertie, I have to make sure that Cabal will not be harmed. Hugh plans to—" She broke off suddenly, her throat closing up, hardly able to say the awful words herself. "Hugh will hang him in the morn for Garrett's death unless I can stop him somehow."

"Oh, milady," Bertie said. "I know that you love this man. We have all come to look upon him with fond regard, and I wager none of us here would want to see him meet with harm. But he was sent by the king to guard you as well as this keep. If the question were to come down to sparing you or himself, what do you think he would choose?"

Emmalyn looked at her nurse, horrified, and anguished to admit to herself that Bertie was likely right in her logic. But it tore Emmalyn to pieces inside to think of Cabal dying. "No," she said, shaking her head. "I don't care that he would want me to go, Bertie. There must be a way for both of us to be free. I have to find a way."

"Milady, so long as you are locked away in here, you can help no one. We have to see you away from Fallonmour. Only then will you have a chance of getting help for Sir Cabal." Bertie patted Emmalyn's hand reassuringly. "We will put our heads together, and we are bound to see a solution."

"If there is one, we have but a few hours to find it," Emmalyn answered. "Dawn—and Hugh's wrath—will be upon us before we know it."

The iron grate of the armory stockade clattered shut in Cabal's face, a twist of the key sealing him inside the cell with Fallonmour's dozen knights. He could have fought the guards who had shuffled him away from Emmalyn, but in truth, after seeing her shocked and benumbed expression, he had no interest in fighting. She would fare better without him in her life. Cabal had cooperatively allowed the gang of men-at-arms to throw him in here, resigned to accept whatever fate Hugh had in store for him.

Death, no doubt.

At present he did not care. He already felt like the most vital part of him had died. He only prayed that Emmalyn's involvement with him would not subject her to any further ill at Hugh's hand. If it took his death to appease Hugh and spare Emmalyn, then he would go to it willingly.

His back to the others imprisoned along with him, Cabal stood at the bars, watching as one of the two guards on post went off to deliver the key back to Hugh for safekeeping. Sir Miles was the first of Cabal's cellmates to approach him.

"De Wardeaux arrived early this afternoon with fifty of his knights," the old captain volunteered. "He said Prince John had granted him full rights to Fallonmour and its holdings, and that to bar him entry to the castle was to defy the prince's orders. He said it would be tantamount to treason."

"You had no choice but to let him in, Miles. I'm sure Lady Emmalyn will not fault you for it."

"He also said that he had come to apprehend Lord Garrett's murderer. He said that you are the knight known as Blackheart." When Cabal made no response during the expectant beat that Miles awaited an answer, the captain asked, "Did he speak true?"

"Yes," Cabal replied.

"And what of the rest? Did you kill Lord Garrett?"

Cabal nodded weakly. He sensed the old knight's wariness, felt him take a hesitant half step backward. "I did not plot to murder him, as Hugh is inclined to believe, but he died at my hand. I killed him."

"Hugh said he feared that Lady Emmalyn's life was in jeopardy each moment you were allowed to stay at Fallonmour."

At that, Cabal faced Sir Miles. "Never," he swore. "Never would I have brought any harm to her. Jesu, I love—" He broke off too late to curb the pained admission, turning away from the old captain's gaze lest he also show him the fear of loss in his eyes.

"I did not believe that you would," Sir Miles said, his voice low enough that the conversation remained between the two of them only. "I'm afraid some of the others were harder to convince. That is, until the instant Hugh's men spilled through the gates and he ordered us locked away in this gaol. By then, there was little any of us could do to correct our mistake. Hugh's hold was established, and all we could do was wait until you and our lady returned." The captain swore, grasping the bars and shaking his head. "And now to add salt to the wound, you must wait along with us while Hugh sends Lady Emmalyn off to Wales in the morn to wed one of the prince's cronies."

"What?" Cabal felt as though he had been kicked in the gut. "He has arranged for her to marry?"

Miles's nod was grim. "De Wardeaux boasted how he found Lady Emmalyn a husband in an old earl who's been widowed thrice over and is looking to make an heir. He said the prince agrees with him that Lady Emmalyn cannot be trusted to make sound judgments on her own and that she would benefit from a stern hand."

Cabal did not need to hear any more than that. He grabbed the bars and began shaking the cell door as if to tear it from its hinges. Gone was his apathy toward what might befall him; now his sole intent was to figure a way out of his prison so he could stop Hugh's plan for Emmalyn. Savagely, he yanked on the iron grid, his wild curses jolting the lone guard into action and bringing him running to the cell.

"Get back!" shouted the knight, drawing his sword as he neared. He jabbed at Cabal through the slats. "Get back from the bars, ye bloody cur!"

Cabal dodged the first few thrusts, trying to grab at the guard's head, his sleeve—anything he could get close enough to reach. When Hugh's man made the mistake of catching hold of the bars with his free hand to steady himself, Cabal sprung. He seized the knight's fingers and yanked him forward, dragging the soldier's body flush against the grid.

"Get the sword!" he shouted to anyone who would help him. Several men rushed forth to assist, but the command had already proved Cabal's undoing. The guard threw his blade down, casting it a safe yard from the cell before any of them could reach it.

The weapon lost, Cabal wrapped his forearm around the knight's neck, cutting off his air with the muscled crook of his elbow. The guard thrashed and clawed and spluttered, but Cabal was unrelenting. He felt enraged, enlivened, fully prepared to kill or be killed if it meant a chance at saving Emmalyn. Snarling with fury, he tightened his hold on the man's throat. "Open this damned door or I vow I will choke the life out of you!"

"I cannot!" the knight croaked. "Jus . . . just the one key!"

Cabal cursed and brought his fist nearly to his chest, pinning the guard in a certain death squeeze. Frustrated and angered, he did not hear the second knight return from his errand until the man was nearly upon him. The Wardeaux man drew a dagger and sliced it across Cabal's forearm before he even knew what hit him. Instantly, his grip fell away and the guard he had nearly killed scrambled a safe distance out of his reach, sprawled and coughing on the floor.

"Try something stupid like that again—any of you—and you die," the second knight warned.

Panting with exertion and rage, Cabal stared down at the bleeding wound on his right arm and watched with a certain morbid pleasure as the deep cut stained his tunic sleeve crimson. As long as he bled, he was alive. And as long as he lived, there was hope that he would get to Emmalyn in time. But suddenly he realized something that doused his hopes and cooled his head better than a face full of icy water.

Even if he should manage a way out of his prison, he had likely just lost the use of his sword arm.

Chapter Twenty-six

The tallow candle in Emmalyn's chamber had burned for nearly two hours after Bertie and the other maids had left, and Emmalyn was still no closer to resolving the dire situation facing them all. Staring at her four walls, she had gotten so desperate to act that she had actually considered escape through her open window, a plot that would have surely gotten her killed if Hugh's ten guards on the wall walk did not catch her first.

Where was Cabal's midsummer magic when she needed it? If only she could vanish from out of her prison as the lion in his story had done. Dieu, but it seemed a lifetime ago that he had been sitting at the village bonfire spinning yarns. And at present, Cabal was about as far away as possible from being able to spirit her out of her confinement the way he had helped the old lion in Palestine. Now they were both caged, and it would take more than magic and wishing to free them from Hugh's devious plans. But certainly a bit of prayer could not hurt matters, she thought, sending a silent plea heavenward.

It was answered by approaching footsteps, then the sound of Father Bryce's voice in the corridor outside her barred door.

"Ah, good eve, my son. I am Father Bryce and this is Brother George—"

"What do ye want, priest?" her guard growled.

"We have come to provide the lady with religious counsel, my son. Her maid informs me that Lady Emmalyn is somewhat troubled over the news she has received today and would seek solace and advice from the Scriptures."

There was a scrape of a stool on the floor and the muted jingle of armor as the knight evidently came to his feet. "Begging pardon, Father. But I don't think Lord Hugh would approve of this. . . ."

"Not approve? Did you hear that, Brother?" Father Bryce's chuckle was disbelieving. "What would he not approve of, do you reckon, my son? Lady Emmalyn's seeking the church's counsel, or our providing it to her in this time of obvious need?"

The guard cleared his throat as if discomfited with the question. "Lord Hugh said permit no one inside tonight, Father. The Brother and ye will have to go now."

"My son," Father Bryce said gently, "I am a man of God, bound by my vows to serve my flock. So long as this woman is among my parish, 'tis my duty to be available to her. Now Brother George and I will thank you to let us pass so that we may see to her, as she has requested."

"If 'tis all the same to ye, Father, I think I'd better go check with Lord Hugh first."

Father Bryce gave an impatient-sounding huff. "Very well, my son. If you feel you cannot make this decision yourself, I quite understand. . . ."

A long beat ticked by before the chamber door creaked open. "Ye've got a quarter hour, Father, no more."

"Bless you, my son," Father Bryce said as he and a slight-built hooded monk crossed the threshold. "If you don't mind, this is a rather private matter." That said, the priest pushed the oak panel closed on the knight's scowling visage.

"Father Bryce," Emmalyn whispered, greeting him warmly, though her gaze kept straying to the queer little fellow at his side. Fallonmour had only one priest, and she had never heard of this Brother George, whose face was obscured in the deep cowl of his brown robe. "What's going on, Father? Did Bertie send you?"

"Aye, my girl, she did," the old priest whispered. "But we must act swiftly if we are to get you out of here. Come the both of you, move away from the door."

She did as instructed, watching in astonishment as "Brother George" removed his concealing vestments and within scant moments stood before Emmalyn as Nell. The young maid was garbed in a russet wool tunic much like the one Emmalyn wore now, her blond hair plaited in a single braid that fell a scarcely discernible inch or two shorter than Emmalyn's own locks. "Put this on, my lady. Hurry!"

Caught up in the rush of the moment, Emmalyn hastily donned the hooded robe while Father Bryce began to recite from his Bible in Latin, speaking loudly enough that it surely carried under the door to the guard on watch. While he did this, in a voice scarcely above a whisper Nell endeavored to explain the plan for getting Emmalyn out of the castle. "You will leave this chamber dressed as Brother George, exiting with Father Bryce through the postern gate of the keep."

"But to get to the back stairwell will mean passing the chamber where Hugh is stationed," Emmalyn argued. "We will never get past him. He'll not trust this disguise."

Nell shook her head. "We have seen to that already, my lady. The postern is the only way out of the castle, unless you think it safer to walk past the guards in the gatehouse."

"No, 'tis too great a risk to walk out in plain sight. I agree, the postern is the only choice."

"Father Bryce has arranged to send you to the abbey in Wexley, less than four hours away. The queen's bishop is in summer residence there. Tell him your plight; he will see to your safety and get word of Hugh's defiance delivered to London."

"But what about Cabal?" Emmalyn asked frantically. "What about you, Nell? What about everyone else at Fallonmour? I cannot simply leave to save myself when Hugh will doubtless wreak vengeance on the rest of you for aiding in my escape."

Nell simply stared at her without responding, but in the next instant Father Bryce whispered urgently, "There is no time, ladies. Nell, take your place beside the bed. Lady

Emmalyn, kneel before me and bow your head as if in prayer."

They no sooner had positioned themselves as Father Bryce had instructed, their backs to the door, when the panel yawned open and the guard cleared his throat over the priest's murmured prayers. "Ye've had long enough to counsel the lady, Father. Out with ye now, the both of ye."

"Continue your prayers, my lady," Father Bryce instructed Nell as he rose to his feet. "God be with you, child."

"And with you, Father," Nell said softly.

"Come along, Brother George." Emmalyn felt the priest's hand clutch her wide sleeve, and before she knew it she was crossing the threshold of her chamber with him, walking out into the corridor, head bowed, delivered one step closer to freedom. One step farther from Cabal. "This way, Brother," Father Bryce said when Emmalyn stopped in the hallway, considering what lay ahead of her.

With a guiding tug and a shuffling, hasty gait, the old priest led her down the torchlit corridor toward Garrett's solar, the room Hugh had commanded for his own upon arriving. The door was open wide, light spilling into the hall. It felt vaguely familiar to Emmalyn, hearkening back to a night when she had crept along this same space of floor, inching her way toward the room that Cabal had slept in.

As she approached the open chamber now, led by the hand by Fallonmour's clergy, to Emmalyn's amazement, she heard the same female giggle that had so wrenched her all those nights ago. Jane's giggle. Followed by an interested male growl that could only belong to Hugh.

"Oh, my lord!" Jane cried in a wanton purr of delight. "Such wicked things you do to me! Once more, I beg you!"

"As you wish, my greedy little wench," Hugh said.

Father Bryce slanted Emmalyn an uncomfortable look, cautioning her back as he peered around the edge of the door. Evidently satisfied with what he found, he waved her forward. As Emmalyn sidled past, she could not resist a quick glance within.

It was difficult not to laugh at the sight that greeted her.
Jane reclined atop Garrett's desk, looking thoroughly bored,
her bodice half-open while Hugh sprawled over her, feast-
ing on her neck and bosom with blissful abandon. The
sly maid held his head to her as if she meant to prevent
him from looking up at an inconvenient moment. She met
Emmalyn's wide-eyed gaze and winked at her, a gesture of
sheer, unabashed feminine conspiracy.

Returning the maid's broad smile, Emmalyn passed the
doorway and followed along down the passage after Father
Bryce. Within moments they had snaked down the back
stairwell and out of the unguarded postern gate. Once on the
other side of the curtain wall, Emmalyn paused. She looked
back at the tower keep, at the dim candlelight glowing from
within her chamber and the stone castle that was her home.
If she left now, would she ever see it again? Would she ever
see Cabal?

"My lady, go," Father Bryce urged. "You mustn't tarry—
'tis too dangerous for you! Your escort awaits at the village
chapel. Go now, my lady!"

Emmalyn jumped into action, speeding down the back
side of the castle hill, taking care to keep silent and run
swiftly, lest the guards on watch spy the small blotch of
darkness traversing the plains and gullies and heading pell-
mell for the village. She reached the small chapel nearly out
of breath, her heart pounding, throat burning.

James, one of the two Fallonmour knights who had
returned with her from the market, stood armed and holding
the reins of his destrier. A gray palfrey was saddled beside
him and ready for Emmalyn's use. "I am to take you to
Wexley abbey posthaste, my lady. We should be there before
matins if we leave now and encounter no delays on the road."

"Thank you," she murmured, almost dizzy from the pace
at which these events of the past few hours were transpiring.

As James grasped her waist to help her mount, Emmalyn
began to think about all she was leaving behind. Not just
Cabal but everyone at Fallonmour: Bertie, Wat, Father Bryce,

Nell . . . even Jane. All of the people who had become such vital parts of her life. And then there were the villeins, the folk who worked her lands and filled her coffers and her stores. How could she just walk away from them? How could she leave everything she loved without a true fight?

Father Bryce said to plead her case to the bishop, but what sort of case did she really have? Just her word that the queen had granted her the rights to Fallonmour; she had nothing to prove it. Even if he believed her and sent word to London, how long would that take? Days, certainly, but more likely weeks. Mayhap months. And in the meanwhile, she would seek to appeal to the bishop to return with her to Fallonmour forthwith to spare the life of her lover, the man who had confessed to killing her husband? He would think her mad.

It would never work, and it was far too risky to attempt it when Hugh planned to see Cabal dead in the morning.

That, much more than the thought of being carted off to Wales to wed the beast Hugh described, weighed heavy on her heart. Somehow, her future seemed less important if she was to be forced to live it without him. Regardless that he had admitted to killing Garrett, regardless of his dark past and all that had gone between them, Emmalyn loved Cabal just the same.

She loved him, and she determined then and there that she would have the chance to prove it to him.

"James, wait." When the knight turned to her, she shook her head. "I cannot go."

"Is anything wrong, my lady?"

"Yes. Everything is wrong, and I can't leave without trying to make it right. Help me gather the villeins, James. Tell them to fetch torches, and every pitchfork, scythe, and cudgel they can find. Bring the supply cart around; we will need the weapons we bought at market, too. We'll assemble here in the chapel once everyone is present."

Chapter Twenty-seven

Something strange was happening inside the castle. For more than the past quarter hour, Cabal had been listening to what sounded like some countless dozens of men stumbling out into the bailey, their muffled pained groans and racking coughs carrying through the sole window of the armory. Finally, the swelling ruckus proved enough to make the stockade guards look up from their second portions of stew.

The larger of the duo set aside his bowl, pausing to wash down another greedy mouthful with a swig of ale. "Keep your eye on them," he told the one Cabal had attacked earlier. "I'm going to find out what all that noise is about."

The guard left behind glared at Cabal from his seat a safe distance across the room. He belched then, a terrible, deep rumble that made him lean forward slightly, clutching his stomach. He was still hunched over and grimacing when the other knight came racing back inside. "They've poisoned us! Don't eat another bite! The damned wenches have poisoned the stew!"

"Oh, Jesu!" the second man cried, toppling his stool as he vaulted to his feet in a panic. "Where's the well? I need water!"

His companion pushed him back. "Nay! I'll fetch you water right after I get some for me. You stay here—someone's got to man the post or Hugh will have both our heads!"

"Then you stay!" the knight shouted as he shoved his way out the door. "I'm not about to sit here and die for de Wardeaux!"

That said, both of them fled the building. Sir Miles and the others had since crowded around the front of the cell with Cabal, watching and listening in total astonishment. "Do you think 'tis true?" Miles asked. "Do you reckon the women are hatching some sort of plan?"

Cabal shook his head. "For Lady Emmalyn's sake, I certainly hope not. 'Tis madness to risk it."

He put his shoulder into the iron grid in frustration, cursing when the grate hardly shook under the impact. As if the others had similar thoughts, the rest joined in, twelve bodies slamming against the bars in unison, all of them determined to break their way out of the prison. Thrice they had hit the iron wall; thrice to no avail. No one said the situation was hopeless, but Cabal could see the futility of it reflecting in every pair of eyes that looked to him for leadership.

"Someone's coming," Miles said, calling attention to the sound of hasty footsteps padding alongside the outbuilding.

"Bertie!" shouted half the garrison in one elated voice when she entered in a rush.

"What the devil is going on out there?" Cabal demanded as the big nurse loped up to the bars. "What have you done to the guards?"

"No time to explain now, milord." She withdrew a large iron key from the sleeve of her bliaut, and in a few short moments, the lock fell away and the cell door creaked open.

"Hugh had that key. How did you get it?"

"Jane's been keeping him busy abovestairs in the castle," she said with a grin. "He won't notice the key is missing for some time yet, I reckon."

While Fallonmour's garrison poured out into the armory, following Cabal's direction to grab weapons from the stalls, he pulled Bertie aside. "Where is Emmalyn? Is she all right?"

"She's gone. But don't fret, milord—she'll be fine. Father Bryce had Sir James escort her to the abbey at Wexley about an hour ago. She'll be safe there with the bishop. Now you must see to your own safety. Take the postern gate and go, before de Wardeaux realizes what's happening out here."

"Leave?" Cabal shook his head. "Not so long as he remains."

"But milord, you must go! 'Twas all milady could think of when last I saw her: your well-being. She would want to know that you are safe and out of Hugh's clutches."

"No, Bertie. I'm not going anywhere. Not until I'm certain Fallonmour will be Emmalyn's for good."

Ignoring the nurse's further protests, Cabal headed off toward the keep to root out Hugh. As he crossed the bailey, he noted that his men were already rushing the guards posted on the wall walk, shooting some down with their crossbows and scrambling up to battle the ones that yet stood ready to fight. The inner courtyard was littered with dozens of Hugh's incapacitated knights, most of them retching into the grass or running to find relief from their ailing stomachs. More of the same sight greeted him as he passed the great hall on his way to the stairwell.

Hugh had not given Fallonmour's folk—or its women—enough credit, he thought with wry satisfaction. Nor had he ever shown Fallonmour's lady her due respect. Cabal meant to teach the blackguard that very lesson, and without further delay. He pulled a sword from the scabbard of a semiconscious Wardeaux guard, then with a roar, raced up the stairs two at a time.

"De Wardeaux!" he bellowed as he reached the second floor. With the sword gripped tightly in his left hand, Cabal stalked down the corridor toward the sounds of Hugh's voice, pitched high in startled confusion.

There was a flurry of commotion and curses coming from within one of the chambers before Jane was brutally shoved out into the corridor, half-dressed. Running past Cabal to make her escape, she advised, "He's alone but armed. Be careful!"

Cabal found Hugh standing in the center of the chamber, broadsword in hand, wearing just his braies and looking none too amused with the compromising interruption. "So, you managed to escape the gaol with naught but a scrape on the arm, did you? Evidently the slut must have aided someone in stealing my key." He shrugged, smiling thinly. "I'll kill her for that. But first, Blackheart, 'twill be my pleasure to see you dead."

Cabal stepped inside and Hugh charged, cleaving his blade through the air and connecting with Cabal's. Unaccustomed to the left-handed hold, Cabal's arm jolted with the impact, the shock rattling all the way down to his fingers and nearly losing him the weapon. He gripped it tighter and brought the blade up, deflecting Hugh's sword with a skyward thrust of his arm. Hugh stumbled back a pace, then came at him again, snarling his rage.

Twice more their blades clashed as both men circled the center of the chamber, waiting for an opportunity, each man striking when it belonged to him. Intermittently, Hugh shouted for his guards, looking incensed and confounded when no one reported to his aid. He lunged forward, throwing his body weight into his strike as his sword crashed down on Cabal's.

The force proved too much. Cabal was driven to one knee by the blow, his blade wrenched cleanly from his left hand. It hit the floor and Hugh chuckled, moving in for the kill. As he stepped forward, his bare foot came to rest atop the tunic he had evidently shed during his time with Jane. Cabal seized the edge of the silk shirt and yanked the fabric out from under him, sending Hugh down like a felled tree.

Cabal got to his feet and stood over him, the deadly blade poised at the center of Hugh's bared chest. Every muscle in his body twitched in anticipation of his skewering the bastard right there on the floor. He thought about everything Garrett had put Emmalyn through, all the cruelties Hugh was prepared to subject her to, and he wanted nothing more than to see this brother speeding on his way to hell to rot with the other.

But let it be at someone else's hand.

Cabal was through killing. He knew it for certain now, staring down at the terrified expression of Hugh de Wardeaux, a man who surely deserved to die. He deserved to die, but his death was not worth the price. Blackheart was dead, and Cabal would not let his loathing for Garrett's brother resurrect him.

"Get up." Hugh stared wildly at the retreating blade as Cabal backed off, giving him space to come to his feet. He tried to reach for his clothing, but Cabal jabbed the blade closer to him in warning. "Get out."

"You should kill me, Blackheart, for I mean to have my guards kill you the moment you set foot belowstairs."

"Get out," Cabal repeated, and urged Hugh toward the door, following behind him, the sword at his back. He walked Hugh down the spiraling stairwell, intent to eject him bodily from Fallonmour.

"You'll have Prince John's wrath to contend with for this affront, Blackheart."

"And you will have the queen's."

A nudge to Hugh's shoulder kept him moving through the heart of the keep, where Fallonmour's maids gaped in astonishment at the sight of the powerful Baron de Wardeaux so disgraced. Some could not hold back their delight, making tittering jests about the baron's state of attire—or lack thereof—as he passed.

But those same giggling maids drew their breath in sheer fright when, a moment later, Arlo emerged from within the great hall. He stood in the corridor, blocking the path to the keep's exit, a loaded crossbow in his hands. "Release him or die, cur."

Now it was Hugh's turn to laugh. He started to sidle away, but Cabal pressed his sword against Hugh's tender back, one hand on his shoulder as if to force him onto the blade. "You heard him, Blackheart. Release me, or you die."

"Either way I die, isn't that your meaning, Hugh?"

"Do as Arlo says and perhaps I can be persuaded to be lenient with you," Hugh bargained, a bead of sweat trickling down his spine.

Cabal held fast. "Your kind doesn't know the meaning of the word."

"Let him go!" Arlo shouted, an edge of hysteria in his voice. "You have no choice, Blackheart. You have lost."

What happened next would surely be talked about at Fallonmour for generations to come. Emerging from out of the shadows like some ancient female warrior, Bertie stepped into the narrow corridor. Without a word, the big nurse pulled back her arm and let fly a punch that knocked Arlo off his feet and sent him sprawling against the opposite wall in an unconscious heap.

Bertie shook out her hand, her smirk nigh as wide as the English Channel. "I reckon I have been wanting to do that for years."

Grinning wryly, Cabal urged the slumped and defeated Hugh past the great hall, pausing only long enough to let him see the wasteland that remained of his mighty garrison of just a few hours before. Head hung low, Hugh marched before Cabal toward the keep's exit.

As they neared the open door, Cabal noticed that a queer orange light illuminated the night outside the keep, filling the bailey and washing nearly to the castle steps. From the stunning intensity of the fiery glow, it appeared that one of the outbuildings had been set ablaze during the struggle with the Wardeaux guards. Guiding Hugh toward the portal, Cabal was not at all sure what would greet them on the other side.

Never would he have guessed it to be this.

Standing shoulder to shoulder in the courtyard, pitch torches blazing, was an army of more than two hundred peasants. Every man and woman, young and old, who lived or worked on Fallonmour's lands was now here, assembled and ready to defend it. Armed with the tools of their stations and the supply of weapons bought at Lincolnshire, the villeins had grouped together and stormed the keep en masse. Twelve crossbows leveled on Hugh as Cabal pushed him into the courtyard, countless pitchforks and scythes gleamed their warning in the torchlight.

At the front and center of this formidable throng of unlikely heroes was Emmalyn, her shoulders squared, chin held high, looking even more awesome to Cabal than the extraordinary group she led. Despite her delicate frame, Emmalyn's presence seemed to fill the expansive yard.

Like a lioness prepared to defend her kin, she stood protectively at the fore, her braided golden hair in wild disarray, errant tendrils lifting in the night breeze, every inch of her gilded in the ethereal glow of torchlight and sheer tenacity. She bore no weapons to this confrontation, facing Hugh instead with faith in her people, faith in herself. Strong, capable, courageous. Here was Fallonmour's true champion.

Cabal had never been so humbled, nor so proud.

Emmalyn glanced at him and smiled, a little smile, which made him want to think she might be relieved to see him standing before her now. That she might forgive him his foolishness of the night before. That she might forgive him everything. The gentle light reflecting in her eyes made him want to hope that he had not lost her after all.

Hugh, however, could construe no fond regard in the look he weathered from this intrepid lady. Emmalyn pinned him with an icy stare, pointing her finger toward the open gates, and ordered simply, "Go."

He hesitated, looking to where Sir Miles and the rest of the garrison had gathered Rannulf and the bulk of his ailing knights in the yard, easily holding them at bay. He looked to the sea of hard-faced peasants, ready to plug him with bolts on Emmalyn's command, and he took the first step down into the courtyard.

"You are making a dire mistake, Emmalyn," he warned as he descended fully and began the slow trek through the parting crowd. Several villein warriors fell in behind him, urging him forth with pitchforks at his back. "I'll not abide this insult!" he called to her over his shoulder. "Not even your precious queen will be able to protect you now!"

The lady scarcely blinked under the threat. Instead, she motioned to one of the Fallonmour knights at her side. "James, fetch the supply cart and bring it around to the bailey. Hugh and his men will need use of it for transport back to Wardeaux."

As the cart was being loaded with Hugh's defeated army, Cabal stepped down the keep stairs and walked to Emmalyn's side.

"Are you badly hurt?" she asked, indicating the gash on his arm.

He shook his head, frowning. " 'Tis nothing." In truth, he had not even recalled the wound, could not feel the throbbing pain of it, now that he was looking at her. "Emmalyn, you must know, what Hugh said about Garrett's death—"

"You killed him to save the girl," Emmalyn replied. "Your honor would never have allowed him to harm her. I know that much about you without your telling me, Cabal."

"I should have told you everything from the start."

When she glanced away from him and drew a steadying breath, it was all Cabal could do to keep from taking her into his arms. He fisted his hands at his side, lest he reach for her and feel her justifiable rejection of him.

"How much more will you keep from me? What else will I have to find out on my own?" she asked brokenly. "I love you, Cabal, but I cannot love you in pieces. I want all of you: your past, your future, and every moment in between. You have to trust me. You have to be willing to give me that."

"You have me, Emmalyn. God knows why you would want me, but I vow I am yours. I was yours from the moment I first saw you. I have never known love like this before, my lady."

"You could shatter my heart in a thousand pieces if you wanted to," she whispered. "You already did, when you pushed me away last night."

"Ah, Emmalyn," he whispered, full of reverence and devotion. "Let me make it right." Putting one knee to the ground at her feet, he reached out and grasped her hand in his, placing a kiss in her palm. "I love you, my lady. Nothing would make me happier than to spend the rest of my days proving it to you. And so I beg you now, on my knees before all of these witnesses, will you give me that chance?"

Cabal could feel the hundreds of faces peering at the two of them, could feel the hush of silence fall over the bailey as everyone—himself included—held their breath in anticipation of Emmalyn's answer. She looked down at him, her enchanting eyes shimmering with emotion, her pretty lower lip caught between her teeth as if she were moved beyond words.

"I am yours, my lady . . . body, heart, and soul. Will you have me?"

Finally, laughing through her tears, she managed a faint nod. It was all Cabal needed. As the crowd erupted in a triumphant cheer, he surged to his feet and swept Emmalyn into his arms, kissing her as though he had been denied her sweetness for an eternity. She clung to him, matching his ardor, whispering her affection, her tenderness casting away every fear and doubt that had haunted him in the hours they had been separated.

His beautiful, valorous lady loved him, and the future, at last, looked bright.

Epilogue

April 1194

That particular day dawned much the same as the hundreds that had come before it. Still, Baron Cabal of Fallonmour felt an odd quickening in his veins—a queer sense of hopeful anticipation that roused him before the sun's first rays lit the chamber he shared with his lady wife. Something was in the air; he could feel it.

Would today be the day?

Eager to find out, he inched closer to the beauty who lay beside him and traced the line of her bare shoulder. Her sleepy sigh was a balm to his soul. The kiss he placed against the tender skin at the back of her neck was soft, meant more in gratitude for the joy she had given him these past months than as a means of rousing her, but she stirred, smiling as she rolled onto her back.

"I did not mean to wake you," he whispered, smoothing a tendril of silky hair from her brow.

" 'Tis all right, although I was enjoying a lovely dream."

"Were you?" He could not resist pressing his lips to the creamy softness of her breast.

"Mmm," she said with a weak nod. She reached up and caressed his grizzled jaw, the dark-jeweled silver ring on her right hand glinting in the morning sunlight. As promised, Emmalyn had accepted this and everything else about him without reservation, embracing his battered heart no matter how scarred and flawed it had once been. "I was dreaming

311

that you and I were in a field of violets," she told him now, her voice a silky whisper that warmed him from the inside out. "We were making love under a blue, blue sky."

Cabal growled just thinking of the idea. "It has been torture not being able to love you fully these past weeks," he admitted. "But I reckon this makes it worth every moment." He caressed the perfect swell of her belly, his heart gladdening for the impertinent kick that rippled beneath his palm.

Fallonmour awaited a new arrival.

" 'Twill not be much longer, my lord. This baby is ready to meet his father."

"Her father," Cabal countered, revisiting a lighthearted disagreement they had been having for the past nine months. He kissed his wife and moved down on the mattress so that his ear rested against the place where his child slumbered. And in that moment, with the sun peeking in through the shutters and Emmalyn's fingers stroking his hair, Cabal knew the meaning of true bliss. He knew, for the first time and for always, the meaning of home.

PRINCE CHARMING

by Gaelen Foley

Destiny casts its hand one perfect moonlit night when Ascension's most elusive highwayman, the Masked Rider, chooses the wrong coach to rob. For inside is Rafael, the prince of the kingdom, renowned for his hot-blooded pursuits of women and other decadent pleasures. The failed raid leaves the equally notorious Masked Rider wounded and facing a hangman's noose. Then Rafe realizes his captive criminal is Lady Daniela Chiaramonte, a defiant beauty who torments him, awakening his senses and his heart as no woman has before.

Dani can only wonder if she's been delivered to heaven or hell once she agrees to marry the most desirable man in the Mediterranean—until forces of treachery threaten to destroy their tenuous alliance and bring down the throne itself. . . .

Published by The Ballantine Publishing Group.
Available at bookstores everywhere.

Lance St. Leger is defying his destiny. The eldest son and heir to Castle Leger, he has returned from the army determined to continue his role as rakehell and black sheep. He is plagued by an infernal restlessness that cannot be appeased, perhaps because the St. Leger legacy of strange powers is most pronounced in Lance's own dubious gift. He calls it night drifting—his ability to separate his body from his soul, to spirit into the night while flesh and bone remain behind. And it is on one wild night's mad search for a magnificent stolen sword—the icon of the St. Leger power—that he finds her. . . .

THE NIGHT DRIFTER

Rosalind, a young, sheltered widow with a passion for the Arthurian legend, mistakes Lance's "drifting" soul for the ghost of Sir Lancelot. Seeing that she is in need of a champion, the St. Leger rogue assumes the role of the tragic knight, not knowing that this woman is his destiny, his perfect mate.

by Susan Carroll

But deep down in her heart, Rosalind is all too aware she is a mortal woman with very real desires that only a man of flesh and blood can fulfill—a man like Lance St. Leger. As a murderous enemy challenges the St. Leger power, Rosalind must tempt magic herself to save her beloved from the cold depths of eternal damnation.

Published by The Ballantine Publishing Group.
Available in bookstores everywhere.